TRIPLE REINCARNATION

A Novel By:
H.D. DEXTER

ABOUT CREEKHOPPERS PRESS

A portion of all profits from every book published by Creekhoppers Press will be allocated to environmental initiatives. Creekhoppers supports "pro-environment/pro-jobs," endeavors that aim to resolve environmental issues through the creation of job-spurring new industries and technologies.

To learn more, volunteer, or contribute to Creekhoppers environmental initiatives, please visit:

www.creekhoppers.org

To learn more about Creekhoppers Press, or join the cause, please visit:

www.creekhopperspress.com

The raised hand depicted on the cover is a symbol of Jainism, one of the oldest religions on record, and one that shares many principles in common with those followed by, (arguably), about two thirds of the world's population if you include: Hinduism, Buddhism, the religions of China which are Daoism and Confucianism, and related belief systems[1].

Therefore, the majority of the world's people are likely believers in religions, or aspects of religions, that promote concepts of reincarnation, or rebirth, as a fundamental tenet.

---

[1] The government of China is officially anti-religion. However its people are thought to be primarily followers of Daoism and Confucianism. For factual reference and additional information on world religions, including number of followers and historical background, see, Gibbons, David, "Faith & Religions of the World," p. 25, (2007).

ACKNOWLEDGEMENTS

Thank you to my parents: to my mother for years of encouraging me to read and for hours of help editing; to my father for teaching me how to work hard.

Also, thank you to all those who encouraged me along the way, and to Kristen Tenney for the fantastic help with the cover art.

P lato, a Greek philosopher, shared views that the soul of man was eternal. Plato claimed the soul tends to become impure during bodily inhabitations although a minimal former life knowledge remains. However, if through its transmigrations, the soul continues doing good and eliminates the bodily impurities, it will eventually return to its pre-existence state. But, if the soul continually deteriorates through its bodily inhabitations it will end up in Tartarus, a place of eternal damnation. This appears to be an origination of both the concept of karma[2] and the Christian concept of hell.

---

[2] See: http://www.reincarnationresources.com/karma.html: "Karma is Sanskrit for "deed." In both Hinduism and Buddhism karma includes an individual's physical and mental actions which determine the consequences of the person's present life and sequential lives through rebirth. Karma is based upon the phenomena of cause and effect which denotes both action and reaction that extend through many lifetimes.

Karma is normally thought of as a term used by eastern religions such as previously mentioned. But Plato's usage indicates a broader, more global acceptance of the concept.

The following prologue is based upon confirmed, true to life

events, which took place in India. Similar incidents are

thought to be an ongoing problem, even today.

PROLOGUE

Twenty-Five Years Ago
Atapur Village, Jharkhand
(Rural South-Eastern India)

Jaya was on the track team back home, but nonetheless was panicking as she tired from the chase. Regretting her mischief, she wished that she had listened to the school guidance counselor in charge of the trip and stayed in after the curfew.

Her friend, Gopaja, had run off with the two young men that were hitting on them in that rural part of India. But Jaya, while possessed with a bad kid streak, wasn't ready to give up her virginity (at least not for those particular boys). That made her uninteresting company to the group which left her behind, to sit alone.

At first it wasn't all that scary to her, being stared at endlessly by a family of four. It was better than the unflagging harassment of two overly horny and obnoxious boys as far as she was concerned. And after all, families were non-threatening, *usually*.

A married couple, their young son, who looked to be about five, and their daughter, who looked about seven, had been eavesdropping on her since she rebuffed the two boys' attempted persuasions. Jaya had been talking loudly due to the boys' persistence. She finally lost her patience with them and her promiscuous young girlfriend, Gopaja, and turned heads by screaming in disgust, "I'm not about to waste my time with two losers from the country."

The two boys laughed at the outburst, and convinced her friend Gopaja to go along with them and have fun, unlike, "The prissy virgin." Jaya scornfully glared at her friend for revealing her secret.

Gopaja and the two boys left Jaya behind at the café where she worried about how she would find her way back to the hotel on her own. But her fears soon shifted when she realized she had become the subject of study by an odd looking family sitting a few tables away.

At first, she figured the family was simply staring at her due to the scene she had caused and her public outburst. But after enough time passed to convey their disdain, Jaya started getting nervous.

Gopaja wasn't likely to return from her adventure with the two boys, and so Jaya found herself alone, in a strange village, many miles from home. Eventually her nerves got the best of her. She left the café, and started walking back to the hotel. When she realized the family was following, she began a circuitous route around the village. They were definitely trailing her – but why would a family of four be so upset over a moderately inappropriate public tiff as to follow her around? Eventually she started running, trying to lose them.

Twenty minutes later, Jaya was nearly out of steam, and worse, she was hopelessly lost. Her lack of knowledge of the village kept her going in circles. Eventually, she ran into a dead end. It was dusk, and she found herself in a courtyard of uninviting closed doors. There was little light in the courtyard, which was littered with trash and planters full of dead flowers. The place gave her the creeps and she wasn't about to knock on any of the doors. She turned to back out of the courtyard, planning to resume her aimless running. She wished she could remember how to get back to the hotel where her schoolmates were staying, but in her frantic state, she had completely lost her orientation. Panic consumed her, and she didn't think things could get any worse. It was then, as she turned, that her stomach sank. She saw the mother and her two children blocking the path to the main roadway.

Taking a deep breath, she told herself it was OK. It had to be safe. The man wasn't there. What was the worst a mother and her two kids could possibly do to her? Scorn her for indecency? After all, she had done the right thing by rebuffing indulgence. Gopaja, her friend, was the one they should be scorning. That was what she would tell the family. A quick apology, an explanation, and then surely she would receive praise for maintaining her innocence despite the peer pressure. She walked up to them and put on her best friendly smile.

"I…, I am sorry if I offended your family back at the café, but please, let me explain…" her timid voice did not seem to affect the woman in the slightest. In fact, the stranger's face was stoic, emotionless. It scared Jaya for reasons she did not understand.

This is silly; this is just an offended family. I can handle this.

But she was unprepared for what was next. Without warning, the woman grabbed Jaya by the arm. She slammed her against the stucco covered concrete wall with such force that shock at the sudden violence froze Jaya into a state of confusion and pain. Then the mother, with her children watching, bent over, picked up a nearby flower pot and smashed the terracotta across Jaya's forehead. The force of the blow opened a gash which released a stream of blood across her face.

9

*   *   *

"Mommy, is the girl going to be OK?" Lavanya Singh asked her mother while peering at the tied down, spread eagle, and naked Jaya. She was on a dirt floor in a room with no windows, lit only by candles. The talking caused Jaya to stir and begin to regain consciousness.

"Yes Lavanya. This young woman will be reincarnated by the Gods as a reward for her sacrifice. And it's necessary if we want to help your sick brother."

"Will hurting her make my brother well again Mommy?"

"No, no, no Lavanya, this is what the woman wants… and it is her fate. It will not hurt her, but will give her eternal life, blessed by the Goddess Kali. And we will pray to Kali that her sacrifice helps your brother either in this life, or his next."

The confused child asked, "Then why did Daddy have to tie her down?"

The man young Lavanya called "Daddy" then walked into the room, and they ceased their conversation. He put an obscenely large number of pills in Jaya's mouth, followed by some water, forced her jaw closed, and pinched her nose to get her to swallow.

Standing over Jaya, the man commanded her, "Young girl – tell my daughter eternal life and blessings of the Gods is what you want. Tell her now and be blessed by Kali as the vehicle for reincarnation of your own soul and that of my only son, who is gravely ill."

The mother spoke, "I don't think the drugs are working, that is the third batch you have given."

"They will work. We must have patience." But his face showed the frustration of trying to get a young adolescent in modern India to ask to be a virginal sacrifice. He turned to the immobile Jaya, and slapped her brutally across the face. He then punched her in the stomach causing her to gag from losing her wind. Lavanya witnessed this and noticed bruising already starting on the girl's stomach from the many repeated blows. Lavanya's father then demanded, yelling, "Say it now girl or suffer unimaginable pain! Say you wish to be a sacrifice to the Goddess Kali!"

Jaya, tired of the beatings, and drugged beyond comprehension, murmured the words commanded of her. It was an essential step, as only a willing sacrifice would be accepted by the Gods.

In response, the man sprinkled holy water from the Ganges River across her naked body. He then used a common hack saw to remove Jaya's right arm. The adolescent Jaya screamed a horrific yelp as the man stood on her shoulder with his left foot, pinning her torso to the floor, and ripped her limb from her body. Arcs of blood, from ruptured arteries, streamed across the man's face and chest, and painted the walls, ceiling, and floor of the room with dark red lines of death. Next he sawed off the rest of her limbs. Jaya was dead from the severe blood loss even before he finished placing her body parts in front of a statue of the Goddess Kali. His wife and daughter joined him there in prayer, while his son laid deathly ill in a nearby cot.

He was mid sentence begging Kali for reincarnation for his son when an angry vigilante mob arrived, intending to prevent the human sacrifice, but several minutes too late to save the innocent Jaya[3].

*   *   *

The next day, after learning of Jaya's death, her brother screamed for almost an hour. At the top of his lungs, he

---

[3] The prologue to this book is based upon fact. Ritualistic sacrificial killings are historically verified occurrences in India and have been reported as recently as 2002; see Time Magazine, "Killing for Mother Kali," Alex Perry, 7/22/02, http://www.time.com/time/printout/0,8816,322673,00.html.

cursed the family that took Jaya's life, cursed the Gods, and vowed revenge.

CHAPTER 1

May
Shasta-Trinity Wilderness Area of Northern California
(Off the Grid)

In a remote wilderness area of California, where there was no commercially available power or telephone service, Anja Hunter, a shivering and scared, second grade school teacher from the suburbs of Washington, D.C. wondered why she was not spending her summer break as she had planned. Instead, she sat alone on an unfinished concrete floor in a cold, musty and wet smelling six by six room with no windows, a door with no handle, no light, no food, and only a bowl of dirty water which was occasionally slid through a small opening along the floor of one of the walls. Her clothes were heavily soiled with the smell of desperate fear and consisted of only her panties and a partially torn tank top. The room smelled of her feces. No one had spoken to her or turned on the lights in the pitch black room in over 72 hours, although to her, it seemed like an eternity. Despite her marital problems of the last six months, she longed to be home with her husband Jake, who thought she was merely taking an extended "Outward Bound" adventure retreat, with fellow hard core elementary school teachers from around the country. Ironically, that was just an excuse she fed to Jake in order to get away from him for the summer. The truth was she had planned a romantic affair on the Trinidad coast of Northern California with a man she hardly knew, who was named Gregor Eagon.

Instead of a sultry week of sex, the fear of not knowing why or how she came to be in her current situation was beginning to drive her insane. She didn't know why the man she thought was seducing her had instead put her in a cell with no light, food, or water.

*   *   *

The lights turned on and their brightness stung her. Anja closed her eyes temporarily but was eager to survey the surroundings in which she had been dumped three days earlier while unconscious. The last thing she remembered was a bee sting like prick on the back of her neck while hugging her would be lover, Gregor Eagon.

God only knows where I really am.

Teardrops ran down the side of her face. She couldn't believe she still had the vitality required to produce tears.

The door to her cell flew open with a hard bang and hit the pale grey cinder block wall behind it. Gregor Eagon walked in accompanied by another man whom she did not recognize. Gregor was a tall man, maybe 6'3", a Canadian, and with striking looks that could easily seduce most women. His bulging muscles reinforced his confident demeanor. The man standing next to him was dressed in a pristine suit and tie. Anja recognized the Hickey Freeman suit as it was Jake's favorite brand. The man in the suit had an even stronger demeanor than Gregor, as if he was the one in charge. Anja struggled to gather enough energy to think clearly:

I need to observe and gather information. I should find out

14

*who the man in the suit is... maybe his name will trigger
something, some memory, some incident, anything that might help
explain why they are doing this to me...*

As the two men walked in, Anja wanted to defy them
by showing she could still resist, so she sprang to her feet
intending to charge them. But her weakened state caused
her to immediately fall back down.

"Hello Mrs. Hunter, you don't know why you're here
yet but you soon will. You have nearly completed your first
day of training. Ninety days from now, you will be a new
person, ready to go out into the world and give something
to your country. Here are some pads of paper and some
pens. We need for you to write us a diary. Today's entry
will be no less than one hundred pages. It will state only
positive information about your first day of training..." She
started hysterically yelling at the man she thought was
going to make love to her but was instead delivering her to
hell.

"What is this??!! Are you insane? First day? You've
left me in here at least a week! Who do you think you
are..." They shot her with a stun gun and restarted the
conversation fifteen minutes later.

"Mrs. Hunter, it's imperative that you don't speak
until we tell you to speak." She immediately resumed
yelling, and again was shot with a stun gun. The process
repeated several more times until the pain of the stun gun
suppressed her pride and anger.

"Mrs. Hunter, are you ready to cooperate so that we
can give you more information about your current situation?
You may speak Mrs. Hunter."

"Fuck you."

"We'll take that as a yes. Get to work on your diary
entry. Your first day is not fully complete until we have one
hundred pages of hand written positive insight into your
training. We will come back to see you again in six hours to
critique your progress. You will re-write anything negative

that we find, and the process will continue until you get it right. You will not be allowed to sleep or eat until the first day is fully complete. Do you have any questions?"

"Fuck you, you bastard."

As they walked away, Anja stared at Gregor wondering how the man she had fantasized about having sex with could be treating her so differently. Watching him exit, she again wished to be home with her husband Jake. She felt a touch of guilt for having intended to deceive him.

She rubbed her chest near her heart while recalling how Jake always said, "If you think it, it's just as bad as doing it." But then she told herself that she was justified in her betrayal of her husband and that he deserved what she had intended to do and the things she had done in the past. Lying to herself like that somehow made her feel better, at least for the moment.

The metal door clanked shut with a loud bang and she could hear the bolts of the locking mechanism fall into place as the two men walked away. Anja listened carefully, trying to gather as much information on her captors as she could.

Gregor was addressing the other man in a way that reinforced her suspicion as to who was in charge, "Sir, we've got a proven plan here. In the past, it has worked on almost 65% of the test subjects."

"I see. And what about the other 35% of the subjects? Are you forgetting what happened to them? Seems to me they are all dead Gregor. Dead as a doornail. Do you really think that killing Anja Hunter is going to help our cause?"

"Don't be facetious. Killing her isn't an option in this case and you know I know that already. The fact remains, this is our best option. We really have few viable alternatives given the lack of progress so far. And we're running out of time. You were the one telling me last week that we'll be lucky to have more than a couple more months before our chances of success erode to nil."

"I did say that; so you will get to play doctor Gregor. But for your sake, I hope it works out the way you have planned. I would hate to have to use more extreme methods."

Gregor seemed to stop walking at that moment, paused, and then said, "I don't understand sir. What could possibly be more extreme than this approach that puts her life in serious risk? You wouldn't really consider the same approach used in Nakuru? That lobotomy style butchering of the woman's brain would render her useless. We need her cognitive processing somewhat intact." Anja was writhing in agony over what she was hearing but all she could think was:

Say his name, please say his name, just once. I need to know who is responsible for doing this to me.

But the man in the suit would not be revealed. He told Gregor, "Don't worry. We'll hold off on brain butchering for the time being. But you had better produce results. And don't forget, this is just a school teacher we're talking about here. She is not some fly under the radar super spy, or random derelict, that won't be missed. People are going to be asking questions; people will be looking for her, and it's not going to take long for that to happen. It may be risky, but you get only the time allotment we've discussed. After that, I will have no choice but to move on to the alternatives."

"Yes sir. You can count on me. I'll turn her into a viable backup plan for getting the Digitalis. And I intend to have her telling us all about it before the end of the summer."

"Don't let me down Gregor. You have worked with me long enough that you know how it will play out if you fail. And I'm pretty sure you don't want to go there." The conversation ended and the men walked out of earshot.

Back in the cell, Anja sat and cried. As she wiped the near constant flow of tears from her cheeks, she reminded herself of how she was immensely justified in her behavior, decisions, and actions. She convinced herself so well that she grew increasingly angry at her husband for causing her to fall into such dire circumstances. She vowed to herself that if she ever escaped, she would find some way to spite the man that did everything in his power to make her happy. She promised herself to get revenge against the man willing to die for her and she cursed him out loud.

Gregor watched and listened from a monitor in a nearby room then said out loud to himself, "Not even a week and she's already switching over to our team. What a bad, bad, disloyal, cheating wife you are Anja Hunter! Bad for your husband, but good for me! This is going to be easier than I thought."

I am confident that there truly is such a thing as living again, that the living spring from the dead, and that the souls of the dead are in existence.

–Socrates

CHAPTER 2

July 4
Washington, D.C.

Just as Devon Keyes, a corporate attorney working for Hunter Neurologics was about to leave his prominent K Street law office in downtown Washington, D.C. his cell phone alerted him to an urgent "pin" message. The sender was using a pin instead of a regular text to maintain the confidentiality of the transmission. It read:

SECURITY BREACHED – SOMEONE ELSE KNOWS... running out of time –max 14 days left - get to secure communication site and send status on DIGITALIS ASAP

Devon stared at the words in frustration, while a bullet of sweat dripped from his forehead and his hands shook. He sat motionless and worried. It was nearly 6 P.M. on a day most sane people were spending with their families, barbecuing, drinking Budweiser, and trying to stay sober enough to avoid blowing off fingers while shooting fireworks. But Devon Keyes was far from sane.

He was working on the final part of a plan he and his childhood friend John Anton had first put into motion over three years earlier. Up until recently, they had experienced nothing but success, despite their devious intentions.

It was all the more reason why Devon was in the office triple checking the details of every minute that would take place over the next two weeks. He intended to be so well prepared that he could beat the deadline he was recently reminded of on his cell phone, even if all hell broke loose, which he knew was almost certain to be the case.

It would be critical he get to Isla Dedaleras at precisely the right time to acquire the Digitalis. He needed a window of weakened security, and the perfect opportunity was only days away. Because his chance would be fleeting, he had set up a launching pad in the Florida Keys so that he could quickly mobilize when the moment struck. Aligning his visit with a hurricane was something he and John were ready to do a year earlier. Unfortunately, the required storm system never developed. It was only in the last twenty-four hours that forecasters had indicated an unexpected shift in weather patterns which would provide exactly what they needed. And his luck improved further when he learned the entire executive board and all the senior doctors and researchers would be off site taking advantage of the inclement weather to announce to the world their stunning breakthroughs. Dr. William Hunter, who was Jake's father and the founder of Hunter Neurologics would be immortalized as the person who had the most positive impact on medicine in the history of mankind, but not if Devon could help it.

Isla Dedaleras, a Caribbean island about one hour by plane from Key West, had been purchased by Hunter Neurologics from the Venezuelan government. The firm used investment monies that Devon arranged through his friend, John Anton. He knew John's family had money, but never thought it to be so extensive, and was perplexed as to where it was all really coming from.

But Devon was so focused on their ulterior motives

for financing the startup biotech, that his eyes were fixated on the prize at the end of the game, rather than the oddness of his childhood friend suddenly having access to limitless cash. An obsessive, greed induced, lack of awareness was a trait Devon displayed often. It would come back to haunt him later.

Devon was lost in thought sitting at his oversized mahogany desk:

All this is possible now because my law school study partner wasn't the best lawyer after all! Jake Hunter, I wish I could have been able to see the look on your face when you found out the truth! If only you could live long enough! Too bad that's not an option.

The intercom on his desk interrupted Devon's reverie. He gave no thought to his wife as he smiled when he realized it was his paralegal buzzing him. Kate Stinson was *very* easy on the eyes, not to mention a good time to be around, and that made her shark bait for every egomaniac lawyer in the firm.

Devon glanced at his wedding band, but only briefly, before responding to the intercom, "Hey Kate, what's going on?"

"Devon, are you leaving? You said you were heading out around six-ish, but you can't leave!" Kate was clearly panicked over something. Her tone left Devon sighing at the thought of dealing with yet another problem when all he really wanted to do was relax with a Gin and Tonic and/or hear how he was the man of her dreams even though he was already married to someone else.

What an arrogant middle aged man I am… 25 lbs over weight and I still think 20-somethings should be groveling over me. Well hell, they should…

"Yes Kate, I was planning on leaving. What's going on? What's the matter? You sound panicked?"

"Devon, there's something happening – near the mall I mean, the Fourth of July scene down there – they think it was a terrorist attack... come see the TV in the conference room." She was almost in tears as Devon Keyes scrambled out of his office into the only conference room on the floor equipped with TV monitors. He found Kate in there weeping, distressed, glued to the TV while wiping her eyes. When he looked at the TV and saw the panic in the news reporter's eyes he had an immediate flashback to September 11th. But then his cell phone rang. It was his wife of a little over a year, Lois.

Damn it, I hate it when she calls me while I'm alone with Kate.

With barely a modicum of guilt, he pushed the "ignore call" button and resumed comforting his twenty-something paralegal who had the looks of a Maxim cover girl, the smarts of a Yale grad, and the poise and polish that made her flirtatious ways soothing to even the most egregious of egomaniacs.

The news ticker summary cruising along the bottom of the screen summed up the gravity of the situation, "Attack near National Mall... hundreds, maybe thousands likely dead with scores injured, many seriously; cause of the multiple explosions currently unknown; unclear if terrorist act at this time. Citizens advised to stay indoors and asked to avoid the city except for medical personnel." D.C. was officially on "lockdown," meaning no suburbanites would be allowed in without an identification card that proved they had business inside city limits. Even then, unless the person worked for a hospital or essential federal agency, they would likely be turned away at border checkpoints setup on every major artery into the city from Maryland and Virginia.

Kate was grabbing on to him tightly, "Devon, I just..., I can't believe this. I... I mean, I really don't want to go home alone tonight," she glared directly into his eyes in a way that said a lot more than being scared of aloneness.

Devon Keyes had been a loyal and honest husband,

but was tired of his wife. He felt she didn't do exactly what he wanted, without him having to tell her what it was he wanted, and that annoyed him. All in all, it made resisting a woman like Kate Stinson, under those circumstances, harder than finding a green light when you're late for work. And that wasn't the only thing that was hard for Devon Keyes.

"Kate, I could use your support for this meeting I have at the Hunter Neurologics research and development site. It's at Isla Dedaleras, which is an island in the Caribbean. I am flying there in a few days, assuming I can beat the hurricane bearing down on the place. We're taking one of the company's private jets. Why don't you call the flight coordinator and tell them to prepare another seat for you? You could also join me on a pit stop I have to make in the Florida Keys. All in all, it would be a great way for you to learn more about the firm while spending a few days island hopping in tropical weather, far from all this chaos." Devon knew she lived alone and that her family and most of her friends were left behind in upstate New York when she moved down to D.C. The innocent, kind, and compassionate side of him was simply giving her the opportunity to divert her attention from a serious and dreadfully depressing national disaster by allowing her to throw herself into "work." But there could be no doubt; there was a part of him that wanted her company on the trip for other reasons.

Kate smiled at the idea and agreed to go, practically hopping out of her shoes from the excitement of seducing a married man. Devon studied her reaction with consternation. For only a fraction of a second he thought there was something strange about the sparkle in Kate's eyes. It was as if she had her own ulterior motives. But he shrugged it off, told himself not to be so insecure and paranoid, and assumed she wouldn't bother going unless she was truly excited.

They agreed to rendezvous back at her place to figure

out the details of the trip. Since Devon planned on spending the night, he phoned his wife to say his business trip was starting early. Just as he hung up from lying to her, in came a call from John Anton, the man who had yet to explain where he was getting the hundreds of millions they had been spending to bankroll Hunter Neurologics.

"Devon – we need to talk, and now. I've been informed the bomb was in the Hunter Neurologics headquarters building downtown. It was in the basement of the building Devon! We need to do something before the situation gets any worse. Clearly someone else is also after the Digitalis or is trying to prevent us from getting it. We're running out of time…"

Devon stepped out of the conference room and into a nearby office, closing the door and leaving Kate behind. Then, in as innocent a voice as he could muster, he replied to his old friend, "Are you kidding me John? They're saying there's over a thousand dead. How can it get any worse? Look, it probably doesn't matter anyway since I'm heading down to the island in a day or two to try to secure the Digitalis once and for all…"

"We don't have a day or two…" John retorted.

"It'll have to do John. You and I both know we need to time this right. We have to wait for that severe weather system. It will prevent any flights into the island for at least a couple days and that's when we can strike."

"So be it. But you had better find what we're looking for because this bombing tells me we have a much bigger obstacle in our way than we ever anticipated. And if we can't produce the Digitalis or something that leads us to it, then we're going to be in one hell of a mess. We could potentially lose everything…"

Devon mumbled, then interrupted, "Don't be so dramatic John. We are in control here, not some antisocial bomber. Besides, that explosion probably was a terrorist attack and had nothing to do with us. It is the Fourth of July after all."

"Don't be such a naïve idiot Devon. It was meant to look like an unrelated terrorist attack. There's no doubt about that. But everything is at stake here, including our lives if we can't deliver the Digitalis as we promised to the buyer."

"Take it easy with the complements there buddy."

"No, you take it easy Devon. I need you to understand the reality we're in. We cannot waste even an hour. And you need to be extremely careful when you go down to the island. There is obviously some inside person working against us. I'd watch out for that whack job, Dr. Jansen if I were you. I don't trust him one bit. And another thing, I hope it's clear to you that unless we get the Digitalis before anyone else, we might never be safe again. Because it's clear to me, that this is way over our heads now."

"You are rambling. Try switching to decaf John. And I agree, Jansen is a whack job, but he's the last person I'm worried about. There's a reason I told you to get the guy a job on the island. He will serve his purpose when the time is right. As for who's giving away inside information, I don't know the answer to that… yet. But I'll get to the bottom of it. We'll secure what we've been working for, and we'll figure out how to stop the people trying to get in our way. We can't give up because of a few minor challenges when we're this close. Keep your head on straight and we will work through this."

"I am not sure if it's even possible any longer. If we can't deliver, it will be the skin off our backs. And I do mean that literally."

"I'll call you John, don't worry. Keep your cell handy. Oh and by the way, don't forget, the big man's son used to be my law partner… we still have our backup plan if we need it."

"You and I both know that backup plan could unravel if Jake starts to figure things out. He didn't strike me as a complete idiot. Sooner or later, he's going to start putting two and two together about his disbarment and the malpractice case…"

"None of that should matter given the steps we've taken."

"It shouldn't. But it could. So we need to control things by taking action. We can't sit back and hope. Please, just do what you do best Devon, and it'll be drinks and stogies on me – the usual routine."

John can't possibly know, can he? How could he know about the pin message and the fourteen day deadline? I've been too careful, there's no way…

Before either of them could say anything more, the phone went dead, and the nefarious "signal lost" message blinked across Devon's cell while all bars disappeared from the coverage meter. They were not coming back, most likely due to the chaos downtown. Since it wasn't a topic for unsecured land lines, Devon Keyes decided he would wait to call his childhood friend back.

Thankful the interruption was over, and heading for the door to leave, Devon reunited with Kate Stinson and took one last look at the television monitor. They stared intently at the news ticker flashing across the bottom of the screen with the latest updates on the bombing, "…President Wilson's whereabouts cannot be confirmed and only the Vice President's office has contacted the media. Vice President Johnson indicates there will be a press conference tonight at 10 P.M. Eastern time to address the day's events."

I died as a mineral and became a plant, I died as a

plant and rose to animal, I died as animal and I was man.

Why should I fear? When was I less by dying?

–Jalalu 'D-Din Rumi, (Sufi Poet)

CHAPTER 3

Hunter Neurologics Corporate Jet "HN2" Crash Site
Unknown Island in the Caribbean
(Flight from Caracas, Venezuela to Foreign Registered Isla
de Las Dedaleras)

Jakob Hunter was crawling on his hands and knees trying to avoid the heavy smoke that filled the air and stung his eyes. Emergency lighting was barely visible along both edges of the aisle, but his affinity for the lights was unbreakable. Each light further along the path was all that mattered.

Jake knew the mere handful of other passengers on board the corporate jet as his friends and colleagues from the company his father had built over two decades, Hunter Neurologics. There was also a single flight attendant and two apparently less than capable pilots who were lifeless and dangling from their chairs. Jake thought it odd that they were not wearing their seatbelts. But with the smoke thickening, and panic setting in, he had other things to worry about.

Fortunately a strange calmness overtook him as he moved from a crawling position to a standing one, and without thinking, he reached to his right and released the emergency exit door hatch on the starboard side of the defunct plane. The smoke cleared and he saw a heavy rain outside which he assumed had contributed to the crash.

The last time he had checked the navigation system, they were somewhere over northern Venezuela. That was about fifteen minutes into the flight path which took them along Venezuela's northern coast, before turning into the Caribbean Sea toward their destination, Isla de Las Dedaleras, or simply "Isla Dedaleras." The island, which was a former territory of Venezuela, was a small spec of land that only made the cut for local maps. It was purchased by John Anton from the Venezuelan government two years earlier. Since it was a foreign registered territory, clinical trial oversight by the United States FDA could be skirted with some fancy legal work. That was why Hunter Neurologics maintained an office in Caracas and used Isla Dedaleras as their research and development headquarters. The heavy investments were about to pay off as the company was nearing an announcement about a significant breakthrough in memory restoration for those with Alzheimer's, amnesia, and other head traumas.

Jake figured they were probably not more than another twenty minutes from finishing the flight at the time of the crash. It also meant they likely landed on some other island in the middle of the Caribbean. Staring at the vast tropical jungle in front him, Jake was overwhelmed at the lack of civilization.

I suppose this is better than crashing in the ocean.

The automatically inflating slide failed to inflate. But it didn't matter as the emergency exit door was on the ground. The landing gear had been torn off and the plane's belly was resting directly in the tropical foliage which engulfed them. This allowed Jake to walk right out into the jungle and peer back at what used to be a luxury corporate jet.

Where is everyone else? What are they doing? Are the others OK? Why isn't anyone else moving around and trying to get out?

There wasn't a single human built structure anywhere within eye sight. Jake realized he was in the middle of an extremely remote jungle, staring at a crashed airplane – desperately alone. He wished his wife Anja, who was with him for everything else important in life, was at his side, but was thankful she was safely attending to her wilderness retreat back in the U.S. Although a part of him was also a little bitter.

If she hadn't signed up for that, I would have stayed home and tried to improve things in our marriage and wouldn't even be in this mess. Our first time apart and I'm in a plane crash. If she hadn't left, I would never have been on this damn flight and wouldn't be stuck in a tropical jungle.

He knew he had to climb back into the wrecked plane to check on the others. Eyeballing the wreckage, he looked around for signs of flames or leaking fuel. He couldn't see any real significant damage at all, and the smoke had almost completely cleared out from the cabin. Jake was surprised to see his father's chair was empty. Dr. William Hunter was nowhere to be found. He did notice a strange bi-fold card holder near his father's chair. On it was a gold embossed symbol he didn't recognize which looked like two monkeys embracing and the word, "Moksha." He didn't think much of it at the time, other than it seemed out of place. His concern turned back to his father and the other passengers.

Recently disgraced by being temporarily disbarred over his handling of a trial for a former client, Aubrey Doyle, whose estranged husband was also suing him for malpractice, Jake was not about to drop the ball on helping the others onboard the airplane.. He found himself in the middle of an opportunity to earn redemption in his father's eyes. Partly, Jake was only on the flight as he took the position of Corporate Counsel for Hunter Neurologics to try to show his father, and himself, that he was a decent attorney. The other part of it was that no one else would hire a temporarily disbarred lawyer being sued for malpractice in a widely publicized case. No matter how *innocent* Jake claimed he was, the press had already found him guilty, and that meant the public was against him.

Jake checked the overhead compartment near the empty chair. He was looking for his father's steel briefcase. Before takeoff, Dr. Hunter had told his son, "This case holds what we have codenamed, the Digitalis. In a nutshell, it is the compilation of all the results of decades of our work. Its contents will cure Alzheimer's, allow for improving cognitive processing in patients with brain damage, and open the door to a new world of medicine that will change the human race more than any other advance known to man." Jake's heart sank when he saw that the case was missing.

Next, he checked on the other passengers and was even more shocked. His chest felt as if it were about to explode from his increasing blood pressure. He checked the pulses of each of his former colleagues: Janice Hopkins, Chief Psychologist and mother of two, was dead at a young 34; Bill Allison, Chief Medical Officer and recently married was dead; Walter Williams, Senior Vice President – dead, everyone else, even the pilots – all dead. There were twelve dead bodies in total. His father was missing. Besides himself and one other person, the entire team of executives, doctors, and scientists, which comprised the board of directors and leadership group of Hunter Neurologics, was dead. The other survivor was unconscious and not moving.

Jake recognized the woman as Kennedy Taylor, one of the newer research doctors on the team. She was a fresh graduate of Johns Hopkins who had won awards for her research on cognitive processing restoration after brain trauma. For all the respect he had for her and her zillions of credentials, she looked helpless in her disheveled state, strewn across two chairs, unconscious and limp. For the time being, Jakob Hunter was alone.

Puzzled at the light damage to the plane, himself and the dead, Jake peered around in awe at the scene. It momentarily calmed his hysteria. Then it hit him. Just as he felt the throbbing from the concussion in his head, the whole sequence of events leading to the crash landing flashed before him. Nowhere in his memory however, was any rational explanation for the pilots indicating they had to touch down as quickly as possible. There was no sign of an emergency or any communication from the pilots once chaos took hold of their flight. And the passengers were eerily quiet as the plane abruptly descended to its current resting spot in a narrow clearing of otherwise dense Caribbean jungle.

Jake saw meal trays, mostly eaten and empty scattered around each of the other passengers' chairs. He recalled the flight attendant delivering dinner to the pilots well in advance of everyone else. Then he looked back at his chair, the meal tray lying on the floor nearby, still unopened. He glanced at the woman who was alive but unconscious. It struck him that she was remarkably attractive, even in her tattered state. For a second, he wondered how he had never noticed her good looks before. Her meal tray was also untouched. It was then that fear consumed him the most. The crash wasn't just bad luck. It was clearly intentional, and no one was meant to survive it. Overwhelmed by the situation, his world darkened, and Jake passed out.

E gyptians believed in reincarnation or the
transmigration of the soul. They thought the soul
transmigrated from body to body and this was a reason why
they embalmed the body in order to preserve it so that it
could journey along with ka, an animating force that was
believed to be counterpart of the body, which would
accompany it in the next world or life.[4]

---

[4] http://en.wikipedia.org/wiki/Afterlife

CHAPTER 4

Many Weeks Earlier
California Wilderness – Off the Grid
"Day Two"

Anja glanced down to see her watch and started to cry again, at first because she realized she was missing her Cartier, but then she remembered she was barely even clothed. It had taken nearly two weeks to complete what her captors had referred to as, "Day One." The time allotted for her to sleep was interrupted by the loud clanking of the bolts on her door coming unlocked. The light in her cell went on as the door opened. She yawned.

That barely felt like a fifteen minute nap.

The reality was she had no idea how long she had been allowed to rest, nor how long she had been in the cell. She had zero sense of time, day or night, thanks to her captors' efforts at sensory depravation.

Several men wheeled a cart into the room. On it was an iMac with a web conferencing session turned on and the online video showing a masked man in another room somewhere. Two of the men grabbed her by her arms squeezing so hard she yelped out in pain. A third man affixed a metal collar to her neck and locked it in place with a padlock in the back. He hooked electrical wires up to the sides of the collar. Then, dangling the key in front of her eyes, he said to Anja, "I hope someday you realize Anja, this session was simply meant to help you. By that I mean, lessening the time required for you to understand, and subsequently reducing the overall pain and torment you must experience on your road to freedom. You do want freedom, don't you Anja?"

"What I want, is for you to die," she spat on the man and was quickly knocked from her chair by the back of his hand smacking across her face. The men picked her up and sat her back in the chair. They cuffed her hands and her ankles to it so that she could neither move, nor damage the equipment sitting directly in front of her. Then they left. Anja drifted off, her subconscious mind taking over, allowing her to escape to a memory with her husband, Jake. A memory of a day he hugged her just right, in such a way that made her feel so truly loved, secure, and safe. That one hug, more than any other memory, could always make her feel better and always make any problem disappear.

The first electrical shock to her neck collar brought her screaming in agony back to her miserable reality. Her spine went so rigid she swore a few discs popped out of place.

The man on the video screen started talking to her, "We are going to do verbal exercises today. Afterwards, in your day two diary entry, you will be required to report on how you benefited from this learning experience. Are you ready Anja?" The man's sinister appearance was heightened by the leather mask he was wearing which hid any facial expression. But his eyes glowed an incandescent blue as if he was wearing fake colored contacts.

"Yes. I am ready. I am ready to kill you, you sicko." Not quite the answer the man was looking for or expecting as most of the prisoners that survived long enough to sit in that chair were already worn out to a point where their resistance had faded. But Anja Hunter was not a quitter. She was a fighter and was determined to find a way to escape.

Another shock made her spine rigid once again. She recovered, saliva still dripping from her mouth as she stared at the screen.

The man spoke again, "We will learn ten special thoughts today. You will say each thought no less then one thousand times. Later today, you will get to write each thought one thousand times. Let's begin. I want you to repeat after me your first thought Mrs. Hunter. We are displaying it on the monitor in front of you."

My husband Jakob Hunter is a bad man, a very bad man. I cheated on my husband repeatedly because he is a bad man, a killer. I must do everything possible to get justice for his awful actions.

"You're beyond loony. The only thing I am saying is faaaaaaaah," another shock caused her to convulse so hard urine ran down her leg and her wrists bled from being yanked in the metal handcuffs.

"We can take as much time as you like Mrs. Hunter, but we simply cannot begin your day two journal entry until you are able to verbalize each of your ten thoughts one thousand times. Don't worry, we'll send in some water if you start to lose your voice or consciousness. Shall we try it again?"

"What do you want from meeee!" she yelled out.

"Mrs. Hunter, is it not true you've been cheating on your husband with multiple partners for some time?"

"NO! What the hell would that have to do with anything anyways? Whyyyeye do you care about me or my husband!! What is this all about!?!?"

"Mrs. Hunter, what's important is that we work together here. That way, we can avoid having to inform your husband of your indiscretions and risk you loosing a fortune in inheritance from his life insurance. Isn't that something you want to work with us on, Mrs. Hunter?"

She paused and contemplated what the man had just said to her. She had long considered herself nothing more than a trophy wife, although she had no good reason to think that way or be angry towards her husband. In any event, the idea of inheriting money from her husband's insurance policy sounded strange when as far she knew he was in good health. She thought about it for a moment more, and then uttered the phrase, "My husband Jakob Hunter is a bad man, a very bad man. I cheated on my husband repeatedly because he is a bad man, a killer. I must do everything possible to get justice for his awful actions."

Behind the two way mirror on the far side of the wall, Gregor Eagon, joined by his guest, John Anton, watched her begin "day two" as tears dripped down her face. She knew in her heart her husband was the best man she had ever met and the only man that would ever forgive her for her weaknesses, but even on the pedestal upon which she placed him – even there, she didn't think he would be able to forgive her most recent sins against him. So her only choice was to make him the villain, and so it was, in her mind. It was all his fault: if only he had loved her for real, if only he had cared more, if only he had been kinder, if only… if only he had never left her (that he was loyal to her meant nothing when he had left emotionally so long ago). In fact, she started to become convinced. Her mind was repeatedly telling her that it was remarkable she had been able to stay with him, and loyal to him, for as long as she had.

John Anton checked his cell phone and noticed a missed call from Devon Keyes. He wondered how his trip to Isla Dedaleras was proceeding, and then he sent a text message to Lavanya Yashodhara in India:

insurance policy comg along nicely. situation here under ctrl. n route to india this aftnoon. arrive by morng on red i. cant wait 2 c u ;-)

CHAPTER 5

Yashodhara Palace
Rajoli, India
(Remote Area, 2 Hours South-East from Nagpur,
Maharashtra)

Although Jakob didn't know it, his father, Dr. William Hunter, who founded Hunter Neurologics, was alive and being held captive in India.

Dr. Hunter was begrudgingly "escorted" from his "room" by two armed Indian men, each about 6'4" or taller. They refused to answer his questions as to where he was, or why he was there. No one had spoken to him since he regained consciousness and found himself lying in a plush canopy bed overflowing with silk linens. He demanded answers but received only prodding from their AK-47s.

The two guards opened a door to a wood paneled two story library. The tips of their guns in his ribcage told Dr. Hunter to go in. They shut the door and locked it behind him. Moments later, he was greeted by a woman of stunning beauty. Given his age, he was surprised at how he was taken aback by her remarkable appearance and charming demeanor. She was standing near a couch and greeted him, "Hello Dr. Hunter, I am Lavanya Yashodhara. I hope you are recovering well from the injuries you incurred in the plane crash?"

"I am not in the mood for pleasantries. This is obviously not a hospital. I would like to know where I am and what happened to my colleagues." He wanted to scream and shout, and demand. But given the circumstances, he thought politely asking might do him more justice.

Lavanya Yashodhara paused, contemplating her response before calmly looking him in the eyes and informing him, "You are in India, Dr. Hunter, as my guest here in my family home. As for your team, unfortunately, there were no other survivors of the plane crash." William Hunter knew his only child was on that plane, in addition to the team he had worked with for nearly three decades. They were dedicated to, and nearing success on achieving their mission, which was to find effective treatments for cognitive disorders such as Alzheimer's and memory loss due to head traumas. While he never intended for his work to be used for less than noble purposes, he had long known in his heart that the scientific advances he had stumbled upon would draw international attention on a scale never before seen.

He fell to one knee after hearing that his colleagues had given their lives, literally. After pausing to catch his breath, he stood back up and again, calmly asked, "Who are you exactly and why did you bring me here, to India? That flight was on the other side of the world."

"I told you Dr. Hunter, I am Lavanya Yashodhara."

"Ah, I see. The Lavanya part I get." Dr. William Hunter studied world history in his free time, to relax his mind. Through his studies, he found himself focusing on the history of India, because it was the birthplace of so many religious concepts. In the process, he had learned a small amount about Indian culture, including that the name Lavanya typically translated to "beautiful girl." He was only mildly shocked with his cordiality towards a woman young enough to be his grandchild. And he hoped it might help make her more forthcoming. Dr. Hunter continued to pour it on, "Indeed, your beauty lives up to your given name. But it's your family name I am not as familiar with. Perhaps you could enlighten me as to where in India you are from, or better yet, where in India you are hosting me as your guest?"

'Prisoner,' he thought, would be a more accurate word! Just stay calm. Focus. Sharpen my focus and keep the upper hand. This woman is not going to tell me anything useful, unless she thinks I'm going to play ball.

Lavanya laughed, "Ah, Dr. Hunter, you are a flirt, and a clever one at that. Sadly, you are my elder by several generations. My true family name may give you the answers you seek. You see Dr. Hunter, I changed my original family name to hide a horrible stigma brought upon it by my parents when I was only four. What little I recall of the incident, is a memory I will never forget. It is a memory of watching the people I thought of as Gods show their human weaknesses, and which culminated in my growing up as an orphaned child with no family to speak of. So, I chose my new family name. Yashodhara has its origins as a name given to a collection of ancient written works about the fundamental tenets of Jainism[5]."

"Jainism!" he interrupted, "One of the world's oldest religions if I'm not mistaken?"

"Again, you impress Dr. Hunter. The writings about Jainism and the name Yashodhara more closely align with my own personal goals, which now, thankfully, you are going to help me achieve."

He stared at her with the gravest face he could muster, trying to convey through his expression a recalcitrance that would never be tamed.

As if reading his mind, she went on, "Please be assured, Dr. Hunter, there is no need to resist. While I know your wife died years ago, I also know your daughter-in-law is the closest to your heart now."

"That's impossible," he muttered under his breath.

How can she know all these things about me? Who the hell is this woman?

"Do not worry, Dr. Hunter, I will not reveal your sins to your son. They can be our little secret for as long as you cooperate. May I call you William? Of course I may. Many years ago, it was reported in a magazine article, that you found a series of difficult to explain and extremely severe

---

[5] *Yashodhara Charite*, an epic written in the *kandapadya* metre is a unique set of stories in 310 verses dealing with perverted sex and violence and contains cautionary morals on the issue of extreme desires. (See, http://en.wikipedia.org/wiki/Janna#cite_note-sex-4#cite_note-sex-4). Inspired by the Sanskrit writing of the same name by Vadiraja, the Janna transcribes stories of King Yashodhara and his mother and their passing from one life to the next without attaining *Moksha* (liberation from cycle of death and re-birth). (See, http://en.wikipedia.org/wiki/Janna#cite_note-jain-3#cite_note-jain-3). In one of the stories, the king intends to perform a ritual sacrifice of two young boys to a local deity, Mariamma. Taking pity on the boys, the king releases them and gives up the practice of human sacrifice. Nagaraj, D.R., *Critical Tensions in the History of Kannada Literary Culture*, pp. 323–383 (2003). Sheldon I. Pollock. *Literary Cultures in History: Reconstructions from South Asia*, Berkeley and London: University of California Press. p. 1066. ISBN 0520228219. Shiva Prakash, H.S. (1997). "Kannada". in Ayyappapanicker. *Medieval Indian Literature: An Anthology*, Sahitya Akademi. ISBN 8126003650

adverse effects in one of your patients. That article is why you are here."

"Lavanya, I have no idea what on earth you are talking about."

She grew agitated by his unflagging denials. With a tense tone, she attempted to clarify, "More specifically then, Dr. Hunter, you are here to prove once again, that reincarnation is real. Only this time, it will not be considered an unwanted adverse effect. It will be in line with our desired outcome and will forever change humanity."

"Not a chance. Not a chance in hell. Besides, that article was an unauthorized and absurd extrapolation of already exaggerated rumors and conjecture. There was no patient, no clinical trial, and no adverse effects that would confirm something like reincarnation. The whole idea is ludicrous, at best. So again, I say that even if I wanted to, there isn't a chance in hell I could help you with that."

"On the contrary, there is more than a chance. I know for a fact there was a clinical trial at Nakuru in Kenya and that you were a major part of it. And I am quite confident that you are going to change your mind and be more cooperative. In fact, if you would, please turn your attention to the monitor on the wall." On a nearby large screen wall monitor, an image of Anja Hunter, his daughter-in-law appeared. Lavanya used a remote to increase the volume.

On screen, a muffled, male voice, from outside the camera's view, said, "Read the card, now!"

Then Anja said, "My name is Anja Hunter. I am a prisoner against my will," she paused slightly, as if she were going to cry, but then resumed with a more confident tone, as if trying to spite her captors, "I am in a remote location off the grid where there is no electricity, no phones, no roads. My condition is fair, but extremely unpleasant." She wiped tears from her eyes before the camera panned down to show her ragged, barely clothed state.

Dr. William Hunter grew glassy eyed and tears would have flowed, but his mind was distracted by an interruption from Lavanya, "So, do you still say nothing happened at Nakuru, or shall we begin working together to satisfy each others' goals?"

He sat, stunned into silence for a moment, before replying, "What is it you want exactly?"

"Ah, that's more like it Dr. Hunter. It's like I said, I am going to scientifically prove reincarnation, and you are going to help me." She summoned the guards, then continued, "Let's proceed, I'll show you where you will accomplish this feat, which is destined to change the way the world views religion, forever."

T he doctrine of transmigration… was a means of constructing a plausible vindication of the ways of the cosmos to man; …none but the very hasty thinkers will reject it on the grounds of inherent absurdity[6].

–Thomas Huxley[7]

---

[6] See, Thomas H. Huxley, "Essays Upon Some Controverted Questions," 1892.

[7] Thomas Henry Huxley was an English biologist, known as "Darwin's Bulldog," for his advocacy of Charles Darwin's theory of evolution. See, http://en.wikipedia.org/wiki/Thomas_Henry_Huxley

CHAPTER 6

Unknown Island in the Caribbean

Glancing at his watch, Jakob Hunter figured he had passed out for roughly thirty minutes. He pulled his cell phone from his pocket. Hoping it was not in vain, he tried to power it on but there was no signal.

I wish I could talk to Anja. Just the sound of her voice could make this entire mess OK. Maybe I can at least revive Kennedy so I'm not totally alone.

Jake nudged the unconscious Kennedy Taylor. She didn't move. He found a first aid kit and some smelling salts. Waving the salts under her nose caused her to jump from the disturbance.

"What, what the hell are you doi…" she stopped herself mid-sentence realizing rain from outside the plane was coming in while she sat there surrounded by listless bodies and the son of the man who had hired her only a few months earlier. "Jake, what's going on? How long was I out?"

"I would guess about half an hour but I honestly didn't think to check the time. It could have been longer. The good news is that it seems like the storm has died down outside. I'm thinking we may want to check out our surroundings a bit, see if we're alone, before the rain and winds pick up again. What do you think, can you walk?" But all she could do was stare around at the inside of the plane, dumbfounded. Her eyes began to glaze over, as if she were about to turn hysterical.

"Dr. Taylor? Are you with me?! Kennedy?" Her eyes came back to his, but she still didn't look good.

With her face green and stomach queasy, she mustered up the will to state the obvious, "We crashed?"

"Yes, we did. But, the plane is in decent shape. For the most part, it is, remarkably, still in one piece. But everyone is dead."

"Dead? Jake, you're kidding right? This plane is in one piece. How can they all be dead!?"

"No, Dr. Taylor, I'm not kidding. And as for why, your guess is as good as mine. None of them appear to have any significant injuries."

"Would you please stop calling me Dr. Taylor? Please just call me Kennedy. And what about your father? Why is his seat empty?" Tension overtook her voice and demeanor, but it was not as Jake had expected. It was as though she had this strange aura about her, like she knew exactly how to handle a disastrous situation. It was enough to make him wonder:

How could a neuroscientist know what to do about a plane crash in the middle of nowhere? Why is she immediately asking about my father without any care for any of the other passengers? And what kind of a doctor has a healthy enough ego that they can stand to be called by their first name? That's just not normal…

Jake's eyes watered over in response to her question about his father. And Kennedy figured it meant he didn't have any good answers. He said to her, "Kennedy, everyone is dead. Even my father is dead. And his briefcase is gone. He will never be able to present his findings. And he was so close. He was about to end the plague on the human mind caused by Alzheimer's disease. It would have been probably the greatest medical breakthrough in our lifetimes. And now, it will never happen. And I... he will have died thinking of me as nothing more than a failure... a disbarred attorney whose law firm crumbled. I will never be able to make him proud. It's over. It's all over," Jake's eyes started to water and Kennedy realized he was going into a state of shock. She needed to find a way to get him to focus on something else.

Kennedy glanced again at the chair his father had occupied.

There isn't a body. His father's body is gone, and there are no signs of blood or other physical struggle. There's more to this than a simple plane crash.

"I'm so sorry Jake. But I don't get it, everyone is in their chairs, the plane is mostly intact. This doesn't make sense. The fact of the matter is that your father is most likely not dead. We can't be sure when there is no body. But that his briefcase is gone as well, is a good sign."

"Wait!" Jake interrupted her, "Kennedy, just wait a second. Why didn't you eat dinner?"

"I was recovering from food poisoning the night before. What does that have to do with anything? Didn't you eat? Are you hungry? Honestly, I don't get how you can be hungry under these circumstances."

"No, I didn't eat. Yes I am hungry – this starvation diet I'm on means I'm hungry all the time. Hence the name. But apparently it saved my life and not because my cholesterol and body fat percentage are lower."

Kennedy paused, taking in what he said and peering around the plane. She saw the empty meal trays scattered about. "Holy crap," she said, "It was the food. But if the food was poisoned, that would mean everyone was intentionally..."

"Murdered. It sure looks that way. I would say, yes, the entire leadership team of my father's company that he spent a lifetime building, has been killed." Jake jumped up, perplexed at how the pilots could have landed the plane if they too had been murdered. As he ran into the cockpit he saw what happened. A bullet to the back of the head for each of them painted the inside of the cockpit red with blood and brains; although again he saw how they were not wearing their seat belts and the bullet holes in their bodies seemed slightly unaligned with the streaks of blood on the plane's windshield.

Kennedy stood behind him and asked, "But why Jake? Why would someone kill off the entire board of the company?" He wondered what she was really asking and why she was asking it.

Shouldn't she be more concerned with how we're going to get the hell out of here?

Jake replied, "That's the million dollar question Kennedy. I suppose they wanted to steal the biggest medical breakthrough of our lifetimes."

Kennedy replied, "Hmm, possibly. I mean it is far more than a cure for Alzheimer's. You know it's expected to usher in a new era of medicine, where everything doctors do will be based on the breakthroughs your father has developed."

"Yes I know all that. Too bad it's not gonna happen since he's dead."

She looked at him quizzically, "That doesn't make sense. Not like this. There has got to be more to the story. They would never be able to get away with it for one thing, especially with you and I still alive."

"You're forgetting, we are not supposed to be alive. And I'm also willing to bet that whoever has the resources to try something like this, will probably also spend the time and money necessary to follow up and make sure the job was done correctly."

They both sat there for a minute, bewildered by their situation. To Jake, there was something alluring about Dr.

Kennedy Taylor. The way she was looking at him was as if he was her hero.

Shoot, only a few seconds ago, I was amazed at how she seemed so calm and in control. What is it with her?!

It was the first time since meeting his wife that Jake had gotten butterflies in his stomach from another woman. Anja became an afterthought as his attention was sharply focused on Kennedy; even a minor bead of sweat on her forehead was noticeably sexy. His knees went weak as he studied the beautiful contours of her face and body.

She had his undivided attention while asking, "What about your father? We can't just leave this place, wherever we are, without looking for him?"

Jake looked over at his father's chair and again saw the strange card holder with the gold monkeys and the word, "Moksha." He walked over, grabbed the bi-fold card holder, which felt like it was solid gold, as opposed to the flimsy gold painted brands you see all too often, and put it in his pocket. He was unsure of its significance, but was sure it had some.

He had draped blankets over all the bodies. The thought of leaving them there made him want to weep. But the thought of someone coming back to finish him off kept his mind razor sharp. The fact was, Jake didn't know what to do, and yet, he had an overwhelming fear that told him he needed to do something, and fast.

He tried to compose himself and finally said to Kennedy, "No, no, it's OK. I don't think we have a choice. We can't linger here. And even if we did, I have a feeling that wouldn't help us figure out what happened to my father. We should see if we can't find a working cell phone or better yet, maybe there was a satellite phone on board. We'll also need some blankets; if we're lucky, someone's got a backpack in here or something that we can load up with food and water." Kennedy laughed. "What's so funny?" he asked her.

"Maybe we should 86 bringing any food?"

Jake grinned. "Right, scratch the food. And only pack unopened bottled water." They scrambled to find some supplies: warm clothing, sweaters, anything they could easily carry with them, some maps from the cockpit, and then stood outside the plane. They stared at the jungle and tried to figure out where to go. They walked about twenty yards to the edge of the clearing to scope out the jungle to the West. With nothing but tropical foliage in sight, Jake started to second guess their plan and said to Kennedy, "Maybe we should wait here, for a rescue?"

Kennedy responded, "There will be no rescue Jake. Everything about your father's company was top secret. The plane wasn't even registered in the U.S., or any other country for that matter. There will be no one to come looking for us. Didn't you sign the security waivers and confidentiality forms which explained all the risks? We are outside the laws of the U.S., which means we're also outside their protections."

"I suppose my father didn't think it necessary to obtain informed consent from his own son. But still, Devon Keyes was supposed to meet us later this week at Isla Dedaleras. He will look for..." Jake was interrupted with an abruptness that had the two of them hitting the ground so quickly and with such force they were both dazed from concussions.

The flames from the plane exploding stretched high into the sky. The initial explosion was centered inside the cockpit, not in the wings, where the fuel tanks were located, although they exploded next.

After the noise settled and debris stopped falling from the sky, Kennedy said, "I think we're safe now. My guess is that was the special precaution to 'finish the job' if you know what I mean."

"Safe? We're in the middle of nowhere. What if they figure out we survived? They'll hunt us down and kill us."

"There's not a doubt in my mind that you are right Jake. I do believe we would have a problem if anyone knew we were alive."

"Sorry Kennedy. Let's focus on staying that way for now. Assuming we are on an island, if we head away from the hills, we should find a coastline."

I have to stay alive because if they kill me, I'll never be able to set things straight with my disbarment and I need to do that so that I can help Aubrey Doyle. She doesn't stand a chance against her ex-husband and the D.A. without my help, and no one else is going to stand up for her – not against those two. I've got to get back so I can help her..

*　　*　　*

The foliage was dense tropical rainforest. Broad green leafed banana trees were everywhere and created a nice canopy over the underlying ferns. It provided a small amount of protection from the light drizzle that continued to soak them to their bones.

As they walked along, shock from their situation kept them both fairly quiet and deep in thought. Finally Kennedy asked, "Did you check the maps in the cockpit? Did any of them make any sense or seem to match the topography of this place?"

"I couldn't match any of them. It's impossible to say where we are or what island we are on. But I checked the plane's compass before we left the crash site. I'm hoping we can get to the coast and walk the perimeter until we find a town."

"Hmmm, do you think they would crash us on an inhabited island?"

"What do you mean?" Jake responded.

"If it were me, I would find one where there were no people. Just in case, ya know?"

"I know Kennedy, trust me, I get that. But give me a

reason to head another direction, no matter how weak and I'll take you up on it."

"Good point," she responded, "let's keep going. Sorry, I'll try to stay more positive."

"You have to Kennedy. It's the only way. Whether here, or waking up anywhere else. You have to fight. You have to decide to be positive every day. So now, when we have to do it the most, let's be at our best. Deal?"

"Are you lecturing me Jake Hunter? Jeez, I guess thanks for setting me straight," she chuckled slightly before shifting her eyes across his body in way that clearly reinforced her gratitude for his words of encouragement. Jake noticed Kennedy checking him out, thought about his wife running off for a three month adventure without him, and then smiled contently.

*   *   *

When the rain stopped, the bugs came out. Not having prepared for a tropical jungle hike, the best they could do was to entertain each other and try to take their minds off worrying and the mosquitoes. "So Jake, what are you doing here anyway? I thought your father always said you were a lawyer. Didn't he tell me you have your own practice, or something like that?"

"Had. I had my own practice. Well, what I had was a partnership with Devon Keyes, a law school buddy of mine."

"Isn't he the external attorney for Hunter Neurologics that we were supposed to meet with later this week?"

"That's him. He's an attorney in the firm Tate and Gordon now, but works almost exclusively as our external counsel. Just another thing I owe my father for. He did me a favor by helping out my former partner, since I was to blame for our firm folding."

"So what happened? Why did the firm fold?"

"To make a long story short, I've been temporarily disbarred."

"So you screwed up."

"Not exactly. But the world can be an ugly place when you try to do the right thing. Sometimes, even though it's the right thing, it is not always the most *popular* thing."

"Ahh, so in your quest for justice and nobility, you got the short end of the stick."

"I think so, yes. But what I think will not matter one bit unless we get off this island and I can get back to D.C. to appear in court and defend myself."

"And if you don't, you are no longer temporarily disbarred?"

"Exactly. It will switch to permanent by default judgment, if I don't show up."

She was smiling at him now, looking him dead in the eyes before puckering her lips and then after what seemed like an eternity, saying, "But for now, you're only *temporarily* disbarred. As in, you're not dead in the water quite yet. Surely you're going to put up a fight for all that is right in the world?"

Jake smiled back and replied, "As they say, the law only aids the vigilant."

"Huh?"

"In other words, I sure planned to… put up a fight, but it's going to require getting back to D.C. in time. I only have a couple days until the hearing. Plus, it just occurred to me, not even Devon can come looking for us if the pilots were not really the pilots."

"What do you mean?" Kennedy asked.

"Based on how long we were in the air, we should have been over open water at the time of the crash. There was something odd about those pilots. I have to wonder if maybe they deliberately took us off course. That means we could be almost anywhere right now. But then again, what does it matter really? Somehow, I have a feeling if we get out of here, there are going to be more pressing matters to deal with than disbarment. You know, like figuring out who killed everyone in my father's company and where the hell he went."

"Wow, you don't think your father could somehow be involved do you?"

"No. No way. He made too many sacrifices for this company. And he's no killer. I'm surprised you would even say something like that if you were close enough to him to be put on his leadership team."

"Sorry, it was rude of me. I am just trying to put together the pieces of this puzzle. I mean, why take him if you have his briefcase which contained the Digitalis. After all, isn't it the cornerstone of everything? From what I understood, if you have the Digitalis, you have the key to a whole new way of making medicine, from new types of drugs and treatments, to cures for lines of diseases once thought incurable. If you have what is potentially the biggest medical breakthrough ever, why bother kidnapping the man too? It just doesn't make sense. Something is not adding up."

"Maybe it will add up better as soon as we crack into those mini bottles we grabbed from the plane." They both chuckled. Jake went on, "Anyway, so that's why I am here. Mine and Devon's start up law firm tanked. I got sued for malpractice and was temporarily disbarred. Then I ran home. My father gave me this job as an in-house council with his firm to help me make ends meet until I can fix this disbarment thing. Believe me, you wouldn't want to know all the dirty details. You might never look at me the same again."

"Actually Jake, unless you're going to tell me you can see people or the coastline up ahead, I may just have time for the long version. And I love *dirty* details!" a smile ran across her face for the second time since they had crashed. Jake was looking back and caught a glimpse of her seductive smirk and found that, all of a sudden, his legs were not as tired from their incessant hiking.

Why do I feel like this is going somewhere?! I should be figuring out how to fix my marriage when I get home – not how to get in this woman's pants. But wow, there is just something about her, and this place. I cannot put my finger on it. I shouldn't want to put my finger on it. In a few more hours I'm going to be wishing for water, food, and a pillow, not a naked Kennedy, and I probably won't get any of them, which serves me right for thinking like this.

Instead of listening to reason, he decided to indulge his impulses and said to Kennedy, "I have a better idea. I saw you reading a magazine on the flight. I think the cover said something about 50 new sex secrets. So tell me, anything good in there?"

Aw shucks, did I just say that out loud. Darn it, what was I thinking! Now I'll definitely be sleeping on the dirt tonight.

Kennedy gasped in a way that was so blatantly fake it revealed experience and worldliness rather than the naivety and innocence she had intended. Then she countered, "Wow, way to break the ice!"

"Under the circumstances, I would have to argue the ice was already broken by surviving, together, a plane crash, then watching it blow up, and now hiking aimlessly through a tropical jungle!"

She chuckled, "You are a good lawyer. That's a fairly convincing argument!"

They paused in a rainforest opening to feel the light drizzle that had started up again. That was when they first saw it – a low flying helicopter in what appeared to be a search pattern, scouring the area of the plane wreckage. They looked at each other and both yelled out, "Flare gun," simultaneously. Jake had it in his bag; he loaded the gun and fired away.

"Do you think they saw it?" Kennedy asked him, with a hopeful, yet desperate tone.

"Yes, they saw it all right. They made an immediate turn in our direction the second it crossed their line of sight."

"Oh God Jake, what a relief."

"I hope so."

"What? What do you mean you hope so? Would you rather we kept on hiking aimlessly through this rainforest?"

"No, but the second after pulling the trigger, something occurred to me. I'm not quite sure if the people in that helicopter are coming to save us."

"You're kidding?"

"Nope, I am not kidding. We were supposed to die in that plane crash. I am not kidding, not in the slightest."

With most men, unbelief in one thing springs from blind belief in another.

–Georg Christoph Lichtenberg

CHAPTER 7

Yashodhara Palace, India

Jake's father, Dr. William Hunter was escorted by Lavanya and her armed henchmen through a maze of corridors and steps that descended several stories below the above ground levels of her vast palace. Eventually they entered what appeared to be a central corridor with access to a series of laboratories. They went past several doors with various markings and security mechanisms. One with particularly heavy security had a placard that read, "Infected Patients."

At the end of the corridor was an important looking entryway with a biometric security system for authentication. It required proof of identity by fingerprint and retinal scan in order to gain access.

Below the standard placard identifying the room as the "Central Research and Development Lab" was another sign that read, "What we can or cannot do... what we deem possible or impossible, are all choices. Chose to believe and nothing is impossible. Choose a positive outlook, and invariably, success will follow." Another sign, which looked more like one of those motivational posters one would expect to see in corporate America, was on the wall to the right of the door. It listed out now famous men once considered deranged for cockamamie ideas such as inventing electricity (Thomas Edison), creating a device for talking across great distances, the telephone (Alexander Graham Bell), flying, (Wright Brothers), birth of the nuclear age (Ernest Rutherford), and so on. It was a great summary of how the unimaginable was, so many times throughout our history, made into reality.

Lavanya saw Dr. Hunter reading through the list, and seized it as an opportunity to try to persuade him, "We can be on that list Dr. Hunter. If we work together, we can prove reincarnation is real. We can scientifically verify the roots of religion and give billions of people the concrete hope they need for believing in possibilities, if only you would willingly help us."

Dr. Hunter's face turned bright red before he retorted, "You are insane. This is not the way to go about it. And for the record, I will be on a list like that someday, but not for helping you. No, no way. No one, not nobody, ever gets on those lists for self-serving madness. Mark my words, one way or another, one life or another, I will be there for curing Alzheimer's, but I will never be there for involvement with this lunacy you are proposing."

"Lunacy!? Lunacy, and a waste of money, is what they said it was to consider landing on the moon, but of course, that was before Neil Armstrong uttered his famous lines."

CHAPTER 8

City Homeless Shelter at 3rd and F Streets, South East
Washington, D.C.

It was nearly 10:30 A.M. but Aubrey was afraid to leave the homeless shelter. Even during daylight hours, that part of D.C. was not safe, especially not for a battered woman and her fifteen year old daughter, Julia. Besides, she had spotted the District Attorney who was coming to see her. He was nearly an hour late, which added insult to injury, as Aubrey was smart enough to know the D.A. was not there to help her, despite what he claimed. Aubrey knew in her heart, the only person who was trying to help her, and the only person who stood any chance of helping her, was Jake Hunter, her recently disbarred attorney, who was suddenly not returning her phone calls.

While waiting for Milton Strayer, the D.A., to walk across the crowded shelter to find her, Aubrey wiped a tear from her eye. Everything had happened so fast. Not more than a few months ago, she was in a beautiful suburban home living the American dream. Now she was penniless, beaten and raped repeatedly by her own husband, without any allies to help her and unable to get in touch with the one man who could.

Milton was there to gather facts he could use in his effort to permanently disbar Jake Hunter.

"Hello Aubrey. How are you holding up?" Milton always tried to act like her friend, but despite some poor life decisions, Aubrey wasn't nearly naïve enough to believe him.

"Let's just skip the nonsense and get on with this."

"So be it Aubrey. We'll move along quickly then and I'll try to make this as painless as possible for you."

She sighed, knowing full well his intentions were quite the opposite. Milton was a short man, maybe 5'4" with a Napoleon Complex that would have made Bonaparte look like a pillar of self esteem.

"Aubrey, when did Jake first tell you about the made up case he submitted in court on your behalf. This is the case of Sellers v. Griffin Milling, Inc. Are you familiar with that case?"

"I am familiar with it. It was supposed to be what would get me my home, all my family inheritance money back, and give me some security from my wicked husband. I don't understand what the issue is and why the courts can't just accept it."

"We've gone over this before Aubrey. The case of Sellers v. Griffin Milling never happened. Your attorney made it up and lied in court. That's perjury, which is a criminal offense in addition to being grounds for disbarment. I can assure you, one way or another, your attorney, no matter how great you claim he was, will never practice law again."

"So what if it's made up? The point of it still makes sense. Besides, he's not the one who made it up and I told you that already. It was delivered to his office. How many times do I have to tell you this? Why aren't you after the person that sent it to Jake in the first place?!"

"The problem Aubrey is that no attorney worth his

money would use a case without checking its background. And worse, it would be wrong of you to defend him like that at the upcoming disbarment hearing. You would be putting yourself in greater jeopardy and running a risk of being prosecuted yourself. I think we both know you have enough problems already don't we? Another prosecution while you're still on probation is not going to help you."

"Why would it be wrong? It's the truth!"

"It's wrong because you have no real knowledge of those facts. You're simply hypothesizing."

"I'm not hypothesizing! It's what the man told me for God's sake! What are you trying to do here anyways!? What is this, the Spanish Inquisition?!"

"Take it easy Aubrey. Don't you see, Jake told you that to try to protect himself by drawing you into his pitiful game of lies."

"That's not true! Jake Hunter doesn't lie. He wouldn't lie!"

"Aubrey, he did lie to you. And then he lied to the court. And now you're homeless and you've lost your best shot at getting your assets back from your husband."

"You rotten bastard! How can you say that to me when in court you helped to defend my husband! Unless you're gonna arrest me, I am done with this conversation." And Aubrey got up from her cot in the homeless shelter, grabbed the hand of her teenage daughter who heard the whole thing, and turned her back on the District Attorney.

Milton yelled at her as she walked away, "Just remember Aubrey, you have enough problems already. For your sake, I suggest you be very careful about what you say in court, especially when you have no real proof to back yourself up. I wouldn't want to see you sink any lower. Then again, I guess that's not really possible anymore, is it!"

Aubrey stopped walking, turned around, and moved directly in front of Milton Strayer. She stared him in the eye for only a moment. In that instant, she recalled what Jake said about keeping her cool. Then she spat on the District Attorney for the District of Columbia, turned and with her daughter walked away again. Milton gave chase, but three homeless men who had overheard the conversation stepped in front of him, blocking his path.

This time, Milton didn't bother trying to get the last jab, as he was suddenly too distracted by the clock on the nearby wall. He hadn't realized the time and remembered he was supposed to have returned a call to Lavanya Yashodhara almost thirty minutes earlier.

CHAPTER 9

Yashodhara Palace, India

The main lab was a vast room, bigger and better equipped than any Dr. Hunter had seen over the course of a lengthy career. It was an impressive sight, full of scientists and technicians utilizing advanced equipment including several machines that were unfamiliar to Dr. Hunter. He and Lavanya stepped into an office near the main entrance. Lavanya took a seat behind a huge ornate desk and Dr. Hunter sat across from her.

"Dr. Hunter, what you are failing to realize is that your dreams, as you planned them, are over. The only way they will ever become a reality now, is if you first help me. After that, I can give you the means you need to finish your work. You must know in your heart you need my help. Your firm has been so very close, for so long. Close, but no cigar, for over a decade now. And I understand your finances are not doing so well these days either? Just imagine the possibilities. Through team work, we can both get what we want. We can both accomplish ground breaking scientific achievements…."

"STOP IT. Just stop it. This is NOT a win-win, so

stop your simple minded manipulation. I am helping you for one reason and one reason only. And that is to ensure the safety of my daughter-in-law."

"Whatever works Dr. Hunter, or should I just call you Billy then? That is what Anja calls you, isn't it?"

"Let's get one thing straight woman. I am not doing a darn thing until you let Anja go."

"Oh, I see," Lavanya paused for effect, "Dr. Hunter, you're an educated man. Surely you are smarter than that. Why don't we avoid unnecessarily having to hurt your precious Anja, or you, for that matter? Instead, let's focus on the task at hand. Tell me about Nakuru. The reports and rumors about a patient of yours that went, shall we say 'crazy,' are all consistent, which leads me to believe them to be true. So how about it Dr. Hunter? Are you prepared to help your daughter-in-law through an initial demonstration of good will? Are you prepared to tell me about that secret clinical trial of yours? I believe you refer to it as the Nakuru Trial? I do admire the choice of work location, not so conveniently located in one of the most remote parts of Kenya if I understand correctly?" Dr. Hunter sat motionless, displaying his best poker face, although blood was boiling under his skin. Lavanya went on, "So why Kenya, Dr. Hunter? I suppose to avoid drawing attention or something like that? Or did it give you unlimited access to human guinea pigs upon whom you could advance science more quickly by omitting the safety protocols required in any western nation?"

Steam was nearly rising from Dr. Hunter's head. The clinical trial she was asking about had been buried. They had decided, and been ordered, to hide everything and anything that showed any record of it. The consequences, if the truth about what went wrong in the Nakuru Trials, had ever gotten out, even in the scientific community, would have been an apocalypse for the patient she had asked about, and potentially billions of people around the world.

The lengths they went to in hiding any trace of the Nakuru Trials to protect its secrets and dangers, were elaborate, and beyond anything William Hunter thought could have ever been sifted through. Yet somehow, his captor had knowledge of it.

"How the hell do you know about the Nak…" He stopped abruptly, recognizing he had slipped up. He was exhausted and his fatigue caused him to confirm that the trial existed. It was his first major blunder.

Lavanya didn't react however. Instead, she remained cool and acted as if she did not require the confirmation, further strengthening her leverage in the conversation.

Finally she continued, "That does not matter Dr. Hunter. What matters is that you get to work at once reproducing the results. Dr. Rajni Gupta is our Chief Medical Officer. She will bring you up to speed on our attempts at reproducing your work here, the facilities available to you, etc. I know that by working together and combining our joint knowledge, we can accomplish what we both desire." William Hunter cringed, not because of her incessant arrogance, but because he knew he couldn't easily reproduce the results and that trying could lead to cataclysmic outcomes. Then a light bulb went off. Maybe her madness was his way out.

"You don't understand. Even if I wanted to reproduce those results, I wouldn't stand a chance in this lifetime without access to my labs, my files, my notes, and all of my research."

"I figured you would say that, sooner or later. Although I thought you would be more specific and say you need the Digitalis."

She paused to see his reaction, but Dr. Hunter would not bite a second time. Lavanya continued, "Not to worry, I have men in place and can get you whatever you need. Would you like your personal computer from your office in D.C. perhaps? Or would the one from your labs in the

Caribbean be more useful? I believe that facility is on an island called, Isla de Las Dedaleras, or do you just call it Isla Dedaleras for short?" Dr. Hunter was increasingly alarmed and annoyed at how much confidential information she had about him and his company. It could mean only one thing, that she had an inside person or persons helping her.

He knew this because over time, he had increasingly spared no expense on security and secrecy. With each passing year, as he and his team came closer and closer to their cutting edge medical breakthroughs for developing treatments for memory restoration in brain damaged patients and victims of Alzheimer's disease, they knew they needed more and more security to avoid having their work stolen by corporate raiders. Their budget had been drained on what was widely considered the strongest security for any non-governmental organization in the world. But there were hundreds of billions of dollars in new medical procedures and drugs at stake, and with such a huge payoff, elaborate security was essential. It was a model of medical research Dr. Hunter copied from his former involvement in the group that originally organized the Nakuru Trial.

"How the hell do you know all this? How do you know we have a lab in the Caribbean? That is supposed to be top secret!"

"I know everything about you Dr. Hunter, and I do mean everything. I even know there was a steel encased briefcase containing details about the Digitalis traveling with you on your recent flight. The only thing I do not know is what happened to that case. If I did, I wouldn't be bothering with you."

"How can you possibly know that?" He asked, even though he realized an answer was unlikely.

Lavanya continued, ignoring his question, "Dr. Hunter, I even have full knowledge of all the sordid details of your personal affairs as well. Needless to say, you and I both know that should the safety of Anja not be persuasive enough to motivate you, there are additional matters that would be. Matters you would prefer left unsaid, I am guessing. So why not tell me what you need to make this happen, and let's get started. In fact, make a list and leave it on my desk. Be sure it includes instructions for where I can find the Digitalis."

"There is no Digitalis. You're basing all of this on conjecture and rumors that are entertaining to the masses, but far from the truth."

Lavanya showed no reaction to his pleading and instead instructed him, "When you are done, use the speed dial for Dr. Gupta on the desk phone and she'll give you a tour of the facility. I think you'll enjoy meeting, or should I say, reacquainting with Dr. Gupta. Her maiden name might jolt your memory, but maybe I'll just let you wonder and worry for a bit. Oh, and one last thing Dr. Hunter, should you consider trying to fake us out, sandbagging, or simply not making progress quickly enough, then I would suggest keeping in mind that I know your dirty little secrets. I know you are not the innocent hero the American medical community has made you out to be. And we both know how damaging it could be to your only son should certain of your secrets be revealed." He stared at her with resounding anger in his eyes but said nothing, as he didn't want to give away anything else that she might be unsure of or use against him. She went on with her badgering, "So you see, Billy, none of us are innocent, now are we?"

G reek writer Diordus Siculus (c. 60 BC - 30 AD) noted

that the Druids believed, "The souls of men are immortal,

and that after a definite number of years they live a second

life when the soul passes to another body."

CHAPTER 10

Yashodhara Palace, India

Lavanya Yashodhara left the room and proceeded down the corridor that led back to the stairs which would take her three stories up, to the above ground levels of her plush, oversized palace. Even being tucked away, deep in a remote, extremely rural part of central India, which hid her palace from the general public, Lavanya spared no expense to keep her scientific pursuits discreet.

Once upstairs, she rendezvoused with John Anton in her bedroom and immediately fawned all over him, as she always did. Using sex to control men was one of her specialties and John had become her most reliable servant/lover and an indispensable cog in her plans to steal the Digitalis.

John had just got off the phone with his contacts in D.C. including Devon Keyes. He was less than eager to share freshly obtained news with his lover and sheepishly said to her, "Lavanya, sweetheart, how did Dr. Hunter's introductory meeting turn out?"

"It was average, at best. He's still denying the Digitalis. As you predicted, he wants access to his labs and equipment. He claims he can't get anything done otherwise. Can you get his computers, files, whatever medical equipment he needs, and have them delivered here?"

"Honey, you know I would do anything for you, but I'm afraid, well, I'm afraid there's been an incident."

"What do you mean an incident?"

"There was an explosion in D.C. They think it was a terrorist attack. It appears to have destroyed the entire building where Hunter Neurologics was headquartered." There was a moment of shocked silence.

"That's no terrorist attack and you damn well know it. That building blows up just as we get him? What the hell is going on John? I thought you wanted to be with me – have you changed your mind suddenly?"

"Take it easy, take it easy. I agree that it wasn't terrorists. I was simply repeating what the media and the police think. And don't worry. They have that off shore research facility, which *we* funded. I already have Devon in route to see if he can find a copy of the Digitalis. Besides, that is where all the real work took place. If we're going to find or be able to reproduce whatever was in Dr. Hunter's missing briefcase, that's the place that will enable us to do so. Everyone knows that D.C. office was just a superficial front for access to the American markets," he paused, trying to read her face, but like most people, he couldn't, so he asked, "Do you feel better now? Are you happy enough to unwind with me over a few drinks?"

"No. In fact, I am not happy. And we're not unwinding. We're packing. We are going to D.C. tomorrow. In the meantime, you need to focus on finding that briefcase, or better yet, finding the Digitalis, like you promised. For your sake, I hope you work fast Johnny. If the bombing in D.C. was intentional, then you and I both know that means time is of the essence. So if you really want to be with me, and I mean, really *be with me* ever again, then you would do this and deliver everything you can get your hands on from that research facility. Without the Digitalis and all their technology, we might never be able to figure out how to replicate what happened at Nakuru because it sure doesn't seem like the old man is going to willingly tell us."

"I'll drag the whole damn island here for you if I have to."

"You're such an idiot. Listen to me carefully. I want you to get every piece of paper that has ever been printed at that place. Then get every hard drive from every computer; get all their research notes; get everything. If there are any people left alive on that island, get them too. We need to know what they did at those clinical trials at Nakuru, regardless of whether they buried their notebooks in the African savanna or in someone's grave."

"We will have all of that in a matter of days," John responded hoping to earn her praise and affection.

"John, we need to know what exactly they did that caused a patient to consciously recognize information from past lives. If we get the Nakuru files, then we can find that mystery patient, whoever it is. Then maybe we would have some real answers."

"Look, you know we can get their computers, notes, all their research, and most likely even the Digitalis. But Devon has been inside the organization for almost a year now, and he has tried before to get the files on Nakuru. It always turns out the same. That thing is buried so deep, it's like it never happened."

"It happened damn it. God damn it Johnny! I thought you knew how to get things when others couldn't? I thought you cared about me and were going to do this for me? Tell me I wasn't wrong Johnny, please tell me."

"We'll need the old man to help us if you really want to know what happened in the Nakuru trial. What about it? Can you get anything out of him? I need something, some clue to point me in the right direction. What are the chances?"

"I don't know yet. He definitely was concerned when I mentioned it, which tells me we're on the right track. And I think you were right about him in another way as well - he seemed more than fond of his young daughter-in-law. But I'm not sure we're going to be able to tell if he is really helping us or not. So in other words, I am still trying to figure out what buttons to push to get him to talk. Until then, we are probably on our own."

"Right, but overall, that doesn't sound all bad. We have some leverage with the daughter-in-law. If they were lovers, that could turn out to be our ace in the hole. Also," he hesitated, nervous now, "listen, Lavanya, there is something else you should know. At first, I thought this would be bad news, but now, well, it's all going to work out OK I think."

Interrupting him, Lavanya showed her irritation and growing impatience, "I cannot believe you are going to tell me more bad news right now. My blood is already boiling. Let's hear it. Get it over with."

With trepidation John Anton told her about their botched operation with the Hunter Neurologics jet, "There were survivors from the plane wreckage."

"What the... as if it's not bad enough you all lost the damn briefcase with the Digitalis. Now you're telling me there are survivors? Can't anyone do anything without drawing attention?"

"Calm down honey. This is really not bad. It's good in fact. One of the survivors was Dr. Hunter's son, Jakob Hunter."

"You have got to be kidding me. Are you irretrievably incompetent? I guess you never want to sleep with me ever again, do you? Why was he even on the plane? He's not on the list of passengers we went over. Honestly, a fifth grader could do better than this!"

"Look, he wasn't supposed to be there. I guess

Daddy was helping him out with a job after his not so unfortunate disbarment."

She snapped back, "If he had been killed, it could have ruined all the work in California with the wife. What a screw up. So what else? You said survivors. Who were the others? And what are you doing about it?"

"There was a woman, a Dr. Kennedy Taylor. She is fairly new to their team. I'm not sure what her deal is, or where she came from. I come up with blanks every time I search her background. It's as if she didn't exist prior to being hired about six months ago by the old man. The other odd thing is that the pilots were not really the pilots."

"There you go again with your idiot talk. Why don't you try explaining it in a way that someone with at least half a brain can understand?" she snapped back, revealing her deep rooted cruelty.

"It means that through DNA testing on dental remains, the bodies of the pilots were found to belong to two peasants from Venezuela who had been reported missing a few weeks ago. In other words, instead of killing the real pilots after they delivered the old man, someone replaced their bodies to make it look like they had been killed. I don't know yet who or why. But it could be the same people that took the briefcase with the Digitalis in it."

"There's a bright idea," she blurted out rhetorically. "It could be? Don't be so dense. Figure it out. Find the pilots and you find our enemies. And don't be an idiot about the son. The way things are going, we will probably need him to get the Digitalis. If he was working as a corporate attorney for his father, he should have access to everything on Isla Dedaleras. Once we get the Digitalis, we may no longer need to know the secrets of the Nakuru Trials nor will we any longer have a need to deal with Dr. Hunter's holier than thou recalcitrance."

"I'll try Lavanya."

"Don't try Johnny, do it. Make sure Jake Hunter gets

back to D.C. safely. But I don't want him arriving until after we do. You and I will be meeting with him there in a day, two days max, but I want to inspect his home before he returns to it. And one more thing…"

"Yes dear?"

"I am going into town tonight, alone. And I don't want to see you anywhere near this bedroom again until you have a plan for getting me the Digitalis. I sure hope for your sake, the truth about all this didn't disappear in that explosion in D.C. If you're good and find some leads, maybe we can have some fun in D.C. before dealing with Jake Hunter. Now go, and get to work. Then get packed. We're leaving for D.C. tomorrow."

Lavanya threw him out of the bedroom and slammed the door behind him.

John Anton sat downstairs in the palace library, spellbound by the woman, heartbroken at her fury with him, but mostly worried that what she wanted him to acquire, the Digitalis, had already been stolen by someone else, and that any traces of information about the clinical trials in Nakuru, Kenya may have been deliberately destroyed in the bombing in D.C. Either way, he knew the people responsible were more than a few steps ahead when it came to acquiring what his lover asked of him.

W e would accomplish many more things if we did not

think of them as impossible.

–Vince Lombardi

CHAPTER 11

Unknown Caribbean Island

The helicopter landed about fifty yards from Jake and Kennedy. Four commando style looking men with machine guns got out and formed an arc that gave them lines of sight in all forward directions, while two more men covered the rear. They were highly trained and appeared to know what they were doing. Kennedy nudged Jake, "You might be right about them not being here to help us. Why would a rescue team require so many men, and so heavily armed?"

"Maybe, but on the other hand, we don't know where we are. If this is Cuba, or some other island nation hostile to the U.S., this would be the only safe way to rescue us. The bigger question is, since we weren't able to find any working phone, how would anyone even know to come looking. Our flight plan was from one international location to another, meaning it was totally undocumented by U.S. authorities."

"I hear you Jake, but don't they track U.S. planes and citizens anyways?"

"Not when the corporate jet you're on isn't a U.S. registered aircraft. To make matters worse, for a variety of law bending reasons, everyone on board held foreign passports. Bottom line, it might not matter since those guys are heading in our direction and clearly know we are here."

"They're not friendly Jake, we've got to go, now!"

"What did you…, how do you know that? Maybe they're just heavily armed because of…" he was interrupted by a bullet whizzing by, breaking a big tropical looking leaf from its stem. He watched the huge leaf fall to the ground as if life was suddenly in slow motion, until Kennedy hit him in the side full force, like a linebacker, and pile-drove him down to the ground. He was stunned at her tackling ability and momentarily failed to register that he had just been shot at. "Jesus Kennedy, now I know what Troy Aikman felt like when LaVar Arrington ended his career."

"Stay down!" she commanded while pulling a gun from a holster attached to her right ankle.

Jake stared with disbelief at the gun in her hand.

That's it. Now that's just not right. Now I know something is not right about this woman. What kind of doctor carries a gun concealed on her ankle?

He asked, "What the hell is that? Where did you get that?"

"I found it in the cockpit of the plane, when we were looking for a satellite phone. I thought it might come in handy. I'd say, given our circumstances, we are lucky we have it."

"No doubt. But still, I'm impressed."

"You should be!" she said simultaneously with a seductive wink.

Jake was flattered and asked, "Did you just wink at me, even as we're being shot at? I think you did. Damn, you just winked and we could be killed at any moment."

"Don't let it go to your head. First off, you're happily married. Secondly…"

"Whoa there cowgirl. What ever led you to believe I'm *happily* married?"

Bingo!

With exactly the clarification she was hoping for, Kennedy gave a broad smile before finishing her previous thought, "Well, maybe we can fix the happiness part! But right now we've got to focus on staying alive before anything else. I'd say we have just a little bit less than sixty seconds to high tail it out of here back the way we came, before they are on us. Let's move!" That was when another man with a gun showed up seemingly out of nowhere. He had jumped out the far side of the chopper and out-flanked them. His AK-47 was pointing at Jake right between the eyes, as evidenced by the notorious red dot of death.

Jake exhaled a sigh of defeat and fear. His bowels loosened and he thought he might soil himself. Despite the red dot on his head and gun in his face, he turned to see if Kennedy was OK. She was looking directly at him, with fear in her eyes. That was when Jake, more than any other moment in his life, thought he was going die.

It only took a fraction of a second for the most vivid, and disturbing thought he had ever had, to vanish in a streak of red slush that tasted salty. The blood and brains from the man who had previously stood before him, were splattered all over Jake's face. He wiped away what he could from his mouth. Then he turned to Kennedy to see if she was OK.

They looked back towards the field where the four men were previously walking towards them. Kennedy pushed his face down into the dirt and bullets whizzed over head. Not one or two, but a slew of bullets, rapid fire sequence, from multiple machine guns. And then, just as quickly as they started, the bullets stopped.

CHAPTER 12

Washington, D.C.
National Airport

Devon Keyes and Kate Stinson were in the first class lounge at National Airport having a meal and cocktails while waiting for their corporate jet to get fueled up and ready for the flight down to Key West International Airport. Devon excused himself to use the restroom but instead went into a conference room where the District Attorney, Milton Strayer was waiting for him.

Devon greeted him, "Well Milt, what's the latest?"

"She's not been in touch with Jake. And unless she is Oscar winning good at acting like an idiot, she has no idea where the fake case came from. Sellers v. Griffin Milling Inc. is still our ace in the hole, as far I can tell."

"And the disbarment hearing, is that on track? We need to keep the heat on this guy."

"Everything is on track Devon. Not a thing to worry about on my end. How are things on your side?"

"Good. I even got a little extra company to go with me."

"Devon, please tell me you're not putting everything

at risk over some broad."

"Not just any broad. Kate is my new paralegal. And if you took one look at her, you would fully understand why I need to have a paralegal to support me over the next few days." They both laughed.

"Just try not to get distracted. We've been working too hard and waiting too long for this moment."

"No doubt you're right buddy. Not to worry. We are extremely well prepared. In a few days from now, not only will the world be changed, but people will be reading about us in Forbes' list of the richest people in the world."

A viation is proof that given, the will, we have the capacity to achieve the impossible.

–Edward Vernon Rickenbacker

CHAPTER 13

India

A young Lavanya watched as a mob of people stormed her family's religious sanctuary. She was just a little girl, back home, with her parents, where she was normally safe and loved. Their home wasn't much, but they had built it themselves and took pride in it, and appreciated all it had to offer.

Lavanya did not understand why a chaotic mob of people would intrude on her family's sacred ceremony, which was essential to helping her baby brother.

Not even of grade school age, she felt, for the first time, real, pure anger and hatred. Since her older brother, who had been her idol, was killed a year earlier by a carelessly drunk tourist, there was nothing Lavanya wanted more than for her baby brother to be saved.

The mob rushed around, unimpressed by the preschool aged girl's unspoken thoughts. She began to cry. After someone grabbed her and threw her harshly into the corner where her baby brother's cot lay, she grew more scared than angry. She rolled with the force of being thrown and hid under the cot. The mob, in their chaos, was focused only on Lavanya's parents. The mad crowd of people grabbed the two adults and forced them out of the family temple. Her parents fell repeatedly from being brutally shoved, kicked, and poked.

At one point, Lavanya's mother fell to the floor, next to the cot under which she was still hiding. Her mother made eye contact and the look on her face spoke of love and fear. There was also something in her mother's eyes that told young Lavanya to stay put and to stay quiet, and so she did. Hands grabbed her mother and partly picked her back up, partly threw her forward a few more feet, while others kicked her and spat on her. Seconds later, the crowd, and her mother were no longer visible. Lavanya initially repressed her desire to cry and scream with rage at the injustice against her parents. Then, a moment later, she tried her hardest to scream, but when she opened her mouth, nothing would come out. No matter how hard she tried, she could not make any noise. She could not scream for help.

She was running out of breath and about to pass out, when she woke up years into her future, finally able to scream and wailing at her best from the pain of the same nightmare she had been having at least a few nights every week, for most of her life.

Out of frustration, she pounded her fist against her bed, then on the chest of the man lying next to her. It drove her crazy that the nightmares always ended early and she had no idea what really happened to her parents. She wondered if she would ever be healed enough to know. And she wondered if finally getting her hands on the Digitalis would be the key to setting her free from a lifetime of tumultuous nightmares.

The man in bed with her was a very young twenty something tourist she had picked up in town. Lavanya craved sexual conquests like a seventeen year old male. But her fury with John Anton left him sleeping in the palace library, on a couch, where he could be closer to the phone and computers and stay on top of efforts to acquire Jake Hunter, hopefully before anyone else got to him. In the meantime, Lavanya enjoyed her evening of depravity.

Her guest was jolted awake after a night of getting lucky. The bewildered youngster leapt naked from the bed. He was perplexed at the sudden rudeness of Lavanya's behavior.

"How the hell did you sleep through that yelling," she asked the young kid, whose name she did not know.

"What yelling?" he asked while stumbling around, still intoxicated from the previous evening.

"Never mind you idiot. Get out." She coldly responded, as if there was no question or doubt as to what would happen next. Lavanya was done using him and needed to attend to matters around her palace before her trip to D.C. But the young kid just stood there naked, convinced from his misguided and youthful arrogance that he could talk his way into staying a bit longer. He wanted to add more to his experience so that he could lengthen his future recital of hooking up with a woman rich enough to own a lavish palace and beautiful enough to have anyone she wanted.

Within seconds Lavanya was getting dressed and her guards had entered the room. A few moments later, the still naked kid was dragged from her presence. She didn't care and did not ask her guards if they ever gave the tourist back his clothes. Her mind was focused on creativity. She was determined to find a way to get Dr. William Hunter to reveal the secrets of conscious recognition of past lives. She was going to find his long lost mystery patient, learn about the events at Nakuru, or simply steal the Digitalis to make her own medical history.

Her determination and proximity to having what she had worked for all her life energized her into action, without even a sip of coffee.

She left her bedroom and decided to release tension

with some vigorous horseback riding around her estate. While pushing her best thoroughbred to near death, Lavanya contemplated gruesome devices for getting Dr. Hunter to talk. It wasn't long before she was walking back to the palace, as the horse lay on the ground exhausted and unable to walk any further. Lavanya didn't look back and didn't stop to call her vets as she grinned with confidence that her new ideas for torturing Dr. Hunter would leave him begging to reveal the information she had spent a lifetime chasing.

CHAPTER 14

Unknown Caribbean Island

After a minute, maybe longer with no firing, Jake and Kennedy lifted their faces from the mud of the jungle floor. They spotted four bodies in the clearing and saw that the helicopter was flying away, without bothering to collect its crew of fallen commandos.

"What do you think is going on," Jake rhetorically asked Kennedy, not really expecting her to be able to explain the strange sequence of events.

"I don't know, but I think we were just saved by someone."

"I figured out that much. But I'm not sure which part I'm more worried about. The people that saved us, that I would put at no more than fifty yards away and closing fast at 2 o'clock, or the people they saved us from."

Kennedy didn't know either, but decided to think positive, "Well, as of about two minutes ago, we no longer have to worry about the people we were saved from, so I guess that's one good thing."

"Hah," Jake couldn't control his sarcasm, "so now we can just worry about these guys, who honestly, they look the same to me. Same generic no name uniforms."

Kennedy winked at Jake while pointing out, "Their guns are bigger though."

"Ah, so they are. I didn't take you for the type that would notice the size of their guns."

"Ha ha. It just struck me that these look more like government, save your ass types of what do they call them, MK-7s or something." She was clearly pretending not to know what she was talking about, but it was obvious to Jake that she did.

She's no doctor, that's for sure. But I wonder why the charades?

Eventually they realized the new group of men coming towards them had their guns at their sides and appeared less threatening than the previous group. With few options, Jake and Kennedy got up and walked over to them, hoping, more so than knowing, that it was safe to do so.

Before Jake could ask them anything, the taller of the two commandos said, "If the two of you want to live, come with us now."

"Who are you?" Jake asked, wanting some explanations before going anywhere.

"Please Mr. Hunter, follow us now. There will be plenty of time for explanation at the airstrip." With no further conversation, the two men led them to another helicopter.

The chopper looked more hi-tech than anything Jake had ever seen. He was thankful to be riding in it. But he was also uneasy and thought it a little strange that no one would tell him where they were going. Unable to extract any information from his reticent rescuers, Jake struggled to remain calm.

Maybe the closest safe spot is a top secret government base and that is why they can't tell us. But something about these guys makes me feel like I shouldn't trust them.

In and of itself, Jake might have been OK with not knowing the destination. But given the complete anonymity of his "rescuers," their lack of communication, and the numerous gadgets that screamed of the type of money that comes from people that control things outside government boundaries, Jake was utterly terrified. His neck was stiff with fear and he was sweating through his shirt.

The men with the guns all had on radio connected headsets. Jake and Kennedy were given ear protection, but it wasn't wired, which made it impossible for them to talk to each other. He looked over at Kennedy, concerned and desperate for an explanation. Eventually, he realized how silly it was to expect one from her. Instead he did what he could to calm *her* fears. He felt guilty for wanting to calm and protect a woman other than his wife. But he knew he loved Anja unconditionally, and turning his attention to Kennedy was more about taking his mind off his fears than anything else. It could have been anyone sitting next to him.

When things are at their absolute worse, there is still, always something soothing and calming in helping others.

*   *   *

The chopper finally landed at what was clearly some sort of military installation, yet lacked any official government markings. In fact, it lacked any markings at all. It was as incognito as they come. Jake and Kennedy were greeted by a man that introduced himself as Commander Collins but said nothing else.

Collins escorted them to the lobby of a building. Once inside, they were told each would be taken to a locker room to refresh. Jake was escorted through the left rear of the lobby by two soldiers, while Kennedy was escorted by two others through the right rear of the lobby. It didn't make sense to either of them why the escorts were necessary, but neither complained as they were both ecstatic at the thought of taking a hot shower.

After a short walk down a hallway, the soldiers opened a solid steel door and motioned for Jake to go in. As he glanced inside the doorway, what he saw was not a locker room. Instead it was clearly a jail cell. Before he could move to run away the soldiers were on him and forcing him into the room. The door shut and bolted behind him.

At almost the exact same time, another door shut behind Kennedy, locking her into a similar cell on the other side of the building, out of range for any type of communication. Each of them was alone and held captive, with no explanation, and no one to plead with for release.

There was a window on Jake's cell and he watched as the sunlight faded into night. Eventually he tried to rest, but it was hard to sleep. His captives had not given him any food, nor water. His room was barren, with only a stone floor and walls, and a single worn out looking cot. There were no sheets or pillows, just a mattress that looked like a reject from a forty year old sleazy motel. They were still in the tropics, so at least the temperature was warm.

Jake used his shirt as a pillow, closed his eyes, and tried to imagine being home with his wife. But guilt from his recent flirting with Kennedy tarnished thoughts that used to bring him peace.

See that... I merely thought about another woman. I didn't even act upon it. I did nothing, and ultimately, I robbed myself of peace more than Anja. I shouldn't have done that... on the other hand, screw it. She's probably made out with her entire camping party by now, so why should I care. Kennedy is probably a thousand times more loyal. But "it" just isn't there like it is with Anja. Maybe I need to grow up and stop worrying about "it" and start worrying about me. Maybe Kennedy is supposed to be an important part of my life. Maybe...

Jake glanced down at his watch. If he wasn't back in D.C. by the next morning, he would miss the disbarment hearing and a default judgment would be entered against him, permanently ending his legal career. For the time being, there was nothing he could do about it. And after being disbarred, he would not be able to help Aubrey Doyle, a woman whom Jake knew was anything but a saint, and yet, she still was being dealt a sickening amount of injustice. Instead of sleeping, Jake tossed and turned, thinking about how Aubrey had been mistreated: her family wealth stolen by the man she married, rape, theft of her home, the total annihilation of what little was good in her life by someone she trusted. His stomach was cramping from the thoughts of the gross injustice and his inability to help her.

Hours upon hours of restlessness eventually gave way to a morning sunlight which began to brighten the world outside the small window of his cell. He was afraid to wonder what the new day would bring and what his captors would do to him.

CHAPTER 15

Yashodhara Palace, India

Jake's father, Dr. William Hunter was seated at the desk as instructed. But nearly an hour had passed and he had yet to write a single line that would reveal to Lavanya the Digitalis or how it related to the rumors, which she considered real, about a clinical trial in Nakuru, Kenya.

Time moved slowly for Dr. Hunter as he contemplated how to respond and how to escape. His captor had detailed knowledge of him, which made him think his options were limited. Occasionally, he would wonder what he might achieve if he decided to trust Lavanya and work together with her, taking full advantage of the many resources she had available. But he would quickly repress such thinking as an unacceptable moral compromise.

After a clock on a credenza across from him signaled the passing of a second hour, two of Lavanya's armed guards abruptly entered the room. Without saying a word, they walked behind Dr. Hunter and bound his wrists behind him. Then they placed a black bag over his head. Already mentally exhausted and realizing it would be futile, Dr.

Hunter offered little resistance.

The bag on his head was a heavy, thick fabric and had a draw string that closed it tight around his neck so that he was completely shut off from light. The men lifted him and forced him to walk out of the office. Dr. Hunter could not see where he was going, and his captors chuckled while allowing him to bang into walls and doors.

The two men pushed, prodded, and laughed at the world-renowned Dr. William Hunter's futile attempt to walk, from the basement levels of Yashodhara Palace, to the exterior palace grounds and finally through what sounded and felt like straw or hay.

Eventually, a hot, sweaty, and exhausted captive was forced into a chair. Dr. Hunter heard one of the guards chuckle and then say to him with a strong Indian accent, "You are in the barn now just like the animals! There's no waiter to serve you here greedy American."

"I'm neither American, nor greedy, you imbecile." Dr. Hunter responded, but the two guards were already well on their way out of the barn leaving him as he muttered, "I drive a ten year old Chevy for crying out loud."

He was left seated alone, to contemplate his fate, in a horse stall in Lavanya's barn, with the bag still over his head. As the hours passed, the sensory depravation was enough to drive Dr. Hunter a little cuckoo. Being bound up the way he was, left his body stiff and caused both of his arms to fall asleep to such a degree he couldn't be sure they were still attached. Beads of sweat dripped from his forehead as his nerves got the best of him. Extreme anxiety set in, causing his mind to race. He was worried his arms had been cut off; he was worried his daughter-in-law, Anja, had been or would be harmed and would hold it against him in ways that would damage the unique nature of their relationship; he was worried his life's work was either stolen or destroyed at a pivotal time, only days before he had planned to go public with ground breaking achievements, but mostly he was worried about revealing the secrets of what happened in Nakuru, Kenya to a mad woman who would almost certainly exploit the tragedies that took place there for her own agenda, no matter what the costs, and, he was worried, that those costs would be far worse than feared when they first buried all traces of anything ever having happened in Kenya.

*   *   *

It felt to him as though the entire day had passed when he was startled by the sounds of two people announcing their entrance to the horse stall. Dr. Hunter recognized Lavanya's voice, and strangely, also the voice of another woman who accompanied her, although he couldn't quite place it.

Despite his desperate situation and the likelihood of further unpleasantries, there was a modicum of solace in hearing human voices instead of the constant mulling around of barn animals.

Lavanya asked him, "How are you enjoying our barn Dr. Hunter?"

"It's lovely. I particularly enjoyed the sound of Mr. Ed who by my calculations cannot be more than a few feet away."

"I see you still have your sense of humor. That's good. But it will not last. Allow me to introduce Dr. Rajni Gupta. As I mentioned before, she is our Chief Medical Officer." Lavanya removed the black bag from over Dr. Hunter's head and then asked, "Don't you recognize her Billy? If I have my facts straight, it's my understanding you know her, how should we say, intimately?"

Dr. Hunter stared at Rajni Gupta trying to place her face and name, but couldn't despite the prodding from Lavanya. Rajni was beautiful, there could be no doubt, but standing next to Lavanya left her looking like an ugly duckling. In fact, despite his predicament and the mystery of the newcomer, Dr. Hunter was once again distracted by Lavanya's stunningly good looks. She was truly the most beautiful woman he had ever seen. It was hard for him to accept that a woman so beautiful could actually be his enemy.

Maybe she shouldn't be my enemy. Maybe we should be partners. Maybe...but the risks involved with what she wants to do are too great. I could never.

Lavanya noticed the look in his eyes, and smiled, before telling Rajni to enlighten him. Rajni said, "My, my, my, Dr. Hunter, I am so very disappointed you don't remember me after all that time we spent together. I guess it was as I had suspected. I was just company for you in bed, and non-existent by day while you toiled with your tests and research."

Dr. Hunter started to recognize her voice but couldn't believe it. His stomach sank, as he realized the odds were increasingly against him. He asked, "How can this be? Surely they aren't reopening the door to this madness? And if not, surely they didn't just let you leave the organization to work for this madwoman. Why would you work against their directives? You had such a promising... I... I just don't understand... Why would you get involved in this mess?"

Rajni responded, "I could give you some noble explanation, but let's be honest, money talks. Now in return for my honesty, would you please save us some time in this excruciating heat by explaining the Digitalis?"

"Rajni, there is much to which you were not privy at Nakuru. What happened there was a freak aberration from an extremely high risk procedure that hurt more than it helped. To pursue repeating anything from that trial is madness. You know as well as I that once the risks were fully understood, our work there was shutdown immediately."

"Rubbish. In fact, what I know, with the help of others, is that you have spent a lifetime completing what you started at Nakuru, only focused on the wrong parts of the work.

"It is only wrong from your demented point of view! You are just as mad as the woman standing next to you. What is wrong is the pursuit of medical science for personal gain, especially at such a high cost to others. What you are attempting here cannot be done. And it's a pursuit that is going to leave a trail of many, many victims. But judging by your, 'Infected Patients,' lab, I'm guessing you should already know that."

Tired of the bickering, Lavanya broke in, "We know the risks and we know the rewards. And I would expect a man of your background to know that truly significant achievements often come with the high costs of ethical compromise."

"The types of risks you are talking about here are too great. I beg of you to reconsider before many more are hurt."

Lavanya sighed, and then said, "Dr. Hunter, you and I both know that 25 years from now the only thing we will be wondering is why we didn't aim higher, why we procrastinated, and why we doubted for even a second. What appears unlikely today, will seem extravagantly simple minded years from now. But since this is going nowhere, I am going to allow you and Rajni to get re-acquainted. She has picked up some interesting new skills since you last worked with her. Don't worry though; I'll be sitting right over here, as I wouldn't miss this show for the world." Sweat was already dripping from Dr. Hunter's forehead from the heat of India's summer, but his heart rate accelerated rapidly as Rajni pulled into the stall a cart with crude devices that looked capable of inflicting excruciating pain. He tried to remain calm, but fear consumed him and his mind was no longer working rationally. He was, for all intents and purposes, completely overmatched by exhaustion, heat, intimidation, blackmail, and forthcoming torture.

Dr. Hunter couldn't believe his former bedtime companion was preparing to torture him. His mind was furiously trying to figure a way out. There was however, not even a split second where he considered revealing the truth about the Digitalis or what happened at Nakuru.

Rajni leaned in and whispered in Dr. Hunter's ear, "It is going to be a pleasure for me to show you what it feels like to be tossed aside as an unimportant sex toy after I tried so hard to please you, both at work, and in bed."

A startled, shocked, and panicked Dr. Hunter responded, "That's not how it was Rajni. I was straight with you from the start. You knew where I stood. And it was your choice to go along. Regardless, how in the world can you still be angry all these years later?"

Lavanya using her typical calm, confident, almost aloof tone, chimed in, sensing Rajni's pent up rage prevented her from crafting a suitably insulting response, "Dr. Hunter, you should know as well as anyone that being disrespected is something a person never forgets. You can make atonements, but the memories will always haunt both people and the future of their relationship, whatever the nature of it may be. Unfortunately for you, there appears a lack of atonement. And from what I know of Rajni here, I wouldn't want to be sitting in your chair right about now." As she spoke, she had gotten up from her observation chair and placed one hand on Dr. Hunter's shoulder, and one deep inside his right thigh, for added effect. Her neck, which was doused with perfume, was carefully positioned slightly in front of his face. Lavanya knew how to seduce but it hardly calmed him under the circumstances. The words she spoke passed in one ear and out the other while his mind was focused on how to escape.

Dr. Hunter pulled himself together as Lavanya walked back to the other side of the stall and once again sat down. He said to her, "Thank you for that. But you two need to realize you are premising everything on rumors and none of them are real. Whatever you think happened didn't. Would you have me fabricate lies to appease you?"

Rajni whacked him across the face with a slap that sent droplets of sweat flying into a nearby stack of hay. Then she screamed at him in a voice that reeked of out of control madness, "We'll know if you're lying you arrogant old man! I don't recommend it! But I look forward to you being stupid enough to challenge me on this!"

Lavanya barked out, "Get on with it. This heat and his stubbornness are unbearable. It's time to break him."

*   *   *

Rajni continued talking to him, as she grabbed what looked and felt to Dr. Hunter like a dull scalpel and started cutting around his knee cap. She said, "Dr. Hunter, I am confident that together we could make history. There can be no doubt it would be the kind of history that changes the world for the better."

As his blood pressure rose from watching his knee cut open, Dr. Hunter retorted with a shaky voice, trying to maintain some dignity despite the circumstances, "Changes the world for the better? You are so naïve. You have no idea what you have gotten yourself into do you?"

"Oh Dr. Hunter, you worry too much. After we're finished here today, which I doubt will take too much longer, it will be my pleasure to show you exactly what *we* have gotten into. We will start in the Moksha Temple, which will reveal to you the nobility of what we are after. I mention it to you now with the hope that you will reconsider sharing with us the information we need to scientifically prove reincarnation. In lieu of that, the location of the Digitalis will suffice. We know it is real. And we know you and your stupid group of investors have it safely stored away somewhere. Tell us where now, and we can skip the un-pleasantries we have planned for you."

His response was so vehement that he spat as he chastised her. "There is no Digitalis! And no amount of uncivilized brutality can make it exist! Your madness will leave a trail of death, and judging by your desperation, I suspect you already know that. You should stop now before it is too late!"

Lavanya laughed while nudging Rajni Gupta, "See that Dr. Gupta, Americans today are so arrogant, they think they can make demands even while clearly in a position of desperate peril."

"It is astounding, especially in this case. He is in fact a Dutchman if I recall? I would have expected more from a European…" Dr. Gupta responded, in an effort to please her superior.

"You are both insane. I cannot tell you the location of something which does not exist."

Rajni violently slapped the old man across the face. Blood oozed from the side of his upper lip where one of her rings left a gash. Meanwhile, the incision on his leg completely encircled his knee cap. Rajni ripped away the skin covering the bone, without anesthesia but with plenty of warning, so as to allow his mind to focus on the pain. Then she poured a generous amount of alcohol on the open wound as Dr. Hunter screamed with such agony the horses nearby kicked and whinnied.

The crude treatments continued for hours, with Dr. Hunter repeatedly fading into unconsciousness only to be continuously revived. Blood from his wounds soaked the ground around them turning the yellowish hay bright red. His lip was split open; all of his toes smashed; his entire right kneecap removed completely so that even the air caused him pain. Rajni was debating her next steps and asked him to choose between his hands, a precious commodity for a surgeon, or his teeth. Finally she claimed they must leave his hands intact, so prepared to pull out his front tooth with a pair of large metal pliers that further split his lips in the process. Just as she was about to pull, Lavanya ordered, "Enough!" She seldom publicly showed emotion, especially to her enemies, but was clearly on edge.

"This is not how we treat our guests, no matter how unpleasant and recalcitrant their nature. We will try something different." Lavanya pulled a cell phone from her pocket and began to dial.

Before pressing send, she showed the screen to Dr. Hunter who asked, "Why are you calling him?"

"It's time he knew," she replied before leaning in and once again exposing her cleavage while whispering in his ear, "I know your biggest secret and your biggest fear. I know about..." her whisper faded and became indiscernible to Rajni who was eager to hear.

Lavanya recoiled from the smell of Dr. Hunter's fear. She could see, for the first time, tears in his eyes. Lavanya asked him, "Well Billy, should we spill your deepest darkest secret?" She pressed send on the phone and it began connecting to his son Jake's cell phone. The voice mail greeting came on and Lavanya said, "I suppose we'll just have to tell him in a voice mail message. What a pity. What an awful way to find out the worst possible betrayal."

Five hours into his ordeal, Dr. William Hunter was defeated. No amount of physical pain would have caused him to reveal the Digitalis, but he was not willing to risk having his son learn about his secret. With a deflated tone, Dr. Hunter told Lavanya what she wanted to know, "The Digitalis is what you need. It holds the secrets to conscious recognition of past life memories. And it's your best shot at recreating what happened in Nakuru. You can find it in the remote Venezuelan jungle at a highly secure former research site belonging to the investment trust that funded the Nakuru trials. The site in Venezuela is abandoned as a research facility, but still heavily guarded for what it holds inside. It is located in a place called Aguas Muertas and it's extremely difficult to get to as there are no roads in or out. The answers that you seek are there. All the truth about Nakuru, at least what remains of it, is also there."

Rajni gasped, "I can't believe he caved from that, but not the pain."

Lavanya looked at her and said, "Don't be so stupid Rajni. The worst pain a human can feel is never physical. Haven't you ever been in love? Are you really that naïve? Never mind. Don't answer that. Get in touch with John and tell him to confirm this at once. I don't think I can tolerate dealing with him today, but we haven't a minute to lose."

"Yes ma'am," Rajni replied.

"Oh and see that Billy here gets the required medical attention. Once he's healthy, show him the labs and get him started making a new Digitalis. In the meantime, I will line up our next test subject. I have someone in mind that I think will motivate the good Doctor here to try his very best. In fact, I'll be flying to Washington tonight so that I can pick up the test subject myself. I should be back in a couple of days, and expect to see some progress."

CHAPTER 16

Unknown Caribbean Island

The next morning, a bucket of ice water thrown on his body abruptly woke Jake from his slumber. The soldiers were back. This time, they grabbed him roughly and dragged him from the cell, down the hallway, and into another room. He was tied into a chair in the center of the room and surrounded by three standing men, Commander Collins being one of them.

Collins asked, "Mr. Hunter, would you please explain to me what happened to the briefcase containing the Digitalis that was onboard the Hunter Neurologics corporate jet?"

"Wait a second. Just wait a second. You throw me in a cell, then drag me in here and tie me up, with zero explanation as to where I am, why I'm here, or who the hell you are and you're just going to start asking questions? What kind of way is this to start a dialogue? If there are things you want to know and I have the answers, I am sure we can work something out, but this is one hell of a crappy way to get things started."

Collins looked at his two colleagues who were

standing in the room with him and nodded to the bigger of the two men, then said, "Go." At that prompt, Jose moved in front of Jake and cut loose a right hook that sent his head spinning. Blood leaked from his lip.

Jake replied with an anger that came from a part of him he didn't know existed, "Mother... You had better hope I don't get out of this chair! What kind of coward hits a man that can't defend himself? Come on, untie me and let me see you try that again, come on you coward!" Jose hit Jake a second time and started to swing again before Collins pulled him away.

"Mr. Hunter, we can save a lot of time if you would please answer the question."

"I don't know, OK!? I have no idea what the hell happened to my father's briefcase, let alone my father. All I know is I woke up, the plane was on the ground, and they were both missing."

"So the briefcase was nowhere to be found when the plane exploded?"

"NO! THERE WAS NO BRIEFCASE! NOW LET ME OUT OF THIS CHAIR OR I'M NOT ANSWERING ANY OTHER QUESTIONS."

"I'm not sure I'm convinced you're telling the truth Mr. Hunter."

Jake continued with a more defeated tone, "Are you kidding me? Where do you think I'm hiding it? In my back pocket? Don't be so dense!"

"Very well. However, I hope you can understand that we need to be sure of the status of that briefcase before we can return you to the U.S. Jose will be giving you a quick polygraph exam. If you're lying to me, you will not likely leave this facility alive. Are we clear?"

"Clear as mud. And I'm not lying. Let's get on with it then."

*   *   *

An hour later, Collins informed Jake he passed the test with a curt apology for the unpleasant accommodations. "We had no choice Mr. Hunter. I was just obeying orders. Besides, the plane to take you back has only just landed, so we had time to kill. No hard feelings right?" Jake didn't respond.

Obeying whose orders is what I want to know...

*   *   *

A short while later, Jake and Kennedy were back out on the airstrip. The helicopters they had come in on were gone. But they stared in discontent at a Lear jet which had on the side the same embracing golden monkeys and the word, Moksha.

The inside of the jet was beyond luxurious. Their flight home would be in comfort, and they were finally away from the bullet slinging commandos. Collins wished them well and extended his arm to shake Jake's hand, but Jake ignored him and walked right past. On board, the flight crew was limited to only two pilots, who told the couple to make themselves comfortable for the duration of the five hour flight to Washington, D.C. They were finally going home.

Shortly after liftoff, as the plane's wheels were closed into the body of the aircraft, Jake sat back and sipped on a Johnny Walker Blue, impressed they had such good scotch on board.

Kennedy said to him, "What do you suppose that was all about?"

"They asked me this morning what happened to my father's briefcase. They didn't ask about my father, just the briefcase."

"What did you tell them," Kennedy asked.

"I told them the truth, that I didn't know anything about it. But it's weird, this plane, Collins' cufflinks..."

"What's weird?"

"Didn't you see his cufflinks?"

"No I didn't. But so what? Why on earth do you act like you saw the devil because of a man's cufflinks?"

"They had monkeys, gold monkeys. They looked exactly like what I saw on that card holder from the plane crash, right near my father's empty chair." Jake produced the gold cardholder, which he still had in his pocket. "Look, his links, and this airplane, even have this same word engraved on them, "Moksha". What intarnations is a Moksha?"

"That I do not know Jake. But whoever is behind all this, clearly wants us alive as a way to get the Digitalis, at least for the time being."

Jake replied, "After Jose's right hooks to my jaw, I would agree. My only question is what happens to us once they have what they're after?"

"They can't get what they're after Jake. They must never get it. We have to make sure they don't."

"We? Are you kidding me? Look, I don't know who you really are, but I'm just a disbarred lawyer. I've got to figure out how to help Aubrey Doyle and find out what happened to my father before I do anything else."

"Jake, I think this may be bigger than us. Bigger than Aubrey and your father. We may not have a choice is all I am saying."

"There's always choices. Choices are made by the vigilant. And I chose to be vigilant."

Kennedy realized Jake wasn't fully grasping the situation they had been plunged into, but she sensed he was overwhelmed and so let it go for the time being. Then she stroked his arm and leaned into his chest to take a nap during the ride home. Jake did not protest. In fact, he lamented not having experienced the feeling of closeness that comes from human touch in far too long. His wife Anja hadn't nuzzled into him like that in months.

That feels too good. I should push her away. But, I guess I don't want to.

N early every man who develops an idea works it up to the point where it looks impossible, and then he gets discouraged. That's not the place to become discouraged.

-Thomas A. Edison

CHAPTER 17

California Wilderness – Off the Grid

Anja Hunter had not had a moment of peace in over two months. She was sleep deprived as her captors would allow her no more than an hour's rest at a time. It was meant to weaken her mind by preventing REM or deep sleep, and it was working.

In a rare moment of downtime, away from the relentless torture and brainwashing, her mind was reeling. She thought about what haunted her most and wondered if her battle to overcome it would ever end or if she was about to lose it once and for all. She thought about her childhood.

Anja remembered a time, one of many, when her mother came home after having disappeared for four days straight:

It was the usual routine, mom freaked out at dad over what seemed like no big deal: dirty laundry on the floor, thermostat set too high, things that were silly in the grand scheme of happiness. Mom runs out the door, doesn't look back. Mom doesn't call, can't be reached. Dad doesn't seem to mind, doesn't seem worried. Mostly he enjoyed the time with several of his many "girlfriends." Mom comes back and begs for forgiveness. There's an occasional glance thrown towards Anja. In those rare instances, she can see *it* in her eyes. Mom doesn't want to be there. She's begging for forgiveness, but her face reveals she doesn't think she's done anything wrong. Bottom line, she has no where else to go and is using Dad. She looks at Anja as though she's a burden. And Anja realizes she is a lynchpin that is holding her mother back from leaving for good. Never mind that the first thing she does that night is smoke crack cocaine which dad gives her, and makes obscene noises loud enough for the neighbors to hear, not to mention, her seven year old child in the next bedroom over.

Anja strained her neck to look over her shoulder at the permanent reminders of her childhood. They covered most of her back. The scars would always be there to tell her what life was like during those frequent times when mom ran away. She let out an exasperated sigh and said out loud to herself, "Although sometimes I think things were better when she was gone than when she was home…."

If I got through all that, maybe I can get through this. But maybe I never really did get through that. Maybe that's why I'm here now. Maybe I should just give them what they want. If I just believe them, maybe they will help me. Besides, maybe they are right, Jake is responsible for my being here in the first place. In a way, it really is all his fault.

She was starting to crack.

CHAPTER 18

Potomac, Maryland
(Just Outside Washington, D.C.)

Lavanya Yashodhara had John Anton's right shoulder pinned against the stone wall that formed a privacy backdrop and encircled all but a small in/out path to the spa. They were in the backyard of Jake Hunter's suburban Maryland home.

While Jake was still in route in the Leer jet provided by Lavanya, the uninvited guests were making themselves at home. Keeping pressure on John's right shoulder with her right hand, Lavanya moved her left hand to his waist and removed his swim trunks under the water. John, being a bit more conventional than Lavanya tried to move her off of him and muttered something about going inside. She slapped him across the face, pushed his trunks down to his ankles and straddled him. Ultimately, Lavanya was positive that John didn't really mind the location all that much.

Twenty minutes later, after a shower in Jake's master bathroom, she was dropping a summer dress over her body, sans any undergarments when her cell phone alerted them to Jake's impending arrival home. They quickly tidied up the place before Lavanya sent John on his way.

Before he left, Lavanya said, "Let's recap one more time and make sure we've got this straight."

"I've got it Lavanya. Try to relax for once. I'm going to call him and tell him we need him to get the Digitalis from the Research and Development site at Isla Dedaleras. The investors are insisting on it. It's true, you're the "investors" and you're insisting on it, so it should be easy enough to remember."

"It sounds simple enough, but somehow I know you'll find a way to screw it up. If you do, that little episode in the hot tub will be the last of its kind."

"Sometimes, you really are amazingly affectionate Lavanya."

"It's tough love sweetie. Tough love is the best love. Now don't let me down."

"I'll check in with you later. But I really don't understand why you want to stay in the house. And why not just send him straight to that Aguas Muertas place? It seems like an unnecessary risk sending him to the island first."

"John, love, I'm not going over it again. We need to beat our enemies to Isla Dedaleras. Jake is the only one we know for certain will be able to get the Digitalis. Your boy Devon has had plenty of time… too much time in fact. We'll investigate Aguas Muertas later. Now get out of here before he gets home and our cover is blown."

"Fine. See ya." John left the house as they had planned, while Lavanya made herself comfortable in an inconspicuous spot

*   *   *

Jake walked in through the side door to his home in suburban Washington, D.C. as he couldn't find his keys and needed to use the electronic code box on the garage.

Lost my keys... that's just great. I'll add that to the rapidly growing list of frustrations from an otherwise horrible couple of days.

The jet had landed at Reagan National and two limos took him and Kennedy to their respective homes. Jake's mind was still busy contemplating the significance of the embracing golden monkeys and the meaning of the word Moksha. He also had no idea who had provided the flight and limo ride, but he was certain that nothing was ever free, and wondered about the connection between Commander Collins, the crashed plane, and his missing father.

As soon as he could get settled, take a shower, and get some food, he planned to Google the word, "Moksha" in hopes of finding something that might answer some of the mysteries plaguing him.

*   *   *

Jake booted up his web browser, which had its homepage set to the WashingtonPost.com. He immediately saw the type of headline reserved only for major calamities, "Destroyed Hunter Neurologics Building at Center of July 4th Attack." Before he could react, the last living major investor in his father's company called his cell phone.

"This is Jake," he answered.

John Anton greeted him, "Jake, so glad you're OK. Are you home yet?"

"You're glad I'm OK?! Well, yes, I am home John. But I wouldn't exactly say I'm OK. My father is missing you know? And apparently I've been a bit out of the loop the last couple of days. What's this about the office downtown?"

"Are you sitting Jake?"

"Just cut to the chase. What's going on?"

"Apparently, the headquarters building downtown was at the center of a rather large explosion. The police are

trying to figure out how our offices became the source of
enough C-4 plastic explosives to take out a couple of city
blocks. Jake, as you know, there aren't too many executives
from your father's company left alive. I'm afraid the police
are going to have a slew of questions for you. If they
haven't gotten to you already, then consider yourself
warned. You could be in for a week's worth of torment and
interrogations."

"That's ridiculous. I don't know anything about this,
let alone how someone could have stuffed our office full
with explosives."

"Jake, the problem is that building had more security
than Fort Knox. It's no secret your father was on the cusp of
major medical breakthroughs and had that place locked
down tight. The police are going to want to know how the
hell anyone could have pulled this off without inside help.
You're new to the company. So you're going to look guilty
no matter what."

"I don't get it John. What they should be asking is
not who, but why. As in, why pick the most secure building
on the block to hold your bomb. That doesn't make sense. I
mean, unless…" what he was saying hit him like a brick,
"Jesus John! You're telling me someone deliberately blew
up our office building? And you know about the flight
right? This was the same day someone murdered our entire
board of directors by crashing that plane!"

"Listen, try to stay calm. You need to let Devon
handle the police for you. They're not going to respect a
disbarred attorney. So don't go trying to represent yourself.
I hope you know better than that."

"Sure, what's that old saying, only a fool would hire
himself as his lawyer?"

"Something like that. But listen, Devon is en route to
the Isla Dedaleras research site. He flew down to secure the
place after we learned about the plane crash. So he's not
going to be able to help you here in D.C. What's worse, I'm

not sure he's going to know what to do once he gets there, but there is no one left at the site we feel comfortable trusting."

Nor will there be, since they are all dead. Sorry for the inconvenience.

Jake asked, "Are you suggesting I get on another plane? Do you have any idea what I've been through in the last couple days? I haven't even talked to my wife in weeks. Besides, I've only been working for my father for a short time; how am I supposed to know what to do?"

"Come on Jake. You know it's not unusual for Anja to go for days like that without calling. I'm sure she's fine, enjoying her little adventure. But you need to focus on you and your father's lifetime of investment in this company. Unless you want to spend a week in uncomfortable government chairs, with crappy coffee, and worried about saying the right or wrong thing without anyone there to represent you, then I would strongly suggest getting your stuff together, and heading back to the airport. The biggest medical breakthrough of our lifetimes is at stake. Obviously someone is after it. Are you going to let them just get away with this? That doesn't sound like the Jake I know. Besides, I would say you probably don't have more than a few minutes before your place is crawling with feds. If it was me, I would high tail it out the back door."

"John, you know I don't ask for a lot of favors. Can't you pull some strings with your friends in the Governor's office? It's just that Anja, she was supposed to be back tonight. I can't just jet out of here again. I need to see her after everything that's happened."

"You know I would Jake, but all the money in the world can't clean up this mess. There are hundreds of innocent Fourth of July partiers dead. The press is all over this. It makes Sept 11 a distant memory. In fact, I'm surprised they're not at your house right now. And they've gotten wind of your temporary disbarment. That is certainly going to sound like motive to a lot of yahoo detectives bucking for promotion."

"That's ludicrous!"

"You and I know that buddy, but the press is having a field day with it. What's going on with that anyways? What's the latest with your trial? I thought you had some sort of court appearance this week?"

"I don't want to talk about that right now. Listen, what the hell is the point of flying back to that island? I have had my share of the Caribbean at this point. I'm sure Devon can figure out how to lock down the research center."

"No Jake, it's not that simple. We need both of you there buddy. I mean, we know we need the Digitalis. But no one knows what it is exactly. And the only people who did are all dead. We can be certain it's what your father was preparing to present at the upcoming medical conference, and it was being touted as revolutionary and unlike any other medical breakthrough. With all this attention in the media, word is going to get out about that island and the research that was going on there. People will be putting two and two together and that place will be the next target. We've already received threats."

"That just doesn't make…" Jake tried to interrupt but John kept talking.

"Jake, you don't seem to realize the world changing ability of your father's work. People who run the world, the people who really run it Jake… they are going to want this. Right now, if we want to save this company and your father's work, we need you and Devon there locking that place down, and talking to everyone. Someone there must have been an inside man for what happened on that airplane and for what happened to the building in D.C. I need you guys to find out who before we lose everything. And then I need you to find and secure the Digitalis. It's the future of our investment that's at stake."

"I think you meant to say, the future of my father's

lifetime of work that's at stake."

"Absolutely Jake. We've got to protect his years of hard work."

"What the hec…" Jake paused to control his temper before restarting more calmly, "John, I'm just a lawyer for God's sake. I mean a disbarred lawyer at that. I can't go down to some island and play detective."

"Not even to save the family business? Come on Jake. Who else are you going to trust when there's a whole new market of medicine on the line? We're not talking about billions here Jake. We're talking hundreds of billions, maybe more. There are fortunes to be made here Jake. And I'm not talking about fortunes that make a few people show up on the world's richest list. What we're talking about is balance of power shifting fortunes that change the world forever. If someone steals the Digitalis, they're going to control the outcome. I shouldn't have to explain corporate espionage to you. Come on man, I thought you were smarter than this?!"

All he cares about is money. My father's been kidnapped and someone tried or is trying to kill me and all he can talk about is protecting his money. His arrogance is astounding.

Jake retorted, "You thought I was smarter than what, an idiot like you? You're starting to annoy the shit out of me to be honest. You haven't once asked about my father."

"Take it easy Jake. I am not trying to annoy you. I'm simply saying, are you going to sit back and let someone else, someone more aggressive control the outcome of what's going on right now? Or are you going to fight for justice. Fight for what is right. Fight for ensuring the integrity of your father's lifetime of work? The Jake I thought I knew would have been on a plane in a heartbeat."

Jake was happy to have hit the red end call button on his cell without saying another word.

What exactly is the Digitalis? What can be so darn scientifically advanced that people would kill for it? I almost want to go back just to know what it is...

He looked up from the phone and standing in front of him was the most beautiful woman he had ever seen. It was not his wife, however, and he felt uneasy at how captivated he was by the stranger's good looks. The glow of her eyes didn't help Jake in the "till death do you part" category either. The woman was accompanied by two men, each with the same gold cuff links he had seen at the airstrip and on the crashed jet, and bearing the strange symbol with the "Moksha Monkeys."

T o achieve the impossible; it is precisely the

unthinkable that must be thought.

–Tom Robbins

CHAPTER 19

Yashodhara Palace, India

Not more than twelve hours removed from being tortured, Dr. Hunter was led by Dr. Rajni Gupta on a tour of the vast compound that comprised Lavanya Yashodhara's palace and obsessions. He had refused pain killers, as he wanted to be as lucid as possible. While Dr. Gupta led the way, Dr. Hunter hobbled behind on crutches (also refusing to utilize a wheelchair).

He was still muttering his disdain for their work and how they had gotten in over their heads, when Dr. Gupta decided to try again to bond with the man she had only hours earlier physically mutilated. She said to him, "Dr. Hunter, you worry too much. Why don't I show you what we've both gotten ourselves into? We should start in the Moksha Temple. With anything of significance in this world, it is important to have the end vision in mind, even before beginning. Then, we'll head into the labs and show you what we have accomplished towards our goals. We would value your assessment of our progress and our mistakes to date, and it would also give you a good idea of where we are, and what's left to do relative to creating our own special type of Digitalis. To the extent our work does not overlap with your own, we will be that much farther along toward reaching our goals."

"We can start, where ever you want. However, what you cannot control is where we'll end up. It will not be pretty. Rest assured, you will NOT be a hero. There will be no heroes, no prizes, no rewards for what you are attempting to do here. And this idea of using the Digitalis to bring unconscious memories to the surface demonstrates you have no idea of the truth. You have no idea of the dangers inherent in the Digitalis."

"We shall see Dr. Hunter. If you please, would you follow me now? There is much to show you and much we can do even without your personal research notes and equipment." They walked out of the office and back into the long corridor with all the doors. Just past the entrance to the "Infected Patients" lab, they approached a door marked, "Moksha Temple (Backstage Entrance)," about half way down the hall.

His concern and curiosity peaked, Dr. Hunter spoke up, "What was that Infected Patients lab," he asked Dr. Gupta.

"It's a limited access lab where we conduct further research on, well, let's just say our mistakes. It's not something you'll need access to at this time. And hopefully, you can avoid needing access to it in the future."

The backstage entrance to the "Moksha Temple" led them into a world of expert marketing and capitalism that ran counter to the religious principles of humility and conservatism it was meant to promote. Dr. Hunter knew there would be much money to be made from the breakthroughs he was making in neurological medical treatments, but what he saw as he entered the temple was beyond his wildest imagination.

They walked through hallways and rooms that had unfinished ceilings and walls until they came upon the rear entrance to a main temple with a stage and vast auditorium beyond. It looked large enough to hold upwards of a couple thousand people or more. Everything was wired with video cameras and lights more typical of a Hollywood studio than a place of religious sanctity. To their right, was what looked like a control room. To the left, on the opposite side of the back of the main stage, was another room. That one had a sign over the door that read, "Consultation Center." Dr. Gupta led them towards that room.

"What is this place? I thought you were going to show me your research, not take me to church."

"Relax Dr. Hunter; let me show you what we plan to offer to millions of suffering people across the globe."

"What would that be?" He retorted sardonically, "The only thing you're going to be offering are free passes to your 'Infected Patients' lab!" Dr. Gupta didn't laugh.

"You joke about what you cannot understand. It's a common problem for those with lesser minds. It is not, however, the type of response I expected from someone like you. No Dr. Hunter, what we aim to offer is hope. The kind of hope that can give people the fuel required to overcome adversity, to live happy lives, but most importantly, to achieve more than their neighbors. We will give them this hope through scientific validation of their basic fundamental beliefs instilled since childhood. When coupled with the advances you have found possible in cognitive processing, our clientele will leave this facility with mental abilities far superior to even the smartest people in the world."

"You want to use the Digitalis to give people an I.Q. advantage? I thought all this was about using science to prove religion? To prove reincarnation?"

"All this, as you call it, is about both. It's my understanding your work at Nakuru already proved reincarnation… that the woman you dumped me for, Victoria Lake, is living proof. Are you honestly going to deny that to someone who was there?"

"Nothing of the sort was proved. And I couldn't have dumped you because we were never a couple. You have your facts mixed up with grossly exaggerated gossip. Your quest is going to end in misery and unnecessary death."

"Dr. Hunter, I hope for the sake of your family members that is not the case." He sighed in response and bit his tongue.

They entered the Consultation Center and sat in one of several circular information booths. Each booth had a large monitor on one side of the wall opposite the chairs, and a viewing window on the other side. As they walked in, the viewing window was covered but the monitor lit up with a video that started the moment they sat. In the video was Lavanya Yashodhara, thanking them for their patronage and promising conscious recognition of past lives to help reconnect lost family members and to help facilitate something she called, "Moksha."

In the video, a family gathered and smiled next to Lavanya, as soft tranquil music played in the background. All the best marketing gimmicks were on display as she went on to explain, "We all desire, long for, and strive to achieve liberation from the cycle of birth and rebirth. By taking the steps necessary to free your mind through our revolutionary treatments, you can connect the dots of your past lives and speed your passage to liberation from Samsara."

Dr. Hunter reached over to the touch screen monitor to pause the video. Then he turned to Dr. Gupta and asked, "What is that, Samsara?"

"Samsara is the cycle of reincarnation or rebirth commonly accepted by the vast majority of human beings across the globe. Followers of Hinduism, Buddhism, Jainism, Sikhism, and other related religions all subscribe to this concept. In other words, roughly speaking, more than two thirds of the world's population. According to these religions, one's "karmic" account balance at the time of death is inherited in their next life, upon rebirth. During the course of each worldly life, actions for good or bad, determine one's future destiny and the need for rebirth or release. Moksha is the eternal peace or release from that cycle, that is, from Samsara. Since Moksha is usually only earned after many attempts at life and death, we can, in effect, help people get there faster."

"False prophets," he muttered under his breath.

"What did you say?" she snapped at him.

"You're crazy. You want to play with people's brains to try to let them think they can achieve eternal peace more quickly? Don't you realize there are no shortcuts in life? And there certainly are not any shortcuts to eternal peace. What will you charge them for this? And who would be foolish enough to pay?"

"We already have a waiting list of well over two hundred people, each of whom has made the required US$10 million down payment."

"That's one hell of a down payment."

"10% to be exact. In my opinion, it's a very nominal price tag, considering what we offer."

"You all don't seem like you need the money, so why?"

"You are correct; we do not need the money. But we do need discretion. The size of the down payment provides us reasonable assurance we will get it."

"So you're not exactly helping millions of the world's suffering, just the few hundred or so wealthy enough to play your crazy game."

"This is just one part of our planned operations. There is so much more, especially when you fold in advances in cognitive neuroscience that you are going to help us add to our offerings. Doesn't this at least give you a sense of the tremendous potential for our work? Just think, we'll be able to help stupid people become smart."

Dr. Hunter replied, "That's extraordinarily simple minded. You'll have no way of knowing if you're really doing that or the opposite. Haven't you ever read Shakespeare? The fool may guide the wise! And you are nothing but insane to think you can judge another human being's intelligence, let alone manipulate it through science."

Dr. Gupta said, "Sometimes you talk in riddles Dr. Hunter."

"The problem is you are not in a position to understand anyone who isn't of average intelligence. If a person is of far superior or inferior intelligence from the mass population, or near the top or bottom of the bell curve, you will not be able to understand them in the same way you perceive the masses, or "normal" behavior which is only normal by virtue of it being the most common. The very nature of natural variations in how the mind works makes what you are suggesting impossible. It's as if you actually believe a human being could possibly be qualified to judge another human being's intelligence levels. It's impossible, and it's madness. You'll never know if you're destroying a mind, or helping it."

Dr. Gupta looked confused and asked, "Are you trying to say I am stupid Dr. Hunter?"

"I am saying you are crazy to think this is possible. No one can judge another's intelligence; so how can you possibly measure the outcomes! You can't!!!" He was enraged and slammed his fist on the monitor, nearly breaking it before laying into her, "And as for reincarnation, even if I believed in it, and let me be clear about this, I most definitely do NOT believe in it. But even if I did, you need to think about what you are saying. Imagine the lunacy that would ensue from the human mind trying to process memories and thoughts of multiple personalities from multiple lives across different periods in history. It would most definitely drive a person insane. It would be like multiple personality disorder, only exponentially worse."

She looked concerned, "Are you telling me this Dr. Hunter, or simply hypothesizing?" He sat in silence, immediately recognizing the question as a set up, probing for information which he knew was far too dangerous to reveal.

Dr. Gupta continued, "Regardless, this is where you come in Dr. Hunter. You are the leading researcher in the use of electrical stimulation for cognitive neuroscience. I know you will find a way to do this. We must find it. And when we do, this temple will be known across the globe."

"Your temple will be world renowned. There is no doubt about that. But it will NOT be because of helping people. Look, you were there, you have to recognize there are reasons the work at Nakuru was shut down and buried so deep there is not a discernable trace of it having ever existed. I can feel it in my gut; this is the work of the devil."

"Then you must help make it the work of something better Dr. Hunter. Considering the circumstances, you don't really have any alternatives. Besides, we are already very close. You could be a part of something fantastic and that will change the course of history. If you would just open your mind to see the possibilities and opportunities, rather than the negatives, then you might be surprised."

Dr. Hunter replied, "Maybe I have already seen the damage that can be done from attempting to pursue what you suggest…"

Dr. Gupta grew terse and cut him off, "I really wondered for the longest time how one of the founders of the world's leading medical research investment trust could have fallen into its dog house. But now I see the issue. You lack vision. You lack the ability to see a brighter future. I think I've heard enough of your gibberish. So now, if you would, let's watch the rest of the video, it provides an excellent summary of how our proposed treatments might work."

Dr. Hunter mumbled under his breath, "I have plenty

of vision, but not at the cost of the innocent."

*   *   *

They watched the video until the entire pod like booth they were sitting in spun 45 degrees to the right, revealing a window into what looked like a medical suite. The TV monitor playing the video swiveled with them and introduced the "treatments" room. The video image of Lavanya gave way at this point to Dr. Gupta, who looked even better on camera than in person. As she explained the process to would be customers, robotic mannequin doctors and patients repeatedly enacted the steps of the surgery:

After extensive counseling and prep work, your scheduled appointment with our medical team will take place in the room you are viewing now. The procedure itself is painless and relatively quick by today's medical standards. The surgeons will drill a single hole through your skull and use microscopic tools to place tiny electrodes in your brain at precise coordinates, which vary depending on your own personal physiology and genetic makeup. Due to natural differences among us, follow up surgeries may be required to achieve the optimal location for the electrodes.

A remote, and wireless, power pack can be attached at your hip and will send electrical frequencies to the diodes in your brain which in turn stimulate neural activity to achieve the desired results.

It may sound like science fiction, but it is reality, and it has been proven to work. Let us show you more about the different types of results that can be achieved.

We have the science available today, to provide a range of services, from advancing cognitive improvement in memory, logical and analytical reasoning skills, beyond regular known human performance, all the way to conscious recognition of past lives to help you achieve Moksha."

Dr. Hunter's face was bright red as he blurted out, "The implications of doing this in humans is too high risk and you know that. How can you lie like this?"

"My dear Dr. Hunter, we have not been completely devoid of progress here without your input. When we get to the R&D labs, I think you'll be impressed with the work of your former student. Let's continue the tour."

*   *   *

The pod pivoted again another 45 degrees and they were watching rats in a maze. There were two sets. The maze on the right was full of rats that looked disheveled and overwhelmed by their surroundings. On the left, the rats were feasting on the rewards of cheese at the maze exit points. The video started up again, with Dr. Gupta explaining the rats as one of the first successful experiments into the use of electrical stimulation therapy for cognitive regeneration. It was, as she called it, a pioneering first step for a bold new field of cognitive neuroscience.

Dr Hunter interrupted the presentation once again, "You've replicated the Jiang study[8]. That's not exactly difficult to do. But do you realize how simple this is compared to improving cognitive performance in humans, let alone the science fiction you are proposing? Place an electrode in the human brain even a fraction of a millimeter

---

[8] Electrical brain stimulation was shown to ameliorate dysfunction of memory deficits due to age and disease: Jiang, F., Racine, R., and Turnbull, J, "Electrical Stimulation of the Septal Region of Aged Rats Improves Performance in an Open-Field Maze," Physiology & Behavior, Vol 62, No. 6, pp. 1279-1282 (1997).

from the right coordinate, and you can cause irreparable brain damage."

"What we realize Dr. Hunter, is that you are nearly there already in your treatments for Alzheimer's. This is why we brought you here, to share your fabled Digitalis, which makes the process work, and to that end, to greatly speed our progress on our more noble goals. I can thank you now, or can thank you later if you like, but rest assured, you would much rather cooperate with us than not. Should you forget that, just let me know, and I will be happy to give you a pat on that gimpy knee of yours."

Dr. Hunter gritted his teeth wanting to voice an aggressive comeback. But, remembering they had kidnapped Anja, he held his tongue. The pod swiveled again and Dr. Gupta announced, "This last viewing, I think you will find the most impressive. It was specifically added for recruiting down payments from future customers as well as additional money from investors. We wanted to show them real progress, so to speak."

The viewing glass opened to another medical suite. This one was full of real, live patients and doctors. There were three in all, set up in a production line with the different stages of the treatment. The first patient was having a hole drilled in his head. The second, a woman, had a device inserted through the hole, with an image on a monitor next to her, showing the placement of tiny electrodes deep inside her brain's septal region. A holographic image of another doctor was projected next to the real live patient and doctor in mid surgery and spoke to the viewers in the pod. The holographic doctor explained the choice of the diode placement in the septal region as a critical relay point between the midbrain, and the hippocampus. The holographic doctor went on to explain it was in the hippocampus where lesions can cause cognitive disorders such as Alzheimer's, but where expedited brain function in healthy patients, can facilitate far above average brain functions, including stored memory recollection as well as learning and cognitive development. It all sounded eerily familiar to Dr. Hunter as his Digitalis and related treatments for patients with memory problems were based on the same principles.

The third patient sat next to an Electroencephalography machine with electrodes strung between it and the patient's head. The display showed a variety of measures, and a similar, holographic image of a doctor explained the process of figuring out the right electrical frequencies to use for achieving Moksha, which was clearly the focus of their operation, more so than any type of legitimate medical treatment.

"So how exactly do you suppose you will use electrical currents to achieve this Moksha?"

"You tell me Dr. Hunter. We know all about your little incident during the Nakuru clinical trial in Kenya. Our work here would go much more quickly if you would simply come clean and share with us how those results were achieved."

"There was no incident at Nakuru. Again, what you are referring to is purely exaggerated gossip."

"I know that there was. And I know it was the precursor to your current Digitalis that made it possible. I am growing tired of your argumentative denials. Perhaps a greater appreciation of the time sensitive nature of this situation would encourage you to be a bit more revealing," the pod rotated again, and Dr. Gupta escorted him to a nearby conference room with a large LCD screen at the end. She hit play on the remote, which was the lone object on the long ornate table. News clips of the destruction of the Hunter Neurologics building in D.C., and the lost corporate jet played on the screen while Dr. Hunter held his chest and started wheezing. "Believe me when I tell you Dr. Hunter, that this news, that is to say, your learning that everything you've worked for and everyone you have worked with are

130

no longer around is not your chief concern."

He interrupted her, "Damn you to hell woman. Damn you all to hell."

"Please calm down Dr. Hunter. Lavanya is not responsible for the destruction of your building in D.C. In fact, Lavanya saved you from the attempted assassination of your entire executive team on board your jet. Really, you owe her your life."

"Do you honestly expect me to believe this rubbish?"

"It is the truth Dr. Hunter. What you should be concerned about is who was really responsible and why. We have our suspicions, but by working together, we can be better prepared to prevent any more setbacks. The one thing we are certain of, is that whoever is responsible, they have stepped up their attempts at what appears to be a desire for the total annihilation of any traces of you or your work."

"What are you talking about? Why on earth would anyone want to annihilate anything I've been working on?"

"We believe it has to do with whatever happened at Nakuru. We have reason to believe, information so to speak, that a cleanup operation is underway."

"A what? Cleanup operation?"

"Yes, the sort of thing that is assigned a finite amount of time to remove all traces of something or someone. Usually a team of highly trained assassins are given a week, maybe two, never more than three to make things, and people simply disappear." Dr. Hunter slumped over in his chair. His hands moved from rubbing his chest, over his heart, to holding his head in desperation.

T he early Christians taught it (reincarnation), and this can be proved by the words of Saint Gregory, Bishop of Nyssa: 'It is absolutely necessary that the soul shall be healed and purified, and if it doesn't take place in one life on earth, it must be accomplished in future earthly lives.[9]'

---

[9] http://www.lightchamber.org/gfs_bjdocs/spirit/reincarn1a.htm

CHAPTER 20

Potomac, Maryland

Jake turned to face the three strangers that had nonchalantly walked in on his phone call. "What are you doing in my home," he asked them as adrenaline heightened his senses.

"Do not be alarmed Mr. Hunter. We have come to you for help."

"You all want my help? I'm not exactly in a position to help anyone right now. I can't even help myself. I was supposed to be in court this morning for a hearing on my disbarment. Having missed that probably means the end of my legal career. Of course the family business is now gone as well. But I am guessing you already know that. And yet, you think I am somehow in a position to help you?"

Lavanya's demeanor sent chills up the back of his neck. It was the second time in a week that he felt a fleeting pang of guilt at his lust for a woman other than his wife.

She spoke with a charm that was captivating and spell binding. "Mr. Hunter, you are right about that. And please accept my condolences about the recent tragedies. I wish they could have been avoided. But unfortunately, they were not. However, I do have some good news for you about your father."

"Who are you? And if you know anything about my father, you had better tell me immediately." She took a step back as if to make the point that he was in no position to be making demands.

"Really Mr. Hunter, this is not the greeting I expected from you. Won't you join me for a ride and we can discuss this in a civil manner."

"Won't I? Are you asking or telling?"

"I am asking Mr. Hunter. Again, I am not your enemy. Your enemies will not be nearly this courteous towards you. But you should know that already. I understand you've experienced their *hospitality* first hand."

"To where do you want to drive? Wait, let me guess, the airport?"

"You're quick. And you're right. We need you to pick up a few things for us. Well, to be more precise, for your father."

"So he's alive?"

"Yes Mr. Hunter. Or may I call you Jakob?"

"Jake. Call me Jake. Where is he? And I'm not going anywhere until I know who you are."

"I am so sorry Jake. Please accept my apologies for my rudeness. I am Lavanya Yashodhara. As for your father, he is safe, at my home, in India."

"India!? Wait a second. I know your name. Where do I know it from?"

Lavanya replied, "I am a widow of one of the first of my country's tycoons that sprang up from the economic boom at the start of the century."

"Right right, that's it. You married your way into the world's twenty richest, if I remember correctly."

"If that's how you want to put it, yes."

"Married, but then widowed shortly thereafter, under suspicious circumstances if I recall correctly."

She grinned while tossing her hair. Jake was unsure if she was flirting with him, or flaunting her "accomplishments." He asked, "How did my father get to India?"

"Well, we rescued him of course, from his enemies, who, once they know you're alive, will surely hunt you down and kill you. For your own safety, Jake, please come with me? It will not be long until whoever destroyed your family's business in D.C. figures out where you live and that you have survived the plane crash in the Caribbean. It is not safe for any of us to be here in this house." She was as convincing as she was beautiful and it annoyed the hell out of him that she was able to sway him into *doing what she wanted.*

"Let me make a call. Pull your car around back. I will meet you out there in a minute."

"Excellent. Just one thing, may I suggest avoiding the land line?"

"Right of course. Now that I'm wrapped up in the middle of something from out of a movie, I had better think of things like that."

"This is no movie Jake. Unfortunately, it is very real and very dangerous. And the fate of millions of lives and the balance of world's religions is in jeopardy. Make no mistake, my money and wealth pales in comparison to the powers interested in how this turns out. And you are the last person alive that holds the keys to the outcome."

"Great." Sighing with exasperation, "Thanks for the encouraging words. I'm not feeling any pressure at all now – only relief."

She winked and with a half smile said, "Glad you still have your sense of humor Jake."

No doubt about it. She was definitely flirting with me just then. Interesting mix, flirting and at the same time telling me the fate of the world is in my hands. Builds tension and interest, I suppose. It's times like these, where I wish I wasn't married.

*   *   *

Lavanya walked out the front door and into a limo. The two bodyguards accompanying her got into a black Volvo parked immediately behind the stretch job. Jake picked up his cell and tried his wife, Anja.

No answer. He pulled a piece of paper from his pocket and dialed the number written on it. Kennedy Taylor answered.

"Kennedy, is that you? This is Jake."

"Hi Jake. Did you make it home OK?"

"Yes, but listen, did you hear about the office in D.C.?"

"I did, it's awful. I was going to call you but wasn't sure what to say. Between that and your father…"

"Wait, just hold on a second. It's OK. It's going to be OK. But I need your help. I don't think I'm a lawyer any more, after missing my court appearance today. They will probably never let me practice again."

"That's horrible. I'll do anything I can to help you with that Jake."

"That's not what I need help with. In fact, I'm not sure why I just told you that. I guess I needed to tell someone. I needed a friendly ear. The bigger problem, and I hope you can help me with this one, is that I don't know jack about medicine and science. I need your help. We need to go back down to the Caribbean, to the Isla Dedaleras site."

"What's going on Jake?"

"I don't know. But I need to find the Digitalis. Problem is, I have no idea what to look for. The components of the Digitalis were all worked on by separate individuals, each without knowledge of the details of the other parts. For security, only my father had the full picture of all the pieces put together. I'll need your help and well, there really isn't anyone else with executive level medical security clearance left alive, except for my father. But for the time being, he's not going to be able to help us."

"What? So you know he's alive? How do you know this?"

"I can't explain right now. Can you meet me at National Airport in 45 minutes? I'll have a plane waiting for us in the private jet services facility."

"Sure Jake. I'll be there. Whatever you need, you can count on me. Hang in there, OK?"

"I'm trying. It's a little overwhelming right now though."

I wish Anja were here, she could make it all better. Just the touch of her hand on my chest could make all this go away.

* * *

He walked out the back door of his home, disappointed that he wasn't climbing into bed with his wife to catch up on sleep among other things. Instead, he got into Lavanya's limo, leery of what other unimaginable drama the enigmatic woman might usher into his life on their way to the airport. A quick look at her upper thighs protruding from her excessively short skirt took Jake's mind off his missing wife. Gathering his composure, Jake wondered why Kennedy didn't ask more about the Digitalis. Did she already know what it was? If so, shouldn't she have been more concerned that it was in jeopardy?

Anyone who doesn't have something to hide would have inquired further.

CHAPTER 21

Two Weeks Earlier
California, Shasta-Trinity Wilderness
(Off the Grid)

From behind an observation mirror, Gregor Eagon was watching Anja Hunter, the woman he seduced and kidnapped. He really was very attracted to her, which made the initial abduction easy, despite his deep religious convictions. As he watched her, a strange conflict of emotions exhausted him. On the one hand, he wanted to continue his seduction of her. On the other, he pushed aside misguided and superficial thoughts for what he considered a much higher purpose.

On that day however, Gregor needed a break from the overwhelming stress involved with the utter annihilation of another human's psyche. He planned to leave Anja for the day to continue her "rewiring" under the direction of his accomplices.

Given their rural, off the beaten path seclusion, the best escape from a stressful day job, and one he would enjoy, would be a hike through the California wilderness. His journey would serve a double purpose, as he was overdue for a check in with his superiors. It would be a tough five mile hike each way, with dramatic elevation swings capable of bringing even the most fit hikers to their knees. But it was the only safe way for him to make contact and exchange updates on the mission. At 9 A.M. in the morning, he set out from the underground compound where Anja Hunter was a prisoner and headed due west into the heart of the Shasta-Trinity Wilderness Area.

*   *   *

Four hours later, the heat of the California summer was over 100 degrees. Gregor's water supply was low, but he had finally arrived at his destination. He had to enter a code to pass the gated entrance for the Lansing Ranch. It would be another mile down a dirt road before he would see any structures.

Exhausted, he passed by two large buildings, which in the past were always his favorite pit stops during visits, as he enjoyed checking out the new "recruits." But he had more pressing matters on his mind during that particular visit. The buildings were shaped like oversized barns, but clearly built within recent years to a standard that exceeded what one would normally see on a ranch. The first building said Probationary Dormitories. The second read, Junior Grange. Most of the windows on both buildings had wood shutters covering them which were locked from the outside with industrial grade padlocks. There were no people around the outside of the buildings, but he heard noises including screams of agony from within them. He wanted to stop in and encourage the neophytes not to fight their indoctrination, but felt he could not risk it. So he walked on by and eventually approached another structure.

From the outside it looked like an ordinary cabin one would expect to see in the mountains. He walked past the front of the cabin, around to the back, where there was a door to what looked like a kitchen. He punched in a code to the combination lock which granted him access.

Nothing in the kitchen appeared used or even touched. It was more like a display than someone's active cabin. He opened an interior door to a walk in pantry, and closed it behind him. Then he removed a can of diced tomatoes from the corner of the bottom shelf. Next, he grabbed the can behind it and unscrewed the bottom which revealed an electronic key pad.

He punched in two series of codes and put the can back down. Then he replaced the other can. Nothing happened. He remembered the magnetic activation which had been built in as a fail safe mechanism. The two cans had to have their bar codes perfectly aligned so the magnets could trigger wireless transmission of the electronic code. It was meant as a hidden security measure in case the code was ever stolen or recovered by their enemies.

Gregor turned the cans to align the bar codes and the shorter wall of the walk in pantry slid from view to his left. The new opening in the back of the pantry revealed a stone staircase which appeared to descend for two to three stories in a winding fashion. Gregor entered and the pantry wall closed in behind him, sealing him into the dimly lit and musty stone stairwell.

At the bottom, there was another door. That one was more like the type that seals a bank vault. A monitor to the right of the door flickered on with the image of a man who, upon seeing Gregor, stepped into the center of the camera, smiled, and said, "Gregor, my brother, it's been too long."

"It has indeed." He replied. A buzzer sounded and gears cranked for a few seconds before releasing the six inch thick steel door. Inside was a room, nothing like you would expect in a typical mountain cabin. It had more high tech gadgetry than the space shuttle and was decked out with furniture that looked like it should be in some executive office suite. There was the main room, a conference room to the right with a glass wall, and what looked like several offices off the other side of the command and communication station in the center / main room.

They went into the conference room. "How was the hike over?" Aaron Eagon asked his brother.

"No bears."

"That's always a good thing." Aaron responded before asking, "Gregor, how is your work coming with the woman?"

"It's coming along well. It seems we were lucky in a number of ways. She was already disillusioned with her marriage. Hell, some days I think we could have just offered her twenty bucks and asked for her help and we would have got it."

"What a stupid woman! She has no idea how much she's hurting herself with such a lack of loyalty. Honestly, I don't understand why people like that even bother to get married. If it's all fake, how can it be rewarding?"

"I hear ya Aaron. Well, her stupidity is our gain. I think she'll be ready to go in not more than another week or two, at most. We are nearly ready for the next phase."

"That is good news Gregor. But we may need to accelerate that timeline, as our enemies have accelerated theirs and upped the stakes in a number of ways." A serious, concerned and stressed tone overtook the older brother's voice as he spoke.

"What do you mean? What's happened? Is our mission in jeopardy?"

"Yes it is. Time is of the essence. We will need Anja Hunter back in the real world, as soon as possible. A couple of days longer are the most we could safely wait, and even that may be too long."

"It will mean possible tension with John Anton. Are you sure that is worth the risk at this point?

"It is an inevitable conflict. The only question was when, not if, we would have to confront him. Try to find a way to do it without drawing attention to our mission. But if required, take whatever action is necessary to move things forward without letting him get in the way. He is dispensable at this point, although still potentially useful."

"Understood. I will do what I can to accelerate things."

"Good my brother, good."

CHAPTER 22

Potomac, Maryland

Jake entered Lavanya's limo and sat on the rear bench next to her. As he closed the door, he was stunned to see Michael Brooks sitting across from the two of them. "What the hell are you doing here?" Jake asked.

"Wow, what a greeting. It's nice to see you too Jake. We missed you in court today for your disbarment hearing. Judge Henderson was a bit infuriated, although my client thanks you for making his lawsuit against you that much easier."

Michael Brooks was representing Angelo Doyle in a suit against Jake for fraud. The basis was Jake's use of the case, "Sellers v. Griffin Milling, Inc.," while representing Aubrey Doyle in a civil action against her former husband, (Angelo). Unfortunately for Jake, the mysteriously appearing case, which had been over-nighted to him by an unknown sender, never existed. So Jake appeared as a fraud and cheat in court. As a result, Aubrey's case was in jeopardy; Jake had been disbarred; the D.A. Milton Strayer was prosecuting him for perjury, and he still faced a pending civil suit from Angelo and his sleazy attorney

Michael Brooks.

"Enough of this nonsense! What are you doing in this limo?" Jake turned back to Lavanya, "Better yet, what am I doing here! Let's get this straight right now! I'm not flying anywhere or doing anything until I talk to my father! I want to know he is alive and I want to know why the hell this sleaze ball of an attorney is in the car with us."

Lavanya pulled a phone from the console next to the bar and started dialing with the international prefix for India. Then she looked back at Jake, straight in the eyes and said, "As I have said before, we are on your side. I am sorry you have had the unfortunate experience of a prior acquaintance with Mr. Brooks. For what it's worth I feel the same way about him." She paused and turned to face Jake's nemesis, "In fact, Mr. Brooks, if you don't mind, what I have to discuss with Jake is highly confidential. Your services will no longer be needed today." Within seconds, Michael Brook's sleazy, cocky arrogance was replaced with stuttering nervousness.

"Ms. Yashodhara, I must strongly advise against this. You solicited my services to help in this matter from a U.S. and international legal perspective. It would be unwise to walk into the lion's den without your best weapon." Jake laughed at his pitiful attempt at sounding intelligent and persuasive. Lavanya smiled and seemed equally unimpressed.

"Mr. Brooks, if you are my best weapon, then I have no business walking into a lion's den, let alone that of a sickly ill rat. Now, I have asked you politely, please excuse us, before I have you removed. I will be in touch to discuss next steps when the time is right."

"What? You want me to get out here? We're in the middle of the freakin suburbs! I can't exactly hail a cab."

"Bill me then, for the time it takes you to walk." She opened the door and gestured for him to get out. Jake sat and smiled. He enjoyed watching Michael Brooks squirm;

although, he was still alarmed as to what business the two of them had.

The plump, overweight man got out of the limo and slammed the door behind him. The car took off down the street and Lavanya finally looked back at Jake. He couldn't hide his ear to ear grin. Lavanya smiled in response and asked, "Are you feeling any better Jake? Now do you see that I am on your side?"

You're hardly on my side if you have business with the enemy. But then, I guess she did just humiliate the man right in front of me. But why was he here in the first place? I've got to find out what dealings they had together...

Jake replied sternly, "I am not exactly convinced. So, what about that phone call? You started dialing before so gracefully jettisoning Brooks. Can we please call my father?" Jake was momentarily surprised at his use of manners with a woman who claimed to have kidnapped his father, but there was something about her. She charmed him with an air of deep caring.

"Yes we can call your father. And I assure you he is well. I will call him again now and you may speak with him, in confidence in fact. If you like, I will even leave the vehicle to afford you some privacy."

"No, that's fine. I just want to talk to him. I need something, some sort of confirmation that can tell me there's some truth to all this craziness. Not that I think you're crazy. But you'll have to forgive me for being apprehensive at the idea of a stranger walking into my home and telling me they know where my missing father is being held captive. It's not a situation I am accustomed to dealing with." Jake contemplated what he was saying and smirked a bit.

Although this kind of drama is starting to seem normal. What an insane week.

Lavanya dialed the number for Dr. Rajni Gupta who handed the phone over to Jake's father. "This is Dr. William

Hunter, is that you Jake?"

"Yes. Are you OK? Where are you?"

"I'm told I'm in India. I am fine. Where are you?"

"I'm with a woman who claims to be responsible for rescuing you. Lavanya something or other."

"Listen, be careful Jake. These are not your run of the mill criminals. This is big money. Worse than a mob or mafia. It's the type of money that controls the world."

"Dad, they want me to go to the research site. They want me to retrieve the Digitalis from Isla Dedaleras."

"Do as they say Jake. Our options are limited. But take your pocket watch. Take it and go to the place I told you about on the island."

"What? You want me to take my pocket watch from confirmation? What..."

Wait, this is too odd. I better not call attention to it.

His father continued, "Jake, take the watch. You'll figure things out when you get there. Bring the Digitalis back to us so we can get on with our lives."

This doesn't make sense. He's more of a fighter than that. He would never tell me to do this unless...

"Jake, one more thing: don't trust anyone, especially not John Anton."

"You're kidding right? He's our largest investor and a very good friend of Devon's. If we can't trust him then, well... who can we trust? Dad, what's really going on? Why are you telling me to just give up – it's not like you! What is this all about?"

"There's no time for this Jake. Get the watch. Then get what you can from the labs on Isla Dedaleras. Jake, you know what happened in D.C. The same is going to happen to that island any day, if not any hour. Please hurry – everything is at stake Jake, not just everything we've worked for and all the progress, but so much more."

"Is this a joke? Have they drugged you? This doesn't make sense."

"Damn it Jake, just do it. This is about Anja now. Your wife is… is…, she's NOT on a retreat. They have her." Jake froze, his ability to think having evaporated. He was petrified at the thought of his wife being held against her will. He felt defeated, and at the mercy of his enemies, although he wasn't sure exactly who his enemies were. The phone went dead before he could say anything else to his father, so he turned back to Lavanya.

"What the hell have you done to my wife?"

"Relax Jake. It wasn't us. We are working to rescue her. But trust me; I am as honest as they come. I am not capable of lying."

Yah, right, most people that go out of their way to profess their honesty are usually the biggest liars.

"You expect me to trust you?"

"I did just keep my word. I promised you could talk to your father and that he was safe and he was, wasn't he?"

"Are you deranged? What makes you think it's OK that you're holding him against his will in the first place?"

"We are not Jake. We are simply working together to try to secure the release of your wife from her captors. If we knew where she was, or who was holding her, we would of course send in a rescue team. We truly desire nothing more than to partner with you and your father's firm. But as you know, someone is out to destroy him and every trace of the research he has worked on for years. You have my word; it is not me or anyone that works for me." She blinked and gave a strange half smile before continuing, "I believe an associate of yours was asking you to travel to Isla Dedaleras right before I interrupted? So perhaps you can kill two birds with one stone by working with us, rather than against us?" She put her hand on his right thigh, "Don't you trust me Jake?"

He thought for a moment before remembering what one of his former mentors had taught him.

Keep you friends close, and your enemies closer.

Finally, Jake answered, "Of course I do. How could I not trust anyone who shares a common disdain for Michael Brooks."

A little flirting to boot should work wonders for this woman.

"Excellent. I am so glad you want to work with us Jake. I know this must be a tough time for you. When you make it to Isla Dedaleras, be sure to focus on finding any files related to the Nakuru clinical trials in addition to the Digitalis. I'm sure your father mentioned that to you as being critical to our work?"

"Nah ku who? What are you talking about? No he didn't mention it. But fine, I'll look for it. Let me call John Anton and arrange a plane. An associate of mine is already in route. How do I get in touch with you once I have what you want?"

"I'll send my man, Ryan King, who is in the car behind us, along with you. He will arrange for industrial transport cases for packing up as much of the equipment and files from the labs as possible, as well as safe travel back to India. By the time you are done there, it will probably no longer be safe for you to travel commercially, in the public eye that is."

"You expect me to go to India? I have obligations here. I am being disbarred as we speak. I have to get to court and beg and plead for a chance to save my career. And I have a client that is depending on me. I need to help her.

"Aubrey Doyle will be fine Jake. Nothing will happen to her while you're away. I'll see to that."

"You'll what? How do you know Aubrey?! I don't think you understand what it takes to be a lawyer in this country. And when you don't show up for your own disbarment hearing, you're chances for reinstatement disintegrate."

"I do understand Jake. But please believe me; it is

trivial compared to the matters you are inextricably involved with now. Besides, if you're successful in helping me, I'll put the power of all my resources behind helping get you reinstated. You'll have nothing to worry about. So I'll look forward to seeing you at my palace in India a few days from now. And Jake, when you get there, I know we'll finally have a chance to get to know each other much better…you know, on a more *friendly* level." There it was again, that seductive smile. Jake knew it was pointless to discuss things further, as he clearly had to do what this woman wanted if he were to have a chance to save his father, and his wife, let alone deal with whatever world catastrophe was at the bottom of it all. Then he remembered what his father had mentioned about the watch.

"Oh, there's just one thing…"

"What is it?" she asked.

"I need to stop by my condo in town. I need to pick something up." Jake kept a condo in the city, closer to work, to avoid long rush hour commutes.

"What could you possibly need from there that takes precedence at a time like this?" Jake froze; he wasn't good at lying and certainly not deception. He knew he shouldn't tell her about the pocket watch however, so he made something up.

"I have a um…" *cut the stuttering you idiot. Do you want to give yourself away?* "I have a laptop there I need, and my security badge to the labs at Isla Dedaleras. That place has more security than the White House. It wouldn't do me much good to go there without my key card."

"This is unfortunate. We'll have to part ways then, as I'm afraid my schedule simply will not allow for that sort of a side trip. Ryan King, in the car behind us, will take you to your city residence and then accompany you to National Airport. I have a flight back to India to catch out of Dulles. Good luck Jake. We're all counting on you, not just your father."

"You mean my father, and my wife, right."

"Oh right, how *could I* forget about her."

They pulled over and Jake gave a quick and artificially warm goodbye to Lavanya. He then hopped into the car that had been following them, with Lavanya's assistant, Ryan King.

Jake had no idea why his father wanted him to get that pocket watch, but it was driving him crazy as to how or why it would matter under the circumstances.

CHAPTER 23

Sugarloaf Key, Florida
(Stopover in the Florida Keys, in route to Isla de Las
Dedaleras)

Devon Keyes woke up on the patio couch where he had passed out from the previous night's indulgence. He and Kate Stinson had enjoyed many drinks but he was disappointed in not finding her next to him when he awoke.

He searched around the house to figure out where Kate slept, and to find coffee, in that order. Kate had managed to find her way into one of the seven bedrooms in the large house built on the sands that lined Old State Road 4A. They were about eighteen miles east of Key West and two miles west from Pirates Cove on Sugarloaf Key. The location was very secluded and private as most of the lots had a minimum of five acres each.

The two of them had arrived the previous night after a fun filled flight from D.C. The house in the keys was the launching pad that would give Devon quick access to Isla Dedaleras. It also had a secure communication system setup in its library.

As he sipped on some coffee, Devon wondered why

Kate was so accepting of everything. She hadn't once asked who owned the house they were staying in, or why they had to stop there. She was simply a silent companion who appeared to be trying to charm him. In fact, as Devon slowly woke up with each sip of coffee, he grew increasingly alarmed by Kate's nonchalant behavior. Something was definitely not right about her. With his suspicion growing, Devon decided to take care of his business while Kate was still asleep. He was going to attempt to make contact.

He left the kitchen and walked into a large office which was detached from the rest of the house, although a covered walkway lined the path between the two structures. The door to the office required a combination code entered into an LCD touch keypad, in addition to a regular old fashioned key. Once inside, Devon double checked both the door and all the windows to ensure they were fully closed, curtains drawn, and everything securely locked. He then booted up a computer that rested on a large secretary style desk wedged in between floor to ceiling book cases.

Using virtual private network (VPN) software, he secured a connection with an encryption level significantly beyond that which was legally available to U.S. civilians. A screen prompted him for a pass code. He type in the code and hit enter. A message appeared, "Pass code accepted, place eye up to scanner." A biometric eye scanner confirmed he was whom he pretended to be and another message popped up, "Secure Connection Established. Maximum safe communication time remaining: 12 minutes… 11 minutes 59 seconds… 11 minutes 58 seconds…" The countdown timer was running in the corner of the screen.

A text only chat window appeared with the person on the other end using the screen name, "Apogee." In the chat window, Devon read the first message, "Have you obtained the Digitalis?"

Devon typed back, "Delay in acquiring and

delivering product. Need more time. 14 days is not enough. Severe weather system makes acquisition any sooner impossible."

Apogee responded, "11 days is all that remains. It was 14 three days ago. Other suppliers can guarantee delivery. What timeline and guarantees do you offer for the secure and confidential delivery of the Digitalis?"

Devon changed his position and typed back, "No guarantees necessary. We will be in route to acquire the Digitalis within a matter of hours. With any luck, we should have it in far less than 11 days."

Apogee typed back, "What just changed? If in route, why the concern about the timelines? What kind of guarantee is this?"

Devon was sweating as he typed, "There is a large weather system making travel to target risky. I am however, confident we can side step the storm. This is in fact, the perfect time to acquire target, as minimal staff and security will be in place during the storm. Flight will be risky in this weather, but my pilot is the best."

Apogee typed back, "Good to know. Keep me informed. I'll expect your next update in 48 hours max, and remember, there are plenty of others that can competently deliver what you have failed to provide so far."

"Duly noted. You will not be disappointed. I will send you the next update in no more than 48 hours. Get the money ready."

Devon's hands shook as he powered off the computer. To say he was nervous was the understatement of the century. He realized there were no guarantees he would be able to acquire the Digitalis on Isla Dedaleras. He also knew he had not been totally honest about the hurricane. The storm was on a path that could wind up being a direct hit with the island. They were definitely in for one hell of an adventure with Mother Nature.

At least he had some eye candy to distract him for a

bit. He walked back to the main house determined to move beyond innocent banter with Kate Stinson and grinning in thought:

What a stupid girl. She has no idea the mess she has got herself into by lusting after a married man. Not your typical affair, nope, no way. Just a tad bit more life and death. It serves her right. But hmm, it is weird how she just goes with the flow so easily. If it were anyone else, I wouldn't trust them... nah, I'm just being paranoid.

*   *   *

Devon and Kate spent the morning lounging by the pool while a pilot at the nearby Key West International Airport prepared the Hunter Neurologics jet for flying through heavy turbulence. Devon had to hire a new pilot as the prior one refused to risk travelling through such a strong storm. Even the new pilot had initially insisted it could not be done and they were sure to crash or disintegrate in mid air. But after Devon gave him a check for $100,000 as an advance on his total fee, the man was suddenly convinced that they could safely make it to Isla Dedaleras despite the storm.

CHAPTER 24

Georgetown - Washington, D.C.

Jake couldn't stand Ryan King's thick Boston accent, so he tried to avoid any unnecessary conversation. When they arrived at Jake's condo in Georgetown, he told Ryan, "Keep it running, I'll just be a minute." Ryan agreed and Jake scampered into his doorman building, up the elevator, and into his unit. He was struggling to remember what he did with the pocket watch and was worried he would have to tear apart his place in a fury to find it in any reasonable amount of time. But when he walked into the main living area from the foyer, he quickly realized someone had already torn the place apart for him.

Books were all thrown from the bookcases. The kitchen cabinets were emptied out onto the floor. No piece of furniture was in its original position or intact for that matter. All of the closets had been emptied, their contents strewn across the floor.

Who would do this? Why would someone do this? Lavanya didn't seem to know I had this place when I told her I needed to stop here. So it couldn't have been her. But who then?

Jake didn't lead the type of life where he had

experienced fear all too often. But at that moment, he felt it, and it consumed him to the exclusion of all other thought. It was as if time were suddenly frozen. He was afraid to even walk into the different rooms of his condo, unsure if someone was still in the unit.

Once he had thoroughly inspected the place, he laughed at himself for carrying a frying pan from the kitchen.

As if a frying pan would have done me any good against professional home wreckers. Focus. Focus. Where would I have put a gold pocket watch that is about 100 years out of style but of great sentimental value?

He went to his bedroom closet and found the suit he kept just for church. In the right inside pocket was the watch. He pulled it out and examined it, perplexed as to why his father would want him to get it. What meaning did it have? How could it help him? How did it relate to the hidden place on Isla Dedaleras that his father told him to go to? And why was his father afraid to explain it further over the phone?

*   *   *

While staring at the watch, perplexed as to its meaning, Jake heard the front door to his apartment kicked open. The surprise noise caused him to lose his balance while staggering backwards, bumping his head against the wall.

I wonder if it's the same people who trashed the place? What do I do?

He thought about the windows, but he was eight stories above the street. There was a ledge but it was negligible.

I guess my options are confront and fight, or stand on ledge, eventually fall and die.

He grabbed the frying pan again, only slightly laughing at himself this time and announced his presence, hoping that to be safer than a surprise appearance.

"What in the world happened to your condo Jake? We were coming over here to rough it, and you, up. But it looks like someone beat us to it." In Jake's living room were three men, each with handguns drawn. All of them, upon seeing Jake with his frying pan, and the state of his condo, put their guns back in their holsters and chuckled.

"Who are you?" Jake asked, "What do you want?"

"What? You don't recognize me? I thought for sure you would see the family resemblance?"

"Well I don't. And I would say I'm surprised to see three strange men in my condo bearing guns, but really, nothing would surprise me anymore this week."

"Aww, that's too bad. Anyone got a fiddle? The former superstar lawyer has had a tough week," the biggest of the three men was talking in a mocking tone but then switched to a firm, commanding partial yell, "Well tough shit!! See, we think it's bullshit what you did to my brother. We think even if he wins his case against you, that it still won't be proper justice. So what do you say? What are you prepared to do to even things out? Aren't you the one who's always preaching about real justice in the newspapers?"

"Good God. You mean to tell me you're the brother of Angelo Doyle?"

"Bingo! See boys," turning to his two accomplices, the big one rambled on, "Maybe he ain't all that dumb after all. Maybe he'll be smart enough to offer up a more fairer settlement. Whaddya say Jake?"

"A more fair settlement," Jake couldn't help himself. When dealing with people he disliked, his mouth was like a faucet that doesn't shut off properly. The three men just stared at him with confused looks, which only caused Jake to laugh at their lack of language skills. He paused before speaking any further. Jake knew in his heart what he did to defend Aubrey Doyle from her lunatic husband Angelo, was the right thing. And to the extent it wasn't, someone had set him up by sending a fake case to his office. The fact that his career was in jeopardy and that he was being sued over it was already a gross injustice, if the truth were known. But like so many things in life, it had yet to come out.

I've just got to remember, the truth always comes out in the end. Just handle this for the time being. Justice will take its own course on its own schedule.

He looked at his watch. He had only another 30 minutes to catch the flight at National Airport. A member of the flight crew had indicated a storm system approaching the destination required them to take off ASAP; otherwise they would be delayed possibly as long as a week. Because of that, he had instructed Kennedy to go without him if necessary. If nothing else, she could try to figure out what the Digitalis was and how to bring it back.

Jake turned back to the three thugs in his condo and said, "Listen, you guys are right. In fact, it would be presumptuous of me to assume I could know how adversely I've affected your brother and his entire family."

"Look at that boys, he's groveling." The big one said while the other two laughed.

Jake went on, "Listen, why don't we cut to the chase? You tell me, what is a fair and just resolution to this matter? I want to make it right in your eyes for you and your brother."

"Fair and just he says! What a laugh. Ok how about this, you cough up $1 million dollars for me by next week. Then you make sure you lose the case against my brother. After that, we'll consider maybe calling things even."

"Are you deranged? What do I look like, Donald Trump? I don't have a million dollars. I have a mortgage for God's sake. You have me confused with someone who has money."

"That's not our problem bud. Get it. In fact, we want 10% in three days, or we'll show you just how serious we are."

"10%, that's $100,000. Are you forgetting I've been disbarred and have no income!? How am I…"

"Enough with the blabbering excuses. Do it. Or else." And they headed for the door. One of them attempted to destroy the place a bit more on the way out by kicking a hole in the wall, but he stubbed his toe and was clearly hiding severe pain.

I hope he broke his toe, the bastard.

Jake fell to the floor and put his head in his hands. He was utterly overwhelmed at the surreal drama that had engulfed his life. Then he thought of his wife and father and mustered the energy to head back down to the car that was waiting for him. He could still make it to the airport in time. And he could figure out the purpose of the pocket watch during the five hour flight to Isla Dedaleras.

CHAPTER 25

Flight to Isla de Las Dedaleras
Off the Coast of Venezuela

As the plane approached the private landing strip on Isla Dedaleras, Kennedy asked Jake, "Have you ever been to this facility before?"

"No, I haven't. I've only seen the offices we used to have in D.C., and the international office we were at in Venezuela before our little adventure with the plane crash and being stuck in the jungle. Oh yeah, and being shot at. Oh yah, and wearing the brain and blood of another human being. All in all, just a run of the mill average work week. But no, I have never had a visit to the labs here on the island." Kennedy smiled and put her arm around Jake's shoulder. He was clearly exhausted from the recent drama.

"Listen, I know it's been tough. It's been tough on me too. This is not what I signed up for. But your father is a good man. Even though I've only known him a short while, he has influenced me in such a positive way, that I will forever be a better person. And, that's just on a personal level. But there's also his work. You don't understand Jake. The reason this place is so top secret, so secure, is your father is, or was, probably only weeks away from effective treatments for those with Alzheimer's and other memory issues. Think of all the innocent people in car crashes, or even…" she was smiling again and getting excited as she talked, "plane crashes, that have to live through brain trauma. There are no known effective treatments for memory loss from head trauma. But your father can offer them hope. So we have to do this. *WE HAVE TO* figure out what is going on and we have to somehow help your father!" She was fired up, but paused for a quick look behind her to make sure Lavanya's thug, Ryan King wasn't listening. He was out cold, sound asleep in the back of the airplane. "Jake, it's up to us now. We are going to have to play along, find the Digitalis, whatever it is and wherever it is, and somehow get to India so that we can save your father."

"Maybe you're right Kennedy. It's just that, well, it's hard to stay motivated when you spend your whole life building a career, have it taken away in an instant, then in the same week, get shot at, watch your father's life work get destroyed as well, and then to boot, get threatened by thugs that want you to some how cough up money you don't have and never will have since your career has been destroyed by a guilty client that got away with OJ Simpson style injustice, at my expense."

"Jake, you're forgetting something."

"Oh right, how could I forget. Someone is trying to kill me on top of all that, although no one can tell me who or why or when they'll strike next; only that I don't have much time if I want to live."

"No no, that's not what I meant Jake. What I meant was that all of this is within your control right now. We hold the cards. These people making demands of you all want something. It's something you have."

"Doesn't do me any good when I have no idea what it is that I purportedly have, where it is, or how to find it."

"You do though. We just have to keep our heads on straight, and stay on an even keel. So let's think this through. Your father had to have a reason to insist you go out of your way to pick up that watch. May I see it? There's got to be more to that pocket watch than just telling the time."

"Sure, here you go. If you can figure that one out, drinks are on me." Jake handed her the pocket watch with the unusual engraving on the gold cover. It looked like the typical Rod of Asclepius that represents medicine and healing; only the serpent was wrapped around Leonardo da Vinci's Vitruvian Man, instead of a rod. There was some type of writing that encircled the picture, in what looked like Latin. It read, "Scientia Pro Curatio."

Kennedy read the words out loud, "Hmmph. Scientia Pro Curatio. Science to heal. Interesting. And I know this symbol from somewhere, but I can't quite place it."

"How did you know what it said?"

"I was a foreign languages undergrad major before switching to premed in my third year. We had to study Latin, which is how I knew what Scientia pro Curatio meant. But I have never seen that precise phrase before. It's very unusual.

"What does it mean?" Jake asked.

"I don't know. I'll have to research it." She opened up the watch. Inside the front cover was an engraving which read, "Dearest William, thank you for the Foxglove. I owe you everything. – Yours always, Victoria."

She asked Jake, "Is Victoria your mother?"

"No. I actually have no idea who Victoria is. I had asked my father that when he first gave me the watch. Now that you mention it, I remember his response was rather odd. He said something about explaining it all when the time was right."

"Do you think he wants us to find this Victoria now?"

"He did say something about going to this place he

told me about on the far side of the island. Maybe we'll find Victoria there."

Kennedy replied, "Looks like the watch tells time in two time zones. The front of the watch is set to the East Coast. The back appears to be about six hours ahead. That would be mainland Europe."

"I don't know. I guess it could mean we're supposed to go to Europe? But why not just say that then? Why mess around with the watch? Wait a second, what's a Foxglove, maybe that has something to do with it?"

"Holy smokes!" Kennedy exclaimed.

"What is it?" Jake asked.

"Well first off, good point about finding Victoria. He would have just said to find her, not the watch, unless he's trying to protect her for some reason. Here's the kicker… as for Foxglove, it's a flower, sometimes called Digitalis."

"You've got to be kidding?"

"Not kidding. Thing is, there's nothing too special about it. Although a toxin from that plant, called Digitoxin, used to be considered as a treatment for heart disease and was also known to be fatal at higher dosages. Maybe the watch was a thank you for treating a former patient? That is, unless there was some other deeper meaning to it?" The plane landed while they continued to brainstorm the significance of the pocket watch. The passenger door opened and it was time to get out. The weather outside was hot, humid, and deeply overcast with substantial winds from the massive weather system that was only a few miles away.

Jake grinned, "So were you also a flower major before switching to premed, or was learning about flowers just a side effect of breaking a lot of hearts growing up?"

Oh jeesh, I did not just say that. Yes I did… and it was fun. Man, I'm going to hell for that.

"Smart ass." Kennedy slapped him playfully on the leg, clearly pleased that he was joking around with her. She needed the laugh and the flattery, as it had been almost six months since her live in boyfriend of several years suddenly walked out on her. She had recently given up on him and stopped calling, which of course, caused the guy to start calling her again. By then, it was too late; she had already met someone new. In her heart, she knew it was wrong, but she was determined to win over Jake.

C elts were fearless warriors because, "They wish to inculcate this as one of their leading tenets, that souls do not become extinct, but pass after death from one body to another.[10] "

–Julius Caesar.

---

[10] See also,
http://www.newworldcelts.org/index.php?option=com_content&view=categor
y&layout=blog&id=29&Itemid=42

CHAPTER 26

Isla de Las Dedaleras
Off the Coast of Venezuela

As Jake and Kennedy were disembarking the plane, a man was walking towards them. Dr. Marten Jansen came out from what looked like the main reception building in the compound. It was a modern looking, mostly glass, four or five story building with a tall atrium-like lobby. Dr. Jansen was wearing standard white doctor garb, but otherwise looked like he hadn't shaved in a week or cut his hair in months. He was, overall, generally disheveled, almost like a homeless man. It was a strange look for the man who, given recent events, was thrust into being the top dog for a billionaire's prized investment.

Dr. Jansen greeted them in a boisterous voice, "Welcome to Isla de Las Dedaleras or just Isla Dedaleras for short, as most people say!" You must be Jakob Hunter?"

"Just Jake, thanks. Who's in charge here? Is Devon Keyes on site yet?"

"I am the Site Manager. But since the plane crash, I am also the ranking medical officer..."

Jake interrupted him, "Not exactly. Kennedy was on the Executive Operations Committee. That means as long as she's here, she's ranking officer."

"That is correct, of course." Dr. Jansen turned and looked Kennedy dead in the eyes with an eerie glare that gave her goosebumps, "I am so sorry Dr. Taylor. All I meant was that I have been acting in that capacity. It's actually a relief you are here. I am certainly not the type that enjoys the paperwork of executiveness."

"Executiveness? Are you kidding me?" Jake muttered before asking out loud, "What about Devon? Has he arrived yet? He was supposed to be here before us."

"Oh yes, well Devon is not on site yet as his flight has been delayed due to weather. For some reason he was coming from the west side of Florida instead of the normal route down the east coast. Unfortunately, that put him dead in the path of the storm. Last I heard, they were trying to fly around the northwest edge of it and could be here in a few hours time. In fact, I should mention that due to the storm, there are probably less than one or two dozen people on the island. Other than myself, there are just a few patients that we couldn't safely move, and a skeleton crew of staff, our chief security officer, and our head of maintenance. Not to worry though, everything is highly automated. The island can practically run itself. By the way, horrible tragedy, that plane crash. Is there any news yet on your father?" Jake was trying his best to hide his facial expression but was clearly irritated with the quirky Dr Jansen.

The way he tacked on the last comment was as if it were an unimportant afterthought. I don't like this guy. Not one bit.

Trying to avoid saying something rude, Jake responded, "Let's just say, things are more like they are now than they have ever been." He was repeating an old Gerald Ford quote that always made him smile because most of the time people would just think he was misspeaking. But the truth was that Jake was trying to be difficult towards the strange acting Dr. Jansen.

"I'm sorry? What did you say? What do you mean

Mr. Hunter? Things are what?" Jake laughed. He loved watching arrogant people stumble.

"There is no news; not yet anyways." Jake didn't feel comfortable giving away details of his father's whereabouts, especially not to the half hippie, half doctor freak show.

Dr. Jansen felt the tension and decided to change up the conversation, "I understand this is your first visit Jake. So you all have a choice. Based on the latest meteorological data, we have about an hour until the storm gets too severe to allow for going outside. At that point, we will want to take cover in the weather shelter. It's a complete facility, with bunks, showers, and a lounge, all in the underground level of the Recreation Center building. It's designed to withstand even the worst of storms. But, if you like, until then, we could see how far we can get with a tour of the place. What do you say?"

Kennedy had been at the site before, but had only limited exposure to some of the areas. Given their situation, and lack of starting points for finding the Digitalis and Nakuru files, they were eager to see what Dr. Jansen would reveal about the island.

They all agreed to a tour before the weather got worse and headed into what appeared to be the main building. They walked past an empty, un-staffed lobby area and then past a sign that read, "Employees and patients only. No guests allowed. No exceptions."

From there, they were walking down a long hallway which led to the clinical trial reception area. It was lined with commercial propaganda about the potential benefits of cognitive therapies for the mind "under development" by Hunter Neurologics. The ads were extensive and highly unusual in that some were electronic images which flickered and flashed in all sorts of ways. Dr. Jansen noticed Jake closely inspecting the live multi-media images and asked him, "What do you think of the advertisements Mr. Hunter, oh um, Jake? You know, you should be careful not to stare at those ads for too long a time. I did that once it made me cross-eyed." Dr. Jansen actually made a cross-eyed face while speaking.

What a freak!

"Why is that Doc? You afraid I might want to sign up for some cognitive therapy? I had no idea this was part of what my father was working on."

"Well, it's a sort of an on-the-side line of work. It is not part of the primary mission here, but our research has lead to many new possible products that we aim to market to the mass population, when the time is right. Here, look closely at this monitor in particular," he paused to check Jake's eyes to see his line of sight, "Watch it right here, look right in this spot. And don't take your eyes off of it, not even to blink. Tell me, what do you see Jake?"

"All I see is a happy couple on the beach." The whole group of them was staring at the monitor which was playing some sort of travel commercial for a tropical destination.

"Subliminal messages Jake. You can't usually see them with the naked eye. They were banned by the U.S. Government years ago, but modern day technology that we call neural electrical mapping enables us to take the quick, fleeting flickering message across the screen to new levels. And believe me when I say these are levels that will make you a die hard customer faster then you can say, 'Where's my checkbook.'"

It was news to Kennedy as well who asked, "How does it work? What exactly is neural electrical mapping?"

Dr. Jansen replied, "Well in the interest of time, let's just say we have the technology today to create digital recordings of neural activity in the brain. In these particular electronic posters as we call them, we've embedded the digital signals that mimic neural activity during a sexual orgasm[11]."

Kennedy laughed and then said, "Let me see if I understand this. You recorded human brain activity during sex and are using computers to stimulate the same response in viewers of these ads?"

Dr. Jansen patted her on the back and said, "Exactamondo! The longer you watch this ad, the more you should, at least subconsciously, feel like you're having sex. That is, watching the ad should give you good feelings. And our studies show that once a person associates such feelings with a product, they are up to ten thousand times more likely to choose that product, even over superior ones from the competition."

"There's just one problem with that. I bet it doesn't work on Catholic school girls. Too much guilt would be associated with whatever the product is you're selling!"

"Actually we had that same concern. But then we were surprised in test cases to find there was really no issue with that demographic group. In fact, the group we had the most trouble with was…"

Before Dr. Jansen could provide further explanation, Jake jumped in, "Fabulous. So this is what I'm working for, a company that designs ways to brainwash people? I can't believe my father was involved in these types of activities!"

"Not exactly Jake. You are right in that there was way more to your father than mind manipulation. He was certainly much nobler…"

"IS! There *IS* way more to my father… not was. And I thought my father was supposed to be working on treatments for Alzheimer's!"

"Of course Jake. And he was. What you are seeing

---

[11] See, "Neural Pattern Recording & Playback Ushers in New Treatments for Myriad Brain Disorders," Journal of Cognitive Neuroscience & Biometrics, July 2009 (Pp 145-160) which notes several studies in 2008-09 that proved neural pattern playback could trigger standardized responses across disparate patients.

here is called 'cognitive neuroscience,' and it's only possible because of the convergent advances in the last ten years of: (1) super computing power; (2) genetic engineering; and, (3) algorithmic measuring techniques for individual brain cell activities. Again, the technology in those ads was merely an off shoot of the main research that goes on here. The new patient reception area will explain it all and I am confident you will feel relieved about your father's work once you see it."

Jake contemplated, if this is what they're showing the public, then I can't even begin to imagine what they have behind the locked doors.

After seeing the strange advertisements, they all suddenly found themselves very eager to explore the place further.

Jake was bothered by the quirkiness exhibited by Dr. Jansen. He was unlike any of the other men his father had hired and it confused Jake as to how someone so different got into such a high level position in his father's company. Wanting to know more, he asked, "So Dr. Jansen, how long have you worked here? What's your background?"

"Well Mr. Hunter..."

"Really, just Jake will do – thanks."

"Fine, Jake, I have worked here for the last sixteen months. I left a research post in my home country at the request of John Anton, one of the financiers of Hunter Neurologics. He needed someone with my skills to work on special projects here on the island." Jake started laughing, not at Jansen, but at how the words "special project" seemed to make the quirky Dr. Jansen feel important. You could even see his eyes light up as he said it.

Ahh, so John got him the job. I wonder if there is anything special about the projects at all. Hmm, on second thought, knowing John Anton, he probably wanted to protect his investments. I had better find out more about these "special projects." But I knew Dad wouldn't have hired such a kook. And no wonder he said not to trust John.

Still in route to the new patient reception area, they entered a breezeway which appeared to lead to an adjacent building. It was lined with windows on both sides, and had a glass ceiling. Jake peered outside to check on what sounded like low flying aircraft. After the last couple days, he didn't think much of anything could jolt him, but what he saw left him frozen in his steps even as everyone else kept walking. The rest of the group eventually stopped a few steps in front of him, turned back, and almost all in unison, asked, "What's the matter Jake?" He didn't respond. Instead, he just pointed out the windows, at the sky.

CHAPTER 27

India

The cot Lavanya had been hiding under was abruptly pulled away from the wall, exposing her to the mob. An angry, scowling man grabbed her and yelled in Hindi,

परमेश्वर ने अपने क्रोध गवाह को स्वीकृत नहीं है

"The Gods do not approve. Witness their wrath."

He dragged her by the wrist out of her family's home and into the village square. She was forced through the crowd. In front of her and everyone, were her parents, wrists bound, both of them crying, screaming, and trying to explain, in vain, their actions. Young Lavanya started screaming as well. She was screaming for her mother. But her mother's eyes saw men in the crowd that told her not to step towards her young daughter.

*   *   *

Lavanya woke, screaming and in a sweat. She threw John Anton's arm off her naked body and rolled over, turning her back towards him.

He got up out of the bed. Frustrated and humiliated,

he turned on only the cold water in the shower before quasi-slamming the bathroom door behind him.

Lavanya turned her attention to more comforting thoughts in an attempt to block from her mind, the incessant dark and haunting nightmare, which always ended before she could know what really happened to her parents. They were gone and had been for years. Their bodies excavated, at a huge cost to Lavanya, to confirm their deaths. But her nightmare always ended early, never revealing the truth about what happened. A tear flowed from her eye as she wondered if she would ever know, or ever have peace in her present life. She considered that perhaps her present life was cursed so that she must live it out in the Naraka or the Seven Hells as followers of Jainism called the lower part of the universe reserved for demons and the cursed.

The anger which Lavanya felt from not knowing the details that led to her parents' fate caused her to redouble her will to vindicate her family's honor and work towards Moksha, her own liberation from impure living. She was thankful Jake and William Hunter had crossed paths with her and considered it a favorable sign from the Gods. It was a sign she wanted to explore further and more intimately. And finally, at least for that morning, she found a way to escape from her nightmare. With her right hand under the sheets, she whispered to herself, "You are going to love me Jake. You just don't know it yet. And you will love me for eternity through life, after life, and beyond."

CHAPTER 28

Lansing Ranch
Aaron Eagon's Cabin
Rural (off the grid) Northern California

Anja Hunter was nearly done with her "training," and as a result, was moved from her hidden cell back to the main compound at Lansing Ranch. Gregor Eagon watched his naked brother walk out of the guest bedroom of his cabin in a secluded section of the ranch and asked him, "How was she?"

"Not bad brother. I think she's definitely on our team now. Let's put it this way, she sure doesn't seem to be missing her husband any more. They were both chuckling. Aaron went on, "Why don't you spend some quality time with her and let me know what you think." But the younger brother thought what they were doing went too far and hesitated. Aaron said again, "Gregor, you need to get your tail in there and tell me what you think."

Gregor realized his older brother was no longer asking and so he went into the room where Anja Hunter lay naked in a bed. Gregor stripped, knowing full well there was a camera on him, and his brother would be watching from his hi-tech communication center in the basement.

Anja said little. She was utterly defeated and as a result focused only on minimizing any further pain, which meant compliance with what her captors wanted.

Gregor said to her, "Well Anja, we finally get to do what you came here for, or did you forget your original intentions in meeting me?" He looked at her dumbfounded as to how someone who was a successful, married school teacher, only months earlier, could be so defeated. Gregor touched her head, where there was still a little evidence of recent surgery. She had a bald spot where her hair had yet to grow all the way back. It reminded him just how much control they had over Anja's behavior, thoughts, and even her fundamental belief system.

They had sex and when he was done with her, Gregor said, "I think you are finally ready Anja. Ready to take on an assignment. Tell me, would you like to know more about how you can do something meaningful for a change?"

"Yes Gregor, please tell me! I am eager to contribute more to our mission. Please tell me how I can help."

"You remember your husband don't you?"

"Of course. I remember how badly he hurt me, lied to me, and forced me to cheat on him."

"Then it should not be difficult for you to acquire something from him for the betterment of our mission, should it?"

"It would be a pleasure to take from him anything and everything. He deserves no happiness after what he did to me."

"Good. And you know what will happen if you fail, right?"

"My training would have to start all over, back to day one."

"Exactly. Very good Anja. You're definitely ready. Your instructions and everything you need are in a briefcase outside this room. If you run into any problems, there is also a cell phone in there with my number programmed into it. Use it sparingly. And don't forget, we'll be watching you Anja. It would be a pity if we had to start your training over from scratch."

"There's no need to talk like that. No chance of that happening. That man deserves to die."

"No killing, until we have time to confirm we have the real Digitalis. We've discussed this."

"Understood. No killing until after acquiring Digitalis."

"Good luck Anja. You'll find keys to a car and a plane ticket from San Francisco to D.C. Travel safe and know that you have the spirit and will of God on your side."

Gregor Eagon left the room and joined his brother in the hidden basement communication center, which Anja had no idea existed.

Thinking she had been left alone, Anja enthusiastically got up from the bed and grabbed the briefcase, which had embossed on the metal lock the same Latin phrase as on Jake's watch, "Scientia Pro Curatio."

CHAPTER 29

Isla Dedaleras

Still staring out the window, Jake asked, "Dr. Jansen, are you expecting any other guests besides Devon Keyes?"

"No, none that I am aware of."

"Then how do you explain the slew of helicopters that just flew past us?"

"I don't."

With a tone of sarcasm, Jake replied, "Excellent. More good news." Then he turned to Kennedy, "I am so sick of helicopters. If I never see another helicopter as long as I live, I'll be a happy man."

Kennedy smiled at Jake then said, "Maybe we should pick up the pace a bit. You know, see if we can't find the Nakuru files at least." She turned to Dr. Jansen and asked, "Could you take us to the archives?"

He looked annoyed at her request. "Rest assured, you will not find any reference to any Nakuru trial in the archives. That must be the fifth time in the last week someone has inquired about that trial. It simply wasn't a part of the history of this firm. At least, not a part for which there is any trace in our archives room."

Jake chimed in, "He's probably right Kennedy. If it were that easy, we wouldn't be here in the first place."

Although there's no question he's a bit odd. It's almost like he's protecting the files – preventing them from being found. I definitely don't get the sense he's on our team, that's for sure.

Looking at Dr. Jansen, Jake continued, "I'd like to see my father's office, his personal office. Also, where else is there to land on this island beside the airstrip here at the compound?"

Dr. Jansen, with his Dutch accent replied, "There are no other landing spots. But I suppose if one wanted to improvise, they might be able to land on the driving range. One of the executives was a golf fanatic and had it set up so the doctors could have social time. Personally, I don't see what the big deal is with that sport. Chasing balls all over the lawn makes no sense to me. Anyhow, it's on the far side of the island. I can take you there if you like."

Jake was surprised at how he was taking control of the situation, but then, he knew he was always at his best in a crisis. He asked, "How far away is that, in minutes, travel time by foot or car?"

"By four wheel drive, best possible time would be maybe fifteen or twenty minutes. The roads were never developed to cross the island, so it's tough driving. On foot, it would be well over an hour, maybe two, at least."

"I doubt they had SUVs on those helicopters, so we can safely assume we have an hour at most. That's not a lot of time. Show me where my father's office is, and let's move quickly."

"Sure, sure, but the thing is Mr. Hunter, well, you are acting as if you know that whoever is in those helicopters is not friendly."

"Exactly. I would say it's a very safe bet, unless you know something we don't."

"I don't know anything. It certainly doesn't feel right, I mean. A slew of aircraft landing on our private island seems a bit odd. Regardless, in the next sixty minutes, the hurricane will have moved in close enough that we're likely to be stuck for the duration of the storm."

"It's a risk we'll have to take. We can't leave here empty handed. That would be like a death sentence for my father."

"Excuse me?"

"Never mind. Let's go. Take us now… to my father's office. Let's start there."

CHAPTER 30

Yashodhara Palace, India

Dr. Rajni Gupta and Lavanya took Dr. William Hunter to his new office. He wasn't in handcuffs, but might as well have been. He quickly realized they had spared no expense to equip the place with the most cutting edge and technologically advanced equipment. For a moment, he once again considered what might be possible if he did cooperate with Lavanya.

It's too bad how our paths have crossed. With this type of passion, investment, and equipment, we could have accomplished a lot working together. Maybe we still can... maybe we should.

Lavanya, in her commanding way, asked him, "Would you not agree Dr. Hunter, human beings, even the smartest of human beings barely use 20% of their brain's capacity in a given lifetime? Now, let me ask you, what do you suppose is in that other 80%? Is it just unnecessary waste? In a human body where everything has a reason, it's highly unlikely, wouldn't you say."

"You know I would agree. It sounds like something I wrote in fact. So what?"

She laughed, "Hah. It is something you wrote, in the

journal, "Science," back in 1997 when the rumor of the Nakuru Trial first hit the street, back before you went silent and stopped talking publicly about your work."

"Ok, again, so what does this have to do with anything?" He was playing dumb.

"Well, let me ask you another question Dr. Hunter. From where do an infant's dreams come? The mother? The father? If it's either, how are they transmitted from parent to baby? All you have to do is watch a newborn's eyelids, and if you can't find a newborn check out a new puppy. They all dream. Despite their limited exposure to the world, their minds are already active and full of information."

"This is all really basic. I'm not impressed with whatever point you are trying to make."

"You shouldn't be. It's the process to extract the buried information in that 80% of the brain that up until recently, we have not understood. Thanks to you however, we understand it better, and not only can we extract information which would have otherwise remained dormant throughout life, we can help people consciously realize, that is, consciously process imbedded information that would otherwise only affect them through their dreams and through their other subconscious thoughts."

Dr. Hunter interjected, "What you're proposing goes far beyond anything I have done. My work was limited to helping restore normal memory function for victims of Alzheimer's or head traumas. Attempting to elicit cognitive function that exceeds those parameters would most likely be lethal."

Undeterred, Lavanya started to hand him what looked like a brochure.

"What is this," he asked.

"Read it. It's what we give to potential customers to help explain our process. It's the process which we need you to help perfect." The pamphlet fell to the floor in the handoff from Lavanya to Dr. Hunter. He instinctively went to grab for it, but the cast still encasing his damaged knee caused him to fall and swear in frustration. After being helped back up, he skipped over the marketing nonsense which talked about how great Lavanya's Moksha Temple was and how much they only wanted to help people. Instead, he cut straight to the section entitled, "The Science Which Makes it all Possible," and was amazed at how similar it was to his own work:

> The goal of cognitive neuroscience is to understand how the physical mechanisms of the brain give rise to the functions of the mind. This new, but totally safe, field is the remarkable result of significant new technological advances. Those advances are summarized as follows:
>
> (1) Genetic engineering now allows neuroscientists to regulate neural development and function in ways that directly affect human behavior patterns.
>
> (2) Advances in monitoring allow scientists to record the activity of individual brain cells while performing a variety of complex tasks. Through the use of elaborate algorithms processed by high speed super computers, human cognitive thoughts are recorded and can be played back through virtual reality systems developed by our engineers.
>
> (3) Dramatic increases in computing power then allow our scientists to observe, record, and program the functioning patterns of human neural networks. When played back, a patient can re-experience in their conscious mind, past cognitive processing. Thus experiences are also easily transplanted into the minds of others, creating a world of limitless possibilities.

(4) The key to conscious recognition of past life experiences lies in extracting recordings which are naturally embedded in the brain at birth, much like a bird is born, knowing somehow what it takes to fly.

(5) Thus, when these extraordinary scientific advances coalesce with several other significant, yet peripheral medical systems developed by our doctors, you have Conscious Recognition of past life memories, which can be used to pursue Moksha or simply to enhance your present life.

Dr. Hunter threw the marketing pamphlet down. He yelled at Lavanya and Dr. Gupta, "This is insane. You will never be able to make this work." And yet, deep inside, he knew in his heart that what he had just read was already working and involved several components of his highly protected Digitalis.

"Dr. Hunter, you are right about one thing, it's not us that will make it work. But for your sake, and that of Anja, I sure hope you can. Besides, we lifted most of that text straight from your island, Isla Dedaleras, so I have faith that you can do it." He withdrew his recalcitrance and remembered he needed to play along, at least for the time being.

"What is the status of my computers and files? If there is to be any hope for this, I'm going to need my own equipment. My computer at the island facility has a record of every attempted electrical frequency. If I am able to help you, the data we need to do so is on that computer's hard drive."

Lavanya slapped him across the face and the room went silent for a moment. Then she said, "We both know that what you need Dr. Hunter, is the Digitalis. That and only that is what will allow you to repeat your achievements at Nakuru. For your sake, I hope it can be retrieved safely and that you have not mislead us in any way. If you have, then I would suggest you consider the person we have sent to retrieve it for us is your son."

"Jake?! You've sent Jake to Aguas Muertas? But that wasn't discussed. That was not what we talked about. How could you have done this? We've got to stop him."

"Interesting. So I see by your reaction that there were some details you have failed to tell us about Aguas Muertas. For your son's sake, let's hear it."

"I did tell you! It's heavily guarded. The group that built the place was an organization to which I used to belong. It's called Scientia Pro Curatio. It's like a REIT – a real estate investment trust, only this was a MRIT, or 'Medical Research Investment Trust.' It's a group of extremely wealthy investors. Most of them are doctors, descendants of doctors, and other assorted hyper-wealthy people who believe in advancing medical science in ways that most people would find somewhere between unorthodox to unacceptable. In fact, now that I think of it, you would fit right in."

"Honestly Dr. Hunter, with your son's life at stake, do we really have time for color commentary?"

"I thought my son was going to Isla Dedaleras?"

"He is, but you and I both know that the Digitalis we need is not there. We don't care about curing Alzheimer's. What we care about is what you created at Nakuru. We care about scientifically proving reincarnation. So as soon as they are done on the island, my plane will be taking Jake and a small team to Aguas Muertas."

"Please Lavanya, I beg of you not to send my son there. I will equip your team with everything they need to get the Digitalis, but please don't send Jake."

"You're right; you will equip them with what they need. And the reason I know this is because Jake *will* be going with them."

"Please no, it's a death trap. They'll never make it out

185

alive. The site is in territory controlled by a drug cartel which receives money from the investment trust to keep out all intruders. It's been buried and protected. They have standing orders to shoot to kill. Your team doesn't stand a prayer. I beg of you to reconsider."

"Never fear Billy. My men are the best in the business. As long as there are no surprises, they have a good chance of succeeding."

Dr. Hunter wasn't swayed and was clearly in a panic as he continued to plead with her, "You don't understand, that place is not meant to be visited. People have tried. Even the CIA has tried, and failed. The best in the world have tried. They will all be killed."

"My decision is final Dr. Hunter. If you would like to talk to Commander Collins, who will be leading the team, perhaps you can share with him whatever details might help make their mission a successful one. Either way, the mission is going forward, and Jake is going with them."

"Then yes, please let me talk to him. And please let me talk to Jake as well."

"It's so nice to see you so docile and agreeable Dr. Hunter. We'll get you a line to Collins ASAP. But unfortunately, we lost contact with your son after his arrival on the island. We suspect due to a massive weather system in the area. I am told we can expect communications to recover in the next day or two."

"That's ridiculous. That island is prepared for inclement weather. Even if the satellite phones are out, good old fashioned radio communications should still be working."

"We're already looking into that Dr. Hunter. Honestly, we're not sure why we have been unable to re-establish communications with the island through any of the various means we've tried. But believe me, we'll keep trying. In the meantime, I'm sure there is still progress that can be made here."

Sensing a window of opportunity, despite his panicked state, Dr. Hunter said, "Let's start with what is not working. If we focus on the problems, where you're coming up short, then maybe we can construct ways around them that lead us to your goals. Perhaps it's time you all shared with me your Infected Patients lab?"

"Perhaps it is," Lavanya responded, "Dr. Gupta, please make sure the good doctor has a chance to talk with Commander Collins and that he gets what he needs to make some progress preparing for the arrival of the Digitalis. I need to attend to other matters."

"Yes Ms. Yashodhara. I'll update you later this evening."

*   *   *

Lavanya left the two doctors to do their thing and went back to the main level of her palace where a smitten, but naïve John Anton was waiting to talk with her. He asked her, "How did it go with the old man?"

"Not good. He's still not talking. I don't get the sense he really wants to play ball."

John replied, "Oh no? Well perhaps we need to up the ante a bit?"

"Yes John, I think we do. When is his son due to arrive here?"

"If all goes according to plans at the Island and then in Venezuela, I would guess about four days."

"Perfect. We'll have Dr. Gupta keep working with the old man. When his son gets here, he can be our first test patient. That should ensure Dr. Hunter gets his act together. Apparently he cares about the kid more than I would have guessed given his past transgressions."

"What? You want to use Jake as the guinea pig?"

"Why would you care John?"

"I don't. It's just that I thought you… well, never

mind. I guess it's just that if something goes wrong, we've lost our ability to use him as leverage."

"This isn't the little leagues John. And don't be so insecure. It's you I like, not Jake. After all, you don't see me putting you under the knife do you?"

But the truth was, Lavanya had grave reservations about using Jake, and yet, she knew it would force Dr. Hunter to perform his best work. For the time being that was her plan, as she felt it gave her the best chances of turning an obsession into reality, and that would have to take priority over another conquered heart, at least until she could come up with a better solution. Given her feelings for Jake, she was determined to find some alternative.

CHAPTER 31

Isla Dedaleras

Jake asked for a few minutes alone with Kennedy in his father's office and they abruptly shut the door, leaving Ryan and Dr. Jansen on the other side to lurk in the hallway. Inside the office, they closed the blinds on the windows so that no one could see in, although the imminent hurricane meant there were few left on the island to be snooping around.

They mulled around for a bit before Kennedy said, "I figure the chances we're able to find the Digitalis are slim to none. So what are we really doing here Jake?"

"I don't know. But there's some reason my father insisted I get this watch before coming here. And I can tell you this much, when we get our chance, we're going to have to leave the main compound to figure it out."

"Leave the compound! With the hurricane approaching? And some invasion force out there? Why? How? That's not even going to be possible!"

"It's the perfect time. No one will go looking for us. And where we're going, we cannot have any followers."

"Where are we going exactly?"

"Well, that's a good question. I'm not entirely sure. It's a part of the island my father has made reference to only a couple of times. All I know is it's hidden from the rest of the place and he is the only one that knows of it or has access to it."

"Then how will we get in? Maybe the watch?"

"Maybe. For now, let's see what we can find in here. Look for anything that references field work in Nakuru. Finding the Digitalis would be too easy. But maybe we can figure out what this Nakuru thing is all about. If it gets my father back, then it's good enough for me. Why don't you check his files in that credenza over there, and I'll rummage through his desk and computer." The office was not large. It was more functional than fancy. They knew there was slim hope of easily finding anything meaningful.

Jake was spinning his brain trying to figure out how the pocket watch was supposed to help him. He looked at the symbol on it again and read it out loud, "Scientia Pro Curatio, what did you say it means again?"

Kennedy replied, "It's Latin. Translated literally, it means science to heal, but the real meaning is probably along the lines of healing through the use of science."

"Ok and what about this writing around the inside of the cover? It goes in a circle. What's all this mean, 'vires sapientia fides virtus veneratio veritas'"?

"Ahh, you're really testing my memory now. Latin class was a long time ago. Let's see, vires is strength, sapientia, wisdom, fides is faith, virtus is courage, veneratio is respect, and veritas of course, which comes from wine, is the truth!"

"Wow. An A for Kennedy, at least for Latin. So can I help you with your homework or what?"

"Jake Hunter! You are relentless! And that's with a hurricane and uninvited guests looming! Do we really have time for that type of behavior!?" As she said it, Kennedy smiled and walked across the room to stand a paltry couple of inches in front of Jake.

Facing each other eye to eye, they could feel each other's breath. Both of them were smiling until Jake interrupted the moment.

"Hey, I have an idea. What if we search it on the web and see what comes up?" Jake booted up the computer on his father's desk and typed in the Latin phrase from the pocket watch, "vires sapientia fides virtus veneratio veritas." He hit enter.

A site came up with a bold banner across the top that read, "SCIENTIA PRO CURATIO." Jake clicked on the "about" button, then the flag icon for English language, since the default was Dutch. He read the "about" page out loud:

> The Scientia Pro Curatio is a medical and scientific research investment trust or MRIT. It is an international collaboration or pooling of funds with two goals:
>
> (1) Investment returns that far exceed those of commonly available investment platforms; and,
>
> (2) Facilitating medical research that is cutting edge, by eliminating governmental regulations that all too often slow things down.
>
> The more we achieve our second goal, the more we achieve the first. Our organization was founded in Amsterdam, The Netherlands, in the 1960's by a group of prominent doctors, many of whom were of Dutch descent. Its mission is to use unconventional channels for scientific progress that can more rapidly lead to the types of breakthroughs and advances known for providing phenomenal investment returns.
>
> The governing body of our investment trust is called the Global Council and is

headquartered in Amsterdam. The Global Council advises outreach organizations across the world on matters all too often limited by conservative thinking. They range from issues of ethics in medical research (related to such modern day topics as genetic engineering, stem cell research, euthanasia, and abortion), to psychological approaches for helping local memberships thrive while overcoming day to day challenges of life in the current century.

With plentiful initial funding generously bequeathed by the Global Council's founding members, our investment group focuses on offering hope through the use of advanced medical and scientific practices. We utilize our vast network of global resources, colleagues, and localized research sites to ensure medical advancement on issues otherwise restricted by narrow minded laws and regulations.

Jake paused, having read enough, and then said, "Wow, this is wild. I can't see a need for this unless you want to ignore all safety protocols and use human guinea pigs to get really rich, really fast."

Kennedy offered, "I think you're right. It sounds like a way to work around the law."

"I haven't heard of it either. My father certainly never mentioned anything about it. Although he loves 'do good' organizations and is always trying to get me to join the local Rotary. But this seems less, 'do good,' and more 'get rich fast' and never mind the victims along the way. And it's strange that he's never told me about it. Why would he keep it a secret?"

"I can see your father not saying anything in order to protect you. But why do you think he would bother to tell you about this now? It's got to be related in some way, don't you think?"

"I don't know. I don't get any of this. None of it makes sense. And this web site is more cryptic than a Presidential Speech. I say we forget about this stuff and stick to getting the lab equipment and anything we can find about the Nakuru Trial."

"Wait a second Jake. Let's just walk it through one more time. Be patient. So he tells you to get the watch. Surely he's got to know that you'll find out about this investment organization. Then, there's the name inside the watch, Victoria. It's a person you don't know. Don't you think it's strange your father gives you a coming of age family heirloom with a name in it that has no immediate meaning to you and tells you he'll explain it when the time is right?"

"Yes, I think it's very strange. But I'm tired of wasting my time on some re-gift. A woman gets some Foxglove flowers from my Dad and gives him a watch. So what? We need to move on. I'm tired of talking about this stupid watch."

"Jake, calm down. I think the time is right for your father to tell you more about that watch; he just didn't have a chance to. Remember, Foxglove is also known as Digitalis. There's a possible medical link there to Digitoxin. I think your father is telling you that Victoria and maybe this society are important somehow and may be related to whatever this Lavanya woman is after. Maybe Victoria or the society has the Nakuru files? If it were going to be easy to find here, I don't think this woman would have bothered recruiting you to come and get it."

"Lavanya asked us for the Nakuru files. That has nothing to do with flowers or toxins or watches or Amsterdam investment trusts."

"Here's the thing Jake, if it were as easy as coming to this island and walking into the records room, she would have done it herself and we would probably be dead like the rest of the people on that airplane," Kennedy was getting agitated.

Jake, sensing her mounting frustration backed off from his childish displays of frustration, "You're right Kennedy. But we're here now, so we might as well focus on what we can find, while we are here. Besides, knowing what I do about my father and his reluctance to trust computers, I figure there's at least a small chance I just might be able to figure out how to get any secured or confidential files he might have stored as backups. Since this is where he spent most of his time, any backup files could include information about this Nakuru thing, or maybe more information about the Digitalis. Wouldn't you like to know what it is?"

"I absolutely want to know what it is! How about we make a quick search of the database to see if the Nakuru trial is in there? All of the clinical trial information is stored in the application accessed by that pharmacy symbol icon on the computer's desktop." Kennedy took control of the computer from Jake and loaded a program called, TrialCompass. It was clinical trial software used to track patients, adverse events, statistics, and general progress throughout the lifecycle of drug development. It automated the entire process of searching for patterns and predicting success rates for new treatments. The launch screen prompted for a username and password and she typed hers in. The next prompt asked for the name of the trial she wished to access. She typed in Nakuru. The system responded, "No such trial in database."

"Damn, I guess that would have been too easy," she said to Jake.

"Right, so let's see... if you're my father, and you were involved in some kind of clinical drug development trial that you had to keep confidential, of course you wouldn't put it in the main database. But knowing my

194

father, you wouldn't bury it completely either, because it's information. Information is knowledge. Knowledge is the power to advance humanity. At least, that's what my father always said. And the man never, ever, absolutely ever throws anything away. So there's no way it's gone."

"Makes sense. So how do we find *it*."

"Look this is just a database right? I mean the program you're using is just the front end of what they call a client-server program. If it's me, I'm going to keep anything confidential in its own database. Let me take a stab at this for a minute," and Jake took control of the mouse. He checked the computer's registry or hierarchical database used to run the operating system software to see how the TrialCompass program was configured. Sure enough, in the initialization parameters was a path to the database files which existed on a server, presumably in the nearby data center.

If I can log onto that server, maybe I can find another database. There's got to be another one for information Dad wanted to keep secure.

Jake asked Kennedy, "Do you know where the data center is located? Can you get me in there?"

"Yes, I think so. It's in the Utilities Building not too far from here. It's probably not a bad place to be right now. It's supposed to be mother nature proof."

"OK, let's go. And after that, it will be the perfect time to explore the island and find this mystery spot my father told me about."

"Oh yah, the one you know nothing about?"

"That's true, but I know it's somehow extremely important. Maybe it's where we'll find the Digitalis."

*   *   *

They left Jake's father's office expecting to see Ryan King and Dr. Marten Jansen waiting for them in the hallway. But neither of them was there.

"Where the hell did they go?" Jake asked out loud.

"Let's check the vending machines, just around the corner." They walked down the hall and turned the corner, then in unison stumbled backwards, until each of their heads slammed into the wall behind them.

"Is he dead," Jake asked as Kennedy *instinctively* recomposed herself and stepped forward to feel for a pulse on Ryan King's limp body, which was strewn across the ground, with a cup of vending machine coffee spilled nearby.

"Looks like it," she responded, "Single gunshot, to the back of the head. Jake, this is not good. This was a professional hit. Small caliber, so the bullet just bounces around in the head doing maximum damage with minimal mess. Also, obviously a silencer or we would have heard it."

How the hell does she know all this? Is she a doctor or an assassin?

"Do you think Dr. Jansen did it?" Jake asked her.

"Not likely, but possible. In any event, I don't think we should just stand here like a couple of sitting ducks. The Utilities Building is sounding more and more appealing. Let's get going."

"Wait a second," Jake sounded scared, "He was our ride home. Why would someone kill our ride... unless... maybe someone doesn't want us to get the files back to Lavanya?"

"It's possible, I suppose." Kennedy sounded unconvinced.

"Let's get his cell phone, and he should have a walkie talkie on him too. That's what he was using to talk to the pilot. There it is – grab it." They grabbed everything electronic they could find in the dead man's pockets.

*   *   *

196

As discretely as possible, they left the building, while constantly looking over their shoulders. Outside, the storm had gotten much worse. There was a torrential downpour that made it difficult to see more than twenty yards ahead. Trees swayed and leaned heavily from the force of the wind as Jake and Kennedy battled their way down the path, about a quarter mile or so, to the Utilities Building. As they got closer, they could hear strange noises from the building that appeared to be caused by the force of the storm testing its structural integrity, bending the frame and pulling upward on the roof. It seemed as though it might be blown away at any moment. With the winds increasing by the minute, they ran as fast as they could toward the building.

CHAPTER 32

Amsterdam, The Netherlands

Gregor Eagon placed his palm on a biometric scanner and an "access granted" message signaled the opening of a heavy, solid steel, twelve foot door which had engraved, into the center panel, the words, "Scientia Pro Curatio" and below that, in smaller print "Founded 1990." The building, from a distance, looked like a typical canal front row home that lined the older parts of Amsterdam. It was even complete with a hook and pulley system at the top center of the front façade. But up close, electronic surveillance and hi tech security made it obvious there was something unusual about that particular address.

Two men were immediately inside the front door standing guard. They recognized and greeted Gregor in Dutch, "Goedemorgen Mijnheer Eagon."

"Ik zoek Peter Lansing," Gregor responded, also in Dutch, by telling the two armed guards that he was there to meet with a man by the name of Peter Lansing.

"Gelieve te ondertekenen binnen. Droevig, maar het is nieuwe veiligheid om leden van de permanente raad tegen recente bedreigingen te beschermen." The guard on the right asked Gregor to sign in, noting it was a new security measure and a necessary extra precaution because of recent threats against the members of the Global Council. As they were not sure if the threats were external or from someone with inside access, everyone had to sign in who was not part of the Global Council. Moderately offended, Gregor went ahead and signed in on a ledger near the entrance then asked again where he could find Peter Lansing.

"Hij is in de wijnkelder, vloer minus twee," they told Gregor he could find him in the wine cellar, basement level two. From prior visits, Gregor knew his way around the headquarters building, which was discreetly housed in an otherwise normal looking residence at the corner where Stuyvesantstraat runs into Postjeskade in Amsterdam. It was a perfect location right between two stellar parks, Rembrandt Park and Vondelpark. The founders of the society picked the location partly for the proximity to world class museums and the two parks. But they also selected Amsterdam for its extremely central location in Europe which was notorious for liberal tolerance and gave them access to international flights spanning the entire globe through Schiphol Airport. They had, so far, existed with a level of anonymity only pierced by those with whom they desired to communicate.

Gregor made his way to the elevator and descended two floors to sub level two, which housed the wine cellar and cigar lounges along with locker rooms and a gym for those in permanent residence or guests staying overnight in the building. The décor, even on the lower levels demonstrated the vast amounts of money invested in their organization. Gregor recognized original artwork by the likes of Van Gogh, Rembrandt, and other world class artists, as he walked down the hallway towards the wine cellar. A man walking in the opposite direction said hello in Dutch, in a way that indicated he was pleased to see Gregor and wanted to catch up, but Gregor rudely blew him off and through his demeanor made it clear to the passerby that he couldn't have cared less if he had offended him.

Walking into the wine cellar, Gregor found Peter Lansing in a study room, closed off from the main gathering area by glass walls and a glass door. The three other walls were all polished cherry, beautifully crafted. Peter Lansing did not get up to greet Gregor, but instead nodded to him to sit down next to him in the soundproof room.

"Is it safe to talk here?" Gregor asked.

"Yes. I believe it is; however use of discretion is always prudent."

Gregor asked, "When do you next meet with the council?"

Peter responded, "Why Gregor? Is there a problem? You know we cannot afford to have any more delays. We only have ten days until my hearing with the Global Council."

"No, no problems," Gregor hid his hands in his coat to hide their trembling as he lied to the man sitting across from him, "We are making progress Mr. Lansing; however, things have become more complicated. It is possible we could run into problems."

"This is why you have risked our operation to meet with me here? You flew half way around the world to tell me that which could be communicated electronically?" Peter Lansing was exerting his authority over Gregor as he puffed on his Butera cigar, a rare, yet pleasant and mild brand that was his also favorite.

"It's not that simple Mr. Lansing. There is another party or person interfering and she is wreaking havoc on our plans."

"She!" Lansing slammed the crystal double old fashioned glass he had held in his left hand onto the glass table in front of him with enough force that it cracked the glass.

"Please calm down Mr. Lansing. You don't understand. This woman, she appears to be extremely well funded and equipped."

"You would let a woman derail our plans? This is an outrage. My ten year old son could do better than this. Perhaps I should give him a chance at doing your job."

"That will not be necessary. I will take care of this."

"Who is the woman, and what do we know about her?"

"Her name is Lavanya Yashodhara. She has, through inheritance and cunning, access to unlimited wealth. We have an inside track to her operations through her lover and puppet, John Anton. But she may be on to us, as the information flows have slowed to a trickle."

"Information flow is not the issue. The issue is obtaining the Digitalis before she does."

"Of course Mr. Lansing. And we will."

"Does she know we're after it? Do any of them know?"

"They do not. But they've got to know someone else is after it since the bombing in D.C."

"The bombing could have a zillion explanations. Unless it has been linked back to you, then we still have somewhat of an advantage. But you're right. It will not last much longer; not that we have a lot of time left anyway. You know the timeline. You have ten more days. Don't come back here until you have some good news to report. And Gregor, if push comes to shove, and the council finds out about this operation, it will be you that goes down. Make no mistake; I have taken steps to be sure that I will not be taking the fall for your incompetence."

"None of that will be necessary Mr. Lansing. Please rest assured; I will handle this. I already have a team in place to finish things off once and for all."

"Do whatever it takes Gregor. We've worked too hard on this to let a mere woman get in the way. You have all my resources at your disposal. Just tell my man what you need, and it's yours. But fail, and well, you know the consequences."

"Understood. Thank you Mr. Lansing." Gregor left just as quickly as he had arrived. He was furious with the condescending way his employer addressed him. But at the same time, he was pleased that he had gained unfettered access to whatever resources he needed to accomplish their goals. And he prayed it would be enough to level the playing field against Lavanya Yashodhara and John Anton.

*   *   *

After Gregor left, Peter Lansing sent an instant message to Lester Cannes, in Balikpapan, Indonesia, which read:

> Both options for obtaining Digitalis are still in play. And Lavanya still has no idea. We should see results in the next 7 to 10 days. I'll send another update in a day or two. Call me if you learn anything new in the meantime.

CHAPTER 33

Isla Dedaleras

The wind was howling as Jake and Kennedy ran up to the entrance of the Utilities Building. Palm trees were down all over the grounds around them and along the paths connecting the different buildings that comprised the highly secure research compound for Hunter Neurologics. Desperate to get out of the weather, Kennedy swiped her security badge, but the indicator light stayed red. As an executive medical doctor, she could access all the labs, but they never envisioned her needing clearance for the Utilities Building. "We've got a problem Jake. I don't seem to have access to this building."

"No we don't," he calmly responded, pointing off to their right into the pelting rain before grabbing Kennedy's right arm and squeezing it tight enough to make her yelp, "On second thought, what if Dr. Jansen was the one who killed Ryan?"

"Killed who?"

"That man that Lavanya sent along to babysit us. Back at my father's office. You know, the guy we just found dead a few minutes ago. What if Dr. Jansen is the killer? It's not like we've seen many other people around, and I gotta tell you, this guy is weirder than weird. He creeps me out."

"No question about the creep or weirdness factors, but come on, why would one of your father's high level doctors kill someone? And if he did, why didn't he kill us too? You know what, don't answer that." Kennedy abruptly ended their conversation and shifted her eyes behind Jake.

Dr. Jansen greeted them, with a look of fear on his face, which evidently made his slight Dutch accent more pronounced, "Hallo! What are you two doing all the way out here at the Utilities Building in this awful weather! We should get to shelter right away. The weather service is expecting the storm to take a turn for the worse in the next hour. It's supposed to become the strongest hurricane on record. Even though this site was built to withstand tropical weather, enduring the storm of the century was never envisioned. We cannot be sure that any of the buildings can safely stand up to such force."

No one said anything in response. Kennedy finally broke the awkward silence, "Dr. Jansen, we need to get into the data center to check for some additional files that we could not access remotely. Can you let us in please?"

"What? Right now? Don't you see we're in the middle of the mother of all hurricanes? We need to get to the inclement weather shelter. The buildings on the island are going into lockdown. We've got to shut the place down. The structures cannot be expected to hold. It is simply unsafe to be out and about. Please, I urge you to join me at the weather shelter. It's underground in the recreation building, not too far by foot. It's the safest place for us to wait out this storm."

Jake looked at him sternly before clarifying, "We're going into this data center Dr. Jansen. Please give me your security access card now." Dr. Jansen looked confused and stressed, even more so than usual. But he handed Jake his card and the exterior entrance to the Utilities Building was opened. Jake looked back at the doctor, "Is there more security inside that we need to get through to access the servers?" Just then, a huge piece of the siding was torn from a maintenance shed nearby and flew through the air like a bullet, razing leaves and branches along the way. It passed by the group within a few feet of where they were standing. Undeterred, Jake carried on, "Dr. Jansen! Are there more secure doors inside?"

A nervous and scared man, who hardly seemed like a doctor under the circumstances, responded, "Yes, yes, of course. But we need to get to shelter. Don't you understand it's not safe out here or in any of these other buildings! They don't stand a chance against this storm! They are likely to be swept up and blown away!"

"Then we'll need your security badge err, access card, whatever you call it. I'm sorry. You can come with us, or you can go to the rec center shelter. But we're taking your badge."

"I'm going to the shelter. The other remaining staff members are already there. They can let me in. You all should find your way there as quickly as possible."

Jake told him thanks and said, "We will get there as soon as we can. And please, be careful Dr. Jansen. Don't stop anywhere else along the way."

"Why would you say that?"

Jake paused and realized he did not want to reveal Ryan King's death to the man he still suspected of pulling the trigger. Instead he replied, "The weather of course."

Dr. Jansen took off running awkwardly, like a school girl, through the high winds and onslaught of rain. Jake and Kennedy made their way inside the Utilities Building and had to lean into the door with all their weight to get it to close against the Category 5 hurricane winds which were howling around them. Kennedy asked, "Jake, don't you think we should consider riding out the storm and then coming back here?"

"No I don't. I don't think whoever shot Ryan King is going to wait for the storm, so neither should we. We need to find the Nakuru files and free my father, before whoever is trying to stop Lavanya succeeds and risks my father's life in the process. Besides, you heard Dr. Jansen. The kook said it himself; no one ever envisioned a storm of this strength. We may be just as safe in the basement of this building for all we know."

*   *   *

The interior of the Utilities Building lacked the fancy modern touches common to all the other structures on the island. It was mostly steel and very industrial looking. There was a map on the wall immediately inside the front door. It showed a maze of hallways leading to all types of rooms. Everything was, for the most part, underground. Only a few rooms existed on the single above ground level and they were offices and a conference room. The data center was on sub level four, which was the lowest level. Jake and Kennedy walked towards the elevator at the end of the entry hallway and pushed the down arrow button. They heard a chime indicating the elevator arrival. Just as they were about to step in, the lights flickered three times around them. They flickered a fourth time, and then remained off. The elevator panel illumination also shut off. With no windows, they were standing in front of the open elevator, in pitch black darkness. Engulfed in silence, they could hear the wrath of the storm outside. It was tearing apart trees and buildings, throwing their parts through the air and causing loud bangs as they crash landed and further damaged other structures. Both Kennedy and Jake felt unsafe. But both of them also felt a sense of urgency. They needed to find answers before someone prevented them from doing so.

The phone they had taken from Ryan King rang. It was Lavanya Yashodhara's name on the caller ID screen. Jake answered, slightly calmed by the light emitted from the phone's screen in the otherwise completely dark hallway.

"Who is this? Why do you have Ryan King's phone?" Lavanya asked, although it was hard for Jake to decipher the words due to a very patchy connection, probably because of the storm.

"Lavanya, this is Jake. I'm sorry to tell you Ryan appears to have been murdered." It was equally hard for her to understand what Jake was saying.

"Jake? Did you say murdered? Listen Jake, I have information from my sources that tells me there are people trying to kill you and everyone else on that island. They are looking for the Digitalis and they will stop at nothing to get it and will do whatever it takes to prevent anyone else from interfering. Even worse, we understand they are operating against some sort of time schedule."

"Time schedule? What do you mean?"

"I mean, they could be there now. On Isla Dedaleras already. They're coming to kill you Jake. You've got to move quickly. We are monitoring the storm and realize it's bad, but you've got to find the Digitalis and anything you can on Nakuru, then get here to India as quickly as possible. It's probably the only safe place for you now." The connection was worsening and Jake could only hear every second or third word.

"We're trying. Listen, I need to talk to my father. We're having trouble locating the Nakuru files. Can you put him on please?" But then the phone went dead, as the signal cut out. Frustrated, Jake motioned as if he were going to slam the phone into the ground and shatter it into a thousand pieces.

Kennedy yelled out, "Nooo!!" but Jake was only acting and held onto the phone. He knew they needed it to get to India.

Jake commanded, "Let's go, the stairs are over there."

Kennedy noticed a box on the wall and said, "There's a flashlight in with that fire extinguisher. And the data center most likely has backup power systems. Once we're in there, we should see the light."

Jake chuckled, "See the light? Funny woman." As they walked down the staircase, Jake decided to find out the truth about his companion with some prying questions, "So what do you think Kennedy? You seem fairly astute when it comes to guns, ammo, and murders. Is Dr. Jansen our roving island maniac killer?"

"No way. He was far too nervous in an 'I'm scared' sort of way to have been the person responsible for killing Ryan."

"What if he was acting? Don't you think it's odd such a highly educated man having such weird quirks and being so scared over a hurricane?"

"Not really Jake. Many highly educated people have innate, deep rooted fears of natural events, even simple thunderstorms, or heights for example. I don't think he was acting. He seemed legitimately scared to me."

Jake wasn't convinced, "Well, I wasn't buying it. I don't know if he was the killer. But that little scene he just displayed was complete bullshit. He was trying to stop us from getting in here. How the hell did he even know we were here in the first place? There's got to be twenty different buildings on this island. How did he find us in the middle of a hurricane at the one building that is off the beaten path?"

"Oh yeah, that's a good point Jake. Maybe you should work for the FBI. You would be one hec of a special agent."

So that's it? She works for the FBI? Nah, she wouldn't introduce the idea if that were the case. Must be something else. But what? What is her true purpose here?

Jake replied, "Interesting thought. FBI, hmmm. But

do you like special agents? Do you, find them attractive?"

"Why yes Special Agent Hunter. In fact, I find them quite powerful and intriguing."

"Come on Kennedy, let's hurry. You've got to stop flirting with me before I act on it, because I sure can't stop myself from flirting back."

"Oh, so it's all on me is it?"

"Hah, don't be an instigator. You heard Lavanya, we need to hurry. No time for flirting, or worse transgressions."

Oof, did I just suggest sex with this woman? What the hell is wrong with me?

They made their way down the stairs and found the door to the data center. Sure enough, emergency backup lighting illuminated the door. They ran Dr. Jansen's security badge through the scanner and waited for the access light to turn green. Instead they heard a buzz and saw the red light of denial.

"Damn it. He's locked us out. I knew I didn't trust that guy," Jake exclaimed.

"Why would he do that? Maybe it's not him Jake. Maybe someone else has shut us out. Or maybe… he did say the island was going into lockdown. Maybe it's just the automated security mechanisms kicking in."

"You're too assuming of his innocence Kennedy. You got a crush on him or something? Or are you just trying to make me jealous."

Jeesh, am I ever gonna stop this?

Kennedy smiled at him and said, "If I had been trying to make you jealous, we would already be in serious trouble."

Jake laughed and retorted, "You mean you would be in trouble. Not me."

"Sure Jake, whatever you need to tell yourself to avoid feeling guilty."

He laughed and then changed the subject by saying,

"Look, we're going to get into this room one way or another." He grabbed an ax from the nearby fire station and smashed through the door. After a loud series of bangs, it was eerily quiet. There was light inside the room, but the hallway behind them was dark, and the connecting hallways and stairs even darker. They started to walk in but then heard something behind them, back down in one of the hallways. They looked at each other but neither said anything. They simply gestured to the inside of the room.

There were racks of computers that stretched floor to ceiling. They walked around until they found the one labeled, "Clinical Trials Backup Data Files." Jake quickly hacked into the computer and was able to view the file systems.

"So Mr. computer whiz, have you found anything?" Kennedy whispered to him, still worried about the sound they heard outside the room.

"I'm downloading this entire mount point. It's got some encrypted files with an ACL that only allows my father, or whoever has the password, to access them."

"ACL? What? Like when the football players get hurt?"

"Sorry, Access Control List. It's odd that the mount point, which is the entire set of folders, would be so restricted. I also found something else very odd."

"What's that."

"Well there are more backup files than there are active files. It tells me there is a good chance we are on to something here. Plus, the extra backup files are all marked confidential, with an ACL that gives access to a group, instead of just my father. The group is 'glblcouncil.'"

"Can you view it?"

"I did already."

"Well Jake? Was Nakuru in there?"

"I don't know. But I don't think so. At least, I didn't see it in the name of any of the files."

"So what's the big deal then?"

Jake got excited as he explained, "The big deal is that the extra files all seem to be associated with clinical trials held at someplace called, Aguas Muertas. I've never heard of this location. My father has certainly never mentioned it. Do you know anything about it?"

"No, it's not something I was ever told about. Can you get those files too?"

"I am already downloading them. Everything is going to DVD. I just wish it would hurry. I'd like to get the hell out of here before we get boxed in." They heard another noise from out in the hallway. Both of them were watching the download status indicator and wishing it would go faster. It was creeping along. 65%... 75%... a quick jump to 90%, then slow again... finally... 100%.

Kennedy wasted no time saying, "Jake, let's go. Get that disc. There's an emergency exit light in the back. I vote for not going out the way we came in."

"Make that two votes. We need to get this disk into a computer so we can un-encrypt the data. Maybe then we figure out what this Aguas Muertas place is all about, or better yet, maybe the Nakuru files are in there too. But my money says whatever it is we're looking for, Digitalis, or Nakuru or whatever, the real booty is in Aguas Muertas."

Kennedy chuckled then asked, "Booty? Who the hell says booty?"

"Kennedy, there you go again with that flirting..." they were rudely interrupted by the ricochet of a bullet bouncing off computers and the metal racks that housed them. Sparks flew as more bullets short circuited computer servers all around them. Jake and Kennedy hit the ground. They couldn't hear gunshots, just the damage from the bullets. Whoever was shooting at them was using a silencer. Staying ducked down, they crawled to the emergency exit door in the back of the room. Jake made sure it was pushed all the way closed behind them, before they stood up again and ran up the stairs which led back out into the hurricane. At the top, he looked around and was astonished by how much the severity of the storm had increased in the short time they were inside the building.

Out of the frying pan, and into the fire.

CHAPTER 34

Devon's Flight to Isla Dedaleras

Devon leaned away from Kate and into the wall of the plane as he said, "Would you please just zip it! We're going to be fine. And if we're not going to be fine, your yapping isn't going to do us any gooo – ood." Neither of them could talk without choppy voices, as they were bouncing all over the place. The Hunter Neurologics corporate jet was in the middle of fierce turbulence. One particularly severe patch of wind shear caused the plane to drop a hundred feet in mere seconds. Everything not bolted down in the cabin hit the interior ceiling with force. A porcelain coffee cup, which had inadvertently been left out, was smashed to bits not too far from where Devon and Kate were sitting.

More moderate bumps continued although they were periodically interrupted by additional severe changes in altitude that caused both of them to use the sick bags more than once. Devon checked his watch and realized they had at least another ten minutes of flying time. Then he glanced over to the nearby monitor to check the weather radar images. They were not even in the worst part of the storm and the plane felt like it would fall apart at any moment. As the engines whined a strange pitch, Devon reached for the cockpit phone and asked the pilot for an update.

Dexter Mills, who had agreed to fly them through the worst hurricane on record, for a half million dollars, ($100,000 of which had to be paid up front), tried to calm Devon down, "Look Mr. Keyes, we are being tossed around, but all systems are fully functional. We only have another five to ten minutes to get through the worst part. Then we'll reach a pocket in the eye of the storm. We can descend through that, and hopefully land uneventfully."

Devon was agitated and started snapping at the man, "When you use words like 'hopefully' while flying a plane it doesn't exactly build confidence in your passengers. What I need to know is that we can make it there safely with absolute certainty. So what is it flyboy? We can or we can't? Give me a straight answer!"

"Look, I agreed to take on this crazy flight. But I can't tell you we'll make it there safely. I've never seen... no strike that. Probably no one has ever attempted to fly through this kind of weather in this type of bird. But if any type of small commuter jet can make it, my money would be on this one. We have a solid chance. Just hang in there."

"It's hard to hang in there when you're being tossed around like a bouncy ball!" Devon yelled.

"Mr. Keyes! You've got to calm down. If you let me focus on flying instead of talking to you, our chances of making it safely go way up. Now unless you want to tell me something interesting, like why the hell you would be crazy enough to attempt this flight in the first place, then leave me alone so I can fly the plane!" And the line went dead as the pilot slammed down the receiver on his end.

CHAPTER 35

Yashodhara Palace, India

Lavanya walked into her family's kitchen, trying to find the source of the whimpering she heard while out back playing in the yard. She thought maybe it was one of the girls who lived in the house next door. But Lavanya was shocked to see her mother, limp, exhausted, and with tears coating her cheeks. She had never seen her mother cry before, let alone desperate and broken down. The shock prevented her from doing anything other than standing and staring at her in disbelief. Minutes, which seemed like hours, passed before Lavanya's mother looked up and noticed her only daughter paralyzed with fear, standing in front of her, with tears flowing. That was when her maternal instincts took over and she suddenly had the strength to stand and run to her daughter, desperate to provide her with some comfort.

As soon her mother's arms were around her, Lavanya calmed down. But she was still worried and asked, "Mommy, what is wrong? Why were you crying like that?"

"Lavanya darling, I am sorry you saw that sweetheart. I did not mean for you to see that. It is nothing to worry about honey."

"Is it my brother? Is that why you're crying Mommy?"

"Why would I be crying about your brother Lavanya?"

"Because he is sick. It's OK Mommy, I know he is sick."

"Why would you say that darling?"

"I heard you and Daddy talking about it Mommy."

"When did you hear that?"

"Months ago Mommy. Before you and Daddy started to only talk in whispers." When their son had first become ill and there was still hope for his recovery, Lavanya's parents hadn't thought to keep quiet when talking about it. Only after all hope was lost did it occur to them how challenging it might be to have to explain matters to their young daughter. But there she was, already in the know, and seemingly OK with it.

"Do you understand what you are saying Lavanya? Do you understand what this means for your little brother?"

"Yes Mommy. It's like what happened to the kid at school last year. The teacher said he just went to sleep one day but never woke up. Why does that have to happen to my brother Mommy? Can't you stop that from happening?"

"I'm going to try my daughter. I am going to try everything I possibly can, but you must prepare yourself to go on in life, without him. We all must prepare to live our lives without your brother's presence."

"Can't we take him to the doctors Mommy?"

"Unfortunately, we have tried everything we can think of. But we simply cannot afford the operation that could save him. We will have to rely on the Gods instead. And when we are done praying for your brother, we will pray for you, to have a better life than us, so that such a dreadful thing can never happen to you again." Lavanya started crying full force.

*   *   *

For the fourth time that week, Lavanya's whimpering woke up John Anton who was sleeping next to her. He pushed her shoulder to wake her up and asked, "Why are your nightmares increasing?"

"What do you mean?" She replied.

"In the last few weeks, the frequency, it's like you have them almost every night now. And they're worse. Much worse. They go on for hours. You yell, you cry, you yell some more. Sometimes it's yelling in anger, sometimes its fear. A dark fear like, well, like something more sinister than anything I've ever experienced, or even heard of. Why? Why now? Why suddenly so much worse? And what are they about?"

Lavanya just stared at him with a disparaging gaze before getting out of the bed.

"Well, aren't you going to answer me? You wake me up every night, ten times a night. The least you could do is tell me something about them!" John demanded.

"The answer, is, I don't know."

CHAPTER 36

Isla Dedaleras

The ferocity of the rain and wind from the hurricane threw Kennedy and Jake two steps backward for each step they tried to take forward. Debris was flying everywhere. They knew time was limited. Lingering outdoors was not going to be an option without risk of being swept away by the record setting winds.

Briskly running down the only path leading away from the Utilities Building, they came to a signpost with a map of the island. Jake remembered what his father said about going to the place he had told him about years earlier.

He said it's at the far end of the island. Probably near where those choppers landed. Probably too far to reach in this storm. But what choice do we have? And there's some reason I'm supposed to go there. This is actually the perfect time and maybe the only time where we can do it and keep it secret.

Jake screamed over the noise of the high winds, "I don't want to risk going back to the complex and Dr. Jansen. And we need some privacy to dig into these files."

Kennedy replied with a defeated, "Agreed. That rules out the recreation center. But we also don't want to go back to the labs or to any buildings where the shooter might be looking for us. What if we went over here, along the far perimeter of the complex? It seems remote relative to everything else. I've heard that not too far past the perimeter fences there are old buildings from the original plantation that once occupied the island. Maybe we'll find some sort of shelter where we can ride out the storm."

Funny, she's pointing at the precise location where Dad said to go. She can't possibly know more than me, can she? How could she?

Jake punched the signpost with an open hand, hopped backward and momentarily paused, with an annoyed look on his face. He was angry that his father had possibly told some newcomer to his business more than he had told his own son. But he played it off.

Kennedy asked, "What? What are you thinking Jake?"

I am thinking, bingo! I know where we need to go!

Jake replied, "I could never understand why so much of the island was essentially fenced off. But you're right. No one will look for us there."

"Definitely not. The word on the street has always been that wild animals infest the island. That they were all corralled and thrown outside the perimeter fences. Then, they supposedly brought in big cats. Panthers, etc., as an extra security measure."

"Panthers? Like the kind that eat people?" Jake was surprised, "You want us to go outside the fence where there are Panthers?"

"Don't forget the choppers. There were a lot of them. Whoever was in them is probably out there as well."

"Maybe the cats will get them and not be hungry when they see us."

"Jake, it's not going to be safe, but I doubt whoever was shooting at us would look for us out there. No one would be crazy enough to trek past the outer security fences on a sunny day, let alone in the middle of this storm."

Jake replied. "But what choice do we have? We take our chances out there, or we go back and with an extremely high degree of certainty, we face a killer, or possibly more than one killer."

"Let's go," was all Kennedy bothered to say, and they took off running. Neither of them wanted to linger any longer in the storm. As they ran, the force of the wind was behind them and more than once almost face planted them both into the ground. But they managed to hold each other up as they ran, hands locked together, gripping tight, holding on for life, or comfort.

After about five minutes of running, they came upon a Jeep with markings that said, "Maintenance Crew." It was in the mud and appeared to have skidded off the path, sideswiping a tree. Whoever had abandoned it, had left in a hurry, as the lights were still on, the radio still playing, the keys in the ignition, and the engine apparently stalled out. Jake walked around inspecting the tires and looking for damage. Then they got in and tested the engine. It wouldn't start. Jake told Kennedy how to "pop the clutch," and then started pushing, falling in the slick mud several times. Finally they got it going. It was a relief to be in a vehicle although the fabric roof offered only partial protection from the elements and appeared as though it would fly off at any moment.

The route to the west led directly toward the outermost point of the perimeter fences. The second path, to the right of the fork, led to a one time sugarcane field. The fields were marked on the map as, "Sugarcane Range." Most of the leftover sugarcane plants, from the days when the island was a plantation, had been cleared to build a social/sports outlet for helping to maintain the sanity of the staff and employees assigned to work on a very remote and isolated island. The Sugarcane Driving Range was also in the exact spot where they suspected the helicopters had landed earlier. Jake steered the Jeep towards the fields, deciding to take a slight detour from their search for shelter.

As is the case in most hurricanes, Jake and Kennedy could literally see and feel the intensity of the storm increasing by the minute. It caused Jake to drive like he was in a Porsche. But their poor handling Jeep careened around corners only inches from being completely out of control on more than one occasion. It felt as if the winds were going to literally pick the Jeep up off the ground and take it airborne at any minute.

The path ended at a large and wide open field on the northwest corner of the island. Being a former sugarcane field, the ground was already very low relative to sea level. And because of the storm, the area was heavily flooded. Even with four wheel drive, it was unlikely the Jeep would be able to drive across it, which would have been necessary to reach the coastal path that connected the field to outer perimeter fences a mile or so to the South West.

For the moment, while peering out across the field, neither of them was worried about finding the perimeter fence. Instead, they were awe struck, having found themselves gazing at five military style helicopters. None of the aircraft had any identifying markings. There were no signs of people in them or nearby. The choppers were also blatantly modified to be heavily armed with various types of weaponry. Massive machine guns were visible along the sideboards. One thing was clear: whoever had landed in them, was extremely well outfitted, and had already left the landing area to invade some other spot on the island. Jake and Kennedy wanted to take a look inside the aircraft, but would have had to wade through knee deep water to get to them.

Whoever landed in these isn't flying off this island anytime soon. At least, I wouldn't think they can take off while half under water... They're going to be looking for some shelter just like we are. But probably toward the main complex, I would hope...

Trying to distract himself, Jake commented, "You could probably carry forty or fifty people on that many birds."

"Fifty-five to be exact," Kennedy responded, "There are five of them. And each Mi-24 gunship can carry eight soldiers and three crew. It's a relic of the old Soviet Union but a highly regarded design for its ability to transport troops and serve as a gunship simultaneously. It also has superior operability in inclement weather and the dark. In short, it's considered to be one hec of a bird."

"How in the world do you know…" he stopped himself, realizing they really didn't have time to get into a long back and forth of denial and lies. But it was then that Jake knew unequivocally, there was more to Kennedy than a medical degree.

CHAPTER 37

Isla Dedaleras

Jake stared at Kennedy, perplexed as to her true identity and reasons for being there. He asked her, "OK, since you know so much, tell me what are Soviet era helicopters doing here?"

"It's hard to say. I was just about to ask you that. The Mi-24 is in use in about fifty, maybe more countries, around the world. There are at least seven privately owned in the USA in addition to some owned by the U.S. Air Force for adversary training. These have no markings. It tells me they are either privately owned, or being used by some government clandestine service."

"You mean the CIA?" Jake asked?

"Not necessarily U.S. clandestine services. It's impossible to say from here. We would have to wade out there to see."

"Let's not. We've got to get out of this weather. And in any event, I don't want to be around these things if their owners come back."

"Agreed."

With the path forward essentially blocked by the flooded field, Jake and Kennedy decided to backtrack to get to the outer perimeter fence and search for what his father sent him to find. Driving as fast as the winds would allow, several strong gusts nearly blew the Jeep off the path, and sent their blood pressure through the roof. Their hearts were pounding as they finally made it to the iron fence that extended along the perimeter of the Hunter Neurologics research site. It stood ten feet tall from the ground and was lined with military grade barbed wire. Closed circuit cameras monitored thirty foot stretches of fence and appeared to be functioning even though all the other structures on the island had lost power.

Jake found a sledge hammer among the tools in the back of the maintenance crew jeep they were driving. He swung it at the lock on the gate, trying to smash it, but a gust of wind blew just as he swung, causing him to stumble forward and bang his head into the gate. He wiped a stream of blood from across his forehead to stop it from dripping into his eyes. Jake's second attempt was dead on and the massive sledgehammer popped the padlock from its hinges, allowing him to open the iron gate.

Once outside the gate, it took them nearly ten minutes to drive approximately two and half miles on the dirt and gravel road, which was full of flooded potholes. As the odometer turned again, they came upon what looked like a long abandoned plantation house. Its former majesty was hidden under a canopy of Spanish moss and assorted tropical vines that had overgrown the place.

Jake said, "It looks like this thing is ready to fall down at any minute. I'm not sure it's capable of withstanding this storm."

Kennedy responded, "Come on! Jake, do you think we can make it back to the recreation center in this storm? It's not like the winds are slowing down." At that precise moment the canvas roof of the Jeep was torn from the frame of the vehicle and flung up into the nearby tropical foliage.

Jake yelled his response through the wind and rain, "I

guess that settles it. There's no way we can drive back without a roof. We've got to try to wait out the worst of the storm in this house! Maybe we can reach the others on the sat phone."

"Let's give it a shot Jake. We should try to give them a heads up – let them know what happened to Ryan and that we were shot at. Maybe even some kind of warning to be on the look out for whoever was in those helicopters!"

After running to the front door, Kennedy tried the handle.

Jake looked at her quizzically and asked, "What are you doing Kennedy?"

"We've got to at least see if it's open before we bash in the windows!"

"I get that, but what I don't get is why there are poured concrete pillars holding up this front porch."

"What do you mean," Kennedy asked?

"This house is made to look like it's from last century, but those poured concrete pillars are modern. Judging by the lack of wear on the concrete, they can't be more than a few years old."

"That's ridiculous. Besides, who cares? Let's just get out of this storm." Kennedy bashed open the front door using the same sledgehammer Jake had used earlier on the iron gate. They both looked down and were puzzled by a deadbolt locking system that was clearly not from the 1800's. They were utterly drenched, cold, and fatigued from fighting against hurricane force winds. The noise was still dramatic, even after getting inside the house and closing the door behind them.

Once out of the weather, they laughed momentarily before giving each other the type of look that screamed sexual attraction. Kennedy shifted her eyes away and blushed, while Jake watched her closely, studying the lines of her body.

I should be with Anja right now, not some mystery woman

veiled in the disguise of a research doctor. This is like playing with fire and gasoline at the same time.

Breaking the sexual tension, Jake suggested, "This place is obviously not what it was made to look like from the exterior. Let's have a look around and see if we can't figure out what exactly we're dealing with. I am almost positive this is what my father was talking about when he said to go to this island. He meant the edge of the compound. Well here we are, in a fake plantation house."

Kennedy put her hand on the inside of his upper thigh and asked, "You want to see if the bedrooms have fresh linens?"

Do you really have to ask that? You're Vogue cover girl hot. You have a head on your shoulders. And, you have a sense of humor. Ahhh, this HAS got to be a test of some sort. Focus Jake. Focus on staying alive and rescuing your wife and father. Resist temptation. But shucks, no one would know...

"Kennedy, you check this way," Jake ordered, while pointing down the hallway to the right. "I'll go the other way. Let's circle back to this spot in two to three minutes max. Yell out if you find something."

Jake headed down the long hallway towards the back of the house and found a kitchen. Despite the occasional giveaways, the vast majority of the structure was like a replica circa 1850's plantation home. In the center of the back wall of the kitchen was an old fashioned cooking fireplace large enough to walk into. Jake immediately searched all around the fireplace and was not surprised to find a release for a trap door in the brick façade.

The faux brick slid to the right as if it had been spring loaded. In its place was revealed a stone hallway illuminated by gas lamps that kicked in seconds after the wall slid away. Jake yelled for Kennedy and the two of them decided to enter.

*   *   *

Before going into the depths of the structure, they decided to try to reach the others. Using the walkie-talkie they had grabbed off Ryan King, they flipped through the channels trying to contact the recreation center's underground weather shelter. "Hello? Is anyone out there? This is Kennedy Taylor. We're stuck in a hurricane, does anybody copy?"

Time and time again, the equipment crackled in silence before a voice finally came online, "This is Devon Keyes at the Isla Dedaleras weather shelter. Dr. Taylor, what's your location? Do you have the Nakuru files?" Jake grabbed the handset from her before she could respond.

"Why did you do that Jake?"

"Well, what the hell is he doing asking about that file? How does he know we're looking for it? Why is he asking if we have it before asking if we're even OK?"

"I don't know Jake! He's your friend, so you tell me."

"That's my point. He's supposed to be my friend. I haven't talked to him after a week of completely bizarre chaos and the first thing he asks about is some file which, I have no idea how he even knows it exists."

"Not a big deal Jake. You already told me Lavanya had sent someone else right?"

"Right, but for the someone else to be an inside guy that I previously trusted, is a bit weird. There's something not right here."

"What do you want to do Jake? Just ignore him?"

Jake pressed the button to talk, "Devon, how did you make it to the island in this weather?"

"Jake? Is that you? Jake Hunter?"

"Yes Devon it is. You wouldn't believe what I've been through. When did you get here? How did you land in this storm?"

I wonder if he came in on those choppers.

"There was a pocket in the radar of low intensity weather. We basically gunned it in through that pocket a few hours ago, just before the weather got real bad. Believe me when I say it wasn't pretty. In fact, our plane is banged up pretty good. I don't think we can take off until after some repairs. But the thing is Jake, we're in a bind here. John filled me on some of what's happened to you and the others."

"Devon, what the hell are you doing here? The entire board of directors is dead and my father has been kidnapped. So why would you risk flying through a hurricane to get here? I don't understand what's going on."

"Jake, someone had to get here and make sure security protocol was followed. As the corporate counsel, I'm technically the acting CEO now."

"What? Are you kidding?"

"Don't worry buddy, I'm not going to ruin your family's business."

"Damn right. For one thing you're jumping the gun a bit Devon. My father is still alive. That means it's still his company."

"Jake, please calm down. I'm your friend remember? I said, 'acting' officer didn't I? I'm just trying to keep things going until we get your father back. Jesus Jake. You could show some gratitude considering I just risked my life to fly here to help you. Listen, we've got to make sure this place is locked down and tight. Word of what's happened in D.C. is already out. This isn't some kind of new cold medicine they're working on. It's likely to change the world. People will be gunning for us, especially if the word gets out that your father is gone too. We've got to work together and make sure this place is secure. And to make sure the Digitalis is secure."

Jake made sure he wasn't transmitting through the radio, looked at Kennedy, and said, "He's playing us. I'm certain of it."

"How do you know Jake?" she asked.

"Let's just say I've never lost to the man at poker. No

matter how drunk I got, and how sober he was, I could always read him."

Jake pushed the transmit button on the walkie and said, "Devon, this storm has got us trapped in an auxiliary building. We can't make it back to the rec center until it settles down a bit. But you need to know something. This island is not safe. Not by any stretch."

"It's OK Jake, we'll be OK. I'm worried about you though. What's your exact location?"

"No Devon, you don't understand. There are five heavily armed choppers on the northwest side of the island, on the driving range, or what used to be the driving range before this storm. I'm telling you Devon, these are not your typical helicopters. They are big military style birds, capable of carrying probably about fifty five people or so."

"Exactly fifty-five maximum capacity," Kennedy chimed in, as if deliberately reminding Jake there was more to her than scientific and medical research.

Jake went on talking to his former law partner, "Here's the problem Devon. Those choppers are all empty. We don't know where the occupants went. But you know as well as I do, this isn't that big of an island."

"Are you kidding me? Damn it… I thought we had more…" Devon released the transmission button on his end before finishing his sentence.

Kennedy asked Jake, "Does he know something? I think he knows who was in the choppers?"

"Maybe. For now, I think it's best if we play it cool and ride out this storm." Jake pressed the transmit button, "Devon, I need to speak to Dr. Jansen. Could you put him on please?"

"What? I thought he was with you? He's not here Jake."

"What do you mean? He's not with us either. No one there knows where he is?"

"No Jake. Everyone's shaking their head. No one has

seen him since he left with you and Kennedy a few hours back."

"OK, listen, it's too dangerous to be outside. We're going to ride out the storm here. We'll see you in the morning if it clears up. Stay safe. Be alert."

"Roger that Jake. Where are you riding it out? What's your location?" Devon was trying again to figure out where they were. But Jake turned off the radio without saying anything more.

"Jake! What was that sound? Right before you shut it off? It sounded like gun shots on their end?!"

"Let's hope not. Listen, we had better hide the Jeep so it doesn't look like anyone came here. I'm going to go park it behind some trees. It's probably safest if we figure out where that path behind the fireplace goes and try to hide in there."

"What are you talking about Jake? We need to get back to the rec center and help them!"

"How are you going to help them Kennedy? We can't help them. There's 150 mile per hour winds outside. We cannot make the five mile drive back there. That little Jeep would be pitched into the air like a Brett Favre Hail Mary."

Tears started flowing down her cheeks and Jake pulled her next to him. His mind was going a million miles a minute because of their predicament, but he paused briefly to think how good Kennedy's hard, athletic body felt against his own. She was probably the most attractive medical doctor, or whatever she was, he had ever seen. And up until then, she had the confidence and composure to make any guy want her.

"Just calm down Kennedy. Everything's going to be OK."

"Thanks Jake. Sorry to lose it on you. I just feel like, well, like I'm not in control."

"Unfortunately, you're not. And neither am I. It's

one of the worst and scariest feelings in the world isn't it? Not being in control? But you know what, you just have to embrace it and have faith. Have some faith that everything is going to be OK. And I'll tell you what else. Most of the time, things will be more than OK. So let's not waste energy right now worrying about what we cannot control. Let's stay focused on survival, on moving forward, and then that mind of yours will not have time to worry about whoever has been firing guns all over this island."

"Thanks Jake." She kissed him on the side of his face and he did not pull away. He did smile however.

"Speaking of guns, we should see if we can find any in this house. Have a look would you? I'm gonna go move the Jeep. Maybe it will cool me off, seeing as how hot it's getting in here." Kennedy was smiling and blushing again.

CHAPTER 38

Isla Dedaleras

When Jake went running back into the falsely dilapidated plantation house, Kennedy was there to greet him and said, "You seem nervous. Haven't you ever been in a hurricane before?" They were standing in front of the big fireplace in the kitchen with the strange hidden passageway. Jake wondered where it led and he knew it meant there was much more to learn about the imposter plantation house. He wondered how it tied back to the Digitalis and the research trust in Amsterdam. And he wondered why his father had to keep it a secret from the rest of the company and even his own son.

The panes of glass in the windows were vibrating from the ferocity of the high winds, but the fact they had not broken prompted a closer inspection which again revealed modern day engineering cloaked in circa 1800's disguises: hurricane proof glass windows, over an inch thick. Outside, rain drops the size of bullets were pelting down from the sky in all different directions. The power which lit the hidden passage inside the giant fireplace had flickered a few times before shutting off and then resuming along with a humming sound from a backup generator running nearby.

Jake stared in amazement outside the window at the storm swirling around them. While contemplating what would prompt a disguised plantation home outside the secured areas of the island, he finally responded to Kennedy, "Yeah, you could say that I'm just a tad nervous. I've never really experienced a hurricane. Certainly I've never experienced anything like this. And this house… it's not entirely consistent with what my father told me about on this part of the island."

Kennedy asked, "What do you mean? What exactly did he tell you about?"

He ignored her question and turned the conversation back to the storm, "I guess being a small island in the middle of the Caribbean exposes us to the full strength of the storm in a way that's far more intense than what's normally covered by American journalists on the mainland. Oh, add in that there is a killer on the island too. The same island we cannot get off right now because of the weather. Not to mention your fifty-five soldier capacity military style clandestine services helicopters. It's not exactly the typical day at the office for me. So yes, you could say I am just a tad bit nervous!" But inside, Jake was thinking differently:

Truth told, none of that scares me as much as your ongoing attempts at seducing me, and even worse, there is something incredibly tempting about a beautiful woman wanting me to be her hero in the middle of a crisis, especially when she knows about guns and helicopters. Now, if she drinks Manhattans too, then I'm really in trouble.

Jake walked away from the windows back to the center of the kitchen and was staring down into the musty stone passageway when Kennedy wrapped her arms around his chest. Her hands spread to feel his muscles as if she was thinking more about sex than comforting him.

They needed to find some shelter before she could start ripping off his clothes; so she asked, "What do you say we take your mind off your nerves by figuring out where this little secret passageway goes. My guess is, we'll at least find shelter. But maybe we'll also find the Digitalis. What do you say?"

Jake replied, "It's better than standing here. Let's go." And they began walking further into the dank and cold stone passageway.

*   *   *

The tunnel was winding and descended what seemed like at least two floors before ending at a door that by all appearances was highly secure. There was no typical lock on it. Instead, next to the handle was a round indentation about the size of a compass. Around it was engraved the same words Jake had seen on the pocket watch his father had insisted he retrieve. He pulled it from his pocket and realized it fit perfectly into the socket. There were two grooves opposite each other that enabled him to turn the watch counter clockwise. A latch released and the door sprang ajar. They walked in and marveled at what was before them while lights automatically illuminated the room.

They were standing in front of a circular desk that was large enough to accommodate the four chairs that lined its inside edge and faced outwards toward the wall of the room. The whole thing rotated 360 degrees so that while seated, the four individuals would be able to simultaneously face any direction in the oval shaped room. The ceiling was at least 20 feet high. Aside from the entrance, there was one other door. The rest of the walls were lined end to end in an alternating pattern of floor to ceiling bookshelves with illuminated panels in between. The panels looked like high tech monitors that were displaying tranquil nature images. They too were floor to ceiling.

Jake found a control panel in the center drawer of the

desk and realized the whole room was an elaborate video conferencing center. He then saw placards at the top of each of the monitors that had names of people. He wrote them all down, suspecting they were the "Global Council" members he had read about on the web site for the investment trust in Amsterdam. Clearly, his father must be a part of it.

"How is this thing connected? I don't get it," he said to Kennedy.

"It's not a bad thing Jake. So your father was part of a medical investment trust formed by super rich doctors out to save the world, what's wrong with that?"

"What's wrong with that is they're trying to operate outside the laws of civilized nations. There's only one reason to do that in science: human guinea pigs, or worse."

"The laws of civilized nations don't always represent the paths of greatest intelligence Jake. I figured you for the type that would already know that."

"Make no mistake, I am a firm believer that rules were made to be broken, but not at the expense of the innocent, ignorant, or weak. As soon as I am done saving him, my father is going to have to explain all this."

"Jake, let's see where that door goes. It has a window and I think I see some kind of kitchen or lounge area on the other side."

They walked through the other door and found an elaborately decorated lounge with plush leather furniture, some computers and other office equipment, a mini kitchenette area with wet bar, and full bathroom. It was clearly a fully sustainable office meant to be hidden from the rest of the compound. And it was equipped with everything one would need in order to work on a global project without being noticed. The whole place would have cost millions to build and was obviously weather proofed and able to function even in the middle of a record setting Category 5 hurricane.

Jake handed Kennedy the DVD from his backpack

that had the downloaded files from the Utilities Building computers and said, "See if you can get this to load in any of those computers over there. I need to use the restroom, and then I'm making myself a drink."

While each of them was sipping Johnny Walker, in the underground compound, they fumbled through the computers. Jake found a wireless signal to a network that had a satellite uplink to the Internet. He was browsing the web in search of utilities he could use to hack into the encrypted files they had downloaded earlier from the Utilities Building.

After an hour and half, they found one called, "Cyber-Hack," but it warned them at step one in the process that the encryption level on the files was beyond legal limits normally available to the American consumer, which meant whatever they were accessing, was protected to an extent not possible, except by U.S. military and intelligence agencies. In plain English, there was no way they were going to get into those files, at least not that night and not without the encryption keys that would unlock them.

*   *   *

Twenty minutes later, the full effect of being half way through their third scotch was starting to kick in. Jake flung himself into the back of an oversized leather chair and sighed with exhaustion and frustration at their lack of success. Kennedy suggested, "Hey Jake, why don't I make us one more drink, a nightcap, then I'll rub your back for a bit and try to help you relax. There's nothing more we can do until the storm passes. We can climb into our little base camp I set up for us over by the bookcases. It's not the Ritz, but I think I did a pretty good job." Kennedy had arranged pillows and blankets from the couch into a makeshift sleeping area for two.

Jake noticed how it would require them to sleep very

close together and couldn't help but let out a loud, "Hah! Sounds like a great idea. We're not going to get anywhere with these files without some help. And I am going to need another drink if we're sleeping on the floor!"

Kennedy said, "Don't be afraid to sleep naked," paused to see if Jake was smiling (he was), then said, "So great! I'll be right back with our drinks. Warm up our bed for me will ya?" Jake just stared at her for a moment contemplating her devious nature.

What is she talking about, 'our bed'? It would be fine if anyone else said it, but something about the way she said it, jeesh. What I have done? Errr, what am I doing? Probably nothing Anja wouldn't do. I may as well indulge myself.

Kennedy fumbled at the wet bar while Jake dove into their makeshift "bed" on the floor in the corner of the underground secret office.

Kennedy poured two more scotches. Hers was about a quarter of a shot, then a splash of club soda. Jake's was a solid three shots, easy on the ice to give the double rocks glasses enough room. Next, after making sure her back was to Jake, hiding the drinks from his view, she broke a capsule in half and dumped a substance into Jake's drink. With a good stir, the colorless and tasteless drug was fully dissolved.

*   *   *

"Here you go Jake. Just the way you like it." They drank, and talked about their dire situation. They wondered about the importance of Aguas Muertas, and why it was kept secret. From a laptop he had found in the office, Jake was rummaging through the files he did have access to on the DVD, looking for clues, anything that might help explain the Digitalis, Nakuru or the investor group in Amsterdam, to which his father was inextricably linked.

After a few minutes of silence and trenchant thought,

Jake exclaimed, "It just can't be true?!"

"What's got you so fired up all of a sudden," Kennedy asked.

"Well what would cause my father to keep a second site of his company secret from me? First there's this thing he's involved in somehow, Nakuru, which I have never heard of. Now there is an entire set of clinical trials all held at some place in God knows where Venezuela. Aguas Muertas. Waters of death – what a name! Why was all this hidden from me? I am his family, his son, supposedly his corporate attorney for crying out loud. What's wrong with me that he would do this?" Kennedy used his stress as an excuse to put her hand on his chest, pretending to try to calm him down.

"Jake, I think you are looking at it the wrong way. What's more likely is that he was protecting you, and others. Whatever happened in this Nakuru trial was obviously significant enough to kill for. I certainly wouldn't mix my loved ones up in something like that if I didn't have to. Besides, you said yourself those files are encrypted in a way that could only be provided by someone with access to highly classified technology. Not even rich doctors in Amsterdam have access to that type of encryption level. In other words, there may be a whole lot more to your father than he could tell you about without risking your safety. But the fact is, he made sure you got the key to this place by telling you about that pocket watch. So he's counting on you now Jake."

He slurped back the rest of his drink and slammed the glass down on the floor. "Rubbish! He sends us off on a wild goose chase. This is nonsense!"

Kennedy noticed the effects of the drug she had slipped into Jake's drink were starting to kick in. She said to him, "I understand completely." Then she switched to small talk about the site in Venezuela and the secrets it could answer, as Jake gradually grew dizzy. His world turned dark.

Once Jake had passed out completely, Kennedy said out loud, to herself, "That's too bad because he was really starting to grow on me." Then she got up from their makeshift sleeping arrangements, took the laptop Jake had loaded the files onto, and went to work.

CHAPTER 39

Isla Dedaleras
Night of the Hurricane
(Recreation Center - Underground Weather Shelter)

Even though Kate Stinson was only pretending to believe her trip with Devon was for legitimate business purposes, she was still getting way more than she had bargained for. Distracted by her thoughts of seducing the man to win his trust and extract information, she hadn't considered the full impact of life in the middle of a record setting hurricane.

And Devon, excited at the thought of another notch on his belt, to boost his cocky appearing yet immensely weak ego, made sure not to tell her about the real risks of their little adventure.

Earlier, their pilot had managed to land them safely, although no one got off that plane without the need for tranquilizers to calm them down from the rough and tumble of being tossed around and finally slammed into the ground upon landing. Devon wrote the pilot a check for the rest of his extortionate fee and the group moved into the safety of the island's underground weather shelter in the basement of the recreation center building.

The rec center was the most recent building at the Hunter Neurologics research compound. It was built the previous year after three summers in a row of repeated delays from rough hurricane seasons. The building served the double duty of ensuring a safe place for essential staff to stay on site during inclement weather as well as offering a social outlet so that employees wouldn't feel the need to travel home so often, which could also slow progress and create security risks. Being outside the U.S. and breaking most of the laws typically enforced by the FDA, Hunter Neurologics couldn't turn to U.S. authorities regarding security matters, so when it came to speeding progress and ensuring security on the island, no expense was spared.

*   *   *

Despite all the technology and security, Kate was feeling anything but safe in the underground shelter. Devon, observing her fear, saw it as his chance to make a move. He figured there was nothing else to do in the middle of a storm, so why not go for it. A quick call to his wife would buy him at least a couple of hours to spend seducing Kate, without interruption.

He tried to call, but quickly discovered there was no cell signal and that the land lines were down as well.

That's even better. Now I can ignore the wife guilt free. It's Mother Nature's fault!

Devon walked over to the couch where Kate was sitting and said, "Kate, you look nervous. Is everything OK?"

"Yes Devon. I just wasn't expecting this storm to be so bad. It's my first time in a hurricane. But I'm fine. Everything is good. How are you doing?"

"I'm fantastic! Listen, there's a café and bar upstairs. What do you say we head up there and grab a few drinks to keep us warm? And don't worry about spending the night in here. It will be fun. There's sleeping quarters in the back. The rooms are tiny, but at least they offer some privacy. So we don't have to spend the night on the couches!"

"Thanks Devon, a drink would be great. But is it safe for you to go up there?" Just as he was about to answer, the power went out. Besides their pilot, there was only one other man with them in the shelter at the time. It was Tim Hagan, the Chief of Security on the island.

Tim immediately jumped from his chair and offered, "You guys relax. Here are some flashlights. Grab those drinks you were just talking about and I'll take a look at the generator."

"I can go with you." Devon offered, hoping it would impress Kate, but counting on his offer being declined.

In fact, Tim Hagan laughed at him before responding, "What, in a suit? Appreciate that sir, but you had better stay indoors. The latest weather report is showing this to be a class five storm. That's as bad as it gets. In fact, don't linger upstairs. If the roof gets torn off, and sooner or later, I'm guessing it will, you won't want to be there when it happens."

"Roger that Chief Hagan," Devon said with a condescending tone he mistakenly thought would make him appear more macho than the security chief.

Tim Hagan put on his rain slicker and left Kate and Devon with their flashlights.

Devon said to Kate, "Well, how about we work on getting those drinks? I'll be right back Kate."

"No way. You're not leaving me down here by myself, roof or no roof! I'm going with you. Besides, you can't carry two drinks AND a flashlight. You need my help."

"Good point. Let's do it then!" As they started to walk up the stairs to the ground level they saw the door at the top closing behind Tim who had gone up only moments before them. They made their way up and into the lobby of the Recreation Center. On the far side of the lobby, past a receptionist desk, the front door to the building swayed violently in the wind. It appeared Tim hadn't bothered to make sure it latched when he went out only a minute earlier. The rain water was so strong that a fine mist was coating the entire lobby, even a good twenty feet from the flailing front door.

*   *   *

Inside in the nearby café, there was an eerie feeling while pouring their drinks. Neither of them felt quite right under the circumstances, staying inside drinking when Tim was out trying to restore power for them. Kate finally asked, "What do you suppose happened to the generator Devon?"

"I don't know. That's a good question actually. I thought this place had backup everything, especially power to keep all the security systems running. But I'm sure *The Chief* can fix it."

While flashing her most seductive eyes, Kate responded, "Well, I guess it wouldn't be so bad if he can't," as she ran her hand softly from the top of Devon's chest, across his pecs, toward his waistline before flicking her wrist and then letting her fingers take the lead, with a dive down below his belt and under his pants.

Devon looked at her, squinting to see the outline of her face in the darkness before saying, "No, it wouldn't be so bad at all."

"Let's stay up here Devon. It's exciting."

"I don't know Kate. I don't think that's a good idea. You heard Tim, this is a really bad storm."

"I believe his exact words were, 'as bad as it gets,' and that means we have in front of us the chance of a lifetime. We're never going to get this opportunity again. So the only question is," pausing, her hand slid further into his pants and gripped him, "what are you going to do with it Devon?"

A grin of pleasure and excitement consumed Devon's face. But it was vanquished in a fraction of a second as bullets from machine guns suddenly tore through all the exterior windows along the back side of the café, which bordered the rear of the building. Devon and Kate dove to the floor behind the bar.

"That's where the generator is, in the back of the building," Devon said to Kate. Then he added, "We've got a problem Kate."

"No shit, you think? Why are people shooting at us? " Kate asked. But without responding, he gave her the "let's take a peek" hand signal and they both moved to a kneeling position so they could look over the bar towards the window area. She asked again, "Devon, why would someone be shooting at us in the middle of a hurricane?"

He finally replied, "I don't think they were aiming at us. But try to lower your voice would you? Unless you want to just announce to whoever is shooting that we're hiding in here."

"You really are an idiot Devon aren't you?"

"What the, no who do you think you are talking to me like that?' She didn't say anything, but looked at him coldly before finally raising her hand and pointing over his left shoulder to the group of men standing at the entrance of the café and brandishing their machine guns.

There were five men in total. Four in military fatigues, the fifth, who was in a motley assortment of street clothes, was Dr. Marten Jansen.

CHAPTER 40

Isla Dedaleras
(The Plantation House)

By morning, the storm had settled down substantially. There was still rain, but clearly the worst had passed. Kennedy brewed up some coffee. Then she went back to the makeshift bed and felt for a pulse on Jake. He still had one and she breathed a sigh of relief. Next were smelling salts which were followed by coffee that would make even the Master Brewer at Starbucks blush. Jake was alive, and Kennedy's heart was at ease.

"Jake, I think you over did it on the scotch last night. Are you feeling OK?"

"Huh? Urrr umm, OK? Yeah, I feel fantastic," he said facetiously. They drank coffee, talked only briefly, showered, and then agreed it was time to head back to the recreation center to figure out next steps. To save Jake's father, they would need to load whatever equipment and files they could find, get them to India, and hope that it was enough to satisfy Lavanya. Jake was confused and his mind was fuzzy from the previous night.

I don't remember going to sleep or anything leading up to

it. I hope to God I didn't do anything I'll regret. I'm afraid to even ask her what happened.

*   *   *

During the drive in the Jeep, back to the Hunter Neurologics compound on the other side of the island, they both acted like the previous night of flirting and the morning's awkwardness never happened. Other things occupied their minds, as they were both worried about who was on the helicopters they had seen the previous day as well as who had been shooting at them.

Jake was tensely disappointed in not being able to find any information on the Nakuru trial. It was eating away at him that he didn't know what was so important about it as to prompt the kidnapping of his father. Not to mention the mystery surrounding his father's involvement in the investment trust, Scientia Pro Curation, as it was called.

As they neared the final stretch of road leading to the main compound, what was left standing of the tropical foliage by the hurricane, started to give way to a clearing which housed the numerous buildings at the research and development site. But when their Jeep reached that clearing, all of Jake's tension around his father keeping secrets was immediately vanquished from his mind.

In its place was shock and horror from seeing smoldering remnants of the former buildings. Not a single structure was left standing. All of them had been destroyed, but not by the hurricane. It was clearly a result of extreme force from human intervention. Even in the ongoing rain, there were still parts of structures burning.

Jake and Kennedy looked at each other quizzically. Jake, still unaware of having been drugged the night before, said, "Being in that underground room, and the noise of the hurricane, must have prevented us from hearing the destruction."

"Yes, most likely," Kennedy responded, full well knowing that Jake was lucky to be alive, and wouldn't have heard the roof caving in on him that night, had he been in one of those buildings.

They navigated around structural and forest debris until they came up to what was left of the recreation center and its weather proof shelter. "I guess it wasn't bomb proof," Jake said, "And now we'll never be able to get the Digitalis, if it even was here to begin with."

"No we won't," Kennedy replied, "And unfortunately, it would not have been possible to survive this type of destruction. Anyone in there when this happened would not have, could not have survived."

Jake's distrust of Kennedy was growing.

Here we go again. How does she know these things?

CHAPTER 41

Cher-Ae Heights Casino
Trinidad, California

Inside the Firewater Lounge at the Cher-Ae Heights Casino in Trinidad, CA, John Anton was meeting with Milton Strayer. They were on their way back to the Arcata airport. It was a small regional airport that would allow them to take a prop plane back to San Francisco for connecting flights to D.C., and it was the closest airport to where they thought Anja Hunter was being held captive as an insurance policy for acquiring the Digitalis. However, the two of them were angry and confused.

Martin was saying to John, "I can't believe the whole place is just gone. I still say we must have gone the wrong way out there in the wilderness. It's not like it's hard to do."

"It is hard to do however, when you've been there a dozen times already. And the fact that Gregor Eagon, the little double crossing bastard, isn't answering my phone calls confirms that we've lost this one."

"Then what are we going to do John?"

"Keep the disbarment thing going. We can still control Jake with that. By now, if he hasn't figured out that he was framed, we'll just come right out and tell him. We'll tell him the only way he'll ever practice law again is to deliver the Digitalis to us."

"And if he doesn't?"

"Then he'll never practice law again. Believe me; the guy has more compassion for victims of injustice than Gandhi. There is no way he's going to let Aubrey Doyle suffer without putting up a fight. We'll turn his nobility against him and use that to control him."

"I guess we have no choice."

"We really don't. It's our best backup plan at this point. But let's hope we don't need it. And maybe in the meantime we can find Anja or Gregor and retake control of that situation."

"Even if we do, you realize this probably means they've done surgery on her?"

"Yeah, you're probably right. That's a good point. And it means there isn't much value in kidnapping her again. She's under Eagon's control now. We'll just have to wash our hands of that one. But nonetheless, we're going to track down Gregor Eagon and he is going to pay for this."

"Agreed."

CHAPTER 42

Isla Dedaleras

On the tarmac at the Isla Dedaleras airfield, Jake and Kennedy were surprised that the plane they had arrived on was gone. Instead they got on board a luxury jet sent by Lavanya to take them to India. It had arrived that morning, after the force of the hurricane had subsided enough to allow safe passage. There were no other aircraft in sight, which meant everyone else had presumably already left the island or been killed and buried in the destruction of the buildings. Jake was baffled by the strange events.

Where are the other planes? What happened to Devon? And where did Dr. Jansen go? There were no bodies to be found... why?

Once airborne, a quick flyby over the sugarcane fields confirmed all the military choppers were also gone, presumably having completed their mission.

I wonder if they found the Digitalis?

Fifteen minutes into the flight Jake demanded a stopover in D.C. He had been incessantly checking his voice mail, hoping for a message from his wife Anja. She was supposed to have returned home from her trip. Although

Jake had been told by his father she was kidnapped, part of him was in denial.

No matter how many times he called her cell or checked his for a message, there was no hope to be found. And no sign of her safe return home meant she truly was in trouble. He was overwhelmed in a fury of emotions. Guilt for contemplating cheating on her with Kennedy elicited memories of Sunday School as a child, where he recalled a teacher talking about how the bible says thinking it, is as bad as doing it.

I preach it to my clients all the time… and look at me. What an awful role model.

But his feelings were also complicated by insecurity and rage from having suspected for some time that Anja was less than loyal herself. Ultimately, in his heart and head, what overwhelmed him the most was worry. He worried about Anja because he loved her despite her human shortcomings.

In addition to wanting desperately to either reconcile his guilt by being there for his wife, or figuring out how to rescue her, he had another court date to deal with from the malpractice suit against him. He was sure any sane judge would grant a continuance under the bizarre circumstances that had taken over his life. If he could somehow find a way to win that malpractice case, he would have a chance to recover from the disbarment and save his career. But if he lost, there would be no question that he was done as a lawyer. And if he didn't show for court, a default judgment would be issued against him, just as it was for the disbarment hearing. On top of all that, he also needed to figure out a way to come up with a cool million dollars to pay off the thug-like brother of Angelo Doyle.

Jake pleaded with the pilot for a "minor" detour.

But the pilot, Captain Peter Weiss, told Jake to discuss it with Lavanya, "Sorry sir, I am on strict instructions to get us to our destination as quickly as possible. Apparently some type of rendezvous has been setup with a group of experts being sent to help you."

Jake countered, "Look, we can make up the time in the air. The flight to India is long enough, it should be easy to make up the couple of hours I need to check on things." But Captain Weiss showed little interest in listening to Jake plead any further.

"I told you sir. You need to talk to Ms. Yashodhara. We take our orders directly from her. But I can assure you, where we are going, the flight is not long enough to make up for, or hide, a side trip to D.C. You can use the video conferencing satellite uplink at the workstation in the back of the plane. I'm afraid there really is nothing else for us to discuss. Now please, step out of the cockpit." Captain Weiss used one hand to push Jake out of the cockpit, and his other hand to slam the door behind him.

Jake muttered in vain, "Wait! What do you mean where we are going? I thought we were going to India?" But there was no answer from behind the now closed door to the cockpit. "Damn it! You people think you can just kidnap whoever the hell you want. You can't. You cannot get away with this!"

Kennedy came over and put her hand on his shoulder trying to calm him down, "Jake, let's just try calling her. The fact is, under these circumstances, they can get away with doing whatever they want."

"Key words Kennedy, are, 'under these circumstances.' Believe me when I say, these CIRCUMSTANCES are going to change. I've just about had it with this crap."

"What are you going to do Jake? Jump out of a moving plane?"

He stared at her with a look of scorn on his face that shifted to thoughts of *well, maybe*, until she stopped his madness by saying, "Don't even think about it. Even if you could find a parachute, without the proper training, you wouldn't stand a chance jumping out of a moving airplane."

"Why do you do that?"

"Do what?"

Jake was irritated that Kennedy was insinuating he couldn't do something. It was a pet peeve of his that usually led to fights. But he decided to take the high road; so instead, he used humor to keep things cordial.

"You know Kennedy, why don't you help me understand what other way there is to jump out of a plane? They usually are moving when people jump out of them."

Humor, it's still the quickest way to achieve successful diplomacy. You can't be angry and laugh at the same time.

"Ok, OK, you got me. I'm just trying to calm you down and keep you from doing anything stupid. Let's try calling Lavanya. All she wants is this Nakuru file. Maybe we can find a win-win, get your father back, and save your wife, if that's what you really want."

Kennedy's insinuation, regarding his wife, pushed him over the edge. Jake lost it and went on a rampage, yelling, "I am done with your deception. You don't get to talk to me. You just stay away from me. Sit over there and don't talk to me again until you are ready to tell me who you really are. All these lies, all this manipulation, smoke and mirrors, it stops now."

"But Jake…"

"NO, nope, no way. It stops. Not another word until I know who you are, why you were working at my father's company, and why you are here now."

"You asked me to come here Jake, did you forget that?"

"You set me up for that. I don't want to hear another word from you. I'm going to make a call and am asking you to just stay the hell away from me."

Marriage wrecker.

"What did you say?" Kennedy asked while watching Jake storm to the back of the plane, to make the call to India.

"I said, not another word!"

"Hmm, I thought I heard you say something else."

Nope. Not out loud... marriage wrecker.

*   *   *

The jet had a workstation near the back with a videoconferencing setup that the pilot had already remotely activated. As Jake sat down in front of the screen, he read a flashing message, "CONNECTION IN PROGRESS TO: Yashodhara Palace, India."

Lavanya's mug shot appeared on the screen with the type of animation you could see in the original cartoon movies, like she was a robot skipping a step every time her facial expression changed. "Hello Jake. I have been informed of the problems at Isla Dedaleras. I am so sorry you all had to deal with so many challenging situations. Your efforts will not go unrewarded."

"Excellent. Then you will instruct your Nazi pilots to divert at once, from our present course to India, for a stopover in Washington, D.C. Surely you can understand I am due to appear in court and cannot risk another setback with the lawsuits against me."

"Oh Jake, be realistic. Your chances of winning that case are slim to none without my help. Besides, you would never even make it near the courthouse without paying the million dollars you owe to the Doyle brothers. But do a good job helping me, and I'll be sure you never hear from them again."

"How the hell do you know that?"

"Jake, I know everything about you. And I do mean everything. For example, you and I both know that right about now you are most likely starting to crack. The guilt from cheating on your wife eating at your soul..."

He interrupted, "I did not and have never cheated on my wife!"

"Jake, your wife has been kidnapped. The least you could do is show some concern."

He fell back into the chair, in a posture of defeat. His anger and energy had been wiped from his persona in a split second as he began to realize Lavanya couldn't care less about him or his wife. His head was dizzy and he felt nauseous. Lavanya continued, "It's time to come back to reality Jake. Despite your delusions of grandeur, going to D.C. isn't going to help you save your wife. The best way for you to save her now is to deliver to me the Nakuru files and the Digitalis."

Like a defeated school boy in the principal's office he asked, almost rhetorically, "So, you are not going to ask the pilot to divert from India, for at least a brief stopover? I only need a few hours in D.C., please!"

"I would do that if I could Jake, but time is of the essence. We haven't a day to spare, let alone an hour. Besides, your current destination is not India. I could have sworn Captain Weiss told me that he had already informed you of your upcoming rendezvous. I'm getting you some help Jake. Call it reinforcements, if you will. In fact, I believe you've met Commander Collins once already. Consider this my reunion gift to you and Kennedy with the man that saved the two of you after that unfortunate plane crash."

"I don't understand. I thought you wanted us to bring the equipment and files from the lab to my father so you could conduct your little experiments?"

"Jake, I already had access to most of the information that was easily accessible. What we need is for you to deliver the Nakuru Files and the Digitalis. We have ascertained where to find the Digitalis, and we need you to retrieve it. If we have that, we can proceed without the assistance of your father and he will be free to go. This is the last favor I need Jake. Get this for me, and I will make sure you win that pesky malpractice suit being brought against you. I'll make sure your wife and father get home safely as well, assuming you still want that, of course."

Why wouldn't I want that? Just because of one possible indiscretion everyone thinks I'm going to walk away from something so much more significant? No, this woman isn't that shallow. She must know more. I've got to find out what. And I don't care how drunk I was at the plantation house; there is just no way I could have actually done anything to hurt Anja.

Lavanya, continued, "Look Jake, I can see you're disappointed. But there is little point in arguing any further. Your father was gracious enough to share with us some very helpful information about where to find the Digitalis and the Nakuru files. He even confirmed that they exist, which was a huge step forward. Up until now, the whole thing has just been a rumor."

You kidnap people, ruin lives, kill and worse based on a rumor? How freakin insane do you have to be to act like that?!

Jake asked, "Well do tell then. Where are you sending us?"

"Venezuela. Apparently the predecessor organization to Hunter Neurologics at one time had a research facility hidden at a place called Aguas Muertas. But then, you already knew that, didn't you Jake?"

"How do you know this? How could you possibly know that I already know that, when I just figured it out last night?"

Is Kennedy working for Lavanya? Is that how she knows so much?

"There will be men that will meet you in Caracas. They are highly trained for what awaits and will assist you in the voyage to Aguas Muertas. As I said, Commander Collins will coordinate their activities. I would suggest being nice to them because where you are going is not a friendly or safe place Jake. You will need their help. Do try not to get them killed like you did poor Ryan, would you sweetie?"

What a condescending...

Lavanya added, "Oh one more thing, I hope you have some comfortable shoes. I am told the journey to Aguas Muertas can be a bit rough. You'll need to stay sharp Jake. Your father confirmed, there are unique security measures in place to ensure this facility remains undisturbed, or more like buried forever. Through satellite images we have confirmed there are quite a lot of people there. Although we are also fairly sure the facility is not actively used for medical research. So again, unfortunately, we don't know the full extent of what is going on at the site. But Commander Collins is the best. That's why he works for me. Good Luck Jake. I hope I get to see you in one piece, after you're done in Venezuela."

"What's that supposed to mean."

"It means I *really* want to see you Jake. Not just for the Nakuru Files. But you're going into a hell on earth. I cannot stress it enough, you need to be at your best for this. And get some comfortable shoes for God's sake."

I heard ya the first time lady.

He looked down at his feet. His Ferragamo shoes didn't give him the warm fuzzies. The video screen flickered then displayed a message, "CALL ENDED."

What was my father involved in? Why will no one tell me what this is all really about? I'm globetrotting around looking for the Digitalis and I don't even know what it really is... can it make people smarter? Can it prove reincarnation? Was it really meant to cure Alzheimer's or for something more sinister? I cannot wait to find this thing and find out the truth...

Kennedy could practically read his mind from the look of consternation on his face but wasn't much help when she said, "Jake, this is not good. We can't go about things like this."

"Who are you Kennedy!" he snapped back at her, loosing his patience with her charades, "You are most definitely not a medical doctor. Whoever you are, you had better tell me, and now. And after you tell me that, you are going to tell me what you know about where we are going and exactly why it is you think we can't or shouldn't be going there."

"Jake please, I never meant to deceive you in any way. I'm just trying to do my job here. No one had any idea things would play out like this. We went over literally hundreds of scenarios in training, but all this – all these things that have been happening and are happening are way beyond anyone's wildest dreams. We simply didn't prepare for these scenarios."

"Stop that. Stop that crap right now. Who is WE! And what scenarios did you prepare for?"

"Jake, it's better if I don't tell you…" she paused, the look on Jake's face made it clear she was going to have to tell him something, "Ok Jake, OK. I'll tell you what I know." But Jake was enraged and no longer rational. He stammered backwards in a fit of anger and inadvertently fell into the desk and the videoconferencing equipment. The force of his motion knocked the camera off its mount point and onto the floor breaking the lens and sending glass shards all around the airplane's floor.

He picked himself up and went and sat in one of the four plush and vastly oversized passenger chairs that occupied the front half of the passenger cabin. He put on some headphones, and tried to pretend he was in Tahiti. It was a place he went with Anja, before they were married which held fond memories for him. They were memories of time spent with her, back when life was so much simpler. He remembered watching her snorkel, and laying on the lounge chairs under thatched umbrellas, laughing and smiling, without a care in the world.

I wonder if we'll ever have that again or if too much damage has been done. NO! It's never too late to reconcile unless you decide it's too late. I need to stay away from Kennedy, get the

Digitalis, and save my wife.

Live so that thou mayest desire to live again - that is thy duty - for in any case thou wilt live again!

–Freidrich Nietzsche

CHAPTER 43

Caracas, Venezuela
Simon Bolivar International Airport

Dr. Marten Jansen gathered his belongings as the converted Boeing 737 he was riding in was about to land in Caracas, Venezuela. The passenger compartment was devoid of the standard row after row of three by three mini-chairs. Instead, Marten sat in the lounge which occupied the front quarter of the cabin. It was situated between a divider wall with a door to the rear of the aircraft, and the pilot's cockpit up in the front of the aircraft.

Marten checked the door to the pilot's compartment to confirm it was locked from his side of the wall. He then opened the door at the back of the lounge which revealed a hallway. On either side it was lined with doors to fully enclosed sleeping quarters, four in total. Past those were a galley, a standard half bath, and a full bath. The rear of the finished section of the plane was a conference room. It had an ornate table, with a Dutch flag embedded on the wood at both ends. In the center, was painted a modified Rod of Asclepius, identical to the one on Jake's pocket watch. At the rear of this room was another door which had a sign that read, "Cargo Hold."

Marten walked into the Cargo Hold after using a key card to release the lock on the steel reinforced door. Inside was a small room which occupied the rear most portion of the passenger level of the aircraft. It had a staircase leading down into the plane's hull or stowage compartments below. The room itself was utilitarian. The luxurious leather and extensive décor in the forward sections of the plane had given way to metal floors and unfinished surfaces. There was workout equipment on one half of the room. On the other was an elaborate workstation with more computer equipment than Best Buy.

Marten confirmed the hatch covering the stairs to the stowage level was locked. Then, he logged on to the computer at the workstation.

He entered a pass code and a chat window came up with the username Apogee, the same person with whom Devon Keyes had communicated. The Apogee user sent a message that read, "Have you acquired Mr. Keyes?"

Marten typed back, "Yes. There was an unexpected guest however."

"Anything you can't deal with?"

"Should be fine." Marten typed back.

"What about the Digitalis?"

"We're in route now to its location. I should have an update within hours, days at most."

The Apogee user inquired, "What about the team that Ms. Yashodhara sent to the island? What is their status?"

Marten typed, "We could not locate them. However, the entire Hunter Neurologics Island has been neutralized. Chances they survived the storm, without shelter, are remote at best."

"Very good. Now I just need you to locate the Digitalis. If it is not at Aguas Muertas, we will have only one option left. The Eagon brothers tell me we are well prepared should we need to execute it. But it will take time and we cannot be guaranteed of success. I am counting on you Marten. Do not let me down."

"CONNECTION TERMINATED" flashed across his screen.

Marten grabbed a phone handset nearby to the computer monitor and used it to announce over the plane's PA system, "We're about to land. Everyone meet me in the conference room in two minutes for a short debriefing on our next steps. Seems we'll need to be heavily armed and our safety cannot be assured. We are jumping into a bed of thorns here, so grab your vests, and God be with each of you." He had replaced his dorky appearance with confidence and authority.

*   *   *

In the conference room, Marten was joined at the table by three men. They walked in from the lower level of the plane and introduced themselves to Marten as if they had never met him before. Their names were Viktor, Daniel, and Tommy. Finally, from the hallway with the sleeping quarters, emerged Devon Keyes and Kate Stinson.

"Devon, send her back to the room. She'll have to wait there."

A slightly humiliated Kate Stinson left the conference room, slamming the door behind her. Marten explained the details of their mission to acquire the Digitalis and that there would be an extended risk of hostilities from competing interests.

*   *   *

Five minutes later the plane was on the ground in Caracas, Venezuela. As they were deplaning, Kate asked Devon, "What went on in there that I couldn't hear?"

"It was nothing important Kate. Listen, you need to

wear this," he handed her a bullet proof Kevlar vest to put on.

"What is this for?"

"It's just a precaution Kate. Damn it." He stopped talking abruptly.

Kate asked, "What? Damn it what?"

Devon pointed to the plane nearby that had just landed behind them and was taxing on the runway. On the side it had two gold monkeys and the word, "Moksha."

Kate said, "Isn't that the plane you were wondering about back at Isla Dedaleras? That's weird, now it's here. Do you think it's following us?"

Devon replied, "Shut up Kate. That's not the same plane. Don't be so stupid."

"No I'm sure of it. I saw it perfectly before it turned down that taxiway. It had those same cute monkeys on the side. Besides, why are you being so rude all of a sudden?"

"Kate, I told you to shut up. For your own well being, don't mention this again. And believe me when I tell you my rudeness is the least of your worries."

CHAPTER 44

Caracas, Venezuela
Simon Bolivar International Airport

As Jake and Kennedy walked off of Lavanya's Jet and into the tropical humidity of Simon Bolivar International Airport, they were greeted by Commander Collins, just as Lavanya had said. This time, he didn't shake their hands and didn't bother to smile. Instead, he looked them both up and down, laughed, and then said, "I hope you two have something else to wear. If you do, get it, but make it snappy. That's our ride just over there. It leaves in ten minutes," and he pointed to what looked like a circa 1950's propeller cargo plane. It was the type of plane one might see in an aeronautical museum, but not so much on an active runway.

Kennedy exclaimed, "You're kidding right? We're going to take that thing into the jungle? To Beedaz?"

"What the frig did you just say missy?" Commander Collins asked her.

"Well it's just that, it doesn't look like the safest type of plane for flying into an extremely remote and mountainous jungle region inhabited by drug cartels that are known to possess surface to air missiles."

"No, not that part. Just where in the hell do you think you're going?"

"Beedaz?"

Collins turned to a Latin American looking man to his right, "Hear that Jorge? The gringo thinks she's going to Beedaz." Jorge chuckled slightly, a quasi fake laugh meant to please his superior.

Kennedy wasn't accustomed to having miscalculated and so tried to explain herself, "Well, that is the only place on the maps in central Venezuela anywhere near Aguas Muertas. There's nothing else around it for miles except jungles and mountains."

"Missy, did they also tell you there's a spa where we're going?" Kennedy didn't respond, but looked at Collins with disdain. They also had Jake's undivided attention (and worry) when Collins finally explained, "You've been a bit misinformed is what I'm trying to tell ya. We're not going to no town. We're not going anywhere near civilization for that matter. Where we're going is one of the portals to H E double toothpick, HELLL," he drew out the word hell with a long southern Texas accent.

"Wha what are you talking about," Kennedy asked with a slight stutter giving away her newfound insecurity.

Collins went on, "Where we're going is right in the heart of territory controlled by the largest cocaine cartel operating in Venezuela. And it's not a place anyone in their right mind visits without an invitation. Hec, even with an invitation, you still wouldn't catch me there on a good day. Not sure what the hell that's saying about today, but this plane ain't about to take me back to Texas! Anyways, for the record, it's called B D A L or Beedal as we like to say, and there sure ain't nothing bedazzling about it." He turned to Jorge again, "Tell her what it means Jorge, I can never keep it straight myself, something about crying or the cliff to hell or whatever."

Jorge had grown up in the ghettos of Caracas and had a strong accent, but tried to explain, "It say, Borde Donde Angel Llora. I say its in Engleesh for jews: de edges oh where de angelah is being cries. It being whats they say it beings? Waterfallings?" Jorge smiled at them, pleased at what he considered a stellar translation.

Jake leaned in and whispered to Kennedy, "Allow me to translate. I think he said, the edge where the angels cry. No wait, make that the cliff where the angels cry, once you take away the literal translation."

"Hah! That's an impressive translation. Yah, sounded like that to me too," she smiled.

Jake laughed then asked, "What do you think it means? As far as I could tell it's possibly a waterfall at or near Aguas Muertas. But I am curious, exactly where did *you* find out about this Beedal place?"

"I have no idea what it means, or where we're going. And unfortunately, all the research I did on the plane, to prepare, was apparently misguided and worthless. But I will say, the way Collins described it really made it sound more appealing than the last all inclusive resort I went to in Mexico." She was trying to change the subject before he pressed her on how she knew about Beedal.

"Really?! Come on Kennedy! With the beaches they have over there? How can you say something like that?" Jake playfully asked her while brushing his hand across her arm. His prior aversion to flirting with her was suppressed by an overwhelming need to put her ease and try to trick her into revealing the truth, "So tell me Kennedy, where is Beedal and what does it have to do with Aguas Muertas?"

She sighed, realizing she would have to reveal to him at least some information. She explained, "Beedal is simply the name given by the local tribes to the waterfall near Aguas Muertas. It's extremely tucked away in the depths of the jungle. Supposedly so much so that it's impossible to reach by even skilled hikers. Historians think it was an offshoot Mayan settlement. Today, rumors abound as to its use as a headquarters for the most powerful drug cartel in Latin America, just as Collins mentioned. But there are also rumors as to its former use by the CIA for a variety of clandestine projects thought to have been kept off the books."

"Off the books? My father was involved in projects that were off the books?! Are you kidding me? Can this week get any worse?!"

Collins interrupted, "All right you two lovebirds, stop playing games and get yourselves situated on the plane. We only have a few more minutes until take off. Jorge here will help you with your stuff." Collins walked away and boarded the plane. He was soon joined by Jake, Kennedy, and Jorge. There were three other men already on board, in addition to Collins, Jorge, and a single pilot up front. The interior of the plane was as simple as one might have expected, but fortunately, there were no chickens or other strange cargo.

Jake looked at Kennedy as they felt the wheels lift from the ground. Since the plane crash a few days earlier, when looking at each other on takeoff, landing, or just about any other time in flight, both of them shared a unique bond.

The other three men on board were introduced after liftoff. Marcus Wilds was Collin's second in command and a former Army Ranger. His two sidekicks were heavily armed. Robert Mulligan was supposed to be an expert in electronics and especially communications to/from geographically challenging locations, such as the extremely rigorous mountains of Venezuela. Mulligan preferred to be called by his last name, strangely enough. He was an Irishman who bore no shame excessively playing the role, "I'm cool because I drink tons of Guinness," (never mind the beer belly). The other man was a young 30's something Italian looking guy named Johnny Antonelli. He was a, "mountainous terrain field specialist," which was explained to mean he was a wilderness survival expert. Judging by the amount of weaponry he was carrying, they figured he survived not through specialized skills but rather by brut force killing.

What didn't make sense to Jake was why they would need so much weaponry and high tech gadgetry. The risks had been explained with broad strokes that put a veil over the true nature of what they were about to experience. Not knowing the details is what scared Jake the most. Because not knowing meant there was no way to be fully prepared. He was restless and anxious and not only bothered by the weapons, but also by the suddenness of the departure, and the strange characters Lavanya had sent to "help" him in acquiring the Digitalis.

*   *   *

They had been in the air for about an hour when Collins was walking around the plane handing out big oversized and heavy backpacks. Jake asked him, "What are these? What are they for?" But Collins didn't answer.

Instead he simply finished handing them out until each person had one. Another twenty minutes later he returned and asked Jake and Kennedy, "What's wrong with you two? Why haven't you put on your packs yet?"

"What? While we're in our chairs? Don't you think that would be a bit uncomfortable?"

Collins leaned in closer, clinched his jaw, and with a soft tone that resonated decibels louder said, "Kid, you talk back to me one more time and it will be the last time I try to help ya. Now put on the God damn pack."

As a lawyer, Jake thought he had seen every type of personality in the courts of Washington, D.C. And after the events of the last week, he thought he had seen and experienced more than most people read about in their lifetimes. But Collins was unique. Jake had never met anyone like him.

As Collins walked away without looking back, Jake was scrambling to put the pack on, only because he realized Collins was probably withholding information. Something bad was about to happen, although Jake had no idea what.

Kennedy also put on her pack. Then the two of them sat there, with their butts only half on their chairs since the pack occupied most of the seat space. They stared at Collins perplexed by his odd command and stinging personality. They studied him and watched to see what crazy cockamamie gibberish he would spew out next.

Not more than five minutes later, Collins grew excited. It was as if someone had stuck him with a shot of adrenaline intended for a horse. He walked right up to Jake and grabbed him by the backpack, forcing him to stand up in the airplane. Then Collins said while looking him over, "Yup, seems like you got it on right, nice and tight. That should do the trick."

"The trick for what?" Jake asked.

"Damn it man, now what did I tell you a few minutes back about talking back to me?" But as Jake opened his mouth to crack some sort of wise ass comeback, Collins grabbed him again by the backpack and started to swing him around to his left where Jorge had stood behind them a second earlier. Jake's eyes grew wide, when he saw that Jorge was stepping back and releasing the lock on the cabin door. In a matter of seconds, Jorge was swinging it open and Jake was flying through the air before he, or anyone else could say or do anything. He closed his eyes, then opened them, then closed them again as he fell into the sky.

CHAPTER 45

Aguas Muertas, Venezuela
(1 hour by Air from Caracas - Roadless Jungle Region)

While falling through clouds, Jake finally worked up the courage to open his eyes and look back up at the airplane. He saw the others had also jumped out after him. Kennedy was closest, presumably also pushed, although he wondered what reality was when it came to her. She was trailed by the rest of the team. Seeing the others pull their rip cords and realizing what was going on, Jake felt around on the pack's straps for anything that seemed like he should pull it. Because of the force of the wind, it was practically impossible for him to keep his eyes open when looking towards the ground. Eventually he found the rip cord, opened the chute, and began to float slowly into Venezuela's equatorial rainforest below.

On the way down he had time to think. In fact, it seemed like an eternity while his mind was racing with thoughts of his father's past and the possible evil it entailed. He wondered,

What is the Digitalis and how bad did it have to be that they would go to such lengths to hide it? What was so sinful it

had to be tucked away in the depths of hell? How dangerous does it have to be that my own father would have kept it a secret from me?

Jake landed as gracefully as can be expected for a person on their first jump, with zero training or preparation, let alone warning for what they were about to do. Once on the ground, he tried to see where the others were landing. All of them appeared fairly close by, although well out of site after passing the top of the jungle canvas. On the ground around him was dense foliage which included a large number of palm varieties. They were less than pleasant to walk through as the leaves were sharp and would cut the skin. Jake tried to find a route towards where he saw the others land. He made his way through a swath of vegetation which consisted more of broadleaf tropical species such as banana trees, ferns, and the like.

Finally caught up to them, Jake saw they were walking along what looked like an abandoned air strip.

*   *   *

There was a small hangar at the far end, which looked rundown and must have been deprived of maintenance for at least the last fifty years. Other than that structure and the cracked, weed infested pavement of the airstrip, there was nothing but tropical jungle in sight. A closer inspection of the runway showed it was pockmarked and decayed to such an extent that trying to land on it would have been deadly.

Two Jeeps suddenly emerged from the jungle, near the hangar building. Marcus began barking out instructions, and taking control of the situation, "Mulligan, you take the broad and her lover in the first Jeep. Johnny, Collins, Jorge, and I will lead the way in the other one. We don't have a lot of time as we're a little behind schedule, so let's get going."

Why does everyone in this gang keep calling us lovers? It's making me feel guilty when I haven't even done anything. At least, nothing I can recall. Maybe I should try to live up to the perception.

Marcus Wilds and Jorge wasted little time loading hardcover silver metal cases into the Jeeps. When Jake asked what was in the cases, the only response he got was silence. No one in their tight knit group seemed interested in explaining anything to Jake or Kennedy. It was unfortunate because, when things were left up to his imagination, Jake was skilled at coming up with extreme scenarios that were far from the truth. Instead of allowing rational thought to prevail and provide logical explanations, his mind created myriad contorted realities. He figured it wouldn't be a stretch to assume whatever was inside those cases could be the same types of explsoive weapons used to destroy Hunter Neurologics in D.C. and all the buildings at Isla Dedaleras.

I wonder if they're going to destroy this place too? Maybe they don't want to get the Digitalis; maybe they really just want to destroy it? I can't let do that.

*   *   *

The Jeeps came to a stop two hours into the bumpy ride along the dirt roads of the Venezuelan jungle. They took less than five minutes to stretch in what felt like a mosquito nest, but turned out to be considered, "solomente un poco," as described by Jorge. Then, without any further explanation as to where they were going, or how long it would take them to get there, the group set off on foot into the jungle, through a narrow trail that only existed because of Jorge's handiwork with a four foot long machete.

At the second hour and hundredth mosquito bite into their hike it occurred to Jake, there would be insufficient daylight for them to make it back from where they came without spending the night somewhere. Although he was exhausted from their travels and had been operating on fear and adrenaline for the last couple of days, Jake's blood pressure started spiking. He no longer trusted Kennedy and never trusted Commander Collins or his crew. That left him feeling remarkably isolated and alone in the middle of a very rugged and foreign place. With the sun clearly starting to fade into the horizon, and although they were on a stretch of level terrain, his heart was beating so hard it felt as if it were going to pop out from his chest at any moment. Jake stepped off to the side of the trail to allow the others to keep walking. He needed to pause for a moment and regain control. Collins and Marcus Wilds whispered to each other just after passing him, but Jake couldn't make out what they said.

Kennedy stopped walking, and sat near Jake, to try to help him. She said, "Jake, you are having a panic attack. You need to calm down."

The idiocracy of her stating the obvious was all it took. He laughed and was snapped back to calmness just as quickly as he had left.

Hmm, she's either a really dumb blonde for stating the obvious, or brilliant and was trying to help me laugh. Maybe she's not so bad after all. Maybe I should give her more of a chance, all things considered.

Jake and Kennedy pressed on and another twenty minutes later, the group found themselves at the edge of a wide river. To their right, they stared up at an incredible waterfall, the noise of which forced them to yell when talking to one another. Behind them, they peered back at the huge hill they had finished descending. The rocks and dense jungle made it impossible to walk in either direction along the river. Their only options were to navigate across the water, or go back the way they came. Just as Jake was coming to terms with their situation, Marcus came over to him and said, "Anything you want to keep dry, you best take off and put in a pack. Each of you will be carrying at least one pack across."

Jorge was already at the very edge of the river bank with Collins. They were putting things into an open pack, including their pants. Both of them were stripped down to only their underwear and packing everything else, including their side arms. The other two men, Robert Mulligan and Johnny Antonelli were further ahead, and already wading through water up to their chests, while holding the metal cases with back packs stacked on top, over their heads. Jake looked at Kennedy, to see if she was nervous about wading through the water. Instead, he noticed her noticing the biceps and broad shoulders on the two men already in the water.

"See anything good," he asked her.

"Nothing that looks terribly pleasant," Kennedy responded.

Good answer. Wait, stop it. No, I wasn't just jealous. I love my wife, Anja. I wouldn't be in this God awful jungle trying to save her if I didn't.

They stripped down to their underwear, put their clothes in their packs, and proceeded to wade across the river with the others. After they were half way across, but falling behind the rest of the group, Collins yelled out to them, "Don't dawdle out there. This water is known to be infested with piranha, anaconda, and just about every other kind of unpleasant water creature you ever imagined in your worst nightmares."

Jake turned to Kennedy who had taken it to heart and was high tailing her way past him to reach the far bank as quickly as possible, "Now he tells us, eh?" Jake yelled out as she waded awkwardly past him.

She looked back at him as she passed and replied, "Definitely not cool. But I'm not sticking around in this water any longer than necessary to find out if he's telling the truth."

"He's just messin' don't let him scare ya!" Jake responded. Of course, that was the precise moment he felt a sharp pinch on his right calf. He yelped out, "What was that?" And then he too picked up the pace.

Once they were on the far bank, everyone dried off and put their clothes back on. Jake asked Collins, "What now?" But the man continued his theme of only talking when he felt like it. Jorge took pity on Jake and Kennedy and explained their next steps.

"Ahora, we necessario rest. Den, we be walkings into de crying oh de angelas."

"What the hell is he saying," Jake asked Kennedy.

"Well, since he's pointing to that path over there, I think he's saying we have to walk into the waterfall."

"Path? What path? I don't see a path. There's no path over there."

"Just relax Jake. That's a path. Look at the others; they're putting no-slip tape on the bottom of their shoes. Wet rocks are incredibly slippery, especially when covered in moss like those ones. We should get some of that no-slip tape and do the same."

Before they could ask, Marcus Wilds handed each of them a pair of self bonding rubber strips that had a sandpaper like surface and told them to glue them to the bottom of their shoes. "You two are about to see one of Mother Nature's better sights. And believe me, you ain't never gonna read about this one in any books. It's kept off the maps and charts for a reason, so enjoy it while you can. Once we're through the falls and hike up to the top, what you're going to see on the other side isn't quite as visually appealing if you catch my drift."

Jake blurted out, "I don't care how visually appealing anything is if that means we are there."

"Yeah…," Wilds responded, "we'll be there after that. So don't go straying away or we're not likely to ever find you again. At least, not in one piece."

"He's just trying to scare you Jake. Don't worry." Kennedy said, trying to assuage his fear.

"I'm so tired at this point, that being scared is not even possible for me any longer. Let's confront whatever it is we need to confront and get this over with."

Wilds, Collins, Mulligan, and Antonelli all started laughing. Collins said, "Right on Rambo. But hold your horses when we get there, or you WILL wind up dead. And no, I'm not trying to scare you. I'd put your chances of survival, if you're smart and listen to us, at 25% maybe 30. Again, that's if you listen to us and everything goes according to plan."

"What if it doesn't go according to plan," Jake sheepishly asked. But there was no response.

Sobered by Collins' stern warning, no one talked much more until they were about half way along the makeshift path that led directly into the waterfall. That was when Jake said, "So Kennedy, if odds are we're gonna die when we get to this place, are you going to finally come clean and tell me how you know about military choppers, guns, and everything else?"

"Sure Jake, sure. I'll tell youuuu…" her left foot slipped on a wet rock and she fell forward hitting her right knee on the edge of the cliff, hard enough to yelp out loud, before rolling onto her side and clenching the injured knee. Her other leg dropped over the side of the rocks and hung in the air, a hundred feet above the next landing spot.

Jake ran over to grab her and pull her body back fully onto the ledge. He asked, "Are you OK?"

"Yes. I think so. I banged up my knee pretty good, but I think I can still walk on it."

They were able to proceed, although not as quickly as before, and Kennedy miserably whimpered under her breath every so often. Jake took her pack, to free some weight off her injured leg. That left him carrying two of the oversized packs across the perilously slick rocks.

Eventually they reached a crossing point with the waterfall. They were standing directly in front of the surging water. And because of its height, the water came down with such force and noise, that it was nearly impossible for them to hear each other when talking. Jorge pantomimed while Collins, Wilds, Mulligan, and Antonelli all literally plunged themselves into and through the waterfall. Kennedy went next, after asking Jake not leave her behind. And Jorge brought up the rear. Each of them jumped into the fall head first, running as fast as they could. The force of the water was like having a Mack truck dropped onto them. Before their entire bodies made it all the way through, they were pounded into the ground. With their calves still extending through the waterfall, it felt like a saw was slicing them off. The men on the other side grabbed each successive person by the wrists and pulled them the rest of the way through. Every last one of them had a bloodied face from hitting the water and or rocks in the process, even the tough guy Collins. He had a bloodied lip. Mulligan had a full on broken nose which appeared the worst of the injuries. Jake and Kennedy escaped with more superficial scratches, having had the luxury of others to pull them through.

Behind the waterfall was another world. The stone cliff had what looked like a series of houses carved into it. There was a stair case which ascended behind the waterfall to the top of the cliff. It was set back behind the box like houses, which sheltered it from the froth of the waterfall and kept it dry. But it also sheltered it from what little light was left in the day. In their exhausted and beat up states, it would be an agonizing and dangerous walk up to the top.

CHAPTER 46

Borde Donde Angel Llora
Venezuelan Jungle

After making their way to the top of the cliff, they set up camp about a hundred yards from the river. Jorge was pitching tents, while the others were setting up a satellite dish, computers, and a portable generator. Jake didn't bother asking what it was all about, as he was tired of being treated second class. His patience for Commander Collins was at an end. He and Kennedy just sat and rested, and watched the others fiddling with high tech gadgetry.

After a while, Marcus and Collins told "the lovebirds" to come with them. They walked another fifty yards away from the river to the edge of a steep drop off. It wasn't exactly a cliff, but it also was a steep enough hill that any descent without ropes could be impossible or lethal even for highly skilled climbers. Marcus and Collins took turns peering over the edge, down into the valley below, with binoculars.

Jake asked, "So, is this the place where the angels cry? The Beedal?"

"No you moron," Collins replied, "That was the waterfall you just hiked up." Jake wanted to punch the man. But Collins distracted him from his anger by handing him the binoculars and instructing him to have a look down below. Collins went on, "For your sake, you better hope this is where we find the Digitalis."

Jake was shocked to be peering through binoculars at Kate Stinson, the woman he recognized as Devon Keyes' assistant. She was sitting, bound in a chair, in the middle of an open field in front of an industrial looking building made of rusty sheet metal for its roof and window coverings. The walls were plain, pockmarked cinderblock. There was something amiss though with the building's fatigued look. Jake contemplated while examining every detail of the building:

This is like déjà vu. It reminds me of those amusement park replicas where they make things look older then they are, like the wild wild west or old ghost towns. The construction looks solid, secure, and yet someone has tried to make this place look tattered and decrepit just like the plantation house back on Isla Dedaleras.

There were five men, all South American looking, standing around Kate. One of the men was pacing back and forth about five feet from where she sat bound to a chair. While Jake was glued to the binoculars, the electronics and communications expert Robert Mulligan was hastily assembling a super high sensitivity, long distance listening device. Jake's full attention was drawn back to the binoculars as he observed the pacing man down in the valley below abruptly change direction, walk toward Kate and punch her in the jaw closed fisted.

Blood spewed from her mouth before her head followed the stream. She fell sideways, still bound to the chair, and hit the ground hard. She was lying on her side, blood oozing from her mouth and lips, and tears clearly visible on her face, even through binoculars from 250 yards away.

While still on the ground, the same man placed a

hand gun to Kate's temple and was clearly yelling at her. For a split second, Jake started to stand from his kneeling position, thinking he was going to go run down there and help the woman. He said out loud to Marcus and Collins, "We have to do something. We can't let them kill her."

"Relax Rambo. We will keep our cover for now. They might not kill her. They're probably just trying to get information, which is hard to extract from a dead person."

"The word might isn't very reassuring."

Marcus pushed him and said, "Shut up and listen. We need to know just as much as they do." Then he handed Jake a set of wireless headphones which were attached to the mini satellite looking dish he had finished setting up. Jake could hear the conversation down the hill, some two to three hundred yards away with stunning clarity. Each of them had on a head set. But they were all puzzled and confused by what they were hearing.

A gruff, short, but lean looking Latino man took the place of the gun wielding maniac in Kate Stinson's face. This man, unlike the other, was talking calmly, and strangely enough, with virtually perfect English. He had almost no accent, "Agent Stinson, let's go through this one more time. We need to know where to find the missing encryption key to the Digitalis. In order to do that, we need to know where your fascist spy agencies have already looked. We know the CIA, NSA, FBI, all of them have been involved, and we know they all have copies of it. There is no way something so powerful would not have multiple backups. So I suggest you tell us where to find it, or I'll have to let Pedro there practice his boxing a little more."

What are they talking about? CIA? NSA? Encryption keys to what? I thought she was a summer intern at Devon's firm. And why would drug dealers care about the Digitalis?

"What am I watching?" Jake finally asked out loud with a tone that insinuated he wasn't going to tolerate Collins' silent treatment any longer. He wanted answers.

He *needed* answers, as he felt like his life had unraveled. Slowly but surely, everything that used to be his reality, one after another, in an almost planned progression, was turning out to be something completely different than what he had thought.

Good God, it's like I'm in the Truman Show, only with working airplanes and parachutes. This must be a much larger studio set.

There was never a more dizzying moment in Jake's life than that split second, in the middle of nowhere Venezuela, where he first started thinking that there would be absolutely nothing left of his life that he could safely believe was real.

Anja is real. No one can fake real love. She is still real.

Marcus pushed Jake's head to turn his eyes back down to the bottom of the valley and said, "Just keep watching and learning, maybe we'll hear something useful, like where to find the Digitalis. Besides, it's your friend's woman down there. So don't turn to us for answers as to why her new compadres seem to think she's a spook."

Down in the valley, Kate whimpered and grunted. She looked totally exasperated while trying to muster enough energy to voice an answer, "Look, you have my ID, you know I work for the Scientia Pro Curatio. And that means there is going to be hell to pay when they find out how you're treating me. And worse, when they find out you let Devon and Jansen get away. They are the ones who can tell you how to get the Digitalis. I wish I knew myself. That was my primary mission. Believe me, if I did know how to get it already, I wouldn't be in this mosquito infested hell hole."

"Damn it Gringo! You know, Pedro here is a fine boxer! But he's been wasting a lot of his time looking for this encryption key. You and I both know where the Digitalis is, but we cannot get to it without that key. And as for Devon and Dr. Jansen, they are inside having a relaxing meal. In fact, they are the ones that want us to find out what you know, but they didn't give us much time to get answers, so we're working against the clock. Now, the thing is, I'm starting to think we might not find the key, at least not with your help. So maybe to make the best of the situation, we at least let Pedro get some boxing practice." The man talking stood up straight and turned to the others in the group with him, "What do you say boys, do we untie the broad and see how long she can last?"

One of the men responded with, "Awww come on now, that's hardly fair, she's barely half Pedro's size." Pedro was the tallest and bulkiest in the group, probably somewhere around 6'4" and easily 255lbs of what looked like solid muscle. Nonetheless, the leader of the group proceeded to untie Kate while the others repositioned in the opening to make an informal circle around her. Pedro just stood and stared at her, dead in the eyes. Once untied from the chair, Kate was barely able to even stand up straight given the abuses she had already endured.

Jake, witnessing all this grew anxious and panicked. He had seen enough death already. Finally he demanded, "That's it, we go down there now and help this woman. I'm not going to sit here and watch her get beaten to death by that man. There's no freak'n wa…" Marcus cut him off by grabbing his right arm and twisting it behind him in such a way that he was then able to easily push Jake face first into the dirt.

"Now you listen to me you son of a bitch. There are a few things, quite a few things, you don't know about what's going on right now. Apparently one of the most obvious is that you will be doing only what I, Commander Collins, Johnny, Rob, or even Jorge tell you to do. In other words, you don't make any decisions. We make them for you. Another thing, perhaps a less obvious one, you also don't realize – is that you should believe me when I tell you that woman down there knows more than what you heard her telling those men. I would bet my family jewels on it. She ain't no legal secretary. That's for damn sure, and she knew exactly what she was getting into with this mission. The Scientia Pro Curatio doesn't send out amateurs. They have agents that are generally considered far superior to the CIA's best and brightest. If she's still alive when we go into that compound later tonight, then, and only then, will we do our best to save her. But we are not going to sacrifice our own objectives just because you have another crush on yet another hot broad. Hell, if we did that every time you had a crush, we'd have no time left for anything else. Besides, for all we know, what you're watching down there could be completely staged. It could be just a fake scene designed to get some sucker like you to show his cards. I sure hope you haven't already blown our cover."

Jake and Marcus Wilds were locked in a staring contest when their bickering was interrupted by the sound of a single gun shot.

CHAPTER 47

Venezuelan Jungle

Blood gushed from Kate Stinson's temple as her body lay limp in its final resting place. Because of their bickering, none of them saw exactly how Kate went from being a boxing bag to the recipient of a forty-five caliber bullet in the head. The Latino men that had surrounded her all walked away and into the fortress-like building behind them, while Jake Hunter chastised his companions for doing nothing.

Jake's stomach was turning at what he had witnessed and he was nearly hysterical from a loss of control over his own emotions. Kennedy, having heard the gunshot as well, while lingering a few feet away, came running up to the three men on their perch overlooking the execution site in the valley below. As usual, she was by Jake's side at just the right moment. She grabbed him by the shoulders and pushed him ten yards back, deeper into the jungle and further away from Marcus Wilds and Commander Collins.

She kept pushing Jake until he was backed up against a tree with her face directly up in front of his. They could feel each other's breath. Tears were streaming down Jake's cheeks from the shame of not having tried to help another human being in need. Kennedy glanced quickly at his lips then back to his eyes. She could see anger and terror resonating in the glow of his hazel-green eyes. Even under the circumstances she was totally enamored of the man and struggled to think of anything other than wanting to kiss him. Kennedy had caught him, literally, in a moment of weakness and knew two things with complete certainty: first, she could have gotten away with a kiss, and second, she knew that she was going to regret it for the rest of her life if she didn't try.

She pressed her lips to his. At first, Jake didn't move a muscle. He started to reciprocate, for only a fraction of a second. Then, he collapsed to the ground, held his head, and wished Anja still loved him, and wanted him, in the same way Kennedy did.

Their fleeting moment together was officially ended when Marcus Wilds, the ever compassionate commando, yelled out, "Hey marriage wrecker, get that SOB ready. We are going in after dark. That's about an hour from now, maybe two, max."

*   *   *

Each of them was assigned a set of night vision goggles. Unaccustomed to their bulky weight on his head, Jake threw his to the ground and chose to rely on only his own eyesight despite the remarkably dark conditions in the remote jungle. Collins chastised him, "Don't be a fool. Down there in that valley, there won't be any moonlight. It's going to be pitch black. If you don't believe me now, at least take the night vision goggles with you, so once you get down there, you have the option." Jake strapped them to his waist, but was still in a partial state of shock over the killing he had witnessed earlier. Despondency left him lackadaisical and nonchalant about any risks to his own life.

Jorge stayed behind in the camp while Jake and Kennedy rappelled with the four commandos down the side of the hill, which lead to the strange building in the valley below. Collins was in command up in front, Mulligan and Johnny were in the middle, and Marcus Wilds was bringing up the rear, behind Jake and Kennedy.

The four commandos each had machine guns. Kennedy had been given a short Uzi, and Jake was carrying only a handgun, having declined an automatic weapon. He preferred less baggage, thinking it would be more important to travel light and keep his hands free. He also had secretly brought with him a satellite phone from the communications tent Robert Mulligan had set up in their base camp.

About fifty yards from the building, Marcus stopped and looked into a small notebook he was carrying. Then he walked around the side of a large tree and started kicking away scrub brush with his boots. Underneath the jungle vines and foliage were two steel doors with an electronic LED and number pad, which surprisingly, was lit up. Marcus entered a code and another panel opened just below the LED screen. It was a retinal scanner.

Jake lamented out loud, "That's just great. Travel all day, catch a connection, jump out of connection, ride through mosquito breeding grounds, and now this. There is no way we're getting past a retinal scanner. They are not fake-outable."

Marcus stopped what he was doing, gripped Jake's throat so hard he started gasping and then whispered into his ear, "There are plenty of men down here that would be glad to kill ya just for the fun of it, but if you talk again and blow our cover, I'll do you myself. Besides, fake-outable ain't a real word; so shut the hell up." Then he threw Jake to the ground, which did not go over so well, as he promptly jumped up and was about to rush Marcus. At the last second, Collins stepped in between them and diffused the situation.

Marcus dug into a pack he brought with him from the base camp and pulled out what looked like a small portable

DVD player. He powered it on and launched a program which displayed a flash page that read, "Biometric Bypass Utility." Then a message box popped up which said, "Input name and biometric identification type." Marcus typed in the name, "Dr. William Hunter," then, "right retina," and pressed enter. A new screen popped up that read, "Enter desired location," and Marcus typed in, "Borde Donde Angel Llora." The screen displayed a progress bar and flashed the word, "Processing." Finally, a yellow exclamation appeared, along with a new message, WARNING: this location at level ten risk to life rating for previous five years. Use extreme caution. When ready, click the green GO arrow and place device up to scanner."

"What is a risk to life rating," Kennedy asked Collins.

Collins looked her up and down in a way that made her feel sleazy and then said, "What do you think it is? Suffice it to say the worst ranking is a ten, so if you survive this, you're in an elite club. The only problem is, there are no other members."

Marcus clicked the GO arrow and an extremely high definition image of what looked like Jake's father's eye appeared on the screen. Marcus placed the portable device's screen up to the biometric security panel on the steel doors and a green, "Access granted," light turned on.

"What!? How did he just do that?" Jake wondered aloud.

Kennedy didn't want to further reveal her true expertise, but she had fallen for Jake and wanted to spare him the further embarrassment of being ignored once again by the others, so she explained, "It's a biometric impersonation device Jake. It essentially takes a high definition multi-layered digital recording of the biometric input in question, which in this case was your father's right retina, and then it plays it back. It tricks the biometric security scanner on the doors into thinking your father is really here."

"I didn't see that in the Memorex commercials."

"Exactly," she responded, while trying to control her giggling, "You wouldn't have seen this anyway, not even elite U.S. military troops have access to this technology."

Jake went on, "I get it. But I'm afraid to ask why my father's right retina has been recorded in the first place and why exactly, it would open these doors down here in the middle of nowhere."

"It's because we're not in the middle of nowhere. We're in the middle of somewhere very important, and very highly protected. I think the real answers as to why, are exactly what we're about to find out, once we're inside."

CHAPTER 48

Venezuelan Jungle

Inside the steel doors was a dim staircase leading to an underground corridor. The group started in, while Jake and Kennedy lagged just far enough behind to allow some whispering between the two of them.

Jake was asking her what she thought of standing by idly watching a person executed and doing nothing to try to help. He insisted, "Look, I think it's wrong. What I don't know is what everyone else in this motley crew of ours is here for. They claim they want some damn Nakuru file or Digitalis. But what is so special about the Digitalis, that it justifies letting a woman be executed. That's not something I am ever going to forget having witnessed. I mean, what would society say if they knew? What would people think if all of this was front page news on the New York Times? Who knows? They might say it was OK to sacrifice her life under these circumstances. I wouldn't agree. What about you Kennedy? Would you agree?"

"No, I would have fought to save her. We could have saved her and still gotten into this dungy, moldy, musty underground tunnel." They had closed in on the others at that point and decided to cease their conversation. The way forward was blocked by yet another heavily reinforced door. Marcus once again made quick work of getting the green light to proceed and they entered a large room. Collins flicked the light switch and several bulbs popped as if they hadn't been used in years. They were all surprised at what they saw once the room was illuminated.

Jake spoke first, wondering, "How do they power this place? We can't be anywhere near a power plant."

"Solar power," Kennedy informed him, "There were panels on the far side of the roof. What I don't get is who the men were you saw above ground and if this level is isolated from the rest."

The entire floor was contained underground with no exterior windows. Its design was efficient in purpose, containing medical equipment and strange looking accessories right out in the open. It was strikingly similar to the main research lab that used to exist at Isla de Las Dedaleras. But there were a few differences.

For example, lining one of the walls were cages big enough to hold large animals or even seven foot tall humans. And all the operating tables had built in heavy duty restraints.

The room was covered in layers of dust and cobwebs. Generally speaking there were no signs of human presence in the lab for what looked to be a significant amount of time.

A spider that resembled a tarantula was crawling across one of the operating tables. Besides the door they came in through, there was only one other exit, which was an elevator on the opposite side of the room. The indicator panel over the door was working and fully illuminated. It showed the elevator to be on Level One while they were on Sublevel 3.

"We need to secure this place," Marcus said as he walked over to the elevator with Rob Mulligan, the electronics expert. They ripped off the elevator panel, twisted and cut wires, and then pronounced it out of service.

Rob Mulligan, usually not one of the more vocal in the group, then turned to the rest of them and said, "We probably have no more than fifty minutes, or until they figure out the elevator is disabled, to get what we need and get out of here."

Collins gave marching orders, "All right Jake, this is where you come in. According to the schematics we were given, that room to your left there contains an archive of all the work done by your father as well as his previous work on the Nakuru trials in Africa. You get to sort through it and find us the Nakuru files. While you're doing that, my men and I will get the Digitalis. Kennedy, you can do whatever the hell you want in the meantime but stay out of our way."

She muttered under her breath, "Wait, where will you get the Digitalis? How do you know what you're looking for?"

Jake was also getting excited and asked about Nakuru before Collins could even respond to Kennedy, "So are you saying these Nakuru clinical trials took place in Africa?"

"That's what we're told. But we're also told there's nothing left there at Nakuru."

"You mean Nakuru is a place?"

"Some shantytown in Kenya, I am told."

"More mysteries and secrets. Lovely." Jake sighed, overwhelmed at the thought that his father had done so much secret work. He was perplexed as to what it involved. Then it occurred to him, cold blooded murderers were in the same building, only a few floors away. He asked, "What about the elevator? What if they try to use the elevator right away, say like in the next few minutes, rather than fifty?"

Rob Mulligan responded, "If they are able to get it working after my handiwork, then they find us, and we run as fast as we can. There are way too many of them to expect to win in a gun fight with these guys. They're paid to stand guard over this place. Part of that payment involves laundering drug money. Not exactly the type of people we want to mess with. Unfortunately, that's why we couldn't help that woman you saw killed either. But just have a look around this place. No one has been in here in years. They're not very likely to suddenly decide to come snooping around down here tonight unless we tip them off to our presence." Jake was slightly relieved but still not convinced, "OK, so we'll avoid tipping them off that we're down here. But why the fifty minute limit then?"

"Because when this lab was sealed eight years ago, an alarm mechanism was installed on the vault containing the Digitalis. Any tampering with security, cutting wires, etc., triggers the alarm. It will take us about thirty minutes to get into the vault. That leaves another 10 for contingency. That is, if we don't blow it all answering your silly questions."

"I get it. We don't have a lot of time, so you're right, let's not waste it."
Besides, I can't wait to finally know what the Digitalis is made of. What it does… why it's worth killing for.

Jake continued, "One last thing though, how do you know all of this?"

Marcus responded, "Your father told me, personally. It came straight from the horses mouth. When I asked him why he was finally cooperating, he said it was to protect you."

Kennedy grabbed Jake's arm and pulled him away into a nearby office. She said, "Stop prying. They're not likely to tell you the truth. Besides, the only thing that matters right now is getting the Nakuru files, and them getting into that vault. We don't want to spend any longer in here than we have to."

"Roger that General Kennedy."

"Sorry Jake. I didn't mean to be demanding. But let's try to stay focused while we're on the clock."

"Right. Good plan." They started sorting through files. Jake was lost flipping through the paper files when

Kennedy called him to check out her slightly different approach. She asked him to have a look at a video she was playing on a monitor in the office. The box for the video simply had the number 574 written on it. It was an old fashioned Betamax style cassette, covered in dust from years of non-use.

A title screen on the monitor displayed, "Nakuru Clinical Trial Patient #574, Day 77, two days prior to subject termination." What they saw next was beyond their wildest imagination.

CHAPTER 49

Underground Facility in Venezuelan Jungle

Jake stared at the video in total disbelief. It was an older tape and included images of a much younger version of his father, working alongside another man whom he did not recognize.

The two men in the video were observing a patient from behind a mirrored wall. Kennedy turned up the volume on the monitor so they could hear the commentary by Jake's father and his counterpart, who had a nametag reading, Dr. Trevor Coates.

Jake turned it back down just a tad, saying to her, "I don't want to draw the others' attention. Don't need to hand them anything extra on a silver platter. Let's be sure we know every detail of everything we find before sharing."

"Agreed," Kennedy replied.

Jake's father, Dr. William Hunter continued his presentation on the video, "As you can see, patient 574 exhibits all the trademark adverse effects we have seen to date. The control mechanism put in place has only exacerbated the problem by having an unanticipated magnifying effect. At this point in the study, we have no feasible options to pursue as a means of avoiding the irreparable damage to patient psyche that occurs as part of this project."

Jake talked over the video, "Why is the patient's face blocked out? Who do you suppose patient 574 was?"

"Shhh!" Kennedy demanded, "I want to hear this. They probably were protecting the patient's identity for some reason. Listen to the video, maybe we can find out."

Jake's father continued, "When we focus instead on the second branch of the study, which we have dubbed, Digitalis, and which has as it's sole mission the ability to control and shape individual beliefs with regard to right and wrong, terrifying and safe, and other variations of basic perceptions, we see the current approach as remarkably effective. The only caveat being that patient mental stability is not sustainable for prolonged durations." Jake leaned over and pushed pause on the tape player. He was irate.

"You mean to tell me my father helped devise a medical process for brainwashing!? Kennedy, is this really real? Can that really be done? I mean, can science actually be used to change what people think?"

"I don't know Jake. But judging by how well hidden this place is, and by the amount of interest in the, "Digitalis," I would guess this is all real, very real, in fact," she paused then said, "Also, you asked me to be honest with you. Well, the truth is I wouldn't be here if all this weren't real."

Jake thought for a moment, desperately searching for a way to justify and rationalize his father's involvement, "I suppose if we didn't do it, someone else would have – the Russians, the Chinese, someone. In fact, I've always felt terrorist organizations around the world must have something like this in order to be able to constantly recruit and develop an endless supply of suicide bombers." Jake paused again, "My God Kennedy, I hope my father is not responsible for something like that."

"I highly doubt it Jake. I have only worked for your

father a short time, but he is the last person I would suspect of being interested in or even capable of using science for anything other than good. Besides, it looks like your father was young in this video. Clearly he was not in charge. Perhaps whatever happened here is why your father is so dedicated to helping others now."

"Maybe… Let's find out. Let's see how this works. Let's see what exactly he was involved in. I want to know every detail about what kind of twisted perversion of medicine they created in this torture chamber."

In the video, the other man present with Jake's father stepped into the center of the screen and announced:

> "I am Trevor Coates, Managing Director of the Digitalis Project. In this project, our research was premised on cognitive neuropsychology[12], but we took the sum of knowledge in that field and used it for applied medicine; i.e., not only do we use brain imaging on patients with cognitive impairments[13] such as head traumas and illnesses (Alzheimer's being a critical focus area in this study), resulting in memory loss, but also, healthy volunteers in our clinical trial

---

[12] Cognitive Neuropsychology is the scientific investigation of cognition (how the brain functions); i.e., of all mental abilities: perception, attention, learning, memory, processing of spoken and written language, thinking, reasoning and belief formation, *see,* Coltheart, M. (2002). Cognitive Neuropsychology. In Wixted, J. (Ed.) Stevens' Handbook of Experimental Psychology, Third Edition - Volume 4: Methodology. John Wiley & Sons, pp 139-174. **Cognitive Neuropsychology assumes that cognition can… be fully revealed by the scientific method, that is, individual components of mental processes can be identified and understood**, *see,* Fodor, J.A. (1983). The Modularity of Mind: An Essay on Faculty Psychology. Cambridge, Mass.

[13] Cognitive Neuropsychology is concerned with understanding brain functioning through studies of "abnormal cognition," *see,* Eyseneck, Michael and Mark T. Keane, <u>Cognitive Psychology</u> at Pp 18-19, (2005).

allowed substantial progress towards mapping, digitally, standard electronic frequencies for defined brain functions. This then, is the core of the Digitalis project. Defined, scientifically measured, and recorded brain functions[14] that can be transferred to others, and played back, at will, in either healthy or unhealthy brain damaged subjects. The Digitalis project is of course, just one part in a much larger program.

The overarching program has been dubbed the Universal Mind Programming (or UMP) study. It has as it core focus the application of the convergence of these scientific breakthroughs with basic tenets of Cognitive Therapy[15]. That is to say, that behavior is shaped by beliefs. If you can alter a person's fundamental, deep rooted, beliefs, then you, in effect, control their behavioral responses going forward.

For example, take your not so average John Doe who because of a lifetime of exposure to religious extremists, believes

---

[14] Cognitive Neuroscience is the field of medicine that utilizes modern day breakthroughs in technology to understand the sequence of functioning in the human brain when performing a task; i.e., what parts of the brain are used, and in what order, *id,* at Pp. 18-19.

[15] Cognitive therapy seeks to identify and change thinking, behavior, and emotional responses. This involves modifying beliefs, identifying patterns of thinking to change, relating to others in different ways, and changing behaviors. Therapy may consist of testing the assumptions, identifying subject's current beliefs and-unquestioned thoughts that are distorted, unrealistic and unhelpful. Once those thoughts have been challenged, one's feelings about the subject matter of those thoughts are more easily subject to change, *see* Judith S. Beck. "Questions and Answers about Cognitive Therapy". *About Cognitive Therapy.* Beck Institute for Cognitive Therapy and Research.

dying is a joyous honor given only to the immensely fortunate in life. Then convince him that it's even better to die for a particular cause. Convince him the killing of the Chinese Premier is noble and essential relative to his particular cause. Then record his brain functioning through measures of electrical signaling via the neurons[16] in the brain. Converge that recording with technological breakthroughs that allow playback in another human through embedded electrical diodes[17], and you've got yourself one hell of an unlimited supply of assassins, regardless of their upbringing. They could be Harvard graduates that every week attended a church of the polar opposite beliefs, but with a perfected playback, using the Digitalis techniques, they will be obsessed with killing the Chinese Premier in a matter of days, rather than the more typical years it might take to instill that type of thinking."

Kennedy interrupted, "I can't believe what I am hearing. This is crazy. No wonder everyone and their brother wants this thing."

Jake wasn't convinced, "This is rubbish. What about

---

[16] Neurons are responsive cells in the nervous system that process and transmit information by electrochemical signaling, *see* http://en.wikipedia.org/wiki/Neuron

[17] "We can conclude from the phase 3 outcomes... that the extraordinary ability to improve and control cognitive functioning through electrical diode implants transmitting from coordinates [omitted/classified] and frequencies in the range [omitted/classified], which was first reported by Piaget does in fact translate to humans." *See,* Dubonet, Peter, et. Al, "Behavioral Manipulation Through Electrical Diode Stimulation Phase 3 European Union Center for Medical Research," University of Prague Press (10/2008) (previously publicly available, classified 11/2008).

the part he so conveniently glanced over. The bit where he says they couldn't maintain mental stability?"

"I don't know. I guess let's keep listening."

Dr. Trevor Coates continued his presentation, "For the most part, the Digitalis method is flawless. However, on average, mental deterioration of patients was complete within fifteen days of the onset of electrical diode stimulation. Lower frequency transmissions have been proven to prolong sanity. However, even so, the longest recorded deviation was seventy-two days. This critical adverse effect in 100% of test subjects is why we must recommend termination of the project at this time. The remainder of this presentation provides the details on the process and test subject 574."

Jake said, "I think I've seen enough. So… what? Lavanya wants this to brainwash people? I thought she wanted to prove reincarnation. I don't get the connection."

"Well there has got to be more here. There must be more to the Nakuru trial. I mean she asked you for the files on the clinical trial, but didn't say anything about this patient right?"

"Right, but you have to wonder if she really wants this Digitalis stuff. Honestly, do you really think some rich woman who has everything she could ever want would be crazy enough to be worried about proving reincarnation is real?"

Kennedy replied, "Actually, yes, I do think that. I think she's exactly the type of person that would undertake such an extreme activity."

"I don't know," Jake answered, "Maybe it's the factory that produces living death machines she is really after. There's more money in it, if you ask me. And money is always the root of all evil, right?"

"Money is a strong motivational factor. It gives a lot of power over people. But control major religions as a God in the eyes of their followers, and you've got not only money, but eternal devotion from millions, maybe billions, of people across multiple national boundaries. Don't forget, some would say that more than two thirds of the world's population is made up of devout believers in religions which adhere to principles of reincarnation. We're talking the bulk of the people in India and China, the two most populous countries, believe in this. That's just the tip of the iceberg. Many people, in many other countries as well, including a growing percentage of Americans. In other words, far more people believe than don't."

"So someone thinks this is worth killing the two thousand innocent people who were murdered on the National Mall last week?"

"Probably a good chance that is true. Jake, you realize we cannot hand over this tape to anyone." Jake lunged for the Betamax player and grabbed for the tape. Kennedy tried to stop him and get it first, but was unsuccessful.

Jake then said to her, "I don't know who you really are Kennedy, but this tape could be all that is keeping my father and wife alive. It stays with me. And if you try to get in the way of me helping my family again, you are going to see a side of me that I can tell you think doesn't exist. You would be wise to believe me that it does exist and that you don't want to see it – not ever."

"Careful Jake. For one thing you are in way over your head and probably wouldn't even be alive right now without my help. For another, all I was trying to do was restart the tape so we could watch the rest of it. I'm on your side Jake."

"I don't believe you."

CHAPTER 50

Underground Facility in Venezuelan Jungle

When the video resumed, it had moved to a new scene with clips of patient 574 in what looked like an interrogation room. The test subject's face was still blurred to hide their identity. Furthermore, their hair had been cut, Marines style short, and they were wearing clothing that made it impossible to determine gender.

Across from patient 574 were Dr. Trevor Coates and another man that looked a little like Dr. Marten Jansen. The two doctors only referred to the test subject as, "Patient 574," and never used a real name.

Other than the desk and industrial looking chairs there was no other furniture in the room. The walls were padded. Patient 574 was strapped in, bound to the chair which appeared bolted into the floor. The room had no windows and only the one door in and out, with no handle on the inside of the door.

Jake looked at Kennedy and asked, "Call me crazy, but doesn't that guy look a lot like our friend Marten from Isla Dedaleras?"

"I think it's him, only many years younger," She responded.

The test subject, patient 574, was swaying back and forth in their chair in an uneasy and awkward side to front, back to side convoluted motion. 574 looked distressed beyond belief. Tears could be seen falling from the blurry circle hiding their face. There were also some small blood spots on 574's clothing.

"574, do you know where you are right now?"

"I don't know but I need to survive the crash. That's all I know right now."

"574, you are not going to crash. You are safe and sound at <BLEEP>."

"What do you mean? I don't understand. If I don't survive the crash, I can't, I can't, I can't not survive the crash. I can't not complete my mission."

"574, tell me about the crash."

"It wasn't fun Dr. Jansen…"

Jake hit the pause button and exclaimed, "Ah hah! I knew it. It is him."

"You don't know that it's the same Dr. Jansen from Isla Dedaleras. I mean, he looks similar, but still, there is something different about this guy, especially when he talks. It doesn't quite sound like our Dr. Jansen. The accent is strange, definitely not Dutch, and his mouth moves differently."

"I suppose it doesn't matter. Let's keep going." Patient 574 went into excruciating detail about a car crash and a mission.

"What mission 574? What was the primary objective of the mission?" Dr. Jansen asked.

"I had to kill them. I had to kill or… I had to kill the enemy." Patient 574 was crying hysterically at that point.

The doctor interrupted again, "Patient 574, why are you crying?"

"I don't want to kill. I don't like to kill. I mean, I didn't used to kill."

The video went to a split screen with Dr. Jansen

narrating the momentarily frozen dialog between him and patient 574. You can see here, the impact of multiple past lives recognition; i.e., the subject is no longer able to keep his present life and previous two past lives separate and distinct. The mind tries to merge the three, unsuccessfully, which is what we believe is the primary stimulus for the cranial breakdown that begins shortly after the procedure is completed."

The video continued:

"What year is it 574?"

"It's 1986."

"If it's 1986 then what courier are you looking for in Boston and what's so urgent?"

"The revolution depends on it. I have to find the courier and get him to John Adams."

"Are you mixing lives 574."

"Wait, no, yes, no, I just need to find the courier, I can't fail. I must not fail the society."

"What society?"

"It's not important right now."

"574, do I need to convince you that it is important and that you should share it with me? Do you remember the types of things I might do to help remind you of what is important? Do you want me to do those things 574?"

"Yes, I know, please no, there's no courier. This is 1986. I was just confused."

"No 574 you were not confused. Tell me what the courier's message will say?"

"It will say to kill."

"Kill whom 574?" That's when 574 broke loose from the bindings holding them in the chair, jumped up and ran head first into the wall slamming the top of their skull into the two way mirror that was between the camera and the room. The mirror shattered as the patient's head carved a circular hole in the glass. Blood oozed from the patient's ears and jaw, which were cut deeply as they pulled their head back out from the glass. Dr. Trevor Coates, still seated at the table, opened a drawer and pressed a button which appeared to send bolts of electricity through the floor. The shocks did not affect him or Dr. Jansen as they lifted their feet and watched the barefooted patient fall down to the floor. Medics stormed into the room just before the scene in the video froze.

"Jeesh, that looks like a woman, and yet she snapped those bindings like it was no big deal."

"How can you tell Jake?"

"Look at her feet and legs."

*   *   *

They fast forwarded the video to the next section where it cut to a new scene and test subject. It started with an introduction by Dr. Jansen.

He was in the video explaining how patient 1447 was given living quarters near the facility but outside the main building. He explained how there was an elaborate set of video surveillance put in place in 1447's "cottage" and that the following were spliced clips of notable events that would help assess the results of the Digitalis process. He was sullen and melancholy as he concluded his introduction, "The following scenes are graphic and will show why the Digitalis project must be terminated. Due to the shocking and revealing nature of some of the clips, this presentation is for internal, medical staff viewing only. Lastly, we can conclude from the study on 1447 that, the Digitalis is neither salvageable, nor does it provide the requisite data for improvements in any undertaking of future studies. This first scene opens with 1447 at their desk, after six days without sleep, delusional, and wanting to save a person they had never met, at least not during their present life."

At first Jake and Kennedy could only see the back of patient 1447's head. But seconds later the patient fell from

305

their chair and momentarily exposed their face. Jake was the next to fall, collapsing to his knees as he saw a woman that looked remarkably similar to pictures of his mother.

CHAPTER 51

Escape from Aguas Muertas

A loud alarm sounded and gunshots prompted Jake back to his feet. A split second later Kennedy had her hand on the back of his head pushing it down below the bottom of the windows that lined the upper half of the wall between the archives room and the main lab of the underground facility. They carefully moved to the door and saw Marcus Wilds holding his right shoulder about five feet away, crouched down behind a desk. Blood stained his shirt. Something had gone terribly wrong with their attempt to break into the vault containing the Digitalis.

Along the far wall, the elevator doors were opened. The South American men they had seen earlier in the day stood there shooting randomly throughout the room and yelling in Spanish. Marcus Wilds saw Jake and Kennedy and yelled to them, "Get what you can, and get back down the tunnel, the way we came in, NOW!"

Jake and Kennedy ran for the tunnel as Marcus provided cover. Kennedy fired a few shots herself along the way. Collins, Rob Mulligan, and Johnny Antonelli were already a few steps ahead of them. Marcus followed, leaving a trail of blood behind him. Bullets whizzed all around from the gunmen who were chasing them.

As Jake and Kennedy were running toward the steel doors that led above ground, they heard Marcus let out a wail. Jake looked back and saw him face plant. He had been shot a second time. The bullet hit the femoral artery in Marcus' left leg and streaks of blood arced across the tunnel. Marcus tried to stand and keep moving. When he pushed himself to his feet, a third bullet struck him in the back of the head. He immediately went down, motionless. Johnny Antonelli had stepped back as well, and had been in route to help Marcus before watching him go down for good. Antonelli instead turned to Jake and said, "Hurry up unless you want to be like..." when a bullet went into the left side of his jaw and came out through his right ear, splattering brain and blood along the way. Jake didn't linger as bullets continued to fly around him. Many were hitting the concrete and steel that held up the tunnel, and which caused them to ricochet and fly around in all directions. The gunmen were no more then 20 to 30 yards behind Jake, who was at the tail end of the group. If not for the curvature of the tunnel, he probably would have been shot already.

Jake made it to the exterior tunnel door and ran out into the jungle. The rest of the group was already ahead of him, making their way back up the hill to their camp near the waterfall. No one bothered to stop and help him, not even Kennedy. Each of them was in a sheer panic, a flight for life. The tropical jungle forest offered cover from sight, but little protection from bullets. Fortunately, the hill they had to ascend was rocky and the jagged rocks offered many crevices in which to hide for cover from bullets, which continued to fly around.

Jake eventually caught up to Kennedy who was sitting crouched behind some rocks. She had a bullet wound. The bullet did not exit cleanly and was lodged in her shoulder blade causing her excruciating pain every time she moved. They yelled up to Rob Mulligan and Collins for help. Jake saw Mulligan keep on running, but Collins doubled back. Unfortunately, the gunmen were already upon them. Jake and Kennedy stepped further behind the crevice where they had stopped, and opened fire to defend themselves. The pace of bullets intensified into a crescendo until finally stopping, at least for that moment. Jake looked to his left and saw that Kennedy had been hit again. A bullet had grazed through the right side of her throat. She held it with her hand as blood gushed. They both knew she had only minutes to live, at most. Tears welled in their eyes.

Kennedy spoke as blood flooded her mouth, "Jake, I'm sorry. I'm sorry for lying to you. I'm not a doctor Jake. I... I... I..."

"Easy Kennedy. Just rest easy. There's nothing you need to apologize for."

In a gurgled and weakening voice she went on, "Jake, I need to tell you something. I was investigating your father's connection to Nakuru Jake. There's more to it than you know. But your father is unquestionably a good man. You've got to find Victoria Lake in Amsterdam. 176 Witte De Withstraat. It's a home owned by your father. It's near the Scientia Pro Curatio."

"Near what?"

"The investment trust started by your father. Your watch Jake. It's the group where your watch came from. Just get to Victoria. She can explain it all. She knows about the Digitalis. When you find her Jake, protect her and the Digitalis at all costs. She can fix all this. She's the only one left that can help you. And Jake, whatever you do, don't give the Digitalis to anyone except your father. Not anyone else can be trusted with the power that it holds."

"Investigating my father? For what? What happened at Nakuru?"

"Jake, I am sorry about your..." and then she was gone.

You're sorry about my what? Was that my mother in that video? Sorry about wrecking my marriage – maybe something did happen that night on Isla Dedaleras? How about sorry for dying when it sure seemed like you loved me? How about that!? How about sorry for leaving me here alone?!

Jake had no choice but to pull himself together. He peered around the edge of the rocks. He could see no gunmen, so made his way back to the trail leading up the hill to their camp. He found Commander Collins a bit further up, laying on the ground, motionless, on his stomach. Jake flipped him over.

Collins looked Jake dead in the eyes and begged him, "Please help me."

"Of course," Jake responded before throwing him over his right shoulder in the classic fireman's carry. Jake lifted him up the trail, passing Rob Mulligan's dead body along the way. The two of them were the only ones that made it back to the camp.

Jorge greeted them and applied remedial first aid to Collins. He would need to be airlifted out, as he had been shot twice in his right leg, once in the buttocks, and once in his side. All of the bullets, miraculously, had gone in and out cleanly. Chances were good Collins would live, if he could be stitched up quickly enough.

Jake used the satellite phone to call for help. He left a voicemail for Lavanya, and then another for John Anton. Frustrated that he was unable to reach either of the two people most likely to be able to get him and Collins airlifted out of the jungle, he decided to hold his ground for the time being. Since their cover had already been blown, it mattered little that a noisy chopper would call attention to their presence. But until help arrived, Jake knew it was essential to conceal their camp as much as possible. He and Jorge frantically dismantled the tents and equipment and hid everything in the dense tropical foliage. Once satisfied they had made their former encampment look abandoned, they sat and waited for a call back.

While waiting, Jake's mind was going crazy. He wondered what was happening to his wife. Despite thinking it was in vain, he decided to use the satellite phone to call her once again. He fell to his knees when she answered.

"Anja? Is that you? Is that really you?" he asked.

"Jake? Where are you honey? I've been worried sick. I got home yesterday and you were not here. I was about to file a missing person's report. For God sakes Jake, you could have at least left me a note or something."

I could have left a note? Is she kidding? And were they bluffing when they told me they had kidnapped her?

"I um… I um, thought you had been kidnapped. Are you safe? Are you really home? What happened to you?"

"Kidnapped? Are you smoking crack? You know where I was. The retreat was off the grid. I told you I would have limited access to phones before I left. Why on earth would you think I was kidnapped? No, never mind that. The real question is where are you and why haven't you been answering your cell?"

Jake laughed, nearly hysterical.

Why haven't I been answering my cell! Why haven't I! I never thought it would be so nice to be nagged about that! But something's not right about this. Even my father was convinced she was held against her will.

"I'm just glad you're OK Anja. I'll be home soon sweetheart. I'll be home soon."

"Where are you Jake? Why aren't you answering my question?"

"You wouldn't believe me if I told you."

"Try."

"I'm in Venezuela. Listen Anja, my father's in trouble. His company has been destroyed by someone or some group. I don't really know who yet. But I am going to find out. And I am going to put a stop to this. The thing is, to do so, I may have to go to India. No, make that I have to go to India… to help my father."

"India? Venezuela? What's going on Jake? Are you saying you're not coming home?"

"No. I am coming home, immediately. I need to see you. I need to know it's really you."

"It is really me Jake. Please come home. You're scaring the hell out of me."

"Listen Anja, keep the doors and windows locked. And if you see anything or anyone strange, don't hesitate to call the police. I should be home in 24 hours. I love you Anja."

"Jake, please wait, don't get off the phone yet." But the sound of choppers overhead made it impossible to hear or talk any longer. Jake pressed the end call button.

CHAPTER 52

Departure from Venezuela

The choppers were there to help. It didn't take long for Jake and Jorge to load their equipment. The choppers quickly lifted off. A wounded Commander Collins lay on a gurney fading in and out of consciousness. Jake and Jorge peered out the chopper's windows at the grandness of the nearby waterfall, amazed at how such a beautiful site coexisted next to such dark secrets guarded by the hounds of hell.

They were both thankful for escaping a part of the world few ventured to visit and even fewer safely returned from. Teardrops in the corners of their eyes paid homage to those no longer with them. Jake knew for certain that Kennedy had died. In addition, also either dead, or likely soon to be, were the three other men they left behind, Johnny Antonelli, Robert Mulligan, and Marcus Wilds. All of them seemed decent enough. And at the end of the day, each of them was just trying to make a buck and get through life the best way they knew how. Jorge was talking in his hard to decipher slang, but Jake was lost in a sea of painful thoughts:

*This isn't part of the deal I signed up for. I need to do
something before more innocent people die. I'm responsible
for those four people's deaths. I'm responsible for Kate
Stinson's death too. I should have helped her. I should
have prevented all of this. I need to be the aggressor for
once instead of simply playing right into the hands of
Lavanya and everyone else using me to get the Digitalis. I
am going to serve justice on these people for what they have
done and the countless lives and families they have ruined.
I am going to make sure they do not get what they want
and they are not able to kill again.*

From the ground below, Devon Keyes and Dr.
Marten Jansen watched the helicopter carrying Jake and the
others liftoff from an area of dense tropical jungle foliage.
Unfazed by their escape, Devon said to Dr. Jansen, "Don't
worry Marten, we have a backup plan. The man's wife is
waiting for him at home. Boy is she going to have a nice
surprise for him."

"What are you talking about? Dinner? What do I
care about that man's dinner right now when the Digitalis
just slipped right out from under us? Sometimes I wonder
why we're even doing business with you."

Devon was a rock, "Shut up Marten. Not everything
is what it seems ya silly Dutchman. Just get your boys ready
to deliver the payment. Tell them they'll have their Digitalis
in the next 48 hours and to be prepared to make the full
payment, as agreed upon. I'll be in touch with them
through the secured channel. We're about to wrap this
thing up once and for all. And then we can wipe these rats
from the face of the earth."

"Wow Devon, what did they ever do to you?"

"They irritated me by delaying the inevitable. And
worse, they made it a royal pain in the ass for me to get my
money. They're liabilities now. Ultimately, we have no
choice." A sinister grin consumed Devon's face.

*   *   *

Jake could see an ambulance approach, as the chopper descended onto the helipad at the international airport. Collins struggled to talk, "Jake, come closer, I need to tell you something." He was barely conscious, but Jake leaned in and put his ear next to Collin's mouth. He went on, "Right leg, calf pocket." Jake looked down at his leg. His pants had a big utility pocket sewn into them. Jake made sure no one was watching. Jorge was, but Jake didn't think him a threat, so he went ahead and retrieved a rectangular metal box from Collin's pocket.

"What is it?" Jake asked him.

"It's the schematics for the Digitalis."

"So you did get it! I can't believe it. The mission wasn't in vain."

"Don't loose it Jake. I've already sent a communication to inform Lavanya that it's in your possession. If you double cross her, she will find you, and kill you and your family."

"She'll find me?! Not if I can find her first."

T he soul comes from without into the human body, as into a temporary abode, and it goes out of it anew as it passes into other habitations, for the soul is immortal. It is the secret of the world that all things subsist and do not die, but only retire a little from sight and afterwards return again. Nothing is dead; men feign themselves dead, and endure mock funerals... and there they stand looking out of the window, sound and well, in some strange new disguise.

–Ralph Waldo Emerson

CHAPTER 53

Potomac, Maryland
(Suburbs of Washington, D.C.)

After consulting with Lavanya, Jake insisted on a chance to stop off at his home before returning to India. Lavanya resisted fiercely, but ultimately relented, as Jake used the Digitalis as leverage to take control and get what *he* wanted for a change. He did not mention to Lavanya that he had spoken with his wife. It was the first time he thought far enough ahead to use good judgment. Jake suspected something odd in his wife's sudden freedom and he was right.

Lavanya meanwhile knew Anja was by then under the control of her rivals and enemies led by Peter Lansing and the Eagon brothers. She never would have allowed the stopover in D.C. had she known Anja was waiting to greet Jake because she would have known it was a trap.

Back in Potomac, Maryland, Jake got out of the taxi and approached the front door to his suburban home, just outside of D.C. He was eager to see his wife no matter how suspicious the circumstances.

He was exhausted and bruised both physically and

mentally and it didn't help when he found taped to the outside of his front door a summons for yet another court date in the malpractice suit and disbarment cases against him. On the back of it was hand written, "I know you're back. You outta time. Deliver the money in 24 hours." Jake knew it was the writing of Jessie Doyle, the mobster who had ransacked his apartment downtown only days earlier. Jessie was the brother of Angelo Doyle who was suing Jake for malpractice and was responsible for his disbarment.

Jake wanted to pour himself a stiff scotch and run away from the world. He was going on two weeks of nothing but new disasters on a daily basis. The simple pleasure of sleeping in his own bed sounded like heaven. But despite his mental and physical exhaustion, he was still eager to see his wife, flesh and blood, and know that she was OK. He knew that her simple touch could wipe away all his problems.

When he walked through the front door of his home, Jake found his wife Anja waiting for him in the living room. She was wearing nothing more than a see through lace nightgown. It was the type that hugged her body in all the right spots but hung loose in all the others. It drooped down along her curves to just above her knees. It showed a lot, while leaving the best for further investigation. Normally, Jake would have been grinning, but instead he was aghast at how much weight Anja had lost since the last time he saw her. She looked like a tweaker, all boney and starved. But her seductive stare was unusually captivating. Jake's concern for her well being elicited his deep rooted love for her. And with each batting of the eyelashes and each smile, his mind slowly shifted from concern for his wife's well being to triple-x rated sex. In fact, he wasn't sure he had ever lusted after her so strongly. Perhaps not ever, not even before they were married. For a while, all Jake did was stare at her with an awkward silence while his mind undressed her, groped her, kissed her.

I don't know why I had such awful thoughts or did such terrible things in the Caribbean with Kennedy, but I am going to save this marriage. Something brought me back here, in the middle of unimaginable chaos, something brought me to this woman, even while my father is being held against his will half way around the globe. And that something is what's going to save us.

Anja finally broke the silence, "Well honey, are you gonna stare at me all night or are ya gonna fuck me?" She was grinning seductively and in a way Jake had never seen from her before. It was strangely, almost evil, but in a way that excited him.

And the way she talked – not just her uncharacteristic words, but her tone and demeanor - Jake had never heard her talk like that in the fourteen years since they first met. He didn't know what to think, but wondered just what kind of adventure camp for teachers it was that she had spent two months visiting. Answers to his questions about where she had been, why she had lost so much weight, why he couldn't reach her at all for months, were all suddenly unimportant. He walked up to her and began to kiss her on the lips, passionately. He gently bit her lower lip and tasted her mouth. She immediately went to jello, knowing that to Jake, kissing on the lips was something he considered the most intimate expression of deep, true love.

Jake grabbed the back of her neck and massaged it with his right hand, while his left pulled her hips close to him. All he could think about was making up for the time apart.

Never leaving their living room, they spent the night there, having sex, resting, cuddling, and having sex again. Talk was sporadic or mostly done through looks of lust and love. There were only short intermissions to their complete undivided attention on each other. The evening was intense and one of the most passionate and memorable Jake had ever had, with Anja or anyone in his life.

But something was bothering him. It started as just a minor irritation like a fly on the back of his neck. As the night grew old, whatever bothered him also grew. Something was different about Anja. He couldn't quite pinpoint what it was. Certainly the sex was different. It wasn't more than half way through the evening before he knew with complete certainty that Anja had been with another man. The subtle differences in their love making gave her away. But that wasn't what was bothering Jake the most, as he had long suspected infidelity and was determined to save his marriage at all costs. What was bothering him was something far worse.

His gut was telling him that something more sinister was wrong with his wife. He couldn't figure out what, but in the way that only a person in true love can, Jake knew his wife was no longer who he thought she was. Even so, he would not waiver, not ever, from his perseverance to save his marriage. Brushing aside his unknown fears he was able to enjoy his wife's embrace. In each other's arms, both of them eventually passed out on the living room floor.

Only a couple of short hours before sunrise, they finally made their way to the bedroom to collapse into a bed that they hadn't occupied as a couple in months. Jake closed his eyes and quickly fell back asleep. Meanwhile, Anja rolled over, reached under the mattress on her side of the bed, and grabbed the gun she had placed there before her husband's arrival.

CHAPTER 54

Potomac, Maryland

Anja held in her left hand a Heckler and Kock MK23 semiautomatic handgun with a high tech silencer attachment. The HK MK23 was generally thought to be one of the best semi-automatic handguns available and was widely used by U.S. Special Ops. It was considered capable of accuracy within two inches from as far away as fifty yards, which is exceptional for a handgun. But accuracy would not be an issue, as Anja had the nose of the silencer practically touching Jake's left temple while he lay sleeping.

Also under the bed was a PDA the Eagons had given to her. She glanced at its screen one more time, and re-read the same message she had been staring at for hours, "Acquire the Digitalis and the disc in your husband's possession with the Nakuru files, then terminate him as you have begged to do for so long now, as you were born to do, and achieve your salvation. Report back immediately when mission complete."

Anja released the safety mechanism on the gun. She glanced at her sleeping husband who looked peaceful and content, then glanced back again at the phone message.

Streaks of water drew lines across the sides of her face.

Something inside prevented Anja from pulling the trigger. Rationalizing her internal conflict, she told herself that she must first make sure the disc Jake came home with contained the Nakuru files. She could not kill the man who had risked everything to come home to her before attempting to save his own father. At least, not so quickly.

The Heckler and Kock went back under the mattress, and the phone stayed in quiet mode. For the time being, Jake would live.

*   *   *

The next morning, a buzzer sounded on the coffee maker as a plume of steam escaped from the grounds. Jake poured two cups of coffee, put them on a breakfast tray next to a plate of scrambled eggs and bacon and went back to the bedroom. Anja smiled as she rolled over to see him walking in with the tray. Jake smiled back, happy to have another morning with his wife, happy to be alive, happy to have another day to fight to regain everything that had been taken from him. Happy in knowing there was hope that the new day could bring positive change and could be better than yesterday.

"What if this is normal?" Jake asked Anja.

"What if what is normal?" she responded.

"What if all of this: all this lunacy, all this chaos, the killings, the malpractice suit, the bombing in D.C., the plane crash, all of it, my father's kidnapping, what if all of this is normal? What if it is just part of the price we pay for the eradication of a major disease? I mean, if it is normal, then we need to learn to fight back. We need to learn an effective offense that can…"

"Wait. Stop right there," Anja interrupted, "Did you say your father has been kidnapped?"

"You mean, you didn't know? For some reason, I

thought you knew. I guess because he knew you had been kidnapped, I figured vice versa."

"That's absurd! I wasn't kidnapped Jake. I was on a retreat. I told you that. It was a camp site off the grid. There was no cell coverage or even land line phone service. It was impossible to call you, but I told you that before I left. More importantly, what is going on with your father? Is he OK? Where is he?"

"No he is not OK. He's in India."

"India? Is he safe? I thought you had said India over the phone before, but nothing you were saying made sense, nor does it now."

"You've never seemed like you cared about or even liked my father before. Why this sudden show of deep concern?"

"Jake, don't be silly. He's your father. Of course I'm concerned. Just tell me what you know please. Is he safe or not? What do the kidnappers want?"

What do the kidnappers want? They want what everyone around me seems to want. The Digitalis. The key to restoring memory functions for victims of Alzheimer's; or the key to proving reincarnation is real; or the key to brainwashing people, depending on who you ask. It's a key to whole new field of medical technology that is going to make someone a billionaire a thousand times over. The key that even my beloved wife, appears to be after.

"Anja, what they want is already in transit to them. I sent it from Isla Dedaleras on a private plane."

It was the first time in his life that Jake lied to his wife. But his instincts were telling him that she could not be trusted with the truth about the Digitalis.

"What is that Jake, what did you send?"

"Why are you asking Anja? Are you wondering if they'll release my father, or do you just want to know what it is that prompted my father to be taken hostage and shipped across the globe?"

"Well both, I guess. Honestly, I just want to know if

they're going to let him go."

"I don't know. But I'm not going to sit around wishing for it to happen. I am going to go to India myself, and I am going to make sure he is released, one way or another. It's time for me to live what I always preach to my clients, that if a person doesn't take action and make the difficult choices, then the passage of time will make them for him, and he'll have to live with the results thrust upon him, instead of influencing the outcomes through vigilance, perseverance, determination, and belief in the possibilities."

There was a pause. Anja looked momentarily sullen.

She mumbled under her breath, "But you stopped off here first to see me, even with your father waiting for you to help him."

"What did you just say," Jake snapped, "Don't tell me that was nothing," he demanded.

"Nothing, nothing. It's just that, well, I love you Jakob Hunter."

Before Jake could respond, or even smile, a glass window pane from the side door to the kitchen shattered, sending shards inward in all directions. They could hear the ruckus from their upstairs bedroom and quickly ran down to the kitchen to investigate.

CHAPTER 55

Potomac, Maryland

A gloved hand reached through the broken window in Jake Hunter's kitchen and opened the exterior door to his home. The silent alarm system in the home was triggered, although the intruder didn't seem to care.

Jake and Anja were both running in to see what all the noise was about. Their heart rates accelerated as they became gripped with fear. Although Jake had been through extraordinary events over the previous few days, he still found it an unnerving invasion of his privacy to be observing someone breaking into his home. That the intruder was there during daylight hours could only mean the danger was far more severe than a typical break in.

What they saw when they got downstairs, was Gregor Eagon walking into their kitchen, with a gun aimed at Jake. He used a walkie-talkie to radio to an accomplice, "I'm in, and I've got both of them in the kitchen, over."

"We're coming in the front then, no sign of Devon, over?"

"No, not yet, over, out." He powered off his walkie-talkie then smiled at Anja, patted her on the butt like only a lover would do, and said, "Hello Anja. We've missed you." Jake's stomach felt like someone had just thrown a bowling ball into it.

But with one gun wielding man in his face, and by the sounds of things, at least two more on their way, Jake knew he would need to focus on some creative thinking to get out of the mess he was in.

Questions as to how his wife knew the intruder would have to wait, as Jake wasn't about to show any signs of weakness or concern. He focused on what the men had just talked about. They were looking for Devon. Not a coincidence. Clearly the same Devon that Jake had once trusted enough to build a law firm with. They weren't looking for him at Devon's house, either. That could have meant only one thing.

No wonder he wanted to dissolve the law firm at the first sign of trouble. The bastard has been playing me for who knows how long. Focus focus... there will be plenty of time after I'm away from these gun toting a-holes to be angry. Where's the opportunity in this. There's always an opportunity in every crisis if you just look hard enough. Ahh, yes...

Gregor Eagon grabbed Anja by the hair and threw her into the front entrance of the home. Jake was ordered up into the foyer as well. Gregor opened the door and let two other men in, neither of whom Jake nor Anja recognized. Gregor barked out to them, "We'll wait here, in the living room. These two stay with us until we have everything we need and can verify its authenticity. Did you guys finish the wiring?"

"It's done. Detonators are in the car."

Detonators. Jeesh, opportunities are fading fast. I need to do something, before Devon gets here.

Jake finally decided what to say and asked them, "Devon didn't tell you guys about the Digitalis?"

Gregor responded, "He told us he would be giving it to us here at your home and to keep you alive until he gets here. If you have it, and you value your life at all, I would suggest you hand it over."

"I don't have it. But neither does he. You guys are being played. Whatever he hands to you will be totally worthless without the codes that unlock the encrypted files. And there's only one set of those. Sadly, they are not here."

"Bullshit. I'm calling bullshit on that. We wait for Devon, we get the Digitalis, and we finish this." Gregor wasn't falling for it.

*   *   *

Devon rang the doorbell and Jake was told to answer. "Hey Jake," Devon was acting like there was nothing unusual going on, "Can I come in? I need to talk to you."

"Yes you can come in," Jake responded while glancing at the alarm system's control panel near the door. He noticed it had been triggered by the break in through the Kitchen.

It's only a matter of time until the police arrive. I've just got to stall them.

Jake greeted Devon, "As a matter of fact, we've all been waiting for you." A look of slight displeasure flashed across Devon's face as he walked in and saw the whole group.

"Perfect. You're already here then," Devon said to Gregor, "Do you have the money?"

"We've got it," Gregor responded while displaying a large duffel bag which appeared to be overflowing with wads of cash, "Where's the Digitalis?"

Devon turned to Jake and said, "Well partner, this is it. See, I'm brokering a deal. The Digitalis for early retirement. So if you would, please get the hard drive that has the schematics for creating the Digitalis."

Jake blurted out, "Bullshit! How could you do this Devon?" They looked at each other, both surprised.

Devon replied by firing a gun shot into Anja's leg. Then he said to Jake, "There's a lot more where that came from. Don't make me ask again. I know you have the hard drive from Aguas Muertas. That's what these men want. If you give it to them in the next 15 seconds, then I'll refrain from shooting your whore of a wife a second time."

Jake ran into his office, opened a safe tucked into the wall in the back of a closet and produced the rectangular metal box that Commander Collins had given to him. He realized it was a hard drive to a computer and contained the schematics for recreating the Digitalis that was used at Aguas Muertas.

Can this little drive really contain everything needed to make the Digitalis? Somehow that doesn't seem right to me. I bet it's not that simple. These men cannot leave here with this. My father's life, my life depends on it. Besides, they'll kill me the second they have it.

Jake handed it to Gregor who then asked, "Where's the codes required to un-encrypt the files?" He turned to Devon and said, "You don't get one cent until we know we can access these files."

Jake chimed in, "Never mind the codes, you don't even have the real Digitalis."

Devon blurted out, "Shut the… just shut up. How would you know anything about it?"

Jake countered, "Because the real Digitalis was on board on the Hunter Neurologics jet that was intentionally crashed and blown to smithereens. But before it was blown up, someone took the Digitalis and my father."

"Where Jake? Where did they take the Digitalis?" his wife asked.

Jake looked at her, immensely disappointed, "No way. How can you be asking me for that? What is the matter with you?"

Devon pointed his gun and shot Anja in the leg a second time. He aimed for the same spot as the first bullet to magnify the pain and damage. She yelped in agony.

Gregor commanded, "Don't shoot her again without my permission."

"What's it to you?"

"She's still valuable to us."

Then Devon said to Jake, "Worry about your double crossing whore of wife later Jake. Right now, you owe me. Get the codes and verify this hard drive for the man." Jake just stood there. Devon fired a third shot into Anja's leg, defying Gregor's orders. She screamed in agony and begged Jake to comply.

Faint police sirens could be heard in the distance. Gregor noticed them and said, "Damn it, we've been here too long. It's time to wrap this up once and for all."

The sound of suppressed bullets from a silencer whooshed by a couple times, followed by the thud of Devon Keyes against the wall in the foyer. Blood stained the spot where he pressed against the wall before hitting the hardwood floor and laying limp.

"Let's go! Run!" Jake whispered to his wife while the others were watching Devon spew blood. But even in her injured state, Anja intentionally tripped Jake, trying to prevent his escape. Jake looked at her with an expression of utter and complete heartbreak. He was nearly destroyed by her actions, trying to stop him. But when he peered into her eyes, he saw pain and confusion. He knew his wife was being manipulated, or at least he felt there was a small chance something like that could explain her erratic behavior. A simple, remote sliver of hope that she still loved him was enough to give him the energy to get back up and try again. He was determined to escape, regroup, and figure out a plan to save his wife, and then his father. As Jake lunged to his feet, bullets resumed. He was near the bag of money and grabbed it as he scrambled toward the kitchen.

Gregor shouted, "Get the girl. She's coming with us." But then, out of the corner of Jake's eye, he saw his wife hit twice more with bullets as she resisted the intruders, but couldn't tell the severity of her wounds. He ducked behind the wall separating the entrance foyer from the kitchen. Jake was also hit in his leg. The wound made it difficult to stand or walk. So Jake crawled through the kitchen trying to get out through the back door. He could hear Gregor in the background scolding his thugs for shooting Anja. "You idiots. You've gone and killed a perfectly good and highly trained soldier."

Tears clouded Jake's vision upon hearing those words. But he knew that while he was unarmed, the chances of him doing anything to save her, if she still had a chance to live, were non-existent. He needed to escape, reset, and try again later.

Jake grabbed his car keys hanging on the wall, and pushed himself out the kitchen door into the backyard of his home. He tried to walk around to the side, where the cars were parked. He fell, and tried to get up but it hurt too much. He kept crawling, looking back every so often, surprised that no one was coming out after him. As he reached the driveway on the side of the house, still crawling, an explosion blew out all the windows and sent pieces of the roof into the air. In the nick of time, he was able to roll under one of the parked cars, a Chevy Tahoe. He watched as debris fell everywhere and the house went up in flames. No one inside would have been able to survive. And Jake only just got into the Tahoe and drove away from the flames, as they quickly grew large enough to ignite the other car still parked in the driveway.

CHAPTER 56

Washington D.C. Area

Sirens wailed as fire trucks and policemen drove towards what was left of Jake's house. He was fleeing the scene and looking for any sign of the intruders who had shot him. He was flying through turns so fast that several of the wheels on his big Tahoe SUV left the ground on more than one occasion. Eventually, the radius of his search had extended far enough from his house, that he was forced to accept a successful escape by the men who had attacked him, killed his wife, and stolen the hard drive from Aguas Muertas which contained the schematics for the Digitalis. Without it, he no longer had a way to free his father from Lavanya Yashodhara.

Jake pounded the steering wheel and screamed at the top of his lungs. He cried profusely, hysterically. "Anjaaaaaa," he yelled over and over.

* * *

Twenty minutes later, which felt like only seconds, Jake finally calmed down. After glancing at his leg, he drove to a pharmacy to purchase hydrogen peroxide and gauze. At the checkout, his credit card was declined. Next, his debit card was declined. Jake paid in cash and looked in his wallet. He had ten dollars left to his name. But then he remembered the bag of money in his car. After wrapping the wound, and with nowhere else to go, Jake drove into the city and stopped at the "K Street Tavern," which was his favorite pub and was near his condo in Georgetown. He needed a scotch to calm his nerves and needed to think. He walked into the pub, taking the bag of cash with him, which was an odd sight.

There was an open stool at the far end of the bar, near some pool tables. Jake sat down, oblivious to the other patrons who were staring at him in his tattered state. Two men playing pool were paying particularly close attention to Jake as he ordered a Johnny Walker.

The bartended greeted him, "Hey Jake, you want your regular, the Black label?"

Just as he was about answer, the two men playing pool grabbed Jake and the bag of money and dragged him out the back door of the bar and into the alleyway. Forced to pay attention, Jake immediately recognized the one man as, Jessie Doyle, the mobster brother of Angelo Doyle who was suing Jake for malpractice.

"Well well well, Jake Hunter. We didn't think you'd be dumb enough to show up here without paying us our money first. This sure is an unpleasant surprise! Now you're gonna pay with some broken bones!" Jessie spat at Jake after throwing him on the ground. Jake jumped to his feet and yelped at the pain in his right leg.

"Boy if you was smart, you would have stayed down on the ground!"

"Hold on Jessie. You got your money right there. That bag has your money and then some. I'm offering you a deal."

"What kind of deal?"

"You asked for one million. That bag has ten million dollars in it. In return for the nine extra million, you get your brother to withdraw his malpractice suit against me and recommend reinstatement of my license to the judge."

"My brother will be happy to recommend you for the attorney of the year award when he sees this much dough. Consider it done. But if any of these bills come back with tracked serial numbers, we're gonna hunt you down like tonight's dinner, only you're gonna suffer before you die. Got it?"

It's so nice to see that the future of America can still be bought with enough money.

"Not a problem. There's not a question in my mind that those bills are not marked, tainted, being tracked or anything else. As long as you don't go running your mouth where you got it, then all the problems with the source of those bills will be for me to worry about."

"I don't how you pulled off getting this much cash so fast, but you got one thing right – it's your problem to deal wid! Nice doing business wid ja!" Jessie Doyle and his sidekick laughed their way down the alley and out to their car.

Jake went back into the bar and sat down. Roger, the bartender, came back over and asked, "Everything OK Jake?"

"Fine Roger. Everything's fine. I just haven't figured out how to see the rose petals yet. I'm stuck on the thorns. Oh and what's worse, I'm gonna have to settle for the Red label. I was a millionaire a few minutes ago, but now I'm down to ten bucks."

"No worries Jake, I got the difference. And this one will be a double. You look like you could use it."

"If you only knew Roger ol buddy. If you only knew."

Jake sipped on his scotch while glancing up at the television. A commercial was just ending. The news came on after it. Next to the news anchor, was a picture of Jake.

His mug shot was on the FBI's most wanted list. The newscaster was explaining a story about charred human remains that were found in Jake's burnt down home. The damage from the intense heat was so severe it would take a couple of days to positively identify the body. Witnesses reported having spotted Jake recklessly speeding away from his home just after the explosion. The local authorities were considering him the primary suspect in the presumed killing of his wife but were working closely with the FBI on related matters. Then the anchor turned it over to a field reporter who was capturing a press conference by District Attorney Milton Strayer and Special Agent Jeremy Nielson at FBI headquarters in D.C.

"We believe Mr. Hunter is armed and extremely dangerous. We believe he is very well funded, and we have evidence that leads us to conclude he has an elaborate international support network. At this point, we believe he may be responsible for the deaths of the Hunter Neurologics board of directors, his own father's disappearance, the tragedy in D.C., and now possibly the death of Anja Hunter, his wife. In addition, a Special Agent assigned to his case, Kennedy Taylor has also gone missing. The FBI has taken steps to apprehend this suspect but needs the public's help."

Jake's glass dropped, tumbled for a second teasing the edge of the bar, half on, half over the edge, then hit the floor and shattered. He didn't flinch but just kept staring at the television.

But they only found one body at my home?

While Jake had other lawyer friends, he knew his situation was beyond any legal problem they could or would want to help with. Further, he couldn't fathom the idea of dragging anyone he cared about into the middle of such an awful mess. So Jake did the only thing he knew how to do when things were at their worst. He made lists. He grabbed a bar napkin and wrote down what he still had.

Thirty seconds later, he had a list of three things: $10 bucks, a pocket watch his father advised him to collect, and Kennedy Taylor's dying words.

Roger the bartender came up to Jake, "Hey buddy, I know there's no way any of this stuff they're saying about you is true, but you're drawing the attention of the locals. You might want to consider getting the hec out of dodge for a bit."

"I have a name Roger. I have a name and an address. I've got to find Victoria Lake. She can explain all of this. And the person who told me that, wouldn't lie." Jake downed the rest of his scotch. Then he folded up his list, put it in his pocket, and stood up as if he were going to walk out of the bar. He was determined to find Victoria Lake.

Roger the bartender asked him, "Anything I can do to help you Jake?"

"Yes Roger, as a matter of fact there is. You still keep a stash of IDs and credit cards that drunkards forget to collect at the end of the night?"

"Bigger stash than ever. These days, weeks go by before some of these people realize they left them behind."

"Find me an ID Roger. I need one that looks at least a little like me. It should be close in age… that's all they really look at in the Airport. Then I need some credit cards and if you can spare it, a couple grand. I'm good for it. I'll pay you back double."

"Jake I don't know man. I don't know about doling out a couple grand. Sure sounds like some serious mess you're in."

"Come on Roger. How long have I been coming here?"

"Long enough to believe me when I say that if you go into an airport and shuck out a thousand bucks cash, you're going to draw more scrutiny than a terrorist holding hand grenades. I'll give you the cash but let me book you a flight. Where you going?"

"Amsterdam."

"You'll need a passport. There are couple in here from some tourists. Oh here's a good one right here. Victor Skolintsky from Poland. He's a couple years older than you, but I think it looks close enough. I think it'll work."

"No worries. Back in the day, when I was in my prime, I had many years of experience using other people's IDs that were far older than me. I should be able to get by. Thanks Roger!" He chuckled.

"You couldn't have pulled that fake ID crap on me brother! But anyways, no thanking me. Hec, it's nothing. This bar wouldn't be here if you hadn't helped me with that lawsuit thing a few years back. I owe you."

"No seriously. I knew you were good for an emergency loan and a bailout. But thanks… thanks for believing in me Roger. You're probably the only person left that does."

"Come on now Jake. Just remember what you always used to tell me, that the truth will come out in the end. It always comes out, in the end."

"Let's just hope it comes out soon enough to do me some good. I seem to be running on borrowed time."

"Use my car Jake. Go to the airport now. And call me if there's anything else I can do." Roger threw him the keys, they did the typical manly half hug thing and Jake ditched out the back of the bar. He got in Roger's car, an old beat up Chevy Malibu, and drove to Dulles International Airport.

CHAPTER 57

Amsterdam, The Netherlands

"Coffee, with milk," Jake ordered from the waitress at the breakfast café in the lobby of the Krasnapolsky Hotel at Dam Square in the center of downtown Amsterdam. The Krasnapolsky was a luxurious hotel in a central location, walking distance to all the places Jake intended to visit. The timing of his red eye flight put him on the ground early in the morning. It was only 6:45 A.M. when he sat down for some coffee. He needed to kill a few hours before finding his way to the home of Victoria Lake.

While sipping his coffee, Jake played with the pocket watch his father had given to him.

There has to be something more to this reincarnation stuff. But why would my father keep it a secret?

*   *   *

Unable to wait any longer for answers, it was around 9:30 AM when Jake finally walked to 176 Witte De Withstraat. After he knocked, a woman answered in Dutch from behind the closed front door, "Hallo?"

"Is this the home of Victoria Lake?"

"Who is that? How did you get this address? What do you want?" she responded, with a Dutch accent, although switching to English.

"This is Jakob Hunter. Ms. Lake, it's imperative that I speak with you about..."

"You have the wrong person Sir."

"Please Ms. Lake. My father was a friend of yours. He is in grave danger..."

"I don't care who is in trouble. This is not the home of Victoria Lake. Now please go away."

There was a moment of silence, but then Jake knocked again and said, "Ms. Lake, my father desperately needs your help. He has been kidnapped and taken to India. He told me to seek you out. He said that you were a close friend of his. He gave me a watch that you once gave to him."

"A watch? What kind of watch?" she asked.

"It's a pocket watch to be exact."

"What does this pocket watch say on it?"

"It says, vires sapientia fides virtus veneration veritas."

"What did you say your father's name is?"

"Dr. William Hunter. The watch is also engraved with a gift message from you to him. But he gave it to me and told me to use it, just last week. I didn't know what he meant at first, but events have... well, desperation has led me to you. Please Ms. Lake, I am out of options for helping my father. We desperately need your assistance." Jake flashed the watch in front of the view from the peephole.

"Fine, OK. You may come in. But I am not sure I'll be able to help you much. It is your father who always helps me." And she opened the door to her row home on the quaint cobblestone street overlooking the canals of Amsterdam. Jake went in and was greeted with a cup of tea and some biscuits by a woman in her 50's who was in remarkably good shape for her age.

*   *   *

After some very brief small talk, Jake got to the point of his visit and asked Victoria Lake, "Were you a patient in the Nakuru Trials?"

"No. But what I witnessed there was enough to cause them to want me dead."

"You look fairly alive to me."

"I am relatively safe, for the moment. And that's assuming you haven't blown my cover by coming here. But twenty years ago, when the Nakuru trial was in full operation, I was shot in the side of the head while working on the project as a nurse. The bullet grazed my brain and left me in a coma for over a week. When I came out of the coma, I couldn't remember my name, where I was from, nor anything from my past. I had no recollection of being shot at, or the atrocities I had witnessed. The doctors said I would never regain my memory. In retrospect, it was that awful prognosis that probably saved my life, at first."

Jake's face lit up, "With no memory, you were no longer a threat."

"Exactly. But then your father came along. I didn't know it at the time, but we were already closely acquainted from our work together on the trial."

"What was that about? My father was responsible for your being shot at?"

"Not at all. Have some patience young man. Give me a minute and you'll understand all that is troubling you. Your father gave me a reason for living. Hmm, let me see, how can I better explain this? You see, although I've only lived in Amsterdam a short while, I've come to know several of the city's unique personalities. There is much talk about the liberal application of marijuana laws here. And it's true that it does a great deal for the tourism. But there was a man I met recently, with whom I had a lovely, albeit sad conversation for almost an entire afternoon. I met him in one of the coffee shops. I wasn't there for the same reasons he was. I simply wanted a coffee and lacked the energy that day to make it down the street to my favorite café. Well low and behold, this kind man entertained me for hours."

"So you enjoy conversations with intoxicated people. And that is somehow important?"

"Not exactly. You see, what this man had, was a lifetime of excessive marijuana smoking. You could see it in his skin which made him look twenty years older than he was. But the real point is that his drug use robbed him of reasonable judgment, without him even knowing. In other words, he likely believed it was easier to propagate his problem through continued escape rather than to clean up his act and have a shot at actually appreciating what is important in life."

"Again, I'm not sure where you're going with this."

"Jake, when I went back a week later to talk with that lonely man, what do you think happened?"

"He probably was happy to see a familiar face and make a friend?"

"Jakob, this man started telling me his story all over again, as if he had never met me a week earlier."

"Wow. His memory was that damaged from the drug use?! That is sad."

"Very sad indeed. This man was not suffering from any medical illness other than having destroyed his mind from overindulgence. His quick and easy escapes from reality had turned his life into a living hell, and I'm not sure he even realized it."

"OK, that makes sense Ms. Lake. But still, how does this relate to you and my father?"

"Your father Jakob, came to me one day and said there was a small chance he could give me back my memories. He said it was highly experimental and the risk was so great, that I was just as likely, perhaps more likely, to wind up insane or dead."

"But you took the chance?"

"I did. I was only thirty-two at the time. But if I live to be eighty, without having had the treatment, it would have meant that about half my life was erased. I would have been just like that man in the coffee shop, only not by free will. In other words, there was no choice to be made in my opinion. There was enough left up there in my head to know that any chance of repairing my mind was worth it, no matter what the risk, no matter how challenging, no matter what. But your father Jake, is a brilliant man. In the weeks leading up to the procedure, my confidence in his work grew."

"You're too kind Ms. Lake."

"No Jake. I don't exaggerate. They say I was smiling contently, like a child on a birthday, when I was carted into the room where your father gave me my life back."

"So it worked?"

"It worked. And to my horror, I woke up a few days later, screaming at the memories it brought back to me. Memories of atrocities you couldn't or wouldn't ever want to imagine."

"At Nakuru?"

"Yes. Crimes against humanity committed during western sponsored medical trials at Nakuru, in a remote area of Kenya."

"Africa. So it is true. I would say that's unbelievable, but I guess nothing is anymore."

"Why is Africa unbelievable as the location? Don't you see, by working in such a remote area, they almost got away with using human guinea pigs?"

"It's not that. I mean, I get that part. It's just the past week has been a bit unusual for me. I've been in planes more than I've been on the ground. I mean, I knew my father was a doctor, but I had no idea any of this was ever a remote possibility. I just never imagined my father to be wrapped up in these kinds of things. Anyways, so what caused you to be here, in Amsterdam?"

"The problem was that the procedure performed by your father was ground breaking. It gathered wide-spread attention. Matters were not helped by my sense of ethics, which forced me to go public with information on what I knew about at Nakuru," she paused, to wipe a tear from her eye, "At first, I pretended not to know. I didn't even tell your father. I knew that Peter Lansing would kill to protect his secrets, and the last thing I wanted to do was put your father's life in danger. After a few weeks, I could no longer sleep. Shortly after that, I could no longer eat. Eventually, I spent all day crying. I was falling apart with the knowledge of burying an atrocity. I had to act, or I would have been as bad as them. What is it they say, 'Intentional ignorance by great men is worse than atrocities by weak men' or something like that?"

Jake grinned and joked, "I think you just made that up, but it sounds good." They smiled at each other.

"Your father helped me again. He put me in touch with friends of his that live here in Amsterdam. And then he gave me this place to stay, close by, so they can protect me. They told me I had implicated the most dangerous man since Al Capone. I am supposed to testify next week. That's what makes it so strange meeting you now, only days before a trial that could put Peter Lansing behind bars for the rest of his life."

Jake sat back in his chair and let out a huge, "HAH! No, not strange at all. I can assure you, there is no coincidence in the timing of our meeting today. Listen, we had better get in touch with whoever it is protecting you and find you a new hiding spot."

"Why? This one works and I've grown to love Amsterdam. It gets talked about for all the wrong reasons. It should be talked about for how beautiful it is, being one of the few European cities not destroyed in the wars. And besides, I've been safe here so far."

"I understand Ms. Lake. But the thing is, I'm a nobody. I'm just a washed up lawyer. Well, at least I may still get to be a lawyer again, but I'm not likely to have any clients. The point is, if I was able to find you, so can they, whoever they are. And for all I know, *they* may have been following me."

"Oh my, you think you were followed?"

"I don't know. But please don't panic. I am pretty sure I wasn't. Right now, they probably think I am dead. But I've seen too much go wrong in the last week to take any chances. We cannot risk you being exposed. Can you call your contacts and get a new hiding spot? Would you do it for me?"

"Sure Jake. You know, you sure do remind me of your father!"

"After you make the call, would you be comfortable telling me exactly what happened at Nakuru and how my father was involved? I mean, was he somehow responsible directly or even indirectly for crimes against humanity?"

"Easy Jakob. Your father is probably the best human being I know, so just rest easy. But yes, I will tell you everything. Drink your tea while I make the call. I'll just be upstairs in my office."

She walked upstairs to make the call while Jake sipped on what he guessed was Earl Grey, which was by then lukewarm. The biscuits however, were delicious, especially for a guy that hadn't slept or had a proper meal in over a week. Jake wondered what Victoria witnessed in Kenya that would warrant ongoing attempts at killing her. A bead of sweat dripped from his forehead as his mind then shifted to how his father could have been involved, even indirectly. Left to his imagination was not a good thing. Victoria couldn't get back quickly enough.

CHAPTER 58

Amsterdam, The Netherlands
176 Witte De Withstraat

Victoria walked back down the steps with stress showing on her face. Jake asked, "How did it go?"

"They say they're already over budget with my protection services and that I am worrying for nothing."

"Did you tell them that I was here?"

"I did, and it didn't make any difference in their position. In fact, they started acting weird once I told them."

Jake asked, "How so? How were they weird?"

"They started asking strange questions that seemed irrelevant, such as how long were you staying, how you found me, what you wanted, and so on."

"That is interesting. What else did they ask?"

"It was confusing actually. But I got the feeling they wanted me to keep you here."

"Never a dull moment," Jake sighed, exhausted from the constant drama.

It's no longer safe here. We need to leave.

He suggested, "Why don't we take a stroll and get out of the house for a bit? The last thing I wanted to do was put you or anyone else in more danger, but I didn't come all this way to leave without answers."

They walked a few blocks to a nearby gondola station and paid for a city tour by boat. The canal system in downtown Amsterdam encircles the city center through a series of connected bands of waterways which provide access to most of the neighborhoods. In addition, the canal boat tours provide for a spectacular viewing of the city's prettiest streets, and architecture that is hundreds of years older than the oldest buildings in America. Jake was there with Victoria at the time of year where Amsterdam's northern location provides for fall days full of brilliant sunshine, often lasting as late as 10 PM, with temperatures in the low 70's.

"So Victoria, I need to know, was my father involved in anything unethical during the Nakuru trials? There are people who have killed, many times already, for even the slightest bits of information about what went on there. It's driving me insane to think my father was somehow associated with harming people."

"Rest easy Jake. Your father's involvement was similar to what he has dedicated most of his life towards, which is helping others. He was working for a study, as part of a post medical school internship. I never knew who funded the study, as that information was only given to those at the highest levels. In fact, I'm not sure your father even knew. Everything was, for the most part, very tight lipped."

"So some anonymous companies or people…"

"Or governments," she interjected, "People with power and money and the ability to make things happen thousands of miles away, in the far reaches of a distant continent. Nakuru was a shanty village, nowhere near close to a major airport. We were at liberty to do whatever we wanted there, with our 'volunteers.' And we did. Eventually, I grew suspicious of how we were treating the native peoples."

"Were they treated poorly?"

"No, on the contrary, they were treated in relative royalty compared to what they were used to. It was too much. I knew there was something more to the motives. When I dug a little deeper, I found out that your father's partner in the study..."

Jake interrupted, "Peter Lansing?"

"Exactly. He apparently had a different set of directives from your father."

"What exactly was my father's directive?"

"Jake, you are about as patient as William!" she smiled at him, "That was what I loved about your father. Time was always of the essence; life is too short he would always say. Try to relax, enjoy the ride a bit, it's going to take me a while to explain all this in a way that makes sense."

Jake sat back in the boat and enjoyed the warm sun on his face, while Victoria began to explain, in excruciating detail, the events that took place during the Nakuru trial and why people were willing to kill for that information.

While on the ride in the gondola, Victoria talked Jake into a distant world from her past. It was set in Nakuru, Kenya:

*   *   *

As a young nurse, the opportunity to work on a well funded clinical trial designed to revolutionize treatments for cognitive disorders was Victoria's dream. Dr. William Hunter was only a few years older than Victoria, and her crush on him left her extra motivated to go to work in the mornings.

One day, while at work, Dr. Hunter's partner, Dr. Peter Lansing stopped in and asked if he could borrow a nurse for the day. He was frantic, as he was in the middle of a critical stage of his work and his head nurse had to leave the project unexpectedly, due to some sort of family emergency. As it was, most of William's team was out sick that week, dealing with an assortment of illnesses native to the African continent. That left only Victoria to assist, which she willingly agreed to, thinking it would be an opportunity to learn more about the other studies that made up the Nakuru project.

Mid day rounds involved checking drug dosages from the prior day and administering new dosages. Victoria would read and update the charts hanging from the patients' beds, while Dr. Lansing, would instruct her what medicines to administer. They navigated a tent lined with beds on both sides, pushing a rolling metal cart stacked full of vials of experimental intravenous drugs. Curious as to the differences in the medicines, she asked Dr. Lansing, "Why haven't I heard of all these drugs? I thought your project was supposed to be essentially parallel to ours except with a few minor variations to form control groups."

"You're curious. That can be good and bad," he responded while barely glancing at her. His coldness gave her the chills and she did not press for more of an answer even though his response spiked her curiosity. "Read the next chart please nurse," Dr. Lansing instructed, trying to further dissuade her from any more questions.

"Patient 27.54… what is this numbering system?" she asked.

"27 is the line of drugs we are testing. The numbers after the decimal indicate the attempt."

"You mean to tell me this is the 54th patient you have tried this drug on? What happened to the others?"

"That's irrelevant. Please nurse, if you will, the dosage from yesterday's administration? I don't have all day for this."

"Sorry Dr. Lansing. It reads, 200 g of… what on earth is corticoselegeline tropica 9z?"

"Again you persist with the questions. It's a drug we are testing to accelerate memory restoration. It has proven highly effective in monkeys. But we cannot seem to get it to work in humans without extreme adverse effects, often resulting in death by suicide. Now then, do you really want to ask more questions? You see, the world isn't always the bed of rose petals you've no doubt grown accustomed to while working with Dr. Hunter. Someone has to do the dirty work, and this is where it's done. If you cannot handle it, you may be excused."

"Sorry, no, it's fine. I was just curious."

"Let that be the last time you forget what curiosity did for the cat."

"Yes sir," a young Victoria Lake responded like a chastised child.

They continued their rounds until interrupted by a circus of activity. A man known only by the name, Kanja, was carried into the medical tent. Screams for help beckoned Dr. Lansing and Victoria to his attention. The man had fallen from a cliff and had severe head trauma. Initial diagnosis based on accepted medical procedures was a 100% likelihood that he would have severe brain damage, loss of memory, probable loss of most cognitive processing. Dr. Lansing and the patient's family members argued over letting the man die in peace, rather than live a life of essentially brainless functioning, with Lansing repeatedly telling the family he could do nothing. A native African woman who appeared to be the injured man's wife was begging him, on her knees, crying and pleading for help. Finally Dr Lansing said, with a translator next to him repeating his words in Swahili, "There is nothing we can do, I am sorry. We will minimize his pain and suffering, but I'm afraid that is the best we can offer."

An hour later, Victoria left the tent where Lansing was conducting his studies to take a lunch break. On her way back to her dorm, she realized she had left her journal back in the tent. Obsessed with her journal and determined to keep it private, she scampered back to retrieve it. As she walked in, a startled Dr. Lansing asked her what she was doing back.

"I forgot my journal," she replied before freezing in place, confused at what she saw in front of her, "What are you doing to that patient? Isn't that the man they brought in earlier today," she timidly asked.

Lansing was performing surgery on the man. He had just drilled two holes in his skull and was feeding a very thin tube into the man's brain. It was a procedure that normally required two sets of hands, but Lansing had rigged his equipment so that he could perform it unassisted. He did not want Victoria observing what he was doing but just as he was about to send her away, the patient started regaining consciousness. It was fortuitous in a way, that she had happened back into the tent, otherwise, the procedure would have been completely botched and the patient likely left completely brain dead. "Get over here and assist. Can't you see this patient needs more anesthesia?"

"Yes sir, Dr. Lansing. I'm on it." Victoria knocked the patient back to unconsciousness while staring in wonder at the procedure she was observing. A video monitor showed real time MRI images of the inserted probe and the target location for the diodes Lansing was implanting. Strangely, as she watched Dr. Lansing work, he positioned the diodes in the man's brain away from the targets marked on the monitor.

"Doctor, do you realize you are deviating from the proscribed coordinates displayed on the monitor?"

"Shut up. If you repeat any of what you've seen today, even one word, it will be your last day on the job. Understand?"

"Yes sir."

*   *   *

Two weeks of sleepless nights passed before Victoria finally worked up the courage to try to figure out what Dr. Lansing had been up to. She waited until a Saturday night, while Lansing was in the make-shift pub they had in town. Then, she went into his cabin. Lansing had his own private communications station which was odd, considering everyone had access to the one in the main research building. At his desk, she found records of his medical work that he had apparently been transmitting to someplace called Balikpapan, Indonesia.

Intrigued as to why he needed to transmit to that location and in secret, she started flipping through the journals and medical logs. She was stunned at the experiments he had been performing. They were gross deviations from what she understood the objectives of the project to include. Engrossed in the unbelievable, she lost of track of time.

Almost a half hour later she was startled when she heard, "I warned you about curiosity, didn't I young lady. I see it's gotten the best of you," coming from an intoxicated Dr. Peter Lansing who was slurring profusely while holding his handgun at his side.

"Oh Dr. Lansing, I am so sorry; I just wanted to find out what happened to that man we were working on the other day. I looked for him in the recovery tent but he was gone and there was no record of him ever having been there. So then I came here to ask you but you were out."

"Save your squabbling lies for someone dumb enough to believe them. Now get up! If you don't mind, I'd rather not get blood all over the inside of my cabin." Victoria trembled uncontrollably as she stood. Peter Lansing grabbed her with his left hand and whipped her around. She flew towards the door of his cabin. He was behind her instantly, pushing her out the door, and around to the back of the building. There was only African jungle behind his building as it was at the edge of the makeshift research center that had been setup.

Lansing fired one shot which hit her in the head and sent her to the ground. Then he went back inside his cabin and retrieved a small box, about the size of a shoe box. He made sure Victoria's fingerprints were all over the box before throwing it down on the ground next to her limp body. Ivory artifacts fell from the box. It contained a wealth of the internationally banned treasures. He looked back at his handiwork, convinced the authorities would conclude she had accidentally become entangled with poachers trading illegally in forbidden ivory. Back inside his cabin, he washed his hands and went to bed and slept peacefully, as if nothing had happened. His heart rate never went above normal and he fell asleep within two minutes of putting his head on his pillow.

*   *   *

Back on the gondola ride, in the present, Jake asked, "So then my father saved you?"

"Yes. He did. First he saved my life. Then he restored my memory which was initially lost from the damage done by being shot in the head. Lansing's inebriation probably saved me from a lethal shot. His aim was off and the bullet entered my left cheek with a slight downward trajectory. It exited the back of my skull having inflicted minimal damage to my brain's septal region. That's the part responsible for memory."

"Got it. Something I will never forget after this week."

"So why kill you? What exactly was Lansing doing that could be so incriminating that would…." Jake was interrupted by a loud bang and then the splash of the gondolier falling into the canal. There was a man on a nearby embankment that was taking aim and readying to fire again. Without thinking, Jake flipped the gondola sending him and Victoria backwards into the filthy canal, but also putting the upside down boat in between them and the shooter. "Hold on to the boat and keep your head down," he said to Victoria while maneuvering it to a nearby dock. Crowds of people screaming alerted nearby police who could do little to immediately help them, as street officers in Amsterdam do not carry weapons. But they had bought enough time by flipping the boat. Eventually the man got nervous and fled. Jake never got a good look at him.

As they climbed out of the filthy water, Jake asked pointedly, "Listen Victoria, I want to know more about what happened at Nakuru. I want to know all of it. But what I need right now is access to the medical files from Nakuru. And if you have it, I need something called a Digitalis. Does that have any meaning to you?"

Victoria brushed aside her dripping hair and looked at Jake, with concern in her eyes, she said, "Yes Jake. I have a copy of the Digitalis. Your father asked me to keep it safe. He told me there were only two copies of it. One he kept with him at all times, and this one. You can take it if you think it will save his life. In any case, it is evidently, no longer safe with me."

"Thank you Victoria. You have probably just saved my father. But what about Aguas Muertas? Supposedly we retrieved a copy of the Digitalis from there a few days ago."

"Anything retrieved from Aguas Muertas would be extremely antiquated compared to your father's recent work. If anyone is able to un-encrypt files from that site, they will be in for a huge surprise. And it certainly will not include knowing what makes up the Digitalis. There's a reason why the Scientia Pro Curatio's Global Council shut that place down and brokered a deal to keep it hidden and highly guarded. And that reason was strong enough that they made sure no one could ever get the Digitalis out of there.

"I don't get it, then what is on that hard drive that we got from the vault?"

"That's a good question. It's one I would love to know the answer to."

"You and me both," Jake replied, "It will have to wait for now however. I need to go help my father."

"Bring him back to me safely Jake. Please."

"Bring him back to you? You mean you two were...? Um, OK, will you be OK? It doesn't seem safe for you here any longer?"

"I'll be fine Jake. Like your father, my family is originally from the Netherlands. I have places I can go outside the city for a while that should be safe. Besides, I only need a few more days and then hopefully all this will be over."

"I don't know Victoria. 'All this' doesn't seem like the type of thing that is, well, ever over. Not with what's at stake. At least, if I'm guessing correctly as to what's at stake. I mean, you're living proof that memory can be restored. I can't believe my father never told me about you. Why would he keep you a secret from the world?"

"Well, you know, Jake, I think you are right about one thing. The people after the Digitalis will probably never stop trying to steal what your father worked so hard on for so many years. Don't let anyone but your father know you have it Jake. Once it becomes public knowledge, certain groups of people will stop at nothing to remove any traces of its true origins, including anyone that could explain them, which would include your father."

"You mean they would have to kill him and probably us as well?"

"I'm afraid so Jake."

"Thank you Victoria, for all your help."

"Not sure I helped much Jake, but I hope so. Please take care of yourself and get your father to safety for me. I need to see him back in one piece."

"I will." And Jake started to walk away, but at the last second paused and turned back to ask, "You know Victoria, there is just one thing I don't get?"

"Yes? What's that?"

"Well I get the part about Peter Lansing wanting to kill you to hide crimes against humanity. I even get that my father has created something called a Digitalis that everyone and their brother wants."

"Ok, so what's your question Jake."

"Well, the thing is, the person who wants me to get the Digitalis doesn't seem to care about restoring memory for victims of Alzheimer's or head trauma, or even for the irretrievably dim-witted. Nor do they care about brainwashing people."

"Oh? What do they care about Jake?"

"Something in my gut tells me you already know, so why don't I hear your version of the truth first? How about it? Are you going to tell me, or do I have to pry it out of you?"

"I don't know what you are talking about Jake. Is this really a time for games and riddles?"

"Reincarnation is what I am talking about. How are you, no, how is the Digitalis and whatever happened at Nakuru related to reincarnation?"

"Jake, you're a good man, like your father, whom I love. So I will tell you this much, I am not the world renown neurosurgeon. Your father gets that prestige. So you will have to ask him to explain it to you Jake. All I know is that I got half my life back... and a whole lot more."

"So you're telling me it's real. All this is really real? You can recall memories from lives other than your own – verifiable memories? You are telling me you are living proof that reincarnation exists?"

"Yes Jake. That is what I am telling you."

CHAPTER 59

Amsterdam, The Netherlands

Jake and Victoria got into separate cabs. Jake wondered if he would ever see her alive again. And he couldn't believe a woman he had never heard of had professed to love his father. Tears streamed down his face at how desperate his situation had become. Everything was real, too real, and still unbelievable. Having lost the satellite phone that kept him in touch with Lavanya, he had no way to know if he was too late, or if there was still a chance to save his father.

For the first time in his life he felt truly overwhelmed, but only until the cabbie distracted him by asking what airline he wanted. He held the Digitalis in his hand, which Victoria Lake had given to him upon his departure. It was a stainless steel canister that looked and felt like a coffee thermos. Jake did not open it up, at first because part of him didn't want to know what was inside or risk exposure to it, but also because he didn't have the combination to the digital lock that kept the top on. When it shook, it made sounds as if it were a liquid, although it was impossible to know if that was part of the disguise or was from the Digitalis itself. Jake figured he would have plenty of time to contemplate what could be inside the canister during the long flight to India. In any case, he felt a sense of relief in finally having in his possession the key to saving his father's life, and possibly the only remaining asset from his life's work.

*　　　*　　　*

Being trapped on an airplane for eighteen hours, Jake found reason for concern in Victoria's statement that only she and his father had copies of the Digitalis. If that were true, with his father's copy still missing since the plane crash, then what Jake had in his luggage was in fact all that remained of Hunter Neurologics. The risk of checking baggage was to risk his father's life, but he had no choice. Airport security wasn't going to make an exception for someone wanted by the FBI. Jake checked a suitcase containing the Digitalis, using the same passport he got from his bartender friend in Georgetown. He worried about lost luggage. He worried about staying alive.

I wonder who has the other copy?

His mind was replaying over and over the injustice of the past few weeks and it left his blood boiling. Eighteen hours was too long for that so Jake put his mind to work formulating a plan for retaking control of his life. One way or another, he would find Lavanya Yashodhara and begin to set things straight.

It is not more surprising to be born twice than once; everything in nature is resurrection.

–Voltaire

CHAPTER 60

Nagpur, India
(Maharashtra State – Geographic Center of India)

Jake knew the closest city of entry to Yashodhara Palace was Nagpur in the Maharashtra state, also known for being the geographic center of India. From conversational small talk, Jake was under the impression the palace was a good distance from Nagpur. After a connecting flight from Mumbai, he was surprised to find upon arrival in Nagpur that Lavanya had a car waiting for him.

How could she have known I was in route? How can anyone be that well informed?

It was a heavily armored limousine. In the front, was an AK-47 toting guard in addition to the driver. Two more men rode in the passenger compartment with Jake. Another car followed behind them. Jake had not mentioned his trip to Amsterdam. He wondered how she could have picked up his trail and if she was responsible for the shooter in Amsterdam. But it didn't make sense. Why would Lavanya want Victoria dead? She was to testify against Peter Lansing, not Lavanya. Perhaps they were working together? Or maybe they were archrivals going after the same prize, the Digitalis. Jake hoped having the actual Digitalis would be enough to free his father. And in a way, he was relieved that maybe soon he could find out what it was made of... how it worked, and what else it could do.

He also wanted freedom from the nightmare he had been dragged into. And worse, even though he knew it was wrong and could come at a cost that would be regretted later, Jake wanted revenge.

As a lawyer, he had seen people destroy themselves, ruining their own families in quests for *justice*. No matter how right someone was, and no matter how much money he won in court for some of his clients, they never achieved peace by going after what he always called *'rationalized revenge.'* Unfortunately, with his emotions getting the best of him, Jake began *rationalizing* his own plans, as justice for himself, for his wife, for his father, and for all that was right in the world. Against his better judgment, Jake continued to plot his revenge.

*   *   *

Two hours later, Jake arrived at the well secluded, yet expansive Yashodhara Palace in the remote wilderness of central India. He immediately asked to see his father. But of course there would be a delay while Lavanya probed him for information.

Lavanya was pleased that Jake had the Digitalis and seemed unconcerned about the death of his wife, or the loss of the Nakuru files. Although Lavanya's global resources had informed her of Jake's time in Amsterdam, she did not know why he went there. And Jake did not tell her, instead claiming to have acquired the Digitalis in Venezuela.

After digesting the current state of affairs, Jake was reunited with his father who was in relatively good health and spirits despite the turmoil he had experienced. Without the need for communication, both of them could tell the other had realized it was imperative they win Lavanya's allegiance in order to gain the leverage they would need to ensure their own safety. Further flashes in their eyes also showed a hidden longing for private conversation. Theirs was a communication that could only be understood by family members. But there were additional matters that would require live dialogue.

Unfortunately, no such opportunity came on the first night as Lavanya was keeping a close eye on the father and son and never left them for even a split second to converse in private.

*　　*　　*

After a lengthy dinner that evening, Jake's father went to his sleeping quarters, accompanied by a guard to ensure no attempts at escape. That left Jake alone with Lavanya in the palace library. She got up to get herself a drink from the bar and offered one to Jake. He had not wanted to drink under the circumstances as he wanted his mind keen and alert, but Lavanya was seductive, amazingly attractive and charming. The thought of a scotch with her wasn't half bad, even if she was presenting it in a way that was more romantic than normally acceptable for a married man. But he reminded himself that his wife had been murdered, and he didn't have to feel guilty for using sex to get what he wanted - revenge. With only a fleeting thought that he shouldn't let his ego deceive him into thinking he was the seducer, Jake accepted the offer for a drink.

It was a mistake however, as he was exhausted from the travel, being shot at, etc. The scotch went straight to his head and kept his wife's death fresh on his mind. But she had betrayed his trust through her disloyalty. To him, it meant there could be no reconciliation, no way to talk, communicate, and work towards peace, at least, not in his present life. That was more frustrating than anything else for him. That is, the idea of his wife dying under such unsettling circumstances cursed Jake with feelings of unresolved conflict. And for a person who went to law school so that he could spend his life fighting against injustice, to have no clue how to avenge what was done to his wife, left him in utter despair and anguish. There would be little sleeping for Jake anytime soon, and he would stop at nothing to achieve his new goals.

Lavanya sensed his despair and was intent on using it to her advantage, something she was highly skilled at doing. She wanted to control Jake Hunter, like she controlled most men. That she wasn't immediately able to completely control him, was not only obvious, but also irritated her, and left her obsessed with doing so. She knew alcohol could help her achieve her goals, and poured Jake a double with some added ingredients put in for good measure. She dismissed her remaining guards, but Jake was too enervated to notice the unusual action. Lavanya had him right where she wanted.

"So tell me Jake, what happened in D.C. that caused you to lose the Nakuru files?"

"I'm not sure I ever had them to be honest."

"You reported having acquired them, did you not? Regardless, what happened to you? My people tell me your home was literally blown to bits. Do you know by whom? Was your wife able to survive?"

"My wife died, most likely, in the explosion."

"I'm sorry to hear that. Are you sad?"

"I don't know. I mean, of course I am sad. And I am angry. I am angry at the injustice of it all. Part of her loved me; that much I know. But she also acted very strangely, almost like she wasn't on my side."

"Jake, I don't want to hurt you any further, but if I were in your position I would want to know the truth."

"Well there you go Lavanya. You can't say that without now telling me whatever it is you know. So let's hear it."

"Jake, I had men watching you, your father, your family, for some time. I assume you know that much already. That is, surely you know by now that I do my homework and am extremely well informed."

"I sort of figured as much, yes."

"We have observed that your wife wasn't always loyal to you."

"That's one hell of an accusation!" he paused, downed the rest of his scotch, put his head in his hands in exhaustion and then in a vain attempt to fight the reality he already knew to be true, he did what he was best at, cross examined in an attempt to distort reality, "You personally observed this disloyal behavior? And what exactly was observed? How can you be certain anything more than superficial indiscretions took place?"

"Jake, there are pictures, of the skin on skin variety. I can have one of my men bring them to you if you like. I'm sorry Jake. But apparently this wasn't a one time or one man thing."

Defeated and too weak to fight his despair, Jake acquiesced, "No, I somewhat figured as much. I mean, I could just tell the bond had been violated the last time she was with me, you know, intimately. But at least I got to be with her one last time." Jake tried his best to control his emotions, although his voice cracked a bit at the weight of being told in such unequivocal terms that his deepest trust had been betrayed. The cornerstone in the foundation of everything that was real to him had been unequivocally shattered and destroyed. That was when Lavanya moved closer to him and placed her arm around him.

When Jake finally composed himself again, he looked at Lavanya with glassy eyes while she moved in and kissed him. He was motionless at first, numb with pain. But as she pressed her soft lips against his, Jake felt comforted and warmed. As she slowly and patiently continued her pursuit,

Jake finally gave in and kissed back. Lavanya was an incredible kisser in addition to being perhaps the most beautiful woman he had ever seen. They were alone in the room and indulged in each other before moving to Lavanya's bedroom where they spent several more hours together before Jake fell asleep. Lavanya rested, but never closed her eyes. Her mind was too busy plotting the next day.

CHAPTER 61

Yashodhara Palace

The next morning, Dr. Hunter bought time alone with his son after telling Lavanya it would take him a while to reconstruct the Digitalis from what he claimed were merely raw ingredients in the canister. In the labs far underneath Yashodhara Palace, Jake watched his father punch in a code, from memory. It released the lock on the Digitalis canister given to them by Victoria Lake.

The top, when removed and flipped upside down, doubled as a cup, completing the disguise as a coffee thermos. Dr. Hunter removed a pressed and dried purple flower from inside the cup, rinsed it with water and placed it on the lab table. Next he removed the inner seal on the canister and poured the liquid into the cup. Jake asked, "Is that the Digitalis?" But Jake's father just ignored him, and instead put the cup of liquid on top of a nearby Bunsen Burner. A few seconds later, steam frothing from the top, he brought it back over to where Jake was sitting. Again, he asked, "Dad, what exactly is the Digitalis? Why are you heating it?"

Then his father drank it. Jake gasped and exclaimed,

"What? What are you doing? Why?"

"Son, why shouldn't I drink it? You've met the woman right? Didn't she give you any tea? It's delicious, right? Best tea known to mankind. She knows how much I love her tea."

"You have to be kidding me! You mean there is no Digitalis? That was just a canister of tea?"

"Not just any tea son. But Victoria's tea. For the first time since your mother, I think I may be in love again."

"That's great Pops, but I find it hard to believe people have been getting killed over a cup of tea. I'd like some answers about the Digitalis. After everything I've been through, I deserve some answers. If this isn't it, then where is it?"

"No searching required son. We have what we need, right here." And he held up the purple flower.

Jake stared momentarily before remembering his conversations with Kennedy about Digitoxin. He blurted out, "You've got to be…That's worse than a cup of tea."

"No son, I'm not kidding. This is the common Foxglove flower. It is one of the most beautiful flowers in the world. You may have noticed them all over Isla Dedaleras, which translated, means Island of the Foxglove."

"Isn't it also one of the most deadly plant species, if I recall?"

"Not bad. Your science knowledge isn't half bad for a stinkin' lawyer. You are correct. In fact, its toxins, even in small dosages can kill adult humans. But when just the right amount of pollen falls from a bouquet of flowers next to your favorite patient, who is undergoing surgery for major head trauma, you have what some would call, Nobel Prize winning scientific advances."

"But isn't there a drug, a type of Digitoxin, which is used for heart patients? Wouldn't someone else have discovered this?"

"Not likely Jake. The use of Digitoxin for heart

patients doesn't involve infusing the drug into the brain's septal region, although, it's a similar concept. But instead of a 'turbo boost' for the heart, what I found was through the accidental combination of the raw form of the drug with my work on the Digitalis, I could give a turbo boost, of sorts, to the brain."

"An accident. It was all an accident. This is beyond amazing."

"Hardly," his father replied, "If I had ten grand for every year that passed of intense research where I recalled the story of Alexander Graham Bell accidentally inventing the telephone, I could probably retire. If I had another ten grand for all the other accidents that helped with the invention of things like electricity, for example, I could retire in comfort."

"Enough with the history lecture. Please tell me you've figured out the correct dosage since then?"

"I wish I could. But my work was never meant for unleashing a war of religion. We tried to hide what happened at Nakuru not only to keep Peter Lansing from killing everyone involved, but also because we knew the ramifications of what happened to Victoria could change the map of religion more significantly than any other event since the fall of the Roman Empire."

"Why do you say that? And who is we anyway? Is that the group in Amsterdam?"

"The Scientia Pro Curatio is what we informally call the organization that created the investment trust. But to answer your question, *we* does not include *them*." Without providing any further details, Jake's father drew his attention to the religious impact of the Digitalis, "Think about it Jake. How long have academia and religious authority been at odds with each other? It's always been Darwin versus Jesus, right?"

"I'm familiar with the feud."

Their conversation was abruptly interrupted by

Lavanya strutting in without warning, and interjecting, "But scientifically prove the fundamental tenets of one of the oldest, if not the oldest, of the world's religions and you give it more credibility, more believability, more influence across the globe than any other system of belief known to man. It becomes the de facto, most legitimate, authoritative form of worship. It also officially ends the Darwin debate."

"But why are you doing this, Lavanya? What could you possibly get from all the trauma this would cause to billions of people around the world?" Dr. Hunter asked.

"She gets to lead it Dad. The person who legitimizes what becomes the most powerful and influential organization in the world also gets to rule the world. It's pure, unadulterated greed for power, at its finest."

"Not quite Jake. And frankly, I am disappointed you think so lowly of me. I already have more money than any human being could ever want. No, it's not about money and power for me. It's about the murder of my parents. All of this is so that I get my family's honor back. Surely men of your character can understand that? I get a way for my parents to rest in peace, and at the same time, I earn my personal liberation or Moksha."

"What do your parents have to do with any of this?" Jake asked, confused at how they fit in to all her madness.

Lavanya gave him a deadpan stare that made it clear she was done bantering. Taking control of the conversation, she said, "Never mind the details. Why don't you two pour me a cup of your beloved tea?"

Dr. Hunter stepped backwards, upset that she had found out and asked, "What? But how did you know..."

"You didn't really think I would leave the two of you alone in here without audio-visual monitoring devices in place, did you?" she paused for effect, not expecting an answer to her rhetorical question. "Since you still insist on being unsure of how to repeat your handiwork at Nakuru, and since we are still unable to locate your lover, what was her name again? Oh yes, one Victoria Lake, a childhood sweetheart, I believe? Tell me Dr. Hunter, was she always your sweetheart? For example, was she your sweetheart even while you were married? What about while you were fucking your only son's wife? Was she your sweetheart then as well?"

"No way!" Jake interrupted, "That is bullshit. There is no freak'n way that is true." He turned and faced his father with a look of dreadful fear and worry on his face. Jake asked, "Dad, tell me that isn't true, please?"

Silence ensued. Then Jake continued, "No wait, please don't say anything. I don't think I want to know."

"Guards!" Lavanya beckoned for two of her guards who apparently already had their instructions and were merely waiting for the go ahead to grab Jake and lock him into an operating table. As they walked towards Jake, his father fumbled with the Digitalis canister accidentally knocking it to the ground. He was standing near a table which obstructed Lavanya's line of sight from the waist down. When he bent over to pick up the canister, he twisted the bottom which revealed a small button, he pushed it and a small memory card popped out. He quickly dropped it into his shoe and stood up, pleased that he had retrieved the memory card from the base of the Digitalis canister in a split second, and without being noticed.

Next, Dr. Hunter started yelling at Lavanya, "You are a sick, sick woman. Release him or I will not help you any further."

"On the contrary Dr. Hunter, not only will you continue to help me, but I suspect you are going to be at your absolute finest this afternoon. In fact, since your patient today will be your only son, somehow I suspect this will be the day you finally reveal to the world what it takes to allow a person to experience conscious recognition of past lives. After all, you wouldn't want to betray him twice in one day now would you?"

"Go to hell. You can't make me operate on my own son you sick witch."

"Oh no? Would you prefer I have Dr. Gupta try? Hasn't she shown you the results of her attempts in the Infected Patients lab? She's quite good, but let's face it, her work is amateurish at best when compared to your own. Come now Dr. Hunter, it's do or die time, quite literally, for your son at least. Of course, if you do fail, since you seem to fall in love so easily, I'm sure we can find someone else to use as leverage against you. Maybe Anja will turn up alive, who knows? Of course, I also understand we are very close to locating your dear sweet Victoria. Your son here was recently in Amsterdam and left quite a trail. It shouldn't be too much longer before we're able to use it to find her. I figure she is somewhere near where your beloved Scientia Pro Curatio has its headquarters, in downtown Amsterdam. Who would have thought they could be involved in changing the world forever."

"You'll get no more information from me." Dr. Hunter replied, his face boiling red.

"Well, let's hope it's irrelevant, for your son's sake. Truly, I hope you succeed Dr. Hunter, so that we can put all this hostility behind us. But also, you know," she turned, smiled at Jake, and put one hand on his crotch, as he lay locked into an operating table. Then she looked in his eyes and said, "Jake was awfully good in bed last night. I wouldn't mind rolling around with your son once more. So take care of him Doc? Kay? I'll check in on you boys later this evening. Dr. Gupta and her team will be here to assist you with the procedure. Good luck and let's make history."

Dr. Hunter yelled at Lavanya as she turned her back and walked away, "You know as well as I do, Victoria was an exception! The procedure kills everyone it has been tried on! You cannot make me do this! He will die in a matter of days and nothing will have been accomplished!!"

CHAPTER 62

Yashodhara Palace
(24 Hours Later)

The morning after surgery Jake was lethargic but in remarkably good shape for someone who had holes drilled into his skull followed by the placement of electrical diodes around his brain. His father had whipped together a concoction of Foxglove pollen and a variety of other drugs which he doused the diodes in prior to insertion. Twelve hours after completing the procedure, Jake was given an electrical transponder which could be attached at his hip. Using precise frequencies, it would send electrical currents to his brain through wireless connectivity to the diodes. Lavanya was discussing the outlook with Jake's father and Dr. Gupta.

"So, do we have history doctors?" Lavanya asked them in the post operation observation room where the three of them peered down upon Jake in his recovery bed.

Dr. Hunter was angry and would barely even look at the woman. Instead he focused on analyzing charts and tweaking the frequency of electrical stimulation running into his only son's brain. Dr. Gupta responded to Lavanya, "The procedure itself was a complete success. The only question is whether this drug cocktail Dr. Hunter used will work."

Lavanya asked, "So that was the key? To unleash conscious recognition of past lives, all we needed was a little poisonous flower pollen? Digitoxin. Amazing. All this money and time and we probably never would have figured that out."

Dr. Hunter couldn't look her in the eye. In fact, he was restlessly shifting his gaze left to right as if he was nervous or hiding something. Lavanya noticed, but in her misguided excitement, she failed to register the red flag. She continued, "So this is what will change the world forever then: a Foxglove flower. It is truly fascinating how sometimes the smallest things can have the greatest impacts. What do you think Dr. Gupta, will this craziness really do the trick?"

"It's hard to say this early in the recovery. But it makes sense that the toxin from the flower could trigger an immune system response by the body that essentially super-charges the neurotransmitters in the brain and protects the patient from the cognitive breakdowns we have seen in all our other attempts. Of course, the alternative is still possible as well, that Jake will become overwhelmed from the neural activity and eventually experience a complete psychotic breakdown."

Dr. Hunter finally spoke, "The alternative will not be happening. My son will not wind up in your Infected Patients lab. Not now, not never. Your approaches were barbaric, and that's what left your human guinea pigs deranged and infected. Using engineered viruses the way you did is the type of antiquated quackery that has needlessly killed far too many. It was also why Lansing failed in his similarly psychotic quest. We'll do this my way, and you'll get what you want. I promise you that, but please allow me to control this experiment for his safety, and for the sake of the results you so desperately desire."

Lavanya literally stumbled backwards two steps and smiled, "Wow Dr. Hunter, that's a first. I have never heard you so agreeable and determined to be helpful! This is a pleasant surprise. We'll allow you control, so long as we get results. On that note, when can we expect results from Jake?"

"As you can see, he is already talking to the nurses. Contrary to popular belief, the recovery time from most types of brain surgery is remarkably short. However, it could be days or even weeks before he is able to provide insight into his thoughts in a way that confirms reincarnation."

"Bullshit. We don't have that long. How long did it take for your lover? How long was it until Victoria Lake started asking questions about situations and places that were not a part of her present life?"

"It was about month after the procedure that she first talked about her nightmares. But she said they started almost immediately."

"Good. Then we'll see Jake at breakfast tomorrow. Induce sleep if you have to. And remember Billy, if you want to be in control of your son's fate, I would suggest you produce results."

*   *   *

The next morning, Jake had nothing to report. In fact, he had spent the night restless and unable to achieve REM sleep, due to anxiety, and likely the stress of losing his wife, finding out she had slept with his father (among others), and being forced into action as a human guinea pig.

Later, during that second post-op evening, after the medical team had departed for the night, Lavanya went to Jake's recovery room. He was under 24 hour observation, but Lavanya dismissed the nurse on duty. She then injected Jake with a low dosage drug cocktail of part opium, part stimulant, from a needle that Dr. Gupta had left for her in the nightstand drawer next to Jake's recovery bed.

He woke from the prick in his arm. Startled, but alert, he asked, "What the hell was that? What did you just do?"

"Just relax Jake. Dr. Gupta told me to give you this if your heart rate dropped too low. It will help you relax. How do you feel?"

"I feel, I feel, well actually I feel very relaxed, but energized too!"

"Good Jake, good. Why don't we get you out of this awful hospital room and into a more comfortable bed?" Lavanya asked while stroking his body gently, seductively.

"That would be nice. I am sick of being in here. These darn nurses will not let me leave for even a walk."

"They should be fired then. I'll get you a drink Jake. Come on, come with me." He tried to stand and nearly fell, as he was weakened from the drugs. Lavanya helped him walk by inserting her hand inside his hospital gown and wrapping it low around his waist. Her fingers caressed the front of his pelvic bone in a deliberate attempt to arouse him.

She took him back to her bedroom, gave him a double Johnny Walker and made love to him all night. When Jake finally passed out, Lavanya took the electrical transponder that provided the stimulation to the diodes implanted in his brain, and cranked the dial to the maximum frequency. Then she silently got out of bed and went to meet Dr. Gupta in her office.

*   *   *

Lavanya was irritated at the late night meeting and asked, "What is it you wanted to show me that could not wait until tomorrow?"

"Look here at this security tape. It's Jake and his father during a rare moment together alone, post surgery.

Here, I'll turn up the volume."

In the video, they saw Jake ask his father, "Dad, we are not through. This thing with Anja is not OK."

"I know son. We'll deal with that and I'll understand no matter what the consequences. And I'll face them. But first let me finish helping you. If I leave you to Dr. Gupta you will surely die."

Jake showed little patience for anything his father had to say, but then asked, "There's just one more thing I don't get."

"What's that Jake?"

Jake went on, in a whisper, and Dr. Gupta turned the volume up to the maximum level, "There is more to the Digitalis than some poisonous plant. I'm not dumb enough to believe that's all there was. There is no way all this killing, all this drama could be caused by just this. And what about changing the world of medicine more dramatically than anything ever seen by mankind? Proving reincarnation is amazing no doubt. But I feel, no…, I know, there is more."

His father replied full volume, "No Jake. This is it. This is all there is to it. Minor variations are all it will take to treat Alzheimer's and advance the world of cognitive neuroscience."

Lavanya yelled at Dr. Gupta, "So what? This is what you pull me out of bed for in the middle of the night?"

"No, you must not have seen. Let me replay it. This time, watch Dr. Hunter's eyes while he answers Jake."

Lavanya watched more closely and said, "My God. I saw it. He winked at him. The bastard is lying. So if we still don't have the Digitalis, then where is it? For that matter, what is it? What could it possibly be?"

"I don't know Lavanya. But clearly it's something much more remarkable than even this. Should we take him back to the barn?"

"No, I'll find out what we need to know when the

time is right. Besides, from my perspective I already have what I want."

"Understood. But what about Peter Lansing? He's going to be furious."

"Why should I care any longer! He was, like everyone else, just a means to an end. And the end is near."

They didn't bother watching the other surveillance videos from before the operation, and so never saw Dr. Hunter retrieve the memory card from the base of the Digitalis canister. But it was caught on camera. And only luck saved Dr. Hunter from losing the key to the real Digitalis. Lavanya had no idea, and for the time being, Dr. Hunter's prized possession was safe.

CHAPTER 63

At precisely 8:14 P.M., a tall, athletic man left a bar in a building that was made from fire heated mud bricks. It looked like the typical third world African village with limited utilities, no windows or floors in the structures, and none of the basic amenities Westerners are used to. The man walked at a brisk pace. He was not drunk, but had the confidence of a couple of drinks in him. He was following a map through the village's dirt streets. The man checked under his t-shirt at the back of his waist and confirmed his gun was there, loaded, with the safety off. He walked another 200 yards before turning to his right and heading into an alleyway. It was dark, very narrow, and strewn with litter.

Thirty yards into the alley, the light of the street behind him was no longer visible due to a slight curve in the path. The buildings on either side had no windows and were tall enough and close enough together so as to block out any possible light from the moon. The man walked in complete darkness another ten yards. Then he stopped abruptly, thinking he heard something, or someone else. But there was no other sound, so he resumed walking again.

Ten more yards, then twenty, then three pairs of hands grabbed him and yanked him into a building. Lights went on and illuminated a room with a tall African man sitting behind a desk, smoking a cigar. Three other men stood to the rear, blocking the exit back to the alley.

The man behind the desk spoke in English, but with a strong African accent, "You have not kept your end of the bargain, and yet, you have taken two payments already. Do you take me for a fool?"

"No General, it's not like that…"

The man behind the desk slammed his fist down on it so hard, a glass bounced up, off, and shattered on the nearby floor.

"General, I assure you, I am on my way now to complete the work. If you will, look under my shirt, you will see I am armed, and ready to finish this." The general viewed his weapon and then sent the man back on his way.

Another fifty yards down the alley, and he was in a courtyard. There were two doors, one to the left, and one to the right. Straight ahead was a wall, with openings for windows. As was typical in that village, being in a third world nation, the windows did not have glass. Rather, they had simple wood shutters that were open to allow in air during the hot summer night. Mosquito curtains covered the opening but were largely transparent. The man walked straight, pushed aside the curtain, and climbed in through the window. He was standing in a bedroom where an American looking man slept with an African woman at his side. The tall intruder pulled his gun from his waistline and fired two shots, one into each of their heads. Then he ran.

*   *   *

"Jake, Jake, are you OK?" Lavanya placed her hand on Jake's chest rubbing it softly, in a comforting, calming manner, "You were screaming Jake. You must have been having a nightmare?"

"I was," he replied while looking surprised to find himself in bed with the woman who had only a couple of days earlier assigned him to be a human guinea pig, "What am I doing here in your bed," he asked her.

"Jake, you wanted to get out of the patient recovery room, so I snuck you here, against doctors' orders, but you were begging me, and I felt awful for you. But it was a great night," she snickered and smiled while pinching him, "Surely you remember that part, don't you Jake?"

"Vaguely, yes, I think so. But still, this doesn't make sense..."

She interrupted, "Everything is going to be OK Jake. Just try to relax. The nurses said your memory of the last few weeks might be a bit skewed since your accident, but fortunately your father was here to help you. Tell me though, what was your dream about?"

"I, I, I don't remember any accident. What accident?"

"Damn it Jake, why were you screaming just now? Your father said there is no way you'll be able to remember the accident this quickly. Just relax and explain to me why you were screaming and woke me up! How am I supposed to help you if you don't explain yourself!"

"My father said what? I want to see him, where is he?" Lavanya pushed Jake down into the bed. He was still weak from the operation and the drugs she had given him hours earlier.

"Jake, it's barely 5 AM. Why don't we talk with your father at breakfast? But you really worried me with all that yelling. You were screaming, 'Help me, help me, help me,' over and over."

"That is weird, and interesting. I don't remember that from the dream. I do remember a man shooting two people. And there was also a General of some sort. It was all very odd. Just bits and pieces of a story really."

"Bits and pieces. That is very interesting."

Jake was confused by her interest and asked, "How so? Why is that so interesting to you Lavanya?"

"Well, it just is. Do you remember anything else?"

Jake did remember more from the dream, but felt something was not quite right with her questioning and his being in her bed. It was as if she was no longer looking for proof of reincarnation, but more so looking for something in particular. The eeriness of her search for specific facts made him want to shut down.

But Lavanya knew what she was doing, and made sure that Jake enjoyed lying next to her. With both of them naked, her hands on his body made him want to talk. Still though, something deep inside him, some inner instinct told him to remain taciturn for the time being, and so he simply said, "That's all I remember. I'll tell if you I can think of anything else. But my heart was really going. Thank you so much for calming me down," and then, to distract her from any more questioning, he began to kiss her. He was using her own tricks against her and she had to play along, but did not mind doing so. In fact, she indulged in what she considered celebratory sex for the next hour, as she was convinced they had succeeded at doing what she had spent her entire life chasing.

*   *   *

Jake went back to sleep and dreamt again. The next dream was about the African woman that was shot in the head. In his second dream, there was a man making love to her in a cabin at a beautiful and luxurious beach resort. The couple was happy and celebrating something. Again Jake's dream was cut short. Only it wasn't Jake screaming in his sleep that ended the second one. That time, it was the sound of explosions in the palace halls.

CHAPTER 64

Yashodhara Palace

John Anton watched the gunmen on the monitor from the security office in Lavanya's palace. He was furiously jealous at her lovemaking with Jake. The two security personnel also in the office picked up the radio to warn the other guards. John ripped it from their hands and said, "No. Let them be."

"Sir, we need to call the other guards before more people are killed by these intruders."

John pulled a gun from inside his blazer and fired off two rounds killing both men. A call came in over the radio, "Headquarters, I think I heard a shot from the upper level. Shall I investigate?"

John replied back, "No need. Just an accidental discharge. Carry on with your rounds." Then he went out to the garage, took one of Lavanya's vehicles and left the palace. As he drove away, he mumbled under his breath, "I'll see you again Lavanya. I'll see you again."

*   *   *

Jake and Lavanya were huddled closely together in her bed. Before either of them could even say anything or get up to get dressed, the door to her bedroom was blown from its hinges by a powerful explosion.

The force was so strong it blew the door half way across the room. In the doorway, staring at Jake and Lavanya stood Marten Jansen and two other men, each of whom held an AK-47. They laughed at the sight of the naked lovers.

Lavanya leapt from the bed, covering herself with a sheet while Jake rolled to the far side of the bed to search for his clothes. Before he could so much as reach for them, Marten fired several shots in his direction. Jake was hit in two spots and fell to the floor.

"Stop!" Lavanya yelled out, "Please stop. This isn't what you think..."

Marten turned and pointed his gun towards her, then said, "How would you know what I think woman? You have no idea. Now then, let's get down to business. You have something that belongs to the Scientia Pro Curatio. I want it back."

"The what?"

"Don't play dumb. You have been colluding with Peter Lansing to steal what rightfully belongs to the Scientia Pro Curatio. It's going to make a lot of people rich. Unfortunately, neither you, nor Peter Lansing will be among them."

"I have no idea what you're talking about."

Marten moved closer to her, placing the tip of his AK-47 on her right cheek bone. "Give me the Digitalis and maybe you'll live. Keep up these charades, then I'll kill you and go find it myself. But one way or the other, we're leaving here with it."

"I DON'T KNOW WHAT YOU'RE TALKING ABOUT!!!" she yelled back at him, "I've never heard of such a thing... a Digitalis."

"But I have," Jake interjected while pulling himself up half way onto the bed, "I'll give you the Digitalis, if you'll simply tell me who you are working for." Blood was leaking from a bullet hole in his shoulder and another on the right side of his stomach.

"Jake, what are you doing?" Lavanya asked, baffled at his confession but happy he was still alive.

"What I have been meaning to do for some time now. I am taking control of my own fate, rather than leaving it to chance, which really means leaving it to the will of others."

"Hand it over then," Marten demanded.

"First tell me who you work for and why you want it."

"No problem Jake. I work for the same organization as your father. Only I'm not trying to steal from them."

"The Scientia Pro Curatio? Is that it?"

"That's the one."

There's no way my father would steal from them or anyone. There has got to be more to this story.

"And what about my wife. Are you all responsible for what's happened to her?"

"No Jake. That would be your lover there and her accomplice, Peter Lansing. He has your wife. She's his prisoner at his brainwashing ranch in California. But you're probably too late to be of much help to her. I would forget about her if I were you. Besides, word on the street is she's moved on with more than just a couple of men."

"Where can I find Lansing? And where can I find my wife? Tell me and I'll make sure you get the Digitalis."

"The man your father betrayed, Peter Lansing, is very dangerous Jake. And like I said, from what I hear, your wife has the hots for the two Eagon brothers. I'm sure all four of them are having one hec of a good time at the ranch in California. So there you go Jake, now where is the Digitalis?"

"If my wife is alive, I need to know a more exact

location where I can find her. Then I'll give you the Digitalis."

"Look Jake, you're not exactly in the position of power right now. In case you haven't noticed, there are three of us here with guns. Meanwhile, there's only two of you left, and neither of you have any clothes, let alone weapons. Seems to me, you're also a bit incapacitated. You should probably be focused on getting to a doctor."

"Right, but there's things you'll need to make the Digitalis work. I can give you those as well. Without them, it's worthless. All I'm asking for is the location of my wife, please."

Marten laughed and said to his two accomplices, "Don't worry Jake, as far as I could tell, she seemed to be enjoying her new life. But I'll tell ya what, get me that Digitalis and whatever else I need to make it work, and I'll be happy to tell you where you can go meet your own death in a vain attempt to save some slut who doesn't even want to be rescued." Jake's blood was boiling, but on the exterior, he appeared unfazed by the vulgarities thrown at him.

To make matters worse, Lavanya spat at Jake, literally, and then said, "Jake how could you? How could you still care for her? She has slept with everyone in the neighborhood and your own father and you still want to help her?"

"Yes. I do. And if you want what you're after, you're going to help me give this man whatever he needs to take the Digitalis and have safe passage out of here. I suggest you call whatever is left of your security force and inform them of what we are doing; otherwise, you'll get no further cooperation from me. And let's face it, *I* am what you're after."

CHAPTER 65

Yashodhara Palace

Jake convinced Lavanya his first dream was a positive sign and that he would do whatever it took to help with her goals, if she would allow him to cut the deal with Marten and then go after his wife. Lavanya had money like most people have bills, and would have been eager to part with it in return for any help in achieving what she desired, regardless of the circumstances. But part of her sincerely wanted to help Jake. It was a feeling she was neither familiar with, nor comfortable about. She was uneasy about losing control over the Digitalis and over her heart. Jake assured her that not only would he be getting it back, but that it would be worthless to the men without his father's knowledge as to how to make it work.

Jake got some remedial first aid and then he and Lavanya met Marten in the library of the palace with two bags. The first was stuffed with Euros. The second contained the Digitalis canister, minus the memory card which was still in his father's possession. Jake did however provide a notebook with the codes to its electronic lock and made sure a fresh Foxglove flower was inside.

They handed the bags to Marten who in return gave Jake a map with precise coordinates to Lansing Ranch in a remote part of Northern California, off the grid. It was the same place where his wife had supposedly gone for a retreat, but instead was kidnapped, tortured, and brainwashed.

Marten explained to Jake, "Peter Lansing runs a ranch out in the middle of nowhere. Personally, I'd say it's more of a cult for giving losers some purpose in life, although not necessarily a good purpose. The place is hidden in the remote wilderness of California. It's off the grid, which means there's no electricity, at least not without generators. No phone lines either. Roads are limited. It'll be tough to get to, but if you really want to save your wife, that's where you'll find her, or what's left of her anyways. Here's a map that should help you. You should know she is there under the supervision of Gregor Eagon," then he warned Jake again, "You're an idiot if you go after her. Haven't you figured it out man? A malpractice case was filed against you? A disbarment trial followed? Your law firm then conveniently dissolves, all at just the right time. Come on Jake, don't you think if your wife wanted rescuing she would have figured out a way to contact you?"

Jake replied, "There's another side to this story and I am going to find out the truth."

"Well I admire your will. Impressive for a bum American," Marten replied, "And the fact is, you'll be saving me some work if you take out Lansing. He's not exactly in good graces with us. So good luck. But of course, if you're duping me in any way with regard to the Digitalis, I'll hunt you down."

"Are you finished?" Jake asked rhetorically.

"Yes. It's been nice doing business with ya then. Good luck with your kamikaze mission, because that's what it's going to be – pure suicide, if you're lucky. By the way Jake, you know how your wife met Gregor Eagon right?

Surely you're not that naïve?"

"That's cruel," Lavanya interjected.

Marten retorted, "And that's rich, coming from a woman who uses sex to control and manipulate."

Jake yelled, "Take your money and get out. And if I ever see you again…"

Marten replied, "You'll what? Come on, let me hear it! You'll kill me?" The goofball nerdy scientist from Isla Dedaleras had been completely replaced by a confident egomaniac.

"No, but you'll be hurting so bad you'll wish you were dead. You'll beg to be dead."

"Don't count on it Jake. If you can patch up those bullet holes and actually make it to Lansing Ranch, you don't stand a prayer of leaving there alive. But if you do, I'd welcome a reunion with you. You can find me in Amsterdam. I think you know the address already." Then Marten Jansen left.

Lavanya suggested, "Jake I am worried this is a trap. You said yourself there was no way your wife could have survived the explosion at your home. And Lansing has been out of touch with me for some time now. I'm not sure he and Marten aren't on the same page."

"I am worried about the same thing. But if there is a chance, then I've got to pursue it. Regardless of everything that has happened and how society may judge it right or wrong, she's my wife, and I know that when she is in a clear state of mind, she loves me."

"Then I wish you luck Jake."

Jake explained to Lavanya, "I will keep my word Lavanya. This surgery is already done. And to be honest, I find the possibility of confirming something like reincarnation very intriguing. But I've got to try to help my wife first. Even if our marriage is over, I made a promise before God, before the God I worship. Surely you, as a woman of religion can understand the importance of that?"

"I do, and I believe you Jake. I don't know why, but you are the first person I have ever trusted. Go to your wife. And then come back here to honor your promise."

"Thank you Lavanya. Thank you." Then they kissed. It was a long, slow, lingering kiss, which led to another, and then another. Lavanya was shocked at how she actually wanted to put Jake's desires before her own. And Jake couldn't believe that he was willing and interested in helping a woman who had manipulated him so much, ordered him to be a guinea pig, and kidnapped his father. But the fact remained he had little choice but to come back, as his father had warned him that Victoria was the lone aberration, the only patient out of thousands who lived more than a few months after the type of surgery that was performed on him. Jake's only chance was to get back to the palace as quickly as possible so that his father could try to help him.

After some additional medical attention for his gun shot wounds, Jake departed the palace in Lavanya's private jet which would take him to San Francisco airport. From there, he would travel by car as far as the roads would allow.

Lavanya was left behind to deal with a missing John Anton.

CHAPTER 66

Northern California Wilderness
(Off the Grid, Six Hours from San Francisco)

Jake parked his four wheel drive Jeep off to the side of what was once a lumber road. It was a narrow, dirt road, carved into the sides of the mountains. It provided few opportunities to pull off and hide a vehicle. So even though he figured to be a few miles away from the compound, according the map, he took advantage of the first opportunity he could find to ditch the car. He wanted to arrive as quietly as possible, which meant going in on foot.

Jake had plenty of time during the flight from India for his mind to race. He had barely slept at the thought of his wife's betrayals, or the agony she must be in as a prisoner against her will. He also further contemplated that he was being set up and could be walking into a trap that would end his life. He wondered if his wife was really alive; he also wondered if she was there on her own free will, and he wondered how he, as one man, was going to free her from what seemed to be an extremely well funded and armed operation. But even outrageously bad odds could not dissuade him from trying to save her. And despite his indiscretions with Lavanya, what Jake felt for his wife was far more substantial and meaningful.

If there was a chance to save her, he would stop at nothing to take it, even if it meant risking his own life.

The view along the lumber road was spectacular and Jake figured it must provide an alluring backdrop for recruiting those with nothing to lose. He wondered what he would find at the compound that had been described as the home of a cult. Thirty minutes into his hike, Jake tripped on a rock and fell forward; he had bruised his chin and busted open his lip. He wiped the blood from his mouth and slammed his fist into the dirt.

Damn it Anja. Why am I trying to help her? She nearly got me killed in our home, she's never been loyal. Why am I doing this? Is love worth this? I made a promise. I have my honor if I keep my word, regardless of what she's done. Besides, there has to be some explanation for her behaviors. There must be something that would justify it all. Either way, I can show her what promises mean. I will show her. And bottom line, I don't want to live without her.

After wiping away his tears and walking for about another hour, Jake saw the first building of many that comprised Peter Lansing's cult compound. He spent some time observing and walking the perimeter. He wanted to learn his surroundings as well as possible in case he needed to make a quick escape. The compound was big, with several distinct sections and he needed to figure out where his wife might be located. It took him almost an hour and a half to walk the entire perimeter of the place. It was huge. There was one section that was set apart from the rest of the compound which was where Jake witnessed young adults, children almost, maybe teenagers, being marched into a building while chained together, one in front of the other.

Each of the kids was dressed in rags and looked dirty, like they hadn't showered in weeks. It prompted him to take a closer look and what he saw was frightening.

The windows were all taped over, but one of them had a crack, which allowed him to peer in. Inside, Jake saw one of the kids, a young girl, bound to a metal chair, which was bolted into a raised metal platform. In front of the girl was a monitor which flashed questions and prompted the victim to press a button on the chair handle a specific number of times to reflect their choice for an answer. When the girl answered incorrectly, the entire chair and metal platform lit up with electricity sending the young girl's hair straight up into the air. When the shock stopped, tears flowed like Niagara Falls. Perplexed, Jake moved around trying to see the monitor more clearly so he could get a sense of what types of questions were being asked. He wasn't able to read them.

None of it made sense, but saving cult victims from being brainwashed would have to wait. Jake needed to get going and find his wife.

About half a mile from there, was a quiet section of the compound which looked like a series of cabins or dormitories. Those were followed by several buildings that were clearly gathering places, as they were full of people engaged in all sorts of activities ranging from communal pot smoking circles (by the smell of it), to dancing, to a small group listening to a lecture that looked like it was being given by a zealous psycho. But no where did Jake see his wife or anything that looked like a prison. His stomach was churning with anxiety at the thought of her wanting to be there of her own free will.

Growing tired, he decided he needed to go in for a closer look. Jake tore his shirt and cut some holes in his jeans. Then he rolled in the dirt for a bit, making sure to get his hair well soaked in dirty soil. Within minutes, he had the look and feel of a cult member and was able to mix into the place like he belonged.

Walking around the interior of the compound Jake investigated numerous buildings with no luck. Almost two more hours passed before he happened upon what looked like a chapel. It looked relatively quiet, but Jake still used caution while approaching it from the side to peer in through a window. He saw three men, two of whom he recognized from the chaos at his home in D.C. The third he did not recognize, but was surprised at how out of place he looked in his suit and tie, while everyone else had attire more suitable to a bunch of hippies out of the seventies.

With the three men, kneeling in a pew nearby was his wife. She was dressed in a t-shirt and shorts.

It's them. I can't believe I've found all of them in one spot. It's the Eagons and that man in the suit must be Peter Lansing. That means it's time for a homerun, finally something goes my way.

Jake's wife was praying as the three men got up and started to walk away. As they walked past her to leave, the two men Jake recognized as Aaron and Gregor Eagon each kissed his wife on the lips. Then all three exited through the front door of the chapel, leaving his wife behind, still kneeling in a pew. The path from the building back to the other areas of the compound led away from the door, which meant none of them would see Jake peering in from a side window. He momentarily considered accosting them. His anger made him want to go pick a fight. But his recent injuries limited his physical abilities and his love for his wife caused him to focus on a different priority.

Jake waited until the men were clearly gone from view. Then he went inside to talk to Anja. As he walked in, she did not flinch one bit from her position, rather she kept praying, eyes closed, kneeling, hands clasped. Even when Jake was standing right next to her she did not flinch. He looked at her with shock as he saw the reason for her solitude and stillness. Her ankles were clasped into the floor with metal bindings and padlocks. Her thighs had similar metal bindings and padlocks holding them in place. Her elbows also had bindings which locked them into the top of the back of the pew in front of her. Even her wrists and fingers were bound together. She was essentially locked into a position of prayer. Despite her awful condition, Jake felt a sense of ease and peace because he knew then that his wife was not willingly taking part in the madness around her. He felt that his trip to save her had not been in vain.

Jake stared for what seemed like forever before finally whispering her name, "Anja." Her eyes opened and immediately became glassy.

Her face said a lot but her mouth didn't move until she finally said, "I'm sorry Jake."

"Sorry? For what are you sorry? Don't worry about sorry right now. Tell me how to get you out of these bindings."

"No Jake, this is my fate now. I deserve this. You need to go before they come back. These are very dangerous men Jake, and I've done enough damage already."

"The damage would be far greater if I were to leave here without you."

"No Jake, you don't understand the hell on earth these men can inflict. Please get out of here while you still can. Save yourself Jake, please!"

"Listen to me Anja! The only way I am leaving here without you is in a body bag." Upon hearing that, she began to sob uncontrollably. Her body shook and swayed as much as the metal bindings confining her allowed. "Where are the keys Anja. Focus please. Tell me."

"I don't know! I don't know! I don't know!" She was loosing control over her composure and emotions at an increasingly rapid rate. Jake turned and ran towards the altar of the chapel. He found a long metal candle lighting device used to reach the candles placed at high spots in the church. He took it over to her and began trying to use it to pry the bindings free from the wood planks to which they were bolted. He had moderate success, but at great effort, in freeing her left ankle, thigh, and elbow. Then he started untying her hands and wrists. He wanted to feel her embrace. The second she was free, she grabbed his face and pulled him close to her and they kissed. Both of their eyes were open the entire time. They stared into the center depths of each others' eyes while kissing and kissing, and kissing some more. They might have continued indefinitely, but the front door of the church unexpectedly opened.

Gregor and Aaron Eagon, the two brothers who masterminded Anja's kidnapping and brainwashing, were walking into the chapel. They saw and recognized Jake. Both of them reacted with calm smiles and a casual stride as they approached. Their aloof demeanor made Jake very nervous as he knew it meant they would be thinking clearly, while he was in a fit of rage, and more likely to make a mistake. They had Jake at a severe disadvantage.

Jake knew he had but one chance, especially against two very athletic looking men, on their home turf. He waited until they got close and pretended to be as calm as them.

Aaron Eagon stood directly in front of Jake, at the edge of the pew, while Gregor stood to his left. They both saw that Jake had been releasing Anja from her bindings. Aaron produced a stun gun and said directly to Anja, as if Jake were not even there, "You know Anja, we don't allow release until assignments are fully complete. I would have thought you understood that by now." Then he turned to Jake and said, "It's funny, when she first came to us she was so feisty. Now, she's so docile it pains me to have to have to punish her."

As he laughed and turned to stun Anja, Jake grabbed the candle lighter that he had slid under the base of the pew to hide it from sight. In a single lightening fast motion, which was powered by raw adrenaline, Jake jabbed the point of the candle lighter into the carotid artery on the right side of Aaron Eagon's neck. Blood spewed as he yelped and grabbed his neck vainly trying to contain the river of blood.

His younger brother Gregor went into shock and also wrapped his hands around Aaron's neck, trying to help him. Jake saw his chance, grabbed the stun gun from the ground, and a key ring from Aaron's waist. Then he stunned Gregor, followed by Aaron. Jake knew stunning Aaron would result in his death from severe blood loss and that bothered him, not because he didn't want to kill the man, but because he wanted the man to suffer. Jake knew it was wrong, but he wanted justice and he wanted revenge. A quick death for that man was neither in his opinion.

Jake unlocked the rest of his wife's bindings to free her and they embraced for a long time. Then he shocked Gregor one more time with the stun gun. He kicked him in the ribs twice. The second time he heard a loud cracking noise. Anja took several swipes herself, almost falling from the slickness of the growing puddle of blood leaking from Aaron's body.

Jake placed Gregor in another set of metal bindings configured in the pew on the opposite side of the isle. Once locked in, he splashed water in his face, from what looked like some sort of convoluted baptism bath. Gregor awoke and said, "You are going to be very sorry for what you are doing."

Jake punched him once in the upper lip with a right hook releasing teeth and blood into the air. Gregor spat out blood and laughed before saying, "Have your fun, I had mine with your slut wife." Bam, another right hook, more blood, and more laughing.

Anja, grabbed at Jake and said, "Please don't hurt him." Jake looked at her confused as to why she was saying that.

Is she in love with him?

Finally he asked her, "Why did you say that Anja? Why don't you want to hurt this man after what he has done to you?"

"You misunderstand Jake. I do want to hurt him.

But it goes against everything you taught me in life and about your career. You used to always say what set you apart as a lawyer was counseling people away from revenge and towards reconciliation. That the world would be a better place if everyone just tried uplifting each other instead of always wanting 'rationalized justice,' and that in the long run, real justice gives more pain and guilt, than it gives healing and peace. So why would you let this piece of shit of a person take from you the one thing he lacks the power to take through force? He can take it from you, only if you give it. Do you really want to sacrifice your own personal goodness, your honor, your soul for someone like that?" Jake stared at his wife, shocked that she had been listening to him over the years after all. Then he kissed her again.

"Anja, I love you."

"I love you Jake and always have. Never for one second has that not been true."

"HAH! That's not what you said to me when we were…" BAM! Another right hook from Jake knocked Gregor unconscious. More water revived him.

Then Jake took the stun gun and shocked Gregor Eagon in the groin and said, "Now you listen to me you scum of the earth. I want to know who is financing this operation, who the man in the suit was, and why you all wanted the Digitalis. You're going to tell me. You can tell me now, or you can tell me after there's nothing left of you but a charred electrocuted worthless pile of jelly. The choice is yours."

The shocking and beating went on for some time before Gregor finally broke. When he did, he informed Jake and Anja, "Peter Lansing has the money. I don't know why he wanted the Digitalis. All I know is it had something to do with discrediting a witness. He needed to prove some crazy broad was not legally sane to testify against him."

Jake mumbled to himself, "It must be Victoria."

Gregor went on, "His money let us build this place

and I enjoy fucking people figuratively and literally, so it's the perfect match. But he's already gone. You just missed him. And you'll never find him. But believe me, he'll find you, and you'll be sorry."

"I'm already sorry," Jake replied before telling him, "Now you're the one that's going to get a bit of brainwashing. Only yours is going to come from real justice. This particular show is over. I'm going to leave you here locked up. But remember me, because I'll be back to make sure you repay society for your sins."

Anja tugged at Jake's arm, again nervous that he would lose more precious time from his life on a vendetta against a man that she merely wanted to forget.

Jake saw the concern in her eyes and knew it was time to go. He had the information he needed and realized the real battle wasn't there. It was with Peter Lansing. A noble justice founded in good, not revenge, meant he had to protect Victoria Lake.

CHAPTER 67

Yashodhara Palace, India

John Anton was long gone, but Lavanya sent some of her people to track him down. He was not going to get away that easy, if she could help it.

She then turned her attention to Dr. Hunter whom she found in one piece. Fortunately, he was an early riser and had been in the underground medical facilities the morning of the chaos and shootings by Marten Jansen.

Lavanya explained what happened to Dr. Hunter and that his son was gone. She told him that he too was free to go, but that she fully expected Jake to return. Dr. Hunter knew his son would keep his word, and so he decided to stay for the time being, so that he could be prepared to help his son when he did. Most of the patients that had undergone similar procedures had only a limited amount of time before experiencing a complete mental break down and winding up insane or in the "Infected Patients" lab. Dr. Hunter was the only one who knew the truth, which was that he had no real idea why Victoria Lake was the lone aberration. But he was determined to do everything in his power to help his son be the second.

*　　*　　*

A few days later, Jake was on his way back to India, with his wife at his side. He had phoned ahead and told his father of the danger to Victoria. His father confirmed that Peter Lansing was a former colleague who stopped working for the good of mankind many years earlier. He said he would explain all the details when Jake got back to India. Then his father rushed to track down Victoria and bring her to safety. Not knowing what else to do and having few options, Dr. Hunter convinced Lavanya to allow Victoria to stay at her palace. It was an easy sell, once Lavanya learned that Victoria was the original proof of reincarnation.

And it was more than Lavanya ever dreamed of, as it was a chance to meet the woman she thought only existed in the world of exaggerated rumors.

*　　*　　*

While Jake was being poked and prodded by his father, Lavanya couldn't contain her excitement and decided to greet Victoria Lake at the airport herself. She waited with a bouquet of flowers in the international terminal, along with her driver. Many of her body guards had been killed by the rampaging Marten Jansen, so it was just the two of them, but her driver was a big man, and always armed. They met Victoria rather uneventfully and the three of them got in her limo and headed back to the palace.

Twenty minutes into the drive, after leaving the densely populated areas, the limo pulled off the road and into a clearing in the woods. Already there was another vehicle. Only seconds later, two vans approached at rapid speed. One slammed on its brakes and fishtailed, blocking the full width of the road just ahead of the clearing. The second van blocked the road behind the clearing, making escape impossible in either direction.

Three men from the van in the front blasted machine guns at the limo, eventually penetrating the bullet proof windshield and killing the driver. A tall man got out of one of the vans. He walked up to the rear of the limo and opened the door, which had been unlocked by his accomplices reaching into the front of the driver's compartment. He was oblivious to the second car parked deeper in the clearing.

He said to Lavanya, "Do you know who I am?"

She looked at him carefully and considering her options, said, "I am sorry, I do not recognize you sir. However, I am sure that whatever our conflict, it can be resolved fully to your satisfaction. Would you like to come and discuss it?" She placed her hand on his thigh as if to beckon him in and flashed the same smile that she had used to successfully seduce so many men before.

But this man did not get into the limo. Instead, he pulled a handgun and aimed it dead center at Lavanya's head, then said, "Your family killed my only sister Jaya. Good luck with your sick and twisted pursuit of Moksha. Maybe this will help you get there faster." Then he released the safety on his gun. As he pulled the trigger, he simultaneously fell backwards onto the ground with a dull thud. A single bullet to his heart, which came from the other vehicle in the clearing, had taken him out. The rest of the men took off in the vans, leaving behind Jaya's older brother, whose quest for revenge left him dead.

Peter Lansing emerged from the other vehicle and looked at Lavanya's bullet wound. She had been shot in the chest, near her heart. She was twitching and in a state of semi-consciousness, but unable to talk. Lansing turned to the passenger in the limo and said, "You haven't aged well Victoria."

"What are you doing here?" A panicked Victoria Lake responded.

"I have a few things to discuss with you Victoria. Seems you haven't quite understood yet about curiosity killing the cat. As a good friend of mine, I trust you'll enjoy spending the next few days or so with me, instead of Lavanya. Who knows, if you're cooperative, and the surgery we have planned for you goes well, maybe we'll be able to reunite you with your beloved Dr. Hunter."

"You're a madman!" Victoria screamed. As hysterics set in, two other men from Lansing's car grabbed Victoria, bound her wrists and threw her into the back seat of their vehicle.

"Thanks sweetie," Peter Lansing said to a motionless Lavanya as he threw the hard drive from Aguas Muertas into her lap. It was a trade, of what Lavanya thought were schematics for the Digitalis, in exchange for the living proof of reincarnation she had craved for years. Lansing continued, "Someday, I hope we can have ourselves a reunion of sorts, for old time's sake."

Lavanya was unable to reply and faded into unconsciousness.

CHAPTER 68

Washington D.C.
(Georgetown & C & O Canal Park - Great Falls)

The white man and African woman were making
love again, only this time in the heat of an African village.
Just as they finished, the man's face became covered in
blood from the death of the woman next to him. Then
another bullet fired, this time into his head, and darkness
ensued.

*   *   *

Jake woke up screaming, but Anja's touch immediately
calmed him. They were back in D.C., in their Georgetown
Condo, since their suburban home had been destroyed. Jake
would only have a brief amount of time in D.C. before he
had to return to his father's care, but he needed to resolve
some loose ends. Jake planned to use a few days, and a lot
of Lavanya's connections, money, and power, to help
Aubrey Doyle and to get his license to practice law
reinstated. But before he did all that, he was taking a day off
to spend time with his wife.

Anja asked, "What was the dream about this time Jake?"

"It was the same thing. It is always the same. I am not sure, but I think I was the man that pulled the trigger."

"That's impossible. I know you, and I know you could not possibly kill in cold blood, not in this life or any life."

"But maybe that's why I can't in this life? Maybe I'm making up for past sins?"

"No way. I don't think that's how it works anyway."

"Well, they say you can't die in your dreams, so I had to be the killer. But why would I kill a couple in love?"

"You were not the killer Jake. You've had other dreams with just the man and the woman, so clearly you were the man in love and not the killer."

He smiled, and then asked, "What if I was the woman?" They both laughed.

"After last night, I'm pretty sure you were not the woman. It would have taken more than just a few lifetimes of practice to be as good as you were!"

"Great, so that means I was murdered in a past life. As if I don't have enough problems already!"

"Maybe that is why Jake?"

"Maybe what is why what? What are you talking about?"

"Maybe that's why you are like Victoria. It's because you are supposed to be alive still. Maybe you are supposed to find the person that killed you. You have unfinished business."

"Maybe. But right now the only unfinished business I want to think about is rolling around with you one more time before we go hiking. You didn't forget did you? You promised me a trip to Great Falls today!"

Smiling, Anja replied, "Oh you'll get your trip if you keep talking like that. You'll get anything you want!"

*   *   *

Jake Hunter wiped the sweat from his brow as he pushed himself up over the last rock at the top of the hill on the island in the middle of the Potomac River. It was a scenic spot that allowed a view of Virginia to the West, and Maryland and the C & O Canal to the East. He bent down and offered a hand to his wife, Anja. Climbing the rocks at Great Falls Park was one of their favorite past times before the chaos of the last month, and they were happy to be re-living it.

Jake was trying to put aside the terrible vision he had the night before. He knew in his heart that he was, or at least wanted to be, a good person, regardless of whatever mistakes he may have made in any past lives. And after what he had experienced in the last month, he felt blessed to be alive and have a chance to spend time with someone willing to truly love him despite both of their human shortcomings.

But as they sat down to rest in the hot summer sun, Jake could tell Anja's mind was reeling. "What is it?" he asked.

"Jake, it's just everything. It's everything that happened to us. And, all the horrible things I did to you. And yet, you still want to be with me? How can you possibly ever trust me again?"

"Trust doesn't come and go with human shortcomings Anja. It is merely affected by them. But there is a deeper level of trust in the connection we had that goes beyond mere human failings. You control how much I trust you with how you treat me going forward, every day.

I honestly don't know how long it will take to fully resolve all the pain from what has happened. But there are more important things in life. And this I know, unequivocally," he paused to hug her and pull her close to him, then looked her dead in the eyes and said with a tone of confidence that indicated what he was saying to be true, "it is never too late to do the right thing."

While listening to her husband in stunned silence, Anja thought about Polonius' advice to Laertes, and then to herself:

I finally get it. I finally understand what they mean when they say, "the truth shall set you free." Jake will love me, no matter what. I can finally be happy with who I am.

Later, as they made the hike back to their car, Anja wondered what Jake's father was doing, whether he was safe, and if he even knew that his son was having such strange nightmares. And she wondered why Jake's nightmares had such striking similarity to the stories his father used to share with her after having sex. She brushed aside her guilt for having cheated on her husband with his father and accepted that she would do everything possible to make up for it for the rest of her life.

CHAPTER 69

Amsterdam, The Netherlands

Peter Lansing left the headquarters of the Scientia Pro Curatio with a pat on the back from his society appointed attorney. They were heading to a Leidsepleine pub to celebrate their recent victory. Lansing was found innocent of crimes against humanity one day earlier at the International Court of Justice (or ICJ) in The Hague, about an hour's drive from Amsterdam. The primary witness against him, Victoria Lake, had not shown up for trial, which resulted in a default judgment in his favor. In turn he was readmitted to the "Global Council" of the Scientia Pro Curatio, since they lacked any evidence to confirm he had violated their guidelines for medical research.

Lansing intended to spend the evening celebrating his full reinstatement. He planned on a night of indulgence in Amsterdam's vivid nightlife. Then Lansing was going to head back to his ranch in Northern California. He was determined to find Dr. Hunter's briefcase which went missing during the plane crash of the ill fated Hunter Neurologics jet. He was planning on gathering a handful of his finest "recruits" and sending them on a global retrieval mission.

    While in a taxi on the way to the airport, he called Gregor Eagon and asked him what frequency was being transmitted to the diodes they had implanted in Anja Hunter's brain while she was their captive. Gregor replied, "We have bumped it up to the highest one yet. We've never tried it at this level on anyone. And still, there hasn't been any response. It's as if she's suddenly found a way to counteract its effectiveness."

CHAPTER 70

Yashodhara Palace, India

Lavanya Yashodhara was on a bed in the medical center beneath her palace. As the doctors rushed to position her for emergency surgery, a letter fell from her pockets.

Dr. Hunter was present, grabbed the envelope, and was stunned at what he read. For the time being, he would have to wait to think further about it, as he needed Lavanya alive so that he could figure out what happened to Victoria.

The doctors worked feverishly while Lavanya continued to fade in and out of consciousness. As the surgeons worked, she started to vividly see the scene from her childhood, where her parents were taken from her.

Lavanya was back in the courtyard surrounded by the mob, watching her parents as they were stoned to death. The new clarity of understanding about her nightmare – her parents' fate - set her free in one sense. But it simultaneously imprisoned her, as in her heart, she knew that she could never rest until fully avenging her parents' fate.

As she flatlined on the operating table, doctors went to work administering CPR.

Unable to assist any further, Dr. Hunter re-read the letter he had found, "I will never forget nor forgive you for what you have done. This isn't over." It was from his son, Jake, who was supposed to have come back to the palace, but had instead disappeared. Lavanya had attached a sticky note to the bottom of the letter which read, "As far as I'm concerned he broke a promise to me. As a result he'll be dead in 24 hours."

Looking at her surrounded by frantic doctors, Dr. Hunter knew she would be of little help in finding Victoria. And he knew he would not be able to talk her out of trying to kill his son. He had less than 24 hours to find and warn his only child, who probably wanted nothing further to do with him.

Dr. Gupta walked into the room and was handed the hard drive from Agua Muertas by another of the attendants. She turned to Dr. Hunter and laughed, then said, "Sorry about your son, Billy. At least he was able to do one thing right," as she waved the hard drive through the air.

"You're a fool if you believe that thing will help you. Did you really think we would leave that kind of information behind!? That hard drive is nothing more than an elaborate decoy. You'll find nothing useful on there."

"Regardless, I still have you here. You'll repeat your achievement. And if you don't, then I'll find another person you care about to be the next guinea pig. But the fact remains, this hard drive would not have been so well protected if it wasn't what we seek. And now, with Lavanya dying, the accomplishment is mine for the taking."

"Please Rajni; I beg of you, tell me what she's going to do to Jake. Please don't let him be killed."

"Then tell me what happened to your briefcase, the one from your flight that crashed."

Dr. Hunter thought for a moment and then gave in. He told her, "It was taken to Indonesia. There is a man, Lester Cannes who is working with me to protect the

Digitalis from Lansing and the Scientia Pro Curatio. It was a costly measure, but it was the only way to be safe."

She laughed at him. "My how the mighty crumble when the fate of loved ones is at stake. All those deaths of good people and you throw them all out the window to save an ungrateful son." She turned to a guard and barked out orders, "Get someone to retrieve the briefcase from Lester Cannes. Then bring him to me."

CHAPTER 71

Balikpapan, Indonesia

Lester Cannes was meeting with the two pilots that crash landed the Hunter Neurologics corporate jet weeks earlier. They handed Lester a locked briefcase, which he quickly opened.

After glancing through the contents, Lester threw the case at the two pilots and said, "This is NOT the Digitalis! You idiots grabbed the wrong the case! And with the press having gotten wind that it wasn't your bodies that were recovered from the wreckage, there is little point in keeping you around. You're marked men by my enemies."

The two men started shaking and pleading for their lives, but as they talked, each was shot in the back of the head while Lester Cannes watched from behind his desk. He didn't move a muscle, not even as their blood splattered across his face.

Moments later, he watched his gunman also fall to the ground as four intruders surrounded him, put him in cuffs, and loaded him onto a plane bound for Yashodhara Palace, India.

*   *   *

Meanwhile, in a small fishing village of a sparsely populated island off the coast of Haiti, a young boy walked into his family's hut with a strange object. The mother, not recognizing the unfamiliar shape, took Dr. Hunter's briefcase, which was the last remnant of Hunter Neurologics and contained the real Digitalis, and placed it across the top of stone fired mud bricks. Then she sat on it, while weaving straw baskets. And the mother was thrilled to have a new chair, despite being completely oblivious as to the untold wealth it contained within.

To be continued…

Visit, www.triplereincarnation.com to join the, "Triple Reincarnation," mailing list; updates will include announcements on release dates and sneak previews of future books in this series.

LEARN MORE:

If you want to know more about reincarnation, religion, or the rapid advances in neuroscience and related technologies, (upon which this book was based), please visit:

www.triplereincarnation.com

QUESTIONS, COMMENTS, IDEAS?

Your feedback, comments, and ideas about this book are welcome and encouraged. Please send your feedback as plain text email to:

feedback@triplereincarnation.com

NOTE: Due to the risk of Internet viruses, attachments will NOT be opened.

ABOUT THE AUTHOR:

H.D. Dexter is the pen name for the author who lives in the D.C. metro area. H.D. is committed to using invigorating media to provide positive messages. It is the hope of the author that this book promotes religious tolerance and understanding.

H.D. also hopes this book encourages you to pursue your own personal dreams and goals... no matter how far fetched you, or anyone else, may think they are.

The truth is, with hard work and perseverance, your dreams are closer to reality than you realize.

www.hddexter.com

www.ingramcontent.com/pod-product-compliance
Lightning Source LLC
Chambersburg PA
CBHW060141260626
47160CB00001B/71